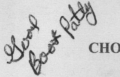

CHOOSING A VICTIM

Lexie was an excellent candidate for eternity. Since their lunch, he'd been on fire with the idea of placing her last breath in the jar he'd finished the night before. He'd made this one especially for Lexie and her smooth, white skin. The glass he had blown had a light, creamy texture and was unlike anything he'd ever placed in his work of art. It fit Lexie perfectly. The jar was wrapped in tissue paper inside a Publix grocery store plastic bag along with a bouquet of flowers. He knew she'd immediately assume the decorative jar was some kind of vase for the flowers. And that's what he wanted her to think. He wanted her to stay calm right up until the very end.

He turned the corner and instinctively looked in every direction. It was the middle of a workday and there was no one wandering the streets. Lexie had the day off from the animal hospital and didn't have to work at Sal's Smoothie Shack tonight. He had no pressing jobs to complete and felt as if the stars had aligned to provide him with this chance to complete another section of his work of art. He loved that Lexie cared so much about animals.

Along with her angelic face, it was the quality he'd latched onto . . .

Books by James Andrus

THE PERFECT WOMAN

THE PERFECT PREY

THE PERFECT DEATH

Published by Kensington Publishing Corporation

THE
PERFECT
DEATH

JAMES ANDRUS

PINNACLE BOOKS
Kensington Publishing Corp.
www.kensingtonbooks.com

PINNACLE BOOKS are published by

Kensington Publishing Corp.
119 West 40th Street
New York, NY 10018

All Kensington titles, imprints, and distributed lines are available at special quantity discounts for bulk purchases for sales promotions, premiums, fund-raising, educational, or institutional use. Special book excerpts or customized printings can also be created to fit specific needs. For details, write or phone the office of the Kensington special sales manager: Kensington Publishing Corp., 119 West 40th Street, New York, NY 10018, attn: Special Sales Department; phone 1-800-221-2647.

ISBN-13: 978-0-7860-2769-9
ISBN-10: 0-7860-2769-X

First printing: February 2012

10 0 8 7 6 5 4 3 2 1

Printed in the United States of America

ONE

Human anatomy is simple. It only requires time to study and a mind to grasp the complex organs God had stuffed into the body. Lots and lots of study time. That's what Kathy Mizell had done for weeks. Nothing else but study, eat, and a little sleep. Cranial nerves, respiratory system, lymphatic system. She'd learned it all and doubted she could ever look at people the same way again. But the test had been last Friday and she'd scored a solid B. Human anatomy was the big hurdle for most nursing students and she had cleared it. Now she had to face tests on prescription drugs, diseases of the pulmonary system, and taking effective case notes.

Kathy considered her anatomy score as she sat on the scarred wooden bench with the name DANNY carved into it. The only cover from the constant Jacksonville drizzle was the pockmarked plastic bus stop with an ad for the *Jacksonville Times-Union* plastered across the inside: a smattering of famous headlines beneath an image of a young, professional-looking couple reading the paper and drinking coffee. The other nursing students called the bus stop wedged between the two buildings "creep central" because it felt so isolated. Kathy had checked with security and there had never been any problems reported.

The eight o'clock shuttle was running late and her brand-new Nissan SUV was at the dealer having its transmission fixed. Her spacey little brother had forgotten to pick her up. So the simple nursing seminar on electronic patient notes at the off-campus College of Health Care had turned into an ordeal. Thank God she'd gotten the anatomy test out of the way Friday. Kathy decided the shuttle back to the main University of North Florida campus was at least in the direction of home, where her mom would have a hot meal ready for her. Maybe spaghetti, or her favorite, pot roast.

Kathy wore the white and pink uniform of a student nurse and carried three thick textbooks in her Nike backpack. She was too exhausted to study for the prescription-drug test she had tomorrow. At least the cozy bus stop kept her relatively dry.

A man in a white commercial van drove past her slowly, stopped down the street, and got out at the bus stop that protected riders headed back to Jacksonville. The van blocked most of her view, but she could tell the man was doing a repair to the plastic cover. After a few minutes he hopped back into the van, drove to the end of the short street, and turned back in her direction. The plain white van pulled to a stop directly in front of Kathy. The passenger window rolled down and a man called out from the driver's seat. "Sorry, miss, but I'm supposed to install a sheet of glass in the back of the booth."

Kathy looked around for a dry place to wait and saw nothing or no one near by. "Can I stay under the roof?"

"Let me get out the glass and you can slide to one side. I'll only be a second."

Kathy evaluated his speech and manner. Her psychology class had a whole section on initial impressions. Her assessment was this guy didn't want her to get soaked. She smiled and scooted to one side, watching as the man stepped through his van and opened the side, sliding door. She could see sheets of glass as well as intricate glass shapes. He held a small glass cylinder in his left, gloved hand as he popped out of the van.

Kathy pointed at the jar. "What's that?"

He held it up. "An airtight jar." The man, in his mid-thirties, had a warm smile and bright blue eyes set deep in a handsome face. He grabbed a leather strap out of the van and turned back to Kathy. His heavy canvas work gloves were well worn to the shape of his fingers.

She huddled to one side, waiting for the man to measure or use the strap on the back of the bus stop booth, or whatever repairmen did.

Instead, he leaned in close to her and looped the strap over her head. At that moment she realized it was a belt. Before she could say anything he jerked it tight around her neck.

The surprise and force of the belt stunned her. It took a second for her to realize what was happening. She was being choked. It wasn't only the lack of oxygen to her brain, but the speed of her panicked heart and reaction of her body to the assault. Her nursing classes had taught her how the human body needed oxygen as fuel. Now that knowledge gave her an odd, analytical view of her body shutting down. She flailed her arms, trying to work her fingers under the belt around her throat. The man shifted and she was able to gasp once and release the breath. When she exhaled, he held the funky glass jar to her mouth with his left hand. He used his right hand to yank the strap tight across her throat again. There was no oxygen available. Nothing.

The man secured the belt and moved away from her, sealing the jar with a lid. He lifted her jerking body in strong arms and transferred her to the open floor of the van.

She heard a slight gurgle but didn't know if it was out loud or only in her head. The last image she saw was the man looking back at her from the front seat of the van. She wanted to see her mom and dad. She even wanted to see her brother to tell him it wasn't his fault.

Then everything went dark.

Detective John Stallings swerved as the tires of his county-issued Impala splashed into a puddle at the end of the long, curving brick driveway in front of a house that looked like an English manor on top of the hill. He wondered how much it cost to put a hill on the flat wetlands near the beach. Three cars blocked the driveway. A blue Jaguar XJ12 sat closest to the front door. A black Cadillac was right behind that, and at the end of the driveway next to where he parked was a beat-up Ford Explorer. He figured that must belong to one of the help.

He paused a second while his partner, Patty Levine, navigated across the damp surface, her metal notepad cover in her hands. She never went anywhere without the scuffed and dented metal notebook that housed not only her notes from work, but most of the rest of her life as well. She always seemed to have it together, never looking distracted or nervous. With straight blond hair hanging down her back she could've been a young lawyer or doctor walking into her private practice. Instead, she was an overworked missing persons detective with the Jacksonville Sheriff's Office. Stallings thanked God for it every day he walked into the office.

They'd composed a few questions Patty pulled out of her metal notebook as they approached the wide, ornate wooden doors. How many times had he done this in the past three years? He'd lost track. And none of them seem to get any easier. There were only a few variations of how this could go. Distraught parents missing their child. Detached parents doing what was expected to report a missing child. Distracted parents who had other issues. Or parents who had something to do with the child's disappearance. None of them were pleasant situations, but all required Stallings's complete attention. He'd been there as a cop *and* a parent. He lived the real, visceral fear of not knowing exactly where his child is or what kind of danger she might be in. In the three years since his own Jeanie had disappeared, that fear still ate at him every minute of every day. As he knocked on the door he once again thought of his missing daughter. He also muttered his affirmation to keep him sharp and alert: "Is today the day that changes my life?"

A chubby black woman with a narrow face and dark, intelligent eyes answered the door. He was about to identify himself when she stepped back and ushered him and Patty into the wide, tiled foyer. The woman hurried off, leaving the two of them standing in silence. Stallings noticed the bookshelves crammed with antique books and knickknacks. In one corner of the foyer he saw his first clue as to what kind of parents he was dealing with: an entire row of sports trophies and children's drawings. He made a snap judgment that these were terrified, caring parents he needed to help right now.

Stallings and Patty looked up as a flabby, bald man in a white button-down shirt and dark pants waddled toward them, his hand extended. "I'm Bob Tischler. Thank you for coming out to talk to us. The sheriff told me you were the two best missing persons detectives he had."

Stallings took the man's smothering hand and nodded, not bothering to tell him that he and Patty were the *only* two missing persons detectives. But Tischler's subtle comment on his political connections were clear. The well-known and wealthy attorney had juice, but that didn't matter one bit to Stallings. The only thing that mattered was Tischler's missing daughter, Leah. Over the years Stallings had found social status meant nothing when a child was missing. All scared parents were the same, so he sat down to listen to this story.

Bob Tischler was joined by his younger wife, Lois, and Stallings realized this was a second family for the man. They had two young boys and Leah, who was fifteen. As their story unfolded, Stallings saw the similarities to his own situation and felt a chill.

Leah was a student at an upscale private school; she had a few problems with her parents and had been caught smoking pot. Her parents thought she was throwing a tantrum when she didn't come home after school Friday. By the time she was reported missing on Saturday, the responding officer thought she was just a spoiled runaway. Now, on Monday, there'd been no sign of her. The whole situation felt far too familiar to

Stallings. He had to wonder if the answer to Leah Tischler's disappearance might lead to answers about his own daughter's disappearance. The odds were astronomical, but he was a father of a missing daughter. At this point he'd do anything to learn what had happened to his Jeanie.

Patty handled all the sensitive questions about relations within the family and the reasons Leah might have to run away. And that was the most obvious answer, she had run away. It was the circumstances of her running away and what might happen to her on the street that caused Stallings to shudder. The chances of a child being kidnapped in the United States were extraordinarily low, but the chances of a runaway falling in with someone who might cause harm were much, much greater. These were not the issues he wanted to discuss with frightened parents right now. All he and Patty wanted to discover was a lead to where the girl might have gone.

Stallings studied the parents as they each told different parts of the sad, familiar story. The mother—red eyed and tired looking, blond hair unkempt but natural good looks shining through—had the composure to write out some notes. Stallings guessed she'd been Tischler's legal secretary and was probably twenty years younger than the sixty-year-old attorney.

Patty asked the key question, "Is there anyone that Leah would have run to?"

Bob Tischler shook his head and looked off in space, but Lois Tischler knew how important all these questions were. She said, "Leah has an older half sister named Susan who lives in Fernandina Beach. We've already talked to her and she hasn't seen her and promised to call us." The woman sniffed, using a Kleenex to wipe her eyes. "There's a music teacher at her school she's close to. I guess there's a chance she could've gone to her house."

Patty wrote down the name of the teacher from the prestigious Thomas School as well as the sister's phone number.

Stallings had already asked about any calls to Leah's cell phone. That was his first clue that she'd run away. The Tischlers had taken away her cell phone as punishment. The modern grounding. Even Stallings knew you didn't mess with a kid's cell phone unless there was a serious issue. It had also cut off one way to track the teenager.

Patty looked up from her notes and told the Tischlers she needed to see Leah's room and access her computer.

Stallings liked how direct and forceful she was, not asking permission but telling them what she was going to do. As Lois Tischler led Patty and Stallings up the hardwood staircase he caught a glimpse of a boy about six or seven peering at them through the banister before scampering away. That made Stallings think of his own son, Charlie, who had been only four the day JSO detectives asked him and Maria basically the same questions he and Patty had asked tonight.

Once in the room, Patty went right to a Toshiba laptop computer on the small white desk near the bed. Stallings glanced at photos on the wall of Leah and her friends. She had long dark hair and an intense gaze. Something about her eyes said that she had street smarts and experience far beyond the wealthy trappings of her family. He hoped that was true because it might keep her safe on the streets of Jacksonville. He let Mrs. Tischler show him through her daughter's closet and draw her own conclusions about any missing clothes.

Finally Mrs. Tischler was able to say that there was nothing missing and that meant Leah was wearing the Thomas School uniform the last time she was seen. Mrs. Tischler pulled out a gray and white plaid skirt, white shirt and a black belt with an ornate and distinctive silver-plated buckle.

She said, "This is exactly what Leah wore everyday to school. She has three skirts and one is missing. She has five shirts and one is missing. She has two belts and one is missing. Every student is issued the same number of uniforms."

Stallings photographed the clothes laid out on the bed and took several close-ups of the distinctive belt buckle. They'd print an information sheet with several photos of Leah and the clothes to hand out to other detectives and the road patrolmen who covered the downtown areas of Jacksonville.

Patty turned from the computer and said, "We're gonna need to take the computer into the lab at JSO."

Mrs. Tischler looked at her and said, "Why?"

"Every time a teenager goes missing it's standard to go through their personal computers. She might have kept e-mails or text messages to whoever she ran off with or information about a place she might want to go. But this computer has too many passwords and I'm gonna need one of our techs to break them."

Stallings may not have been technologically up-to-date, but he'd learned enough to tell every parent of a teenager to make sure they knew the passwords necessary to get into a computer and occasionally take a look in the computer. It might be sneaky but it could help them avoid a lot of problems in the future. At this

point in his life, sneaky was the least of Stallings's worries.

Then Mrs. Tischler, like all parents in a similar situation, looked at Stallings and said, "Please, Detective,
bring my little girl home."

Stallings knew there would be nothing else he could
concentrate on.

TWO

The thrill of feeling the girl's life run out of her was still fresh when reality smacked him in the face. He'd been impetuous and acted without thought. But that was what he needed to do sometimes. He had to run free. Now he had the reality of a corpse in his van and a need to dump it. Fast.

Hauling around the body had left him nervous and shaken—two things he rarely felt. There was no one to blame but himself. It had all happened so fast when he saw her sitting alone in the dark bus stop. Something, some instinct, told him to take a better look so he pulled over down the street like he was working on the empty bus stop. That gave him time to think. A pair of mini sports binoculars helped him assess the girl. The extra time allowed him to come up with his cover story about changing out the glass. He made a number of snap judgments, perhaps not all of them smart, but sometimes there was no fighting instinct. The girl was too perfect a candidate for his project. Her clear skin and trim figure indicated she was health-conscious.

Her face had a certain innocent quality to it that he found irresistible. Only a certain type of woman turned his head. Of those, only a select few rose to the level of being added to his lifelong work of art. Circumstances had provided him with several subjects over the past month. That was unusual. But that was the nature of art. It was unpredictable, thrilling, and could not be contained once human passion started to flow. Besides he had no idea how long he'd have to work on his masterpiece. Ultimately the biggest challenge in his art was finding the right type of woman. If he used prostitutes or crack whores from the streets, his art lost all meaning even if the effort he had to make was much less. It was almost like seeing a good actor on-screen; you couldn't always say what made him a good actor. The challenge was finding women worthy of being remembered throughout all eternity. That's what it was all about for him: worthiness. His work of art had to stand the test of time, a testament to his skill, passion, and devotion to beauty. A way of blending his talents and his desires to create something no one could take away. He had to have at least one thing in his life no one could take away.

Other thoughts went into his actions. He'd made a quick assessment of his chances of being caught. The area seemed deserted. There were no construction projects he was working on in the area. There was nothing to tie him to the area. He scanned the building quickly for obvious security cameras and saw none.

Doing something like this was a big deal. He didn't take it lightly. It was not only creating the art he enjoyed. There were other benefits. He greatly preferred to spend time with each of his subjects before they became part of eternity. Over the years, just by chance, he'd gotten to spend time with about half his subjects.

But now, as the wind picked up and rain splashed against his windshield, he had the unpleasant task of disposing of the dead body that had provided what he needed. She was stretched out on the floor of his work van right next to the sliding side door. He thought about dumping her out in the vast wetlands between downtown and the beach, but knew the longer he rode around with her in the van the more dangerous the situation became for him. He wanted to find a place that might hide her body for at least a few days.

He stopped at a red light in the south part of town and noticed a Jacksonville Sheriff's Office patrol car pull in the lane next to him. The white Chevy Malibu with a pleasant yellow and blue seal seemed innocuous enough. He kept his face straight ahead with his eyes cut hard to the left trying to see if the cop noticed him. But the low patrol car provided him no opportunity to look into the passenger compartment. Did the cop move inside the police car? His heart started to beat faster and he felt sweat sprout on his wide forehead. He involuntarily looked over his shoulder at the girl's body. Now it felt like the light was stuck in the red position and the seconds were ticking into long minutes. Had he finally made a stupendous error? He'd always been careful, but he was no criminal. At least not a real criminal like the ones that prowled the streets of Jacksonville and hid their crimes. He just used common sense, and at this moment common sense didn't feel like it was enough.

Finally the light changed and he hesitated before stepping on the gas of the Chevy van. The police car didn't move and that only made him more nervous. He took the first right turn he could, hoping he didn't see lights behind him.

His hand was shaking uncontrollably on the steering wheel and he realized that no matter what, he had to get rid of the body right this minute. One of the big construction companies had been renovating some of the office space down at this end of the city and the site had five large Dumpsters outside the gutted building. This was the best he was going to find in his current condition. He stopped on the edge of the site, careful not to let his tires roll onto the sand and cement material on the ground. He didn't want any kind of imprint of his tires, a commonsense move he'd picked up from a TV police show.

As always, in any construction site, he took a moment to assess the glasswork that was being done. The Hartline Glass Company logo was plastered on a slick, commercially made sign, which meant the glasswork would have no class or style. They were simply a measure-and-fill-the-hole kind of company that used only sheet glass and pre-measured windows. He may have been forced to do the same thing for the most part, but that was only to support his art of glassblowing. Occasionally he did sell a glass sculpture he'd created but never for enough money to live on comfortably.

He sucked in a couple of deep breaths trying to calm down. Not one light was on in any of the office buildings surrounding the project. The Dumpster was about forty feet away and already had construction debris in it. If he was lucky someone would haul away the Dumpster without checking it too closely.

He scurried around the outside of the van, slid open the side door, and looked at the dead girl on the floor of the van. Her face made him smile and nod to himself in acknowledgment that he'd made the right choice and she was worthy of being in his project. He yanked on his work gloves to keep the spread of his DNA to a minimum, then reached down and heaved her over his shoulder like a fireman. The body had cooled considerably, but she wasn't stiff yet. He struggled along the edge of the construction site to the long Dumpster, then laid her down and judged the height of the Dumpster. He lugged over two cinderblocks and built a crude stairway

He knew he had to check the body and untie the belt around her throat and look closely to make sure there was nothing that would speed her identification and lead the cops to him. But before he could start his customary examination, he saw the reflection of headlights coming from a block down the street. He thought of the cop who had been stopped next to him at the red light. This wasn't a time to panic, even though he felt panic rise in his throat. He had to do something and do it quick. Taking the body in his arms he stepped awkwardly onto the two cinderblocks and tossed her into the Dumpster like a sack filled with old pieces of glass. He heard it land on top and then slide down along the side. He took one second to shove some of the construction debris over her and hustled back toward his van.

He could still see the lights, which meant the vehicle on the next block had stopped with its headlights shining ahead. There was no time to waste. None. He threw the van into gear and turned down the street closest to him, hoping to be clear of the site before the mysterious car continued its trek toward the site.

He was careful not to speed, even with every fiber of

his body telling him to mash the gas pedal. Five blocks away he turned onto one of the main roads and headed toward downtown Jacksonville. After a mile a terrible thought struck him. In his haste to dispose of the body, he'd left the belt wrapped around her neck. All he could do now was lay low and hope time would cover his tracks.

Patty Levine looked at her watch and shook her head. She turned toward Stallings and made one last plea. "Don't you think it's a little late to be bothering a teacher, John?"

Stallings looked up at the lights inside the condos along the St. Johns River. "It's not even eleven yet and it looks like most of the building is still awake."

Patty grabbed Stallings by the arm. "Talk to me, John. I understand your interest in pursuing this, but even by your standards this is bizarre. Why are we going to harass this teacher late at night? Why are we doing this without talking to the sergeant? Why have we been working fifteen hours without a break?" She waited while her partner looked at the ground. Whenever he didn't know how to answer a question he looked at the ground to gather his thoughts. She wished he'd do the same thing before he punched people. She waited patiently for him to focus on her and answer.

He started slowly. "I don't know. It's the way the details of the situation hit me. It's so much like when Jeanie disappeared. We'd had an argument, but it wasn't anything serious. We waited to report her missing because there were other problems we were dealing with and no one realized exactly what had happened. I thought we were a close family. We had roots in the area, just like the Tischlers, but somehow it all went bad. And maybe, by working this as hard as I can, I'll see some clue or hint I missed with Jeanie."

Patty didn't reply; she just looked at the teacher's name on the mailbox and rang the buzzer.

A few minutes later they were in the neat living room of the young music teacher. The woman wore a robe over a flowered muumuu. Her long, stringy hair lay limp across her wide shoulders. Patty had wasted no time explaining the situation and the need to bother her at such a late hour.

After listening to the questions, the teacher shook her head and said, "I assumed Leah was home sick. I haven't heard from her since I saw her in class on Friday."

Patty noticed the young teacher sneaking looks at Stallings. She'd seen it before. The way her partner's understated manner and good looks attracted women from all areas of society. Stallings had no clue when this happened.

Stallings said, "You haven't noticed any calls from numbers you don't recognize? Leah doesn't have her cell phone with her."

Then the young teacher sat straighter and snapped her fingers. She rushed into the kitchen and came back out with an iPhone in her hand. She lifted her glasses to look at the screen closely and said, "I was called by a number Friday evening, but I had no idea who it was so I didn't answer." She read the number off her phone as Patty copied it down into her notepad in the beat-up metal cover.

After a few more routine questions Patty said, "Would you call us if you hear from her?"

The teacher turned directly to Stallings and said, "Why don't you give me your business card and cell phone so I can reach you if I hear anything?"

Patty shook her head, thinking about all the times she'd heard women talk about how obvious men could be.

THREE

John Stallings swallowed hard and resisted the urge to grab the motel manager by the collar of his faded flannel shirt. He gave the young man with the soul patch a hard look and said, "You don't need to know *why* we're looking for her, you just need to know that we're looking for her. But here's a simple question." Stallings spoke very slowly to emphasize how close he was to losing his patience. "Have you seen this girl?" He tapped the photo of Leah Tischler he'd laid on the young man's desk.

This time the man's nervous eyes skittered toward the photo and he picked it up with a shaky hand. He took his time looking at the glossy color photo of a dark-haired, smiling seventeen-year-old taken two months earlier at a dance recital. The Tischlers had been very helpful the night before. He and Patty had developed a detailed info sheet in time to get it out to all the road patrol officers before the day shift and to all the detectives. The sheet had Leah Tischler's photo and description, along with photos of the clothes she was wearing and of the gaudy, silver-plated belt the

Thomas School issued. The teacher Leah was close to provided a phone number Stallings had determined to be a public pay phone inside a check-cashing store one block away. Now he and Patty were checking each of the small, low-rent apartment and motel buildings in the area.

Stallings didn't rush the manager now that he'd made his point. This guy who ran the thirty-unit building couldn't grasp the idea that for every runaway or missing person there was someone who missed them and worried every night. Stallings didn't have time to answer stupid questions like why he was looking for someone or what would happen to her if she were found. He'd long since abandoned any pretext of being polite to people who slowed down his efforts to find missing kids. Especially teenage runaways.

This place was the only obvious destination in the area. But she might have been looking into cheap housing. Anywhere along Davis might lead to a clue to her whereabouts. It never ended with a missing persons case. An interview could lead to five more interviews and an address could point to three different houses. The only chance an endangered teenager had was a cop who wouldn't give up. He had to live by that code. The manager handed back the four-by-six photo and shook his head. "I haven't seen her." He held up his right hand like he was testifying at trial. "I swear to God."

Stallings ignored his partner's short snort of laughter behind him. He was on a mission and a little twerp like this wouldn't slow him down. Stallings nodded, collected the photo, turned, and marched out of the grubby lobby of the small motel west of the St. Johns River.

As soon as he stepped out onto the cracked and uneven sidewalk of downtown Jacksonville, a dribble of rain blew onto his face. At least the heat and humidity of late summer in North Florida wasn't making him drip with sweat; the rain kept him cool.

Patty Levine, lingering behind at the manager's office to smooth over any hard feelings, caught up to Stallings on the sidewalk. She said, "You know you can't really treat everyone like they're a sexual predator or someone about to snatch a kid off the street. I appreciate the fact you're scary and get information quickly, but sometimes it wouldn't hurt to answer a question like why we're looking for someone."

He turned and looked at Patty's bright, pretty face framed with shoulder-length blond hair and said, "Maybe I misread what Leah's parents wanted. I thought they wanted to find their daughter. I thought you agreed with me that this was a good case because we could provide the Tischlers with an explanation of what happened to their daughter."

"Actually, I said it would be *nice* to provide the Tischlers with an answer, but I'm not certain we'll find a smart teenager who doesn't want to be found."

"Then will you humor me?"

Patty flashed a perfect smile and nodded her head. She knew what she was doing. It never hurt to avoid complaints, but she also allowed Stallings wide latitude. Maybe too wide sometimes.

Stallings knew his younger partner would like to be involved in bigger cases but was very loyal to him. He also knew she was very sensitive to the fact that one of the few things that gave him any comfort was working on cases like this. He didn't want to take advantage of her, but he certainly didn't want to lose her as his partner either. She could do so many things and get so many more places than he could based on her looks and personality. The world of police work was evolving and he was stuck in the Jurassic period.

Patty said, "What's your gut say about Leah?"

"I still think she ran away, but the fact that there's no sign of her scares me. This was her first time running away so I don't think she'd leave J-Ville. Someone had to have seen her."

They kept walking down North Myrtle Avenue, occasionally stopping to show the photo of Leah to different vendors or low-cost hotel operators.

Stallings said, "My father doesn't live too far from here."

"How's that going?"

Stallings shrugged. "He's got a lot to make up for and a lot to catch up on. We've been taking it slow, but the kids really get a kick out of seeing him. It seems like he takes their minds off my troubles with Maria. They don't hold the resentment my sister and I did toward the old man. Shit, Helen hasn't even spoken to him yet."

Patty nodded, knowing not to say too much about Stallings's screwed-up personal life.

Stallings said, "What's your boyfriend up to?" He liked the face she made when he referred to the chief homicide detective as her boyfriend. Patty and Tony Mazzetti had worked hard to keep their relationship quiet so that no one in management would feel like they had to move either of them off the squad.

Patty said, "He's been on the Rolling Hills homicide since last week."

Stallings thought about the young mother who'd been strangled in her own bed in the upscale community. Thankfully the killer had not bothered her two sleeping children. The case had garnered quite a bit of media attention, which always seemed to please Tony Mazzetti. The community was always outraged when an innocent person was harmed in their own home. It struck a nerve. A primal fear everyone held. The TV stations thrived on shit like that.

Stallings said, "Any new leads?"

"No, but you know what a bulldog Tony can be."

"Yeah, a regular Rottweiler."

"I wish you two could learn to coexist more peacefully."

"Tell him to stop being such an asshole."

"He said the same thing about you last night."

Stallings stopped and turned, making a face like he was hurt. "You don't really care what an asshole like Tony Mazzetti thinks of me, do you?"

"He doesn't know you well enough to realize what an asshole you can be."

Stallings laughed as they kept walking, happy he had a partner with a decent sense of humor.

An hour later, John Stallings sat at a picnic table across the street from the Police Memorial Building or PMB. It was one of the places that many of the detectives used to get away from the office without being away from the office. He considered some of the things Patty had said about being edgy and latching on to the Leah Tischler case like a shark chomping on a chummed baitfish. He knew why he was acting like a maniac. It was the same reason Maria had been even more distant to him. The third anniversary of Jeanie's disappearance was quickly approaching. Next Wednesday would be three long years without his oldest daughter in the house. The first year had gone by so fast it hadn't hit him. He'd been so busy searching for his daughter and so hopeful she'd still somehow be found it didn't seem like a big deal. By the second anniversary everything around the house had settled down and Maria had slipped into that odd, computer-support-group cocoon of hers. They were barely speaking and the daily activity of taking care of Charlie and Lauren kept him so occupied he didn't dwell on it.

This year was another story. The kids didn't need him as much and he wasn't even living at home. He avoided the lonely two-bedroom house he'd rented except to sleep and occasionally eat. So he'd had time to think about his missing daughter and what it was like three years ago. The wave of fear washing through him, the devastating aftermath of the empty bedroom at the top of the stairs, the feeling of failure and despair.

The day Jeanie went missing was easily the worst day of his life. He was once stabbed in a fight with a drunken homeless man. That moment of realization when the blade seemed to appear out of nowhere and plunge into the left side of his stomach was terrifying and painful beyond words. He'd take a knife in the gut every day if he could just have Jeanie back.

He liked to focus on the good times he'd had with his daughter. Not the fights or sleepless nights after he had found a small bag of marijuana in her purse. One of his favorite memories was when she had turned twelve and joined a lacrosse club at her school. One game into the season the coach lost his job and had to move to Dallas. Stallings stepped in as the coach even though he didn't know the rules, strategy, or goals of the game. But all the girls, especially Jeanie, appreciated his effort and he'd never forget those sunny Sunday afternoons when they had practiced until no one had the energy to run up and down the field.

His first week coaching he tried to adjust and not yell at the girls like he had the boys' football team he coached a few years earlier. It didn't take him long to realize the girls were tougher and smarter than the boys their own age. Finally he followed his instincts and the team became one of the most feared lacrosse clubs in the county.

The highlight of the season didn't come after the championship game. It was much earlier, after the second win, during a long Wednesday evening practice. The girls were filling out an order form for photos with the team mom, a lovely woman from East Arlington. Jeanie walked over to her dad and plopped down next to him, just off the field. For no reason she reached across and gave him a big hug. All she said was, "Thanks, Dad." It was among the most precious moments of his whole life and it was the moment he chose to reflect on while sitting on the hard bench across from the Police Memorial Building.

He was glad no one was around when he had to use his shirttail to wipe the tears off his cheeks.

FOUR

After lunch, John Stallings and Patty Levine sat in their office at the Police Memorial Building. The detective bureau on the second floor of the PMB was affectionately referred to as the Land That Time Forgot because the detectives rarely saw the new equipment and innovations the rest of the building enjoyed. Stallings didn't mind it; he had never cared about the condition of the office because he felt like a real detective needed to be out on the street working cases, not sitting around a plush office, chatting with the other cops about how much work they did. In fact, he usually felt antsy at his desk, but it was a necessary evil to keep track of all the leads he and Patty followed every day. He rarely paid attention to the detectives' comings and goings, but today he did notice the bureau was empty and their sergeant, Yvonne Zuni, was not at her desk in the small, separate office at the end of the squad bay.

His cell phone rang and he took a second to screen the call, seeing the name of the lead homicide detective, Tony Mazzetti, appear on the small Motorola phone. He considered not answering because he hated talking to the smug son of a bitch. Then he realized Tony Mazzetti didn't enjoy talking to him either and decided it might be important.

Stallings answered the phone and said, "What's up, Tony?"

"I need your help."

A small smile spread across Stallings's face. "Really now? You need my help? This is an interesting situation. Do you mind saying it again? I like the sound of it."

"I need your help, Stall. That's as much as I'd like to banter back and forth with you. I need your fucking help right now."

Stallings knew when it was time for fun and games; now Mazzetti sounded serious. "What's wrong, Tony?"

"I have a body at a construction site in the south end of town."

"You need help on a homicide?"

"Patty gave me one of the info sheets you made up on the missing girl, Leah Tischler."

"Oh God, you found her body?"

"No. This victim is named Kathy Mizell."

"I don't understand. What'd you need me for?"

"We identified the belt used to strangle her. It's from the swanky private school the missing girl attended."

Stallings didn't say anything as silence held on the crackle of static over the cell phones.

Mazzetti said, "I think it's Leah Tischler's belt."

Patty Levine sat in the passenger seat of John Stallings's county-issued Chevy Impala. She didn't try to engage him in small talk; she knew him too well. His mood always turned dark after hearing about the death of any young woman. This one was more devastating because of the implication that Leah Tischler was dead as well. No cop took a missing girl more seriously or her death harder. Unfortunately it was an all too common event. And that was just one of many concerns Patty had for her partner, who'd endured far too much stress in recent months. Patty looked across at Stallings, who focused his attention on the road, moving fast but not recklessly. His normally short, brown, curly hair barely touched his collar, and his handsome face, with the scar over one eyebrow and a slightly broken nose, gave him the look of a former football star who'd stayed in pretty good shape since college.

He rarely spoke to her about his problems with Maria, but that wasn't the heaviest weight on him right now. Patty didn't think he or his wife had ever moved past the disappearance of Jeanie. No parent really did, and Maria and John Stallings weren't just any parents. They were both trying to change the world in their own ways: Maria by involving herself in peer counseling for other grieving parents and Stallings through his work in Missing Persons. Now Stallings had set up house not far from the family and had been working hard to make time for the kids. Any time something like this happened, Stallings tended to tune out everything by finding the person responsible. For his sake Patty hoped they had a suspect in custody already.

A few blocks after exiting I-95, Patty could see the police activity and the first of the news trucks arriving on the scene. Stallings pulled the car to the curb more than two blocks from the action in an effort to stay under the radar of the news reporters. Based on his history of capturing serial killers, every reporter in Jacksonville tended to focus on Stallings whenever he arrived at a homicide scene. Stallings didn't like it and it drove Tony Mazzetti absolutely crazy. Patty and Stallings slid over to the edge of the scene and gave their names to the patrolman who was keeping a log of everyone who entered the crime scene.

Stressful times like this pushed Patty to reach for a Xanax or some other pharmaceutical crutch. She'd been working hard to ease off the pills and hadn't used an Ambien to sleep in over a week, resulting in about five hours of total sleep in seven days. She had taken one Xanax for anxiety two days ago and purposely hadn't carried any with her the last two days. She'd even allowed her prescription for Vicodin and another painkiller expire. Now, as they faced another traumatic scene, Patty felt the familiar pang of anxiety and desire for her soothing drug. She craved one to calm her down. Instead she focused on the grim task at hand.

Patty did a quick survey of the scene, wondering who was here already. A call like this, happening in the middle of a weekday, when things were generally slow, attracted cops from all parts of the city. But her new sergeant, Yvonne Zuni, did a pretty good job of scaring away anyone who wasn't vital to the investigation. Her reputation and nickname, Yvonne the Terrible, tended to keep people on task. And nothing was more at odds with her nickname than her looks. A petite build and exotic face with long black hair made it hard to believe she was one of the most feared sergeants in the entire Jacksonville Sheriff's Office. And now she was doing her usual efficient job of directing activities.

Patty saw her boyfriend, Tony Mazzetti, standing next to a green construction Dumpster with the two-letter logo of Waste Management on the side. Screens had been erected in front of it to keep the media from getting any direct shots of activity going on inside the Dumpster. Patty headed his way.

As she approached, Patty stepped onto a sidewalk, giving her a view into the Dumpster, which had settled a few feet lower in front of a gutted strip mall with nothing but walls and a roof standing. She saw two crime scene techs working behind the screens and realized the body was still there. She could clearly see the young woman with long, dark hair. The color was drained out of her face and her eyes were ringed with a pale discharge, which sometimes occurred during decomposition. As she stepped next to Mazzetti, Patty realized how the woman had died. A black leather belt with an ornate buckle was wrapped around her throat. She shuddered at the idea of what this woman had gone through.

Patty cut her eyes over to Stallings, who was speaking with the sergeant out of view of the Dumpster. She hoped it stayed that way. He didn't need a vivid reminder of what could've happened to his own daughter. Any time Patty saw him in conversation with a superior she worried. There were rumors around the department about how Stallings had gone crazy and beat up a rich-kid suspect a few months ago. Patty knew it was no rumor. She'd been there when Stallings caught the pharmaceutical rep handing some free samples to a young coed. Because of the incident, the detectives in the crimes/persons unit learned quickly their new sergeant, Yvonne the Terrible, wasn't quite so terrible. She was more of a miracle worker and steered the focus off Stallings so he could continue to work a big case going on at the time.

Patty stepped next to Tony Mazzetti and said, "Where'd you get the screens?"

Mazzetti turned his handsome face on his thick, muscular neck and said, "Paramedics had them for some reason and loaned them to us. Who would've guessed firemen could be helpful on occasion?" His dark brown eyes scanned the immediate area and settled back on Patty. In a much lower voice he said, "You look great, I'm glad I have something to distract me for a few minutes. This one is ugly."

"How're you holding up?"

The big man shrugged, straining his tailored shirt. "I'm getting used to Sparky Taylor as a partner. I can't believe Hoagie accepted the teaching job at the police academy for three months."

"I heard Sparky is really, really smart."

"He's also really, really weird."

Patty let her eyes drift to Mazzetti's new partner. He was built like a giant pear. Patty figured the African American man was about forty, but with the extra weight and floppy clothes he wore, it was very difficult to be accurate. He'd looked the same six years ago when Patty had first met him. Back then he'd been the tech agent for the department. Basically an audiovisual guy who could plant bugs, hide cameras, and work complex wiretap equipment. But all that ended for Sparky Taylor when he got hopelessly wedged in the bathroom window of a suspect's house after planting a microphone for the narcotics unit. Although the suspect had not come home and seen it himself, the neighbors had told him about the fire department and other cops rescuing a heavyset black man squeezing out of a back window. The department had been forced to reveal its court-ordered microphone and wiretap warrants. Since that incident, Sparky, whose real name was Cliff, had floated around different units in the detective bureau. Now he'd landed in homicide.

Patty turned to Mazzetti. "Any ideas on this one yet?"

"Her I.D. says she's Kathy Mizell, nineteen, and a student at UNF. Her parents said she didn't come home last night, which wasn't unusual. She stayed with friends near campus a couple of nights a week."

Patty felt sick at the idea of a bright young student ending up like this. "What about the scene itself?"

"She wasn't killed here, just dumped. I called you guys because of the photo of your missing girl. I recognized the buckle on the belt. Has to be her belt."

"Seems reasonable, but where's her body and why would the killer link two victims?"

Mazzetti sighed, saying, "I'm trying to find any possible link to the body in Rolling Hills. So far, aside from the mode of death being asphyxiation, there's nothing to connect the women. I don't want to make the same mistakes I've made in the past."

Patty was so proud of him for even admitting he'd ever made a mistake she wanted to give him a hug right there on the spot. She looked back up and saw the dead girl's face as one of the crime scene techs moved to one side. She knew she'd see that face in her short periods of dreaming tonight.

FIVE

He sat outside a McDonald's not far from his ware-house with the living quarters above. He had a dream lease. The two-bedroom apartment covered half of the second floor above his shop and was nicer than half the condos in the city. He watched the two little girls in the covered ball pit. Blond heads bobbing up and down out of sight. The clouds and light rain forced him to stay under the overhang, but at least he had time to enjoy his Big Mac, fries, and Coca-Cola. One of the drywall workers he saw on jobs left the McDonald's and waved to him.

The burly young man said, "Hey, Buddy."

He lifted his half-eaten Big Mac as a greeting and nodded. As the only employee of his business he had no need to make close friends. He was either "Buddy" or "the guy from Classic Glass Concepts." That was how most of the construction business worked. Since his custom glass business took him to only the high-end homes and businesses, he usually saw the same companies catering to the wealthy. He had hoped, when he first started out in business, that his glassblowing talents would allow him to make money creating works of art. He quickly learned that to make a living in the glass business, you had to adapt. Now only a few square feet of his warehouse were dedicated to the actual art he had studied for most of his life. The walls of the warehouse held sheets of thick glass, some etched with exotic designs.

That was how he'd found the victim three weeks ago in Rolling Hills. He was working in a fancy house down the street. All the rich people insisted he use an unmarked van so he was parked in a driveway and no one noticed him. The street was crammed with lawn and pool service trucks and three separate construction crews working on remodelings. The gate to the community was unlocked for all the workers. He'd noticed Pamela Kimble walking with her children one day. Tall and graceful, she had the gait of a runner sidetracked by a pregnancy, fast and deliberate with the kids trying to keep up. He waited until he was done with the job, then came back two days later and parked at a house where he had installed an interior etched glass panel. He knew the owner wouldn't be home. He was careful to leave an invoice on the front door handle in case anyone noticed him, but no one did. No one ever did. Rich people use workers but don't notice them.

He'd slipped into Pamela's house in the middle of the day. She hadn't even known someone was inside until he had his hand around her lovely throat. He'd surprised her as she took a nap in her cool, dark bedroom on the mammoth king-sized bed. Sprawled in workout clothes and a loose T-shirt, she was the perfect picture of a suburban mom.

He had used his hands to choke her, requiring him to wear simple rubber surgical gloves, so he fumbled with his homemade glass jar. An exact little cylinder like the others. He opened his fingers slightly to let her gasp, then exhale, only to tighten his grip harder. It was difficult to describe the peace he felt when her body finally went limp and he let her lie across his lap for a few minutes. She was definitely worthy of eternity. He thought, in the long expanse of time, she might see what he was really doing for her. For her essence and memory. He slipped back out of the house, her kids sleeping in front of the TV in the next room. It was a great moment.

He had been shaken by his experience getting rid of the body the night before. The idea that someone might surprise him in such a vulnerable position was terrifying. He'd made some mistakes. He hoped he hadn't left a fingerprint or DNA somewhere on the body. He almost always used some kind of gloves. It was bad enough he had used the belt and been so flustered he left it. Not that it could be linked directly to him, but it was too unusual to be ignored. He liked leaving as little as possible in terms of evidence or clues. He wasn't like the nuts in the movies who enjoyed taunting the police.

For so long he'd been patient and careful never to use a woman who could be linked to him as a subject for his work of art. He wondered if it was really necessary. Were the cops really that good at discovering minute clues? He doubted it. That was one of the reasons he had picked up the pace lately. He realized his work of art would take too long to complete if he only added a piece every other year or so. But last night had spooked him.

The buzz of the encounter had him pumped up. He felt like a kid on Christmas morning as he calculated how many more he needed. Not too many now. Soon he'd have a real monument. A memorial that would be special. He couldn't help but smile as he thought about his work of art in progress for sixteen years.

He finished his Big Mac and took a long swig of Coke. A red plastic ball popped out of the pit and rolled next to his heavy work boot. As he bent down to retrieve it, one of the blond girls scampered out of he ball pit, red ribbons tying her ponytail, flopping over to one side. She skidded to a stop about ten feet away and fixed her blue eyes on him. A smile swept across her face, showing one missing front tooth.

Then his moment of humanity was shattered when he heard an unmistakable voice say, "Look who's here, the squatter."

He looked up slowly, knowing exactly who had the sneer in her voice. He was surprised it wasn't just Cheryl, but her sweet, younger sister too. Poor Donna had a look of horror on her face as Cheryl marched to-ward him.

Buddy mumbled, "Hello, ladies."

Cheryl jumped right to the point. "You ready to ac-cept our offer?"

"I'm looking, but I *do* have six years left on my lease."

"I can have that voided in court."

"You keep saying that. If that's true, why are you after me to move the shop?"

She growled in frustration. Her sharp features flushed red, while Donna looked on silently. He knew Cheryl had a chance to rent the warehouse for twice what he paid and was pissed her late father had made the agreement. But she was stuck. She also hated him because Donna thought he was sweet. Like their father had. Buddy always figured that was one of the reasons the old man had given him an extended lease. He wanted Buddy to hook up with his daughter. The old man's drastically younger Lebanese wife had produced the two pretty daughters after he was fifty. He had done his best to make sure they were secure before their combined drama had sent him to the grave at seventy-seven last year.

Buddy had options in his living arrangements, but he liked annoying Cheryl too. He always kept a cheap apartment downtown. He had a few things there for storage and spent the night there when the power was knocked out to his warehouse and home a few months back. The place was cheap and on the outside chance this crazy chick got him out of his current place at least he'd have somewhere to crash.

Cheryl turned, shoving her sister in front of her, then stooped and wheeled on her heel one last time to say, "This isn't over. We won't be held hostage." She followed Buddy's eyes to her sister and added, "And stay the fuck away from Donna."

John Stallings hung up the phone at his desk before heading into the conference room, where the other detectives had gathered to discuss the leads to be followed on the new homicide. The link to Leah Tischler put everyone into high gear because of the implications of a possible serial killer. He'd called to check on the kids and tell Charlie he wouldn't be able to practice soccer with him. The seven-year-old took the news in stride. His fourteen-year-old, on the other hand, seemed relieved she wouldn't have to put up with her father today. He didn't bother to talk to Maria. She needed some space and he was doing his damnedest to give it to her. But he could tell she appreciated his efforts to stay connected with the kids and didn't mind him swinging by the house almost every day.

Meetings like this, after normal working hours, were the biggest sticking point in his marriage. Although he had never realized how much time it took away from his marriage, police work had found a way to crush his family life. He wondered how cops with young kids ever managed to balance their lives.

The conference room was jammed with detectives. Tony Mazzetti sat at one end of the table, but it was Yvonne Zuni who was clearly in charge. She leaned on the table near the center as she made sure everyone understood his or her role in the investigation. The dynamics of an investigation had changed greatly from when Stallings had first started sixteen years earlier. In these lean economic times, overtime was a premium and management found a way around the expensive program by farming out leads to a number of different detectives. As usual, Tony Mazzetti would run the investigation. His new partner, Sparky Taylor, took notes as Sergeant Zuni explained the plan of attack.

Stallings liked the odd detective. The guy was a virtual reference book of the sheriff's office policy and procedure. He could quote specific statutes under the Florida criminal code for the most common crimes they had to deal with. A graduate of Georgia Tech, with a degree in engineering, Sparky had a different way of looking at things from most detectives. Stallings appreciated new perspectives.

Mazzetti droned on about the scene and his brilliance in noticing the unusual buckle on the belt used in the homicide. He told them the victim's brief background to give them avenues to investigate, like who she hung out with, boyfriends, and creepy guys in her classes, but the biggest detail was Leah Tischler's belt. All Stallings could think about was where Leah was. Dead or alive, he'd like to find her and give her parents some form of closure. Her wealthy attorney father was already blaming his long hours for her disappearance. Stallings could relate. But now Stallings wondered if he thought Leah could hold a clue to his own daughter. Was this what he would find? Had Jeanie run away, then stumbled into a monster like this? He shuddered at the thought and looked back up at the crowd in the room as the sergeant started to talk.

Yvonne Zuni's dark eyes flashed at Stallings. "Stall, we're gonna need you to work your magic. Focus on Leah Tischler and find out if anyone noticed her around. There's a good chance she had run away when this creep found her."

Stallings just nodded. This was his strength and what he was needed for most often. Besides, he owed the new sarge and would do anything she asked. She may have been a pain in the ass administratively, but there was no one he'd rather have backing him up if he ever got in trouble again.

Tony Mazzetti stared down in silence at the plain chicken breast, tiny helping of pasta, and raw vegetables on his plate. It was tough staying fit while trying to make a relationship work. He glanced over at Patty's plate of lasagna and basket of garlic rolls. As a kid in Brooklyn, a meal in a nice Italian joint was a special occasion. Now it was an exercise in restraint. Before he could feel sorry for himself he remembered he needed to talk to a supervisor at public transportation. He pulled out his pocket-sized, leather-bound notepad and scratched a one-line reminder. When he looked back at Patty, her blue eyes were focused on him like lasers.

He stuffed the notepad sheepishly into his coat pocket. "Sorry, I'm not used to having to balance a homicide and a relationship. It's all new to me. And with no overtime to go out and hit the streets you have to make use of any time an idea pops into your head."

She smiled that sweet smile and took another monstrous bite of lasagna. She looked tired, and he worried she pushed herself too hard in her search for runaways with John Stallings. But homicide was no piece of cake either and if she was gonna be running leads on this new case, she wouldn't catch up on her rest anytime soon.

Relationships might be new to him, but homicide was old hat. He wasn't sure what would happen in his romance. It was uncharted territory—a scary, thrilling adventure ride—but he knew he'd never be able to stomach an unsolved homicide. His phenomenal clearance rate was one of the few things he could point to as an accomplishment and he liked everyone at JSO knowing he kicked ass in homicide investigations. He told himself that was why they called him the King of Homicide. The murder he'd been working on until this afternoon had really eaten at him. Pamela Kimble had left behind a husband and two kids. She was no gangbanger or dope dealer gunned down by a competitor. He knew someone else would take up any slack on the Kathy Mizell case. Maybe even Stallings, who seemed to have a thing for young, confused women who ended up in bad situations. Everyone in the S.O. understood Stallings had some kind of deep-seated desire to make up for whatever had happened to his own daughter. He may not have been Mazzetti's best friend, but there was no denying he was a hell of a cop.

Patty set down her fork, wiped her face, and said, "Do you really think the world would come to an end if we went public with our relationship?"

"There's nothing I'd like better than to tell people you're my girlfriend, but based on policy and what they've done in the past, one of us would have to transfer out of the squad. I figured we'd let things go until we have no choice." He didn't want to bring up the recent feeling that they were drifting apart. Maybe it was just the natural rhythm of a relationship and he didn't have the experience to deal with it correctly.

"You mean you wouldn't be willing to work road patrol instead of homicide just for me?"

He hesitated, not only unsure of his answer, but not wanting to upset Patty. She burst out laughing, covering her face with her hand. Then gave him a sly smile.

"I can't believe you'd fall for something like that. I'd never put you in that position." She reached across the small table and clasped his hand.

He liked her playful side and realized he had to loosen up. He'd been out of uniform and stuck working in the detective bureau for so long he'd forgotten what it was like to just play around. Every cop knew half the job was practical jokes, but somehow he had missed out on that because of his ambition. He'd never really minded being on the outside looking in, but now he realized there was nothing wrong with making a beautiful girl like this smile.

Even if it wasn't as much as he had made her smile a month ago.

SIX

Buddy watched the two women as they marched through the small McDonald's courtyard. He had to admire the shape of them walking away, even though in Cheryl's case he didn't want to. Her surgically enhanced body gave her outrageous curves. It was Donna's beautiful innocent eyes he noticed as she glanced over her shoulder at him, stepping into the passenger seat of her sister's Chrysler 300.

He had considered Donna for his work of art on several occasions. Those big brown doe eyes and wide, full lips gave her an innocent look. She just had nothing to offer eternity. Donna was a lost child who followed her sister around like a puppy. Besides, he knew her and she might point police in his direction if she turned up dead. Buddy liked the twenty-four-year-old. Her sweet disposition more than made up for her lack of brainpower.

He knew the pressure to break his lease and move out was a direct result of Cheryl's incessant harping. She'd taken over most of the daily business activities of her father, including the renting of the six warehouses across the city as well as the small apartment complex on the east side of the river. Her mother had been an internationally known model in Lebanon and greatly preferred lounging at their beautiful house in Ponte Vedra Beach to being troubled with the daily burdens of collecting rent and dealing with tenants.

Cheryl, on the other hand, had a ruthless streak that served her well as a landlord. Buddy had only met her mother once and she seemed pleasant enough and certainly the women's father was a gentleman. After Buddy had blown him a special glass vase for his twenty-fifth anniversary, the man had signed a sweetheart ten-year lease with him, which he allowed Buddy to pay up front. Now, with six years left on the lease, he was probably Cheryl's biggest problem.

He caught Cheryl's murderous glare from inside the black sedan and thought to himself how nice it'd be to choke the life out of her. Too bad she wasn't worthy.

John Stallings rolled over for the fifteenth time in the last sixteen minutes and stared at the clock on the nightstand. He flung the covers off in frustration and growled quietly to the empty room, then growled louder, so it filled the empty house. It was nearly midnight and he was no closer to sleep than he had been when he laid down at 10:15. His insomnia was as much a result of having no family and therefore no anchor in his life as it was of picturing Kathy Mizell shoved into a Dumpster and Leah Tischler at the bottom of a canal somewhere. Both families were crushed tonight.

Stallings couldn't shake the feeling he'd failed Leah

Tischler. He knew rationally that wasn't how to look at the situation, but who could stay rational when a young woman was dead? If you stayed rational you went crazy.

He felt like he'd done everything he possibly could to save his own family. Maybe it wasn't the job. Maybe Maria had grown tired of him. But he thought he'd had a handle on both the job and his home after Jeanie disappeared. Now he realized it was just a fantasy. He knew Maria had been through a lot and had her whole life ahead of her. If leaving him on the curb made her feel better, he was prepared to go through it graciously. He'd made no comments when he discovered that Maria had already been out on several dates. All Stallings wanted was the kids to be happy, and right now he wouldn't mind sleeping for a few hours, but he knew it wouldn't happen.

He rolled out of the bed that had been in the room when he'd moved into the small house in Lakewood and slipped on his jeans and a Jacksonville Jaguars T-shirt. It was time to get a jump on interviews of people who might have run into Leah Tischler.

Thirty minutes later he found himself parking his county-issued Impala and walking down West Davis Street. It was never too late to talk to the street people of Jacksonville. Many cops overlooked them as a source of information, but Stallings knew nothing occurred in the city without the street people seeing or hearing about it.

The street population encompassed so much more than the homeless. Anyone out all the time, whether selling drugs or their bodies, came in contact with a lot of people. Even a runaway from a wealthy family, if that's what Leah Tischler was. It was possible the killer had snatched her from society, but Stallings felt it was more likely the young woman had slipped off society's radar for a little while before the killer found her. There was always the chance she was still alive and had discarded her belt, but Stallings wanted to be practical and veer away from fantasy. He had a job to do and had to be reasonable no matter what his hopes were.

Stallings wasn't like most cops. He had relationships with people. He worked the street like a host greeting guests or a bouncer scaring jerks. No one knew Leah Tischler when Stallings showed them her photos. The discovery of her belt wrapped around the afternoon's murder victim had not been released to the public yet.

Then he saw someone who might hold some valuable information. An acquaintance with his ear to the ground and his finger on the pulse of the drug pipeline running through Jacksonville. Stallings watched the man in a wifebeater shirt stop and speak to different people along the street. He handed off baggies to two or three of them and was completely oblivious to Stallings. People didn't notice cops unless there were two of them in a marked cruiser. Stallings waited patiently until the man was only a few feet away; then he stepped from the side of the building where he'd been leaning and said, "Hi, Peep. Whatcha doing out so late?"

The scruffy man jerked his head and looked at Stallings for only an instant before he turned and darted across the street like a sprinter in the Olympics. Stallings realized if he wanted to talk to the man, he'd have to follow.

SEVEN

John Stallings had spent too many years as a cop to waste his energy matching a scared drug dealer step for step. That left him with two options: go back to his car and look for him or figure out where the man was running to and beat him there. Stallings cut down Houston Street to Jefferson and turned left.

The man he was chasing was known on the street as Peep Moran because of his penchant for spying on women while they were urinating. It was a simple hobby in the world of the homeless because bathrooms were not always available. In the consumer-driven society of the United States many businesses purposely used the bathrooms as a perk for customers only. Consequently many street people were forced to use nature as their lavatory whether the middle-class people around them wanted to admit it or not. In his whole career as a road patrolman, Stallings had never arrested anyone for urinating in public. He knew when the need came over you, you had to relieve yourself. He didn't care if the reason was too much beer or no home to go back to; no one should legislate using the restroom.

He also knew Peep wouldn't venture too far or risk crossing one of the freeways on foot. This was an educated guess on Stallings's part, but one he felt pretty comfortable with. As he eased onto Jefferson Street he saw Peep Moran with his head down and his hands on his knees, trying to catch his breath. Stallings never wasted time yelling at someone to stop; instead he closed the distance between them quickly and by the time a suspect realized he'd been seen, it was too late to flee.

Stallings surprised the scrawny man, but instead of showing his shock, Peep acted casual. "Hey, Stall. Looking for runaways?"

Stallings let the scared little man see his smile and said, "Why would you run from me? I thought we were friends."

"Friends don't break other friends' arms."

"And friends don't sell drugs to other friends' wives."

Peep gave him a slight bow and said, "Touché. We've established we're not friends and therefore it should be obvious I ran from you because I'm afraid."

"Afraid of me?"

"Everyone's afraid of you, Stall. Maybe the runaways and hookers like you, but none of the rest of us who make a living off them have ever had a particularly pleasant encounter with you."

"Peep, you sound a lot more articulate. You been going to school?"

"Mostly I haven't taken my own shit. I haven't had any prescription pills in six weeks and I'm down to only smoking pot on the weekends"

"How's that working out for you?"

The smaller man shrugged. "Aside from being a little smarter and saving some money, I'm not sure it's worth the hassle."

"You heard about the girl's body found in the Dumpster this afternoon?"

Peep nodded. He swallowed and his Adam's apple bobbed in his scrawny throat.

Stallings showed him the photo Leah Tischler's parents had provided. He studied Peep's face and realized the dope dealer recognized her.

Peep said, "She's dead?"

"No, but she's connected to the body in the Dumpster."

Peep nervously fumbled with his hair.

"Give it up, Peep. What'd you know about her?"

"I, er, I might've seen her."

"Where?" He placed a hand on Peep's grubby T-shirt.

"C'mon, Stall, I don't remember. There's a flood of scared girls rolling through here. Some leaving home for good and some just throwing a scare into their parents so they can use the Navigator more often or stay out on weeknights."

"Is that all you know about her?"

"Seems like I saw her right around here, but I can't remember."

"When?" He twisted the shirt in his grip and pulled Peep closer to him. The familiar anger bubbling up inside of him

Sweat beaded on Peep's forehead.

"I don't know. Her face is familiar."

Now Stallings had the man on his tiptoes and he thought about how Peep made a living on others' sorrows. He thought about the value of scaring punks like this to get information and Jeanie's cold trail and the slight possibility of reviving it if Leah Tischler had met the same fate.

A woman's voice broke his trance.

"What's going on here?"

Stallings released Peep and turned to see a woman with dark hair in jeans and a Florida State sweatshirt. She locked her eyes with Stallings, not backing down.

Stallings faced her and said, "It's all right, ma'am. I'm a police officer." She had a pretty face and beautiful, oval eyes. She was in her mid-thirties and wore her dark hair in a ponytail.

"Is this how a JSO officer is supposed to act?"

He thought for a moment and wondered if she was right. He let his emotions get the better of him.

Peep blurted out, "I'll keep my ears open and let you know what I hear."

Stallings hardly noticed him scamper past the woman and around the corner.

The woman nodded good-bye and was gone as quickly. Stallings wanted to know who the hell she was.

Buddy arranged the photos on the dreary brown wall of his apartment above his shop. He appreciated art in whatever form it took. In this case it was a photographer who, like him, had an eye for beautiful women. The photographer, named Petter Hegre, shot them in black and white, or as they said in the new millennium, monochrome. He missed simple phrases he'd grown up with. He missed the fact that artists were no longer revered, replaced by guys like Warren Buffett or that insufferable Donald Trump.

Buddy had lived in the apartment since his thirtieth birthday over five years ago. Before that, he shared a house with a coworker at another glass company. His mom had kicked him out of the house at twenty-two. Even though she had plenty of room and was all alone.

She had said it was so he'd become more independent, but mainly it was because she suspected him of killing her two cats. It was true, but he'd never admitted it. Not to anyone. He'd learned it was one of the keys to keep from being caught. It was also where he'd learned another important lesson: what attracted him to killing was that one, last, perfect breath. With his mother's cats he'd used a kitchen knife to stab a tabby called Tiger. He'd stuck it and watched like a scientist as it wiggled on the blade for less than a minute. There wasn't much thrill to killing something that way. But Blackie, a much bigger cat, was another story. He had a plan for this big black beast that rarely got off the couch and followed him with its eyes to let him know he was further down the affection chain in the house. He'd worn thick, canvas gardening gloves when he wrapped his hands around Blackie's furry black throat. The cat had kicked and clawed at his hands and made a tiny squeal, but in the end he knew the feeling of choking something couldn't be replaced: that last moment when his victim was conscious but had no hope. The divine instants when he realized he had the absolute power of life and death. But the whole experiment pissed off his mother. It wasn't until a year later with a neighbor's Yorkie he discovered the art of capturing a breath. He slipped a plastic bag over the dog and released his grip on its throat for just a moment. He noticed the fog of the dog's breath on the inside of the bag and realized it was possible to capture the essence of something. To harness a last breath. Then it was a matter of finding the right container.

He looked around his apartment and considered all he had learned in the past few months. It made him happy to know he had a grasp on eternity. He had a purpose in life that would outlast him. Most things would.

EIGHT

John Stallings picked Patty Levine up at her condo in his Impala so they could cruise along North Davis and talk to the managers for some of the hotels where runaways hung out.

Patty said, "What'd you do last night?"

"Hit the hay early." It wasn't an exact lie. He had gone to bed early, giving up trying to sleep, and come down here for a look around, but Stallings didn't want to hear Patty tell him how he needed time for himself or needed more rest.

Patty said, "I bet Tony five bucks you'd go out on your own time and see what you could discover. I guess I'll pay up this evening."

Stallings turned and frowned at her. She knew him too well. He mumbled, "Don't pay up."

"I knew it. You gotta stop going out on your own. You coulda been hurt and no one would've known where you were."

He hadn't considered that argument.

Patty added, "You need your rest. I told you to get seven or eight hours of sleep a night."

He nodded and listened for the next fifteen minutes as he cut in and out of Jacksonville traffic, taking surface streets and alleys like any good cop would.

Stallings pulled the Impala to the curb in front of a four-story, brick apartment building. Each unit had one window and about twenty percent of those were boarded. Stallings figured there were maybe a hundred tenants in the whole place. He'd heard this was the new runaway central and under new management. Different buildings popped up in the city as mainstays of runaways. Sometimes it was cheap rent that attracted them. Sometimes it was a manager who looked after the runaways. Either way the new manager here might have seen Leah and maybe even if she met with anyone.

They entered the neat lobby with new, cheap carpet and a plain set of Rooms-To-Go furniture in the corner, where people could gather on a couch and three matching chairs around a coffee table.

Stallings stepped to the clean counter and knocked on the countertop. "Hello?"

Like a good partner, Patty wandered to the hallway and casually stood, but in reality it was an instinct that couldn't be taught at the police academy. She was in position in case something surprising happened and she had to cover Stallings, or if someone rushed them from the hallway, Stallings could do the same for her.

He shifted to expose his gun and badge on his hip so they would be seen by anyone coming out of the office behind the counter. He didn't want to waste a lot of time explaining who he was. He had plenty of his own questions that needed answers.

He was about to call out again when he heard a woman's voice say, "I'll be right out."

He stared as she stepped out of the office and behind the counter.

Her dark eyes met his and she gave him a cursory smile.

The woman said, "Hello, Officer."

It was the woman who had scolded him last night.

A stack of small notebooks were spread across the wide conference room table. Tony Mazzetti looked over the mess at his partner, Sparky Taylor. The fact that it looked as if there were two victims had already pushed everyone to the edge. New information was coming at him from three different sets of detectives and everything was piling up fast.

Mazzetti said, "What'd you think, Sparky? It would help to have some kind of viable theory to filter through some of the shit."

Sparky slowly raised his face from the open file he'd been studying intently and focused his brown eyes on his new partner. "We've already checked former boyfriends and possible stalkers. Those would be the most likely suspects in a case like this. But if we look at the circumstances of the body being dumped it leads us in another direction."

Mazzetti slowly sat down in the seat at the opposite end of the table, staring at Sparky. "Go on."

"First, I don't think the killer, which I'll assume is a 'he' based on the nature of the crime and location of the body, lived close to the construction site. I believe he was driving, so why stay in an area that could help identify you if you've already made the risk of transferring a body to the vehicle? He's pretty strong, yet not necessarily tall because he was able to get the body into the Dumpster, but there were two cinder blocks stacked next to the Dumpster where the body was found. With the number of canals and rivers all over Duval County, a construction site is a poor choice to dump a body."

"All right, Columbo, where does that leave us?"

"It leaves us with a lot of suspects if we considered all the construction workers in the city. I wonder what percentage of construction workers are felons?"

Mazzetti let out a snort of laughter and said, "That's like saying 'What's the bad part of Jacksonville?' I have to say, Jacksonville." He laughed at the old joke every cop in the city liked to tell.

Sparky didn't change his expression and said, "I like Jacksonville. I'm raising two boys here."

"Have you ever seen the NBC special on runaways in Jacksonville?"

"We don't really watch TV around our house."

"Really? None at all?"

"We watch one hour a night as a family. Usually half is the national news and the other half is The History Channel."

"What'd you guys do for fun at night?"

"We play games."

"Like Monopoly?"

"Monopoly leaves too much to luck and has too simplistic a view of world economic pressures to be of any value to the children. We like to play a game which combines Trivial Pursuit with Jenga. You have to answer a question that challenges your intellect, then use your spatial abilities to dismantle the wooden tower pieces. The boys enjoy it very much."

Mazzetti couldn't come up with anything to say and continued to stare in silence. After he gathered his thoughts, he decided his only hope was to refocus their attention on the case. He said, "So where does that leave us? We need a jumping-off point. We have all the usual bases covered. I'd like to hear what you think might be a new way of looking at this homicide."

Sparky said, "The logical place to start looking would be at construction sites. If we have no specific leads on a suspect and the other detectives are looking at the victims, you and I can focus on other things. Whoever dumped Kathy Mizell's body specifically picked a construction site with a full Dumpster. It may not have been a coincidence he realized the Dumpster was going to be hauled away and dumped soon. It's just an idea, but one I've been formulating all day."

Mazzetti took a moment to assess his enigmatic new partner. The guy may have been a techno-freak who had spent most of his career in the tech squad, but he had some good insight. Even with a light Southern accent and relatively soft voice, the guy's comments had impact. He was right. Stallings and Patty were busy working the Leah Tischler aspect of the case. Another set of detectives was looking into Kathy Mizell's background and associations. A third set was running leads and interviewing people at UNF and the health center. So far, Mazzetti and Sparky had been out at the health center talking to Kathy Mizell's instructors and classmates. They had also looked through all the available forensic information. Sitting on the table were security-camera shots from ten different cameras at the health center. That was the last place anyone had seen Kathy Mizell alive and it might provide a clue. But this idea of considering a construction worker wasn't half bad.

Sparky Taylor turned in his seat and started to tap on

the keyboard of the Dell laptop he took everywhere with him. He typed at a speed Mazzetti could not comprehend.

Mazzetti thought about what his partner had said and looked down at his legal pad with a list of tasks to accomplish filling most of two pages. But years of experience had taught him to follow his instincts and right now his instincts said Sparky Taylor was more than just a puffy Georgia Tech engineering graduate with odd habits.

Mazzetti said, "I wish there was an easy way to figure out exactly how many large construction sites there are in the city."

Sparky looked from the computer screen and said, "There are thirty-nine sites requiring one or more debris Dumpsters in the downtown area and surrounding residential neighborhoods. There are an additional eighty-two three-yard Dumpsters spread out at smaller sites across the county."

"How in the hell do you know something like that?"

"I accessed Waste Management's website and went to a page designed for city employees. It's supposed to help code enforcement people when they have issues with debris."

Mazzetti sat, openmouthed, and finally said, "How did you know that site was even available?"

"It was in a memo sent out by the Intel squad about six months ago. Don't you read the memos sent out by the other divisions?"

"Why would I do something like that? It's all I can do keep up with my cases as it is."

Sparky calmly looked across at Mazzetti and said, "Because it's in our policy manual we should read memos distributed from other divisions. It also makes sense on a practical level by increasing the number of people looking at any one problem."

"You'd have to prove to me the value of reading memos from other divisions."

"I thought I just did."

NINE

The pretty woman standing behind the counter in the hotel lobby extended her hand to Stallings and smiled politely. "I'm Liz Dubeck and I run this place. You might recall we met last night." Her sly smile conveyed more than any words could.

Stallings took the hand and nodded, avoiding Patty's intense gaze.

Patty whispered to him, "Aren't you glad you told me the truth already? Otherwise this might be an awkward moment."

Stallings felt like a school kid in a parent/teacher conference as both women turned their attention to him.

Patty took the woman's hand and introduced herself, then set her battered metal case on the counter and started to take down contact information.

Stallings liked how professional Patty could be on a moment's notice.

As soon as Patty had finished, the woman looked at Stallings and said, "What was your problem with the man I saw you with last night?"

"Just a miscommunication."

"You seemed to be making your point very clear."

Now Stallings felt a physical pressure from Patty's gaze. He reached across into Patty's metal case and pulled out a photo of Leah Tischler and laid it out on the counter. "We've been trying very hard to find out if anyone saw her in this area in the last few days. We have reason to believe she might've used a pay phone at the check-cashing store down the street and she would've been looking for a place to stay."

The woman leaned down to look at the photo closely. Her dark ponytail slipped across her shoulder. Stallings appreciated the attention she was giving the photo as well as the shape of her shoulders and neck.

She looked up and said, "She said her name was Lee and she was looking for a room for a couple of nights. I told her she had to let someone know she was okay. She didn't have to tell them where she was, but I didn't want whoever was responsible for her worrying. I could tell right away she wasn't a street person. She had on a school uniform of some kind."

Patty turned to him and said, "That must've been why she called the music teacher."

"I offered the phone here, but she said she'd have to think about it and left before I could stop her." The hotel manager paused. "I hate to ask this, but is she okay?"

Patty took this one and Stallings was glad of it. "She's been missing a few days and there's an indication she may have fallen victim to violent crime."

"Oh my goodness. Is there anything else I can do?"

"You can keep your ears open and let us know if you hear anything."

It was clear this woman was concerned. "Of course, of course, anything you want. Almost everyone in this area comes through here at one time or another." She stepped from behind the counter and joined Stallings and Patty in the lobby.

Stallings took in a breath as she walked past and brushed his arm. She gestured toward the couch and two chairs in the corner of the clean lobby. When they were all seated she said, "I work very hard to make this a clean, safe place for people down on their luck. We get a few grants and I don't always have to charge full rates. I would have let Leah stay here for free if she'd come back after I told her to let someone know she was safe."

Patty reached over and gave the woman a gentle squeeze on her shoulder. "You did the right thing."

Stallings looked around the room and said, "It does look like a nice place. That's hard to find if you're lonely, scared, and have no money."

Liz looked around and nodded. "We've come a long way, but there are always a lot of things to finish around here. You can see the linoleum is peeling in the corners and throw rugs only cover so much. About half the rooms need new beds and it'd be nice to do some cosmetics like replacing this front window that's cracked from top to bottom. I've applied for several federal grants to help."

Stallings looked at the bay window and saw a reflection of light from outside and the hairline crack. "There's only so much you can do, and believe me you've already helped us tremendously."

"I'd do anything to help ease the suffering of a parent worried about a child. Even in your job it's probably hard to completely realize the anguish of missing a child."

Stallings leveled his eyes at her and said, "No, I think I can imagine it."

Buddy sat on a hard, carpeted floor of the dentist's office way down in the southern part of the county, on the edge of an area known as Mandarin. Instead of the goofy posters of giant teeth most dentists had used when he was a kid, there were framed, signed cartoons featuring Donald Duck and Mickey Mouse. The office was comfortable and the staff had been very friendly. And it was really good money for simply installing one four-foot, etched-glass divider with a nicely drawn dolphin exactly in the middle. There were also three outside windows he was going to change, but they didn't have the artistic edge this large sheet of glass offered. For some reason he didn't really mind the mundane job on this bright September morning.

He kept trying to focus all of his attention on the thin edge of the wide glass window as it slid into place. The problem was his mind kept racing as he thought about the girl at the bus stop and the hours he had spent with Jessie, the subject he'd found ten days earlier.

Jessie had been so special. The whole experience was magical. Getting to know her and making sure she was right for his work of art. Those had been a precious few hours. He'd seen her not far off Davis and made sure he parked the van well ahead of her before opening the door. This was an impulse on his part. He had no plans to take any violent action. She came closer with that beautiful wet, tangly hair and a few raindrops staining her white T-shirt. The shirt had the logo on it. A giant bright yellow sun bursting over the horizon with the words HILLSIDE FARMS, OCALA, in blue, under the sun. He made some comment about her being soaked.

The bright young woman turned her head to him and looked in the van. She surprised him by saying, "If I could get someone to give me a ride to Orange Park it would save me a long miserable bus ride."

He didn't hesitate. "My shop's down that way." He said it calmly and coolly, but in fact he could see the top of his building down the street where he was standing right at that moment.

She got in the van and immediately started to chatter about how much she appreciated the ride and she had a friend who would let her stay the night in Orange Park. The young lady introduced herself very properly and he could already tell she met his requirements for eternity.

He drove around the block and hit the automatic garage door opener to his warehouse.

Jessie said, "I thought you said your shop was in Orange Park."

"It is. This is just a warehouse for the glass we work with. We have a couple of them around the city. I'll only be a few minutes and then I'll take you wherever you need to go." He kept his demeanor cool and didn't force anything he said. He invited her to step out and have a soda while he walked past the display glass into his private workspace and selected one of his finished jars. The lid was already made for it, but he had to make the rubber seal that sat inside the glass lid. It only took a second to cut a gasket from a large square of industrial rubber. He never hurried through the warehouse as Jessie sat quietly on one of the stools next to the workbench glancing around the large bay. He had left the bay door open to give her a greater sense of ease, but he knew no one ever walked this far down the street or bothered to look into the boring old glass company's warehouse. The only people who ever bothered him were Cheryl and Donna. Those visits had been too frequent lately. They had already ruined one chance he had at adding to his masterpiece. Barged in and made his subject scurry away like a frightened deer. He never even saw her again. Buddy looked on the bright side: another five minutes and they would've caught him with a dead body in his shop. That would've been enough to cancel his lease.

Jessie watched him as he walked back with a small glass jar in his hand and then saw her eyes drift over to the stairway to his private apartment.

She said, "What's up there?"

"The office." He liked the smooth sound of her voice. It had an innocent and youthful quality to it. He set the jar down and glanced around to see if there was a cord or strap he might be able to use. "Why's a girl like you wandering around downtown Jacksonville on a wet, rainy day like this?"

Now she seemed to withdraw a bit. "My ride fell through and I need to get over to my friend's house. Are we gonna head that way soon?"

He knew she was getting anxious and decided it was time to make his move.

Then a voice shook him out of his thoughts and instantly he was back in the dentist's bright office installing a sheet of glass.

"How's it going?"

It sounded like the voice was coming from a fog and it took a moment more to shake him from his daydream about the lovely Jessie. He cut his eyes to the sound of the voice and saw one of the dental assistants leaning over and smiling at him through the opposite side of the glass, the detailed etching of the dolphin obstructing the side of her face.

He had to blink his eyes hard to refocus his thoughts and form a coherent sentence. "It's going pretty well. I'll have this piece in place by lunch and start on the windows this afternoon."

The woman stepped around the glass, keeping that beautiful smile, and said, "I wish I could concentrate like you. You completely blocked me out while you were setting the glass."

He smiled and let out a laugh. "That's the idea sometimes."

The woman's eyes took a quick scan of the room to make sure they were alone and said, "My name is Mary. What's yours?"

Now he turned his full attention to the pretty young woman with long hair and said, "My friends call me Buddy."

It was after lunch and Patty had a doctor's appointment. Stallings sometimes worried about his younger partner, but she knew the best way to deflect any questions about a doctor's visit was to mumble something about "female issues." That tended to shut him up for at least an hour every time.

He decided to use his precious free moments to run a few blocks down and visit his father. In the last four months, since his father had reentered his life after a twenty-year absence, Stallings had learned a lot about poor choices and forgiveness. He'd also learned a lot about his early perceptions of his parents and their relationship. If his mother hadn't told him she frequently spoke to his father and she held no real resentment toward him, he didn't think there was any way he would've ever spoken to the old man again. But his mother, with her abundant patience and open mind, had explained to him she understood the disease of alcoholism and the pressures his father had been under during his career in the Navy. It'd been a slow process, but his father's open adoration of Lauren and Charlie had given Stallings the incentive to risk getting to know him again.

Now sixty-four years old, he was a shell of the belligerent bully Stallings remembered as a child. The hard-drinking, loudmouth jerk had evolved into a conscientious and surprisingly funny older man. He had not had a drink in six years and moderated a number of different groups to help the homeless and alcoholics in the wide area of Jacksonville's southern downtown. The municipal football stadium and St. Johns River bordered the southern edge of his father's little kingdom. Stallings's office sat within his father's kingdom, but he had never run into the old man. Now Stallings realized he hadn't been looking for him and could've very well seen him without recognizing the old man on a number of occasions.

He parked his Impala directly in front of the tall, run-down but stately rooming house where his father had a single room on the second story in the rear of the building. As Stallings walked up the pathway he noticed his father sitting on one of the comfortable chairs on the covered porch of the large house. Two other men sat on a low sofa with a plastic cover.

His father laid a hardcover book he was reading in his lap and smiled as Stallings approached and took the straight-backed wooden chair next to him.

"Hello, Johnny. What brings you by this time of day?"

"Just wanted to see how you were doing."

When his father smiled and his cloudy eyes seemed to clear, Stallings caught a glimpse of the younger man he had known.

Stallings's father said, "How's that girl of yours doing?"

"Which one?"

"The one you married, goofy."

"Dad, we talked about this. She and I are separated right now."

The older man looked down and shook his head. "That's a shame. I really like Helen."

Stallings was about to casually correct him when he realized the old man had no idea he'd confused Stallings's sister with his wife. He checked quickly to make sure his father hadn't slipped back onto the sauce, leaning in to sniff his breath.

Stallings said, "Her name is Maria. Helen is your daughter." He said it lightly, hoping it would clear his father's head.

The elder Stallings gave a grin and a quick wink. "Just pulling your leg, son." He tapped the side of his head and said, "I'm as sharp as ever."

Even with the comment from his father, Stalling decided to use the visit to make sure the old man hadn't lost a few steps mentally.

* * *

Buddy enjoyed the few minutes he spent talking with Mary. She explained the difference between the dental hygienist and assistant as well as several of the key points of protecting your teeth.

She said, "You have good teeth and a very friendly smile."

"Thank you very much. I appreciate the compliment. How long have you worked here?"

"Almost ten years."

"There is no way. You must've started here when you were fourteen years old." He wasn't just flattering her; she did have a very youthful-looking face.

"You are a charmer. I've been here since I was twenty-two years old and graduated from the program out at the community college."

He liked her friendly manner and now that he looked, she had a few wrinkles, which gave her face a very gentle character. He said, "Maybe we could grab a cup of coffee sometime?"

Her smile already told him his answer. "I'd love to. I'm on vacation for two weeks starting Friday so maybe Friday evening. Otherwise we'd have to wait nine days until I got back from my cruise to Cancún."

"Who you going on the cruise with?"

"I'm trying something new and spending the first three nights of the cruise alone, then meeting three girlfriends when they get on in Cancún. It was the only way we could all work out being together and I didn't want to waste a half a week of vacation. It's very exciting."

Buddy did the math and realized this was an opportunity he couldn't ignore. As long as he kept things quiet, no one would realize he'd be the last person she saw before she missed her departure. That would give him several days to spend with the lovely Mary before he had to worry about anyone missing her.

He looked up and forced a gentle smile on his face, saying, "I'd love to meet you somewhere Friday evening."

TEN

It was early evening and Patty Levine sat on the floor of her Jacksonville condo watching a Rodney Yee DVD and trying to master one of the more advanced yoga poses involving balancing on her hands with her torso lifted off the blue mat on top of the light carpet. She breathed in through her mouth and out through her nose, trying to fill her belly with air as well as her diaphragm. She cleared her mind and did everything Rodney said to, and still she felt like shit.

Patty plopped down onto the mat, placing her right foot across her left leg, and twisted her whole upper body, catching her reflection in the mirror of the open closet door in the hallway. She had no idea why she was so critical of herself. She generally didn't care what others thought and her parents were perfectly reasonable about most aspects of her life. It wasn't until she had gotten serious about gymnastics and started to compete at a high level that she expected more and more of herself. Her hair was tied back in a ponytail and although it wasn't the most glamorous look, she liked her blond hair. But she'd always been self-conscious about her wide-set eyes and the scar at the bridge of her nose she'd received falling off a balance beam her senior year in high school. She bared her teeth to her image in the mirror and, despite most of them being straight and white, all she focused on was her left incisor, which turned slightly outward. She shook her head in disgust and followed the next move on the DVD. That Rodney Yee could really spread his legs.

She muttered, "This is bullshit," knowing it had a lot more to do with her own choices in life than with anything Mr. Yee was telling her on the DVD she had picked up at Target for $19.95. She could remember a time, before she started to compete nationally in gymnastics, when she had enjoyed all kinds of exercise and stretching. Now it seemed like one more thing to cram into her already busy day. But she knew the real issue, the core of her problem tonight, was her back pain and her desire to refrain from using one of the assortment of painkillers she had stashed in her bathroom medicine cabinet. She'd let her normal prescription run out but couldn't bring herself to dispose of the random pills she'd acquired over the years. Soon those would be exhausted too. That was why she was forced to do yoga in an effort to relieve lower back pain that had been building since midmorning.

The frantic pace she had kept with Stallings all day didn't help her in any way either. They'd hit a dozen different places where Leah Tischler might have been seen. The only person who'd been of any help was Liz Dubeck, the manager of one of the downtown motels. Patty could tell Liz was attracted to Stallings's good looks and charming manner. That wasn't anything unusual. What surprised Patty was Stallings's interest in the pretty motel manager. Sure, he didn't say anything and avoided any questions about her after they left the motel, but Patty knew her partner as well as anyone and this was the first time since his separation he'd shown any interest at all in another woman.

Patty twisted and crossed her legs in an effort to stretch out the middle of her back. There was definitely an improvement, but she could feel the constant throbbing still coming from lower down her back. If she'd known this would be the result when she was thirteen and practicing one hundred backflips a day, she might not have had the enthusiasm that didn't wane until her second year at the University of Florida. But that was her nature. She threw herself into anything she undertook.

The fact that Tony was working late and she had no real hope of seeing him for anything more than a few minutes over the next week didn't help her mood. Something just wasn't right with their relationship. She glanced at the Krazy Kat clock on her wall and realized it wasn't even eight o'clock yet and she was starting to feel anxious about going to bed. This would be the fourth night in a row she didn't sleep well, unless she took her usual dose of Ambien. And that's what she wanted to do in the worst way. She'd had to take Xanax the last few days as pressure mounted with the discovery of two bodies being linked to one killer. The Xanax helped her get through the day; it was the Ambien that helped her get through the night. And in two or three hours she'd have to make a decision: go another night with almost no sleep and drag through the day, or pop an Ambien and feel pharmaceutically groggy until ten o'clock in the morning. The choices weren't great. She wondered how Stallings functioned so well with as little sleep as he got each night. There was more than enough evidence of his nighttime activities like crawling around different neighborhoods looking for the right lead on a missing person or the tiny piece of forensic evidence that would help identify a killer. Patty also knew he spent a lot of time tracking down leads on his own missing daughter. That was something he couldn't talk about around the sheriff's office because he'd never been assigned to the case. He never would be; it was his own daughter. But he spent a lot of time on the computer and talking to missing persons detectives all across the country, hoping to find some clue as to what had happened to Jeanie after the Friday she walked away without a word to anyone. Poor John Stallings had a lot more to deal with than Patty did and she felt like he was a pretty good example. He was calm and patient, didn't drink, and never took pills.

Her new attitude had caused her to not renew any of her pain-pill prescriptions and now here she was in the early evening, anxious, alone, worried about sleeping, and in pain. Maybe she should've thought this out a little better.

Buddy had cheated and used a mold to blow the glass containers for his work of art. He used a mold so each container would slip into the slot it was made for. Right now he had an extra two containers with lids and rubber gaskets ready to go. Some were a rich blue glass, others a Coca-Cola bottle green. Any of them would make lovely sea glass if they washed up on one of Florida's sandy beaches. He had to have a clock directly above his workbench or he'd lose all track of time when he worked on his glass sculptures.

He ran up and took a quick shower in his apartment and changed into a nice pair of jeans and a button-down shirt. At exactly eight o'clock he heard a car door and the unmistakable rumble of feet on the staircase to the apartment. He felt a sense of dread as he padded to the door across the expensive hardwood floor he had put in two years ago. Somehow having Donna standing in front of her sister made him feel a little better. Buddy almost leaned down and kissed her on the cheek, but once again Cheryl's scowl forced him back. He allowed them to step into the entryway directly in front of his small kitchen.

He started to get annoyed but remembered what the doctor had told him and took a deep breath. At least this time they'd made an appointment and hadn't scared anyone off. He didn't have enough time left to waste potential candidates for his work of art. Cheryl had already cost him a great addition. Even though they had an appointment and were exactly on time, the thought of that woman invading his home pissed him off.

He thought about the precious hours he had spent with Jessie and how he would've felt if they had interrupted him. He had gotten to know the sweet girl from Ocala even after he had to secure her in a chair for more than an hour before he finally used his braided cord. Thinking back on the whole incident he felt a pang of guilt. He'd released the cord to allow her to gasp her final breath but had fumbled with the jar and missed it, so he had to do it a second time. He didn't enjoy terrifying someone like that. But there was nothing else he could have done. She'd been a good candidate to that point and he couldn't just let her walk away. Now she rested in the jar at the bottom left of this work of art.

Buddy was shocked when Cheryl allowed her sister to do the talking. This meant Cheryl really wanted him to move out. Donna's pretty eyes and natural body added impact to anything she asked and he found himself more open to what she had to say. She used that quiet little-girl voice of hers.

"We'd like to buy out your lease, Buddy."

"What if I don't want to?"

"What if we made it worth your while?" She gave him a sweet smile.

He shook his head like he always did.

Apparently that was too much for Cheryl, as she pushed past her sister and poked him in the chest, saying, "Look, asshole, we own this building. Our father left it to us when he died. We have plans for it once you're out of the way."

He didn't react to her bony finger jammed in his chest. She was like an aggressive drunk in a bar, pushing toward him, doing everything but slurring her words. But he kept calm and said, "Your father may have left you the building, but he leased it to me first. If you thought you could get me out of here through a lawsuit you'd already be in court. I have my reasons for staying and not wanting to move right now. I wish you'd respect them."

Cheryl spat out a curse, turned, pushed past her sister, and disappeared out the door. He could hear her heavy footfalls on the rickety wooden stairs and heard something in his shop fall over as she stomped out the door he'd left open for them.

Donna shrugged and gave him a slight smile, turned, and followed her sister.

The image of Cheryl standing in front of him was burned in his mind. She had a superficial beauty—the kind of looks that turned heads in some circles—but she had no inner beauty, no soul, and for that reason she'd never be of use for anything worthwhile.

ELEVEN

John Stallings leaned back in the hard chair at the dining-room table of his family's house. As Charlie raced up the stairs to get ready for bed, he rubbed his eyes hard, trying to block out the trouble fractions still seemed to give him. As much as he disliked relearning all the rules of fractions or long division or any other math problems that he helped Charlie with each night, he wouldn't give up one second of his time with his boy to do anything else.

He looked out into the living room at his fourteen-year-old daughter, Lauren, lounging on the sofa watching TV. Occasionally she rolled onto her back and texted someone on her small phone. She said hello when he came in and grunted a couple times to his inquiries, but she'd had very little contact with him other than those basic communications.

Then he got a surprise, something he hadn't seen in over a week and certainly hadn't expected tonight. At the top of the stairs, his wife of nineteen years stood silently staring down at him. She glided down the stairs one at a time like she was unsure of her footing or carrying a fragile piece of glass. She kept a steady pace, taking the chair directly across from him at the dining-room table, sitting with the grace of a dancer.

She didn't say anything as he stared at her beautiful face with her delicate, defined features and shiny dark hair dripping down over her shoulder. There hadn't been one time since the day he met her at the University of South Florida he didn't think she was the prettiest woman he had ever met. Even tonight, with all the acrimony between them, one look made it all melt away.

Her voice was scratchy like she'd just woken up, but she didn't look like she'd had any recent bouts with drugs or alcohol, which had plagued her since before Jeanie had disappeared.

Maria said, "How's it going, John?"

He shrugged. "Charlie's got a pretty good head for numbers."

"I'm glad somebody does. Thanks for coming over to help him with it."

"No sweat. I was over visiting my dad anyway."

"I'm impressed you've tried to work things out with him. I know the kids get a big kick out of seeing him. How's he doing?"

"I'm not sure, to tell you the truth. He seemed confused when I was over there."

"I can tell you from personal experience that even when you're not drinking or drugging, the effects linger a long, long time. Confusion is the least of an alcoholic's problems."

For the first time in many months she seemed interested and connected and what she said made sense. He felt better already.

* * *

Tony Mazzetti sat quietly in his Crown Vic with Sparky Taylor content reading an issue of *Popular Mechanics*. Mazzetti was almost afraid to engage his new partner in conversation for fear he would learn about something as disturbing as his family not watching TV at night; his organic diet, which had yet to make a dent in his extra eighty-five pounds; his oldest son's ability to deconstruct, then rebuild, any electronic device sold in the United States; or the fact that Jacksonville Sheriff's Office policy drove Sparky's professional life. He enjoyed the chance to think about not only the enormous number of tasks still needed to be completed for his case, but how to move his relationship with Patty further along. How to make it seem completely right again.

It was nine o'clock and he knew the crews had been working almost eighteen hours a day to complete the renovation of this large office building. There were supervisors for every aspect of the job, but tonight he only wanted to speak to one of them. In the construction trailer sitting in front of the hollow building was Joe D'Annunzio, who was also known as Joey Big Balls. Joey Big Balls ran the administration of the construction project, paying vendors and figuring out payroll because he had no building experience whatsoever. No one wanted to screw with Joey Big Balls because, at least down here in Florida, every Italian from New York or New Jersey in the building industry was assumed to be part of the mob. It'd taken Mazzetti years to get used to the suspicious glances he got when locals heard his accent and saw his name written out on credit applications or business cards. It was a relatively mild and benign form of prejudice, which shows like *The Sopranos* hadn't helped one bit.

In the case of Joey Big Balls, Mazzetti knew the real story. He'd been kicked out of the longshoremen's union in New Jersey for his third offense of stealing big-screen TVs from a freight depot in Newark. He'd moved down here and started fresh, first doing manual labor on construction sites but quickly moving up to the ranks to administrator when builders sought to get things done with a glare or a subtle threat. Mazzetti had met him years earlier when he'd been caught for fencing stolen auto parts. To avoid jail time Joey Big Balls had cooperated in the case and given up two different groups who were stealing high-end cars and breaking them down for parts. Joey didn't care about anyone knowing he had an arrest record, but there was no way he'd survive anyone ever finding out he was a snitch. And that's what Mazzetti was counting on today.

Finally it looked like the trailer was empty except for the single light on in the back. Mazzetti turned to Sparky and said, "Looks like it's showtime."

He didn't wait for an answer; instead he popped out of the Crown Vic, hustled across the street and through the construction site. He was surprised to see that Sparky had kept up with him and was right behind him as he knocked on the door and entered.

The giant man behind the desk at the far end of the trailer didn't look up. All he said was, "I'm done paying out vouchers tonight. I'll be back at noon tomorrow."

Mazzetti said, "I don't need any money, Joey."

The fifty-year-old man looked up and focused his red eyes on Mazzetti and Sparky. He didn't smile or show any concern at all. In a flat voice he said, "Whatcha need, Tony?"

Mazzetti eased through the trailer back to the man's cluttered desk. "How are things going, Joey?"

The big man wiped his hand over his face and down his scraggly beard, showing two of his fingers had been broken and never set properly. He sighed and said, "It's a goddamn right-to-work state, how do you think it's going?"

"Jersey is better?"

"At least you knew where you stood with the unions. They may charge three times too much and have to shut down projects, but there was none of this bullshit of hiring guys right off the street or hiring guys you couldn't trust. Sometimes I think the state is stuffed with goddamn morons."

"Look, Joey, I'm from Brooklyn so I feel like I have a pretty good view of things, and I'll admit the state does have a lot of morons, but after a few years you start to realize the worst morons have come from Jersey or New York."

Joey shook his head and rephrased his first question. "Can I help you with something, Tony?"

"I need info on a case. You hear about this girl found over in the Dumpster?"

The big man remained silent but nodded his head.

"I'm looking for someone in the construction business who might notice another worker acting funny. Basically I'm asking you to keep your ears open and help us out if you hear anything."

"If I turned in every felon or guy acting strange, I'd have no drywall or carpet guys left to work with."

The conversation went back and forth for a few minutes with Joey avoiding any commitment to help. Mazzetti felt his patience start to lag and he stood quickly, shooting the chair back with his legs and leaning in close to Joey Big Balls across the desk. "Don't make me do something we'll both regret, Joey. This is serious." Then he leaned closer, catching a whiff of the big man's body odor. But out of the corner of his eye he saw Sparky Taylor shaking his head instead of backing him up on the threat.

Joey Big Balls raised both of his hands and said, "I'll start asking some guys quietly and see if I can come up with a name for you, but in return you can't come around here anytime you want."

"Joey, I don't want to come around here at all, but I don't think you want to feel any responsibility if another girl turns up dead and you're not willing to help us."

After giving Joey his cell phone number and making his good-byes, Mazzetti headed out of the trailer with Sparky in tow. He turned to his partner and said, "What's with the look back there?"

"I don't agree with those kinds of tactics. They're not prescribed in law or the sheriff's policies. There's a reason we have rules, Tony. You're treating that man like a criminal."

"Hello. He is a convicted felon and a snitch."

"Is he a documented source of information?"

"No, I haven't officially listed him as one of my snitches."

"Then by policy he's only a witness and we don't treat witnesses so poorly."

"We don't let killers run free either and if we don't find the guy responsible for Kathy Mizell's murder and maybe Leah Tischler's too, he's gonna kill again. And I can't let that happen. That's my fucking policy."

TWELVE

Stallings could always tell when the whole squad was on one big case by the way detectives tended to focus on reports and information on their desk rather than chatting back and forth. The usual friendly atmosphere of the detective bureau went out the window when cases got serious and detectives got tired. In the past, before the recession, when overtime was plentiful, everyone had been buoyed by the idea they were making a lot of extra money by working such long hours. Some cops had equated the extra hours and pay to specific material things like, "Fifty more hours and I can get a pool." Some cops had built a future on it— "This is Tommy's college fund." Now the detectives seemed to work a lot of hours for comp time or some other bullshit they never got reimbursed for. That was never Stallings's motivation for working hard. He wanted to find who was responsible for Leah Tischler's disappearance and punish him.

He and Patty had been looking for the last person who'd seen Leah. They had a list of friends and intended to go out to the Thomas School for interviews later in the day. Stallings really felt like he needed to know if Leah had run away, and if she had, where she'd run to. Maybe Jeanie had done the same thing and gone to the same place. Leah's mother had called him three or four times since he'd first gone out to their opulent house at the beach. He knew how tough it was and he wasn't going to tell her to stop calling.

Patty stepped over from her desk and said, "Almost done here. Besides going to the school, is there anyone else we need to talk to today?"

"I have a couple more questions for Liz Dubeck."

"I'll bet you do." Patty flashed that perfect smile.

"No, it's not like that at all."

"Really? What is it?"

It surprised Stallings he had to think about his answer, but he was rescued by Sparky Taylor walking past on his midmorning routine of eating organic whole wheat bread and a stack of vitamins.

Stallings said, "Whatcha got there, Sparky?"

"The usual weight-control stuff. Eating a slice of organic, whole wheat bread and drinking two glasses of water helps me keep my weight in check."

Stallings stared at the portly detective and managed to hold his tongue when he saw how sincere Sparky was.

The squad door opened with a bang, and a tall narcotics detective, whose name Stallings couldn't remember right away, stepped in with an armload of packages wrapped in duct tape. The man, in his mid-thirties, was tall and stooped and looked a little like Big Bird with thick glasses. The man glanced around the room until his eyes fell on Sparky. "Hey, Spark. Our sergeant told us to come up here to process evidence and prisoners to keep them away from some meth-lab guys we have down in our office. He cleared it with the Yvonne the Terrible."

Sparky stepped over and helped the man lay out the packages on the desk. Stallings realized they knew each other from the tech unit, where they had obviously shared similar interests.

Stallings wandered over and casually inquired about the prisoners who were on their way.

The nerdy detective said, "We scored big. One of the guys bought fifteen hundred OxyContin from a gang not far from here. They'd been selling them to some dude from Kentucky who resold them and made a fortune. When we took down the guy from Kentucky on the highway he gave up a gang."

Stallings mumbled, "Sweet."

"I knew Yvonne wouldn't mind us using the squad bay. She was our sergeant before she was yours and we hated to see her go."

"Then why'd you name her Yvonne the Terrible?"

"What better way of keeping people from stealing a good sergeant?"

Stallings had to nod, appreciating the simplistic brilliance of their plan. He let the detective sort out his evidence and noticed Patty talking with Mazzetti at his desk. Even though he knew about the relationship, that didn't mean he liked to see her too close to the weasel.

Buddy used his grinding wheel to put an edge on the long knife he intended to use to kill Donna's sister, Cheryl. There was no simple way to say it. He had to kill the dumb bitch before she ruined his life completely. He had to be careful because he might be considered a suspect in this killing. The fact that he knew her and disliked her meant he might have to answer some questions. He'd always been careful in selecting women for his work of art and he didn't think anyone had ever suspected him. He had never really worried about answering questions from the police, but this time he had to plan things out.

Most importantly he'd make sure he'd be able to find her somewhere away from her house and from his shop. He'd never risk letting her contaminate his work of art. She had no business being remembered for all eternity. In fact, he wished he could just forget about her now, but as long as she continued to hound him about the lease and barge in when he needed privacy, he had to take action.

He was going to use the knife because it was so different from the strangulations he'd done in the past. Although it was comfortable using his hands to choke someone, he'd never stabbed anyone and he didn't own a gun so he couldn't shoot her. Guns were too dangerous and he opposed them. His first preference would be to simply run her down, but he wasn't sure he could do it without witnesses and his van was fairly recognizable. That left the knife. He had read several articles on the Internet about stabbing someone to death and knew he'd have to either stick it in under her rib cage and into her heart or into her throat. He had no illusions and knew it'd be a messy job. Stabbings didn't always kill someone; in fact unless they were well-planned and delivered with force it was very difficult to kill someone with a knife attack. But it might make his life a lot easier.

He'd never considered the advantages of murder for convenience. He felt like art was a decent justification, but the idea of stabbing someone because they annoyed him made him uncomfortable.

Patty Levine looked into Tony Mazzetti's intense brown eyes and said, "This is not the time or place to have a talk like this."

"When is the time?"

"Off duty and in private."

Patty noticed Mazzetti's jaw clench and the muscles on each side work. She couldn't believe she'd said something like that, but it was true.

Mazzetti said, "I just want us to take the next step. No one visits either of us. No one would know if you moved in with me. It's not like we'd be adding to our secret."

"Why wouldn't you move in with *me*?" Patty folded her arms like a schoolteacher waiting for a child to answer for some transgression. In fact she was ready to live with anyone, anywhere.

"Because I have a house. With a garage and a yard and a property value that's increasing. There was no sexist meaning in my comment."

Patty considered the sincere offer from her boyfriend, but it really wasn't the right time to accept. She had a lot going on, and until she got a handle on at least her prescription drug problem she didn't want to drag anyone else into it. She also wondered if his offer was an attempt to bridge the chasm that had recently grown between them. She couldn't put it into words, but it just didn't feel right. On the other hand she didn't want to chase him away, either. As she was about to say something conciliatory a crash at the front of the squad bay startled her. Someone flew in through the door, smacking into the table with a thud next to the detective who'd been processing the seized OxyContin.

Stallings's head had jerked up at the sound of the commotion and he saw three young black men in handcuffs held by a mix of tactical, plainclothes officers and narcotics guys, mostly twenty-five- to thirty-year-old hotshots who spent lots of time in the gym. These young, slick detectives seemed to be more in love with the idea of being a cop than with the hard work needed to be a good police officer. They looked good in tailored shirts and low, tactical holsters worn outside their jeans, but any time a big case rolled down the pike those were not the kind of cops he wanted to work with.

One of the prisoners had already been tossed through the door and bumped into the nerdy detective working on the evidence. The prisoner jumped up and kicked the nerdy detective squarely in the head, knocking him sideways, where he struck his head on the corner of the desk on his way down. This emboldened the other two prisoners, who started struggling immediately in the grasp of the muscular cops. One headbutted a young black police officer, shattering his nose and driving him back into the hallway. The third prisoner used his legs to kick off the wall and forced two detectives back with him on the ground, taking them all out of the fight.

As Stallings pushed away from his desk, ready to rush over and help, he saw Patty Levine weigh in from the side, all elbows and knees, cracking one of the prisoners three or four times with effective blows and knocking him out of the fight instantly.

Two other crimes/persons detectives were slow to react. These were non-uniformed detectives and no one carried a Taser. For years the public had cried out about police punching suspects who acted up; then, with the introduction of the Taser it seemed the controversy would die down. Now the public, uneducated in the use of the Taser, viewed it as a near torture device. Stallings wasn't fond of the small devices that delivered electronic shocks—just more equipment to keep track of. He'd punched enough people in his career to know how effective a right cross could be. And that's what he intended to use right now as the last prisoner was able to shake off the detectives holding him.

Stallings crossed the room, raising his hand ready to strike. He looked the prisoner right in the face, giving him a chance to surrender. He saw no surrender in the man's eyes and prepared to strike hard across his face when another detective popped out from behind the door and swung an ASP, missing the prisoner with the metal expandable baton but striking Stallings hard in his left arm.

The blow knocked Stallings to the side. He immediately reached for his arm, feeling the pain shoot through his shoulder. It worked exactly like every training class had ever taught him. The fluid shock of the ASP strike had traveled up his nerves in his arm and felt as if someone had slammed his hand in a car door.

The detective swung the metal ASP again, striking the prisoner in the arm and, after a full backswing, struck him in the leg, dropping the young thug to the ground.

As quickly as it started it was over. Whew. Stallings looked around the room at the various groaning and moaning men on the floor. The only one who seemed to be seriously injured was Sparky Taylor's friend from the tech division. Patty knelt beside him trying to stop the bleeding from his forehead. Evidence was scattered everywhere, and a new form of chaos descended in the room as everyone tried to separate the prisoners, the wounded, and the evidence.

THIRTEEN

The fight at the office had disrupted everyone's day. Unlike the way many TV shows portray police departments, any kind of a scuffle outside the booking area or jail facility is rare. Stallings once explained it to one of his neighbors by saying it would be like having several stockbrokers get into a fight at the Charles Schwab office. It happens, but those in the area are always surprised. Heading north of the city to the Thomas School was an excellent way to break up the day and step away from the chaos of the fight. Not only was Dwight, the nerdy detective, rushed to the hospital with a serious head wound, two of the three prisoners had to be hospitalized. It had been an all-out brawl and injuries happen, but he was sure some reporter trying to make a name would focus on the broken wrist of a prisoner or the fact that they had been handcuffed at the time of the fight. Someone who'd never been hit had no idea how distracting it could be.

The school sat back from the road with a pattern of soccer and baseball fields adding to the stately feel of the buildings. It looked more like a small college than an exclusive, private prep school. Stallings had heard tuition topped thirty thousand dollars a year and it looked as if they had put a fair amount of that money back into the school.

Stallings had let Patty work her magic to get them set up in an administrator's office near the front entrance. It wasn't only her professional manner; he had to admit she could deal with regular people much better than he could. He liked to think he was learning from her. Then they'd get behind on a missing person investigation, and he'd lose his patience and deal with people too bluntly. And like an epileptic seizure creeping into the consciousness, he could feel his patience ebbing away as they made no progress toward finding Leah Tischler. Although there was the strong possibility she'd been a victim of whoever strangled Kathy Mizell, there was no absolute proof she was dead. Either way he felt a burning drive to discover what had happened to her. The rational side of his mind told him there was no greater chance of him finding out what had happened to his own Jeanie by finding out what had happened to Leah, but he recognized he wasn't always rational and sometimes it was an irrational hunch that solved the case. If nothing else, he wanted to give the Tischlers some sense of closure. Something he and Maria had never felt.

With a great deal of assistance from some Thomas School administrators, Stallings and Patty were able to see, in quick succession, a slew of snooty girls all wearing the same uniform as Leah Tischler wore in her final photo. The school had agreed to help in exchange for the Jacksonville Sheriff's Office being clear Leah had not disappeared from school and the school had no liability in the matter. Stallings agreed, knowing it was someone higher than him who would make the call at a news conference and decide whom to throw under the bus. His guess was that if the school had any responsibility at all, they'd be mentioned prominently in the news. But that wasn't his concern. He had one goal. Maybe one of these girls would help him achieve it.

The sixth girl to walk through the door of the small office sighed loudly as she stood there waiting for the detectives to acknowledge her. Stallings looked up from his notes and was surprised to see a girl with piercings all along her ear and the tip of a tattoo on her neck coming out of her collar.

Patty said, "Are you Marcie?"

The girl nodded her head, causing her stringy hair to flop across her forehead as she stepped forward and plopped into the hard wooden chair. Her plaid skirt puffed out as she hit the chair.

Patty said, "I like your piercings."

The girl perked up, shifted from a suspicious glare at Stallings to a more attentive expression toward Patty. "The ears are the only thing that can be pierced around this place. They made me pull out my nose ring and lip stud. I just put them in again as soon as I walked out that stupid gate."

Stallings sat back and let Patty chat with the girl, putting her at ease before turning to the questions they needed answered.

Patty asked about running away, and the girl said, "We all think about it. It's a nice change, a way to get away from our shitty lives."

Stallings had to ask, "What's shitty about your life?" He wasn't judging her, but he really felt he needed to know the answer. He wondered if Jeanie had had the same conversation with someone else before she disappeared.

The girl said, "You know, our parents don't get us. This is a boring backwater of a town. Jesus, this is the best school in North Florida and even it sucks."

Stallings was surprised when Patty scowled and leaned forward. "What's your father do?"

"He owns a Cadillac dealership north of here.

"So you have your own car?"

The girl nodded and mumbled, "A CTX."

"You ever miss a meal?"

"What'd you mean?"

Patty's normally pleasant blue eyes flashed fire, and she said, "Look around you. Look beyond this school and you'll see people are barely getting by. There's real suffering, not the imaginary shit you and your friends dream of."

The girl looked shocked.

"You guys think running away is some kind of romantic escape. Leah Tischler's parents are beside themselves with grief. There is a very real chance Leah has suffered some traumatic shit. We're working our asses off to try and find her and to help her parents get through a rough time. All I've heard from you girls so far is how tough life is. I think you're as disconnected and screwed up as you think this school is. Now cut the shit, Marcie. You know anything that might help us find Leah Tischler?"

The girl looked like she might cry and was fighting to hold it back.

Stallings stared at the girl and noticed the hole for her lip stud on the right side of her wide mouth. But he could see in her face that Patty had struck a chord.

The girl said, "I might know why Leah ran away and maybe even where she ran to."

The way the girl said it made Stallings hope, just for a second, that this meant Leah had discarded her uniform and a killer had found the belt. He leaned forward. "Where is she?"

The girl said, "Ask Tonya Hazell."

It was another lead, and Stallings intended to run with it.

FOURTEEN

Sergeant Yvonne Zuni sat at her desk after having made more than twenty phone calls regarding the fight in the squad bay. Her only real concern was the condition of the injured detective, Dwight. She'd worked with him in narcotics and despite his odd appearance and goofy nature, he was one of the best detectives she'd ever supervised. She was starting to see that the detectives who'd worked in the tech unit all shared the similar attributes of being extremely smart, working hard, staying diligent in their paperwork and steering clear of trouble off-duty. Usually detectives had three of these four attributes. Every detective had a different three. Some were smart and hardworking but ignored paperwork. Some were smart, stayed out of trouble off-duty, were current on their paperwork but also avoided work at all costs. The tech guys seemed to be the only ones who were reliably stable in all departments. She knew even though Sparky Taylor had some odd habits, he fell into that exact mold, spending every night with his family, giving the job everything he had while he was on duty, and definitely staying clear on policy, procedure, and paperwork.

About every fourth call the sergeant made was to find out if there was any new information about the injured detective. Head injuries were a tricky business and could leave lingering issues. Right now all she knew was he was being evaluated at the hospital and had drifted in and out of consciousness since the paramedics took him from the squad room. Sergeant Zuni knew that Dwight had two young girls at home and his wife was a teacher. She shuddered as she considered the worst-case scenario.

She also had to brief command staff on the incident. The agency was blessed with leaders who'd worked their way up through the ranks and understood many of the issues officers and detectives had to deal with. In this case they understood it was necessary to use serious physical force to overcome the disruptive prisoners. All anyone seemed genuinely concerned about was the detective's injury, and that made Sergeant Zuni feel good about the department.

She heard a light rap on her doorframe and looked up quickly to see the senior internal affairs detective, Ronald Bell, standing in the doorway looking like a model who'd just walked off the runway. He was tall and handsome with light gray hair and a rugged smile, but what set him apart from all the other tall, handsome detectives was that he almost always wore extraordinarily expensive, exquisitely cut suits. Today he had a dark blue suit with a white shirt and pale yellow tie. He looked like one of the ads in *Men's Health* about how to become successful and attractive.

Bell said, "Awfully quiet around here?"

"Open homicide cases tend to keep the detectives busy."

"I guess big-ass brawls do too."

"Don't make me go over my whole day. I wish I could have a Bombay Sapphire martini right this second."

Bell said, "Sounds like you had a rough day."

"Please tell me someone hasn't made an official complaint that requires Internal Affairs to come down and look into this thing?"

"By all accounts your detectives did a great job. It wouldn't hurt if they were maybe in a little bit better shape or had a couple more ASPs available. I heard your man Stallings took a pretty big blow to the arm from one of the tactical guys who had an ASP."

"You know Stall. Something like that's not gonna slow him down. He had a bruise, but he wasn't complaining too much when he ran out the door to look for another missing girl."

"I know John Stallings very well. I'm surprised he didn't crack someone's head open."

"Although it may seem like it to you, he's usually not the violent type."

"I have several Jacksonville residents who might disagree with that analysis."

"Have any of them ever filed a complaint?"

Ronald Bell raised his hands in surrender, stepped into the small office, and pulled the door quietly shut behind him.

Sergeant Zuni raised an eyebrow and said, "Is this something serious or are you going to say something romantic?" She stepped from behind her desk and reached to embrace her secret boyfriend. In the two months they'd been seeing each other she was certain no one had become suspicious. She didn't want Bell to get in trouble for dating one of the sergeants in charge of the detective bureau. It was his job to investigate complaints against officers and detectives, and he was known as a ruthless enforcer throughout the department. But she'd seen another side of the fifty-four-year-old internal affairs investigator. Aside from being smart he was extremely sophisticated and had used much of the money he'd inherited from his mother's side of the family to create a lifestyle in stark contrast to that of most of the cops in the agency. But it was the way he treated her that made her want to see him more and more. He made her feel like she was the only woman in the world and would listen as long as she wanted to talk about anything she wanted to talk about.

Bell said, "This is nice."

"Too bad you're in IA and I'm a conflict."

"No one's complained so far."

"That's because you're used to keeping secrets."

Bell said, "If I could, I'd shout it out so everyone would hear."

Sergeant Zuni laughed for the first time all day. She liked this guy and what they had.

But the relationship was not without pitfalls. Sergeant Zuni saw the irony of her keeping a secret relationship with an internal affairs investigator while Patty Levine and Tony Mazzetti struggled to keep their burgeoning relationship under wraps. The sergeant had figured out the two detectives' attraction to each other some time ago, but she didn't like to meddle in other people's affairs, especially two of the top producers in the bureau.

She stepped back from Bell and looked into his handsome face. "This isn't a social visit, is it?"

"I'm afraid not."

"What's up?" She knew better, even with her boy-friend, than to make specific inquiries. If Internal Affairs didn't already know about it she wasn't about to bring something to their attention. Even inadvertently.

"It is somewhat related to the fight this morning in the bureau."

"In what way?"

"Narcotics is missing two hundred fifty of the Oxys they confiscated this morning."

"And this relates to us how?"

"The missing pills were part of the evidence the detective was bringing in to sort out. As close as we can tell they had to go missing from somewhere up here and probably during the fight."

"Have you been able to ask Dwight what he did with them?"

Bell shook his head. "He's still being evaluated and is in and out of consciousness."

"There was no one here but our detectives. No visitors, lawyers, or reporters. Just cops."

"My first thought was some attorney had grabbed them while he was up here talking to a client, but when I checked all the rosters I saw no one had been up to the squad bay this morning."

"So you really think one of the detectives stole seized evidence? You don't think it's more likely they just miscounted?"

"That's what we've been trying to figure out and it's going to take a little more time. But I needed to give you a heads-up either way."

"I appreciate that and I'll try to show my appreciation later. But for now what's our next move?"

Bell pulled his collar like he needed more air and said, "We're gonna keep our inquiry strictly low-profile. We don't want to screw up any cases, especially a murder investigation. The sheriff is conscious of any political fallout."

"What's that mean?"

"It means I have a hell of a lot of work to do."

FIFTEEN

Patty knew she was expected to run the show during this interview. Even though Stallings was a veteran, with commendations and an obsessive interest in all the cases they worked, he knew when to step aside and let her handle things. Despite being a parent, Stallings recognized she'd be better at dealing with a teenage girl.

Unlike the other girls they'd interviewed during the day, Patty sensed this girl, Tonya Hazell, was frightened. She wasn't sure if it was the intimidation factor of having to speak to detectives or something else, but there was no bravado or swagger in this girl.

Tonya, dressed in the school uniform, was small and delicate with intelligent green eyes and shoulder-length blond hair. She had given up looking at Stallings at all and now focused her attention on Patty. She answered the first several questions with mumbled yeses or nos as she appeared to be assessing Patty's reliability.

Tonya said, "Yes, Leah told me she was going to run

away. We talked about it for more than two weeks before she really did."

Patty stole a quick glance at Stallings. "Do you know where she is?"

That's when the girl started to cry, her tears quickly morphing into uncontrollable sobs as Patty yanked on the roll of paper towels sitting on the desk behind her and waited patiently as the girl dabbed her eyes and blew her nose with a deafening honk.

Patty knew that meant the girl didn't know where Leah had gone, but she waited for an answer anyway.

Finally, Tonya looked up and said, "I haven't heard from her since Friday afternoon when we said goodbye at school."

"Do you have any idea why Leah would run away?" She hoped it was a clue as well as a reason.

Tonya looked down at the ground floor and wiped her eyes with the soggy paper towel.

Stallings looked at Patty and shrugged his shoulders, obviously having no idea what to make of the sobbing girl.

Patty placed a hand on the girl's back and said, "Tonya, it's very important we know everything you know. We'll hold anything you tell us in the strictest of confidence. But we have to do everything we can to find Leah now."

After another few seconds the girl lifted her head and said, "I loved her and she loved me."

Patty took a moment to make sure she understood the simple comment. "Why would that make her want to run away?"

The girl sniffled and said, "You think her dad wants to acknowledge a lesbian daughter when he intends to run for the county commission? That's all he ever talks about. He's a big-time lawyer with big-time contacts, and he can get anything he wants done in this county."

Patty listened to what the girl had to say, then moved to the seat next to Tonya and placed her hand on top of the girl's hand. "Tonya, would you tell us if you'd seen Leah since she ran away?"

Tonya stared directly into Patty's eyes. "I swear to God I haven't seen her."

"Any ideas where she might have gone?"

Tonya paused, her eyes shifting between the detectives. "She has a friend in Tennessee or Kentucky."

"How do you know about the friend?"

"We fought about her."

"What's her name?"

"I never got it. I know they met through a music festival in Jacksonville. This other girl came down from Knoxville or Memphis and impressed Leah. She's a college student and blond. That's all I know."

Patty took some quick notes. This was worth following up if they had the time. She looked back at Tonya. "Anything else you can think of?"

She sobbed and grabbed a gulp of air. "Please find her. I'm so worried I can't do anything."

The lump in Patty's throat gave her a hint of what John Stallings must feel every day.

Tony Mazzetti had been hopping all day. Two interviews first thing in the morning, a quick meeting with the medical examiner, an interview on a midday news talk show about how hard it was to be a homicide detective in the Bold New City of the South. The reporter also asked him about what it was like growing up in

New York but living in Jacksonville. Mazzetti worked hard not to use words like "redneck" and "dumb ass."

Now he was glancing over a few reports from the other detectives. He was particularly interested in anything Stallings and Patty had found out about the missing girl and the belt discovered around Kathy Mizell's throat. Patty usually filled him in on stuff in an informal way, but he liked to be on top of things anyway. The fight in the D-bureau had thrown off everyone's schedule. He'd hung around to make sure he wasn't needed. There was nothing he could do to help the situation and he had plenty of leads to investigate.

The phone on his desk rang and it took him a second just to determine which phone was ringing. In the era of cell phones, landline phones had become almost obsolete to most detectives. He picked it up, barking his name in the receiver as a means of greeting.

A voice equally as gruff, said, "Tony, it's me, Joey."

"Joey Big Balls?"

"Yeah, I'm calling about our conversation from the other night."

"You got any names that popped out at you?"

"Like you said, there are always a few weirdos around. I guess in your line of work that's important information, but for me, as long as they can plumb a line or hang drywall halfway decent, I could give a shit less about what they do in their spare time."

"I know, I know. I'm not lookin' to thin out your ranks, but this is a bad guy we're looking for."

"That's why I'm helping out, but you gotta keep this between you and me."

"Joey, do you really think I'd fuck you, a fellow Italian from up north? You're good as gold."

"Were you full of shit growing up, or did it happen after you became a cop?"

"I guess a little of both. What've you got for me?"

There was hesitation on the line and Mazzetti could hear voices in the background so he didn't push it and gave the big man a second until he could speak freely.

Finally Joey Big Balls said, "I got five names I'm gonna give you, but that means you don't come by and bother me anytime you feel like. Capice?"

"Now we're paisanos?"

"Business associates, that's it." Joey went on to give him five names.

Mazzetti said, "You got any identifiers on these guys?"

"Like what?"

"Descriptions would be nice."

"They look like construction workers. All of them. They could double as bikers on the weekends. White guys and all of them have raised red flags with us for something they said or done. And I don't mean like stealin' tools or punching someone in the head. I listened to what you said and gave you names of guys who act a little creepy when it comes to women or kids. You can do whatever you want with the names as long as no one ever knows I gave them to you."

As Mazzetti was about to thank Joey Big Balls, the line went dead. So much for friendship.

It had taken almost an hour to pick up the flat sheets of tempered glass he had for a job next week. These weren't even etched, but he didn't care because they paid up front and he needed the money. He'd never worried much about money except when he had almost starved trying to make a living as a glassblower. But for the last ten years or so, he had lived very comfortably, even saved a little now and then. Now money and saving didn't seem that important to him. He could afford to eat most meals out and appreciated having one less worry.

He stopped at the Starbucks near Shands Jacksonville Medical Center to grab a cup of green tea, which he'd been told to drink on a daily basis. He waited in the short line until the barista greeted him with a big smile.

"Don't I usually see you on Mondays?"

He smiled and nodded, mumbling, "The usual."

The barista produced the local Starbucks version of tea, and he shuffled to an open table in the rear of the store.

Buddy worked on a crossword puzzle he'd downloaded from the *New York Times* site. The *Jacksonville Times-Union* was not known for complicated mind and word games. He enjoyed the few minutes he had to himself while he planned all the things he needed to complete in the next few days. Chiefly among them was finding a place suitable to deal with Donna's sister, Cheryl. He'd blocked off a few hours this afternoon to see what he could do about that.

He glanced at his watch as he filled in the final word in the puzzle. It was "corpulent" for "a fancy fat man." He didn't solve it all in one sitting, but he'd done it in under twenty minutes. He didn't think that was too bad.

From the corner of his eye he saw someone squeezing down a narrow part of the coffee shop to the table directly across from him, so he shifted in his seat. He casually let his gaze drift up and saw it was a nurse on her way into a shift at Shands. He did a double take when he saw the girl's wide, beautiful features and light brown hair braided down the back. She may not have been the kind of girl who turned heads at a party or in the club, but to him she was everything he looked for in a woman. The fact that she was in the nursing profession enhanced her beauty twofold.

She plopped down with a large latte and a pastry, flipping through the *Times-Union* to the crossword. She glanced over to him and saw his completed crossword, saying, "That's not from the local paper, is it?"

"*New York Times*. I downloaded it."

"That's a great idea. I don't know why I waste my time on this silly thing, but I do it every day." She smiled and said, "You look familiar."

"I'm in here all the time and I'll try to remember to bring in a crossword for you next time."

She reached across the narrow aisle and patted his hand and smiled. "That's very nice of you."

He tried not to stare, but all he could think was how beautiful she was. A deep-down, personal beauty. Some would call it an eternal beauty.

SIXTEEN

Tony Mazzetti had to admit it would've taken much longer to go through the detective bureau analyst and run profiles on each of the names Joey Big Balls had given him. But Sparky Taylor had jumped right on it and now had a driver's license photo, personal data sheet, and, for four of the five names, a criminal history.

Mazzetti said, "Are you telling me four out of the five men at a construction site have criminal histories?"

Sparky shook his head. "Statistically that would be quite improbable. The reason so many of these men have histories is their names were brought up specifically because you told your informant to look for potential violent criminals. Your informant wouldn't give us the names of men he had no reason to suspect of a crime. Therefore, it's not surprising four of them have a criminal past."

"Who are you, Spock?"

"You can ridicule logic and reasoned thinking all you want, but the fact remains that not all construction workers have felony convictions. And while we're on the subject, Spock, as portrayed by Leonard Nimoy, is an extraordinarily interesting and complex character, and his actions are based on a well-thought-out literary principle."

Mazzetti really couldn't answer because he was actually afraid to engage his partner in any further conversation.

It was later in the afternoon when Yvonne Zuni found herself standing in the doorway to her small office looking out over the squad bay. The entire detective bureau took up the better part of the second floor and had been called the Land That Time Forgot for as long as she'd been with the Jacksonville Sheriff's Office. Each detective had his or her own desk, no matter what shift they worked. In addition, there were a number of extra desks that were used when people were brought in to help on specific cases. There were four secretaries and four criminal intelligence analysts in the room at any given time, except for the evening and most of the midnight shift. That left a whole lot of potential suspects in the theft of the pills lost during the fight. And that's what she had to keep reminding herself. It was not necessarily a theft, even if she could find no other rational explanation for what had happened to the melting pills.

The use and abuse of, and trafficking in prescription pain medications had risen drastically over the past few years. When she'd first started in narcotics, the unit focused almost solely on cocaine and specifically crack, which had torn apart certain communities worse than anything else. She had noted a sharp rise in the use of heroin. But it was nothing compared to the industry being built around prescription narcotics on the streets. Even though the pills were controlled and supposedly tightly regulated, there was always a way around the system and she felt that drug companies had to be complicit in the wave of painkillers that had swept through the country. The idea they'd become so valuable someone would steal them directly from a police department was unsettling but not unbelievable.

As she eyeballed the room and thought about her own detectives, Sergeant Zuni considered them in a different light. She wondered, *How does Stall keep going at full speed all the time? Is Tony Mazzetti sore from all the weights he lifts?* These were things she'd never considered. She hoped she wouldn't start to look at someone who slept late in the morning as a potential drug user, but Ronald Bell had planted the idea in her head.

She wanted IA to keep things as low-key as he had said they would and resolve the issue before rumors started to run rampant.

As John Stallings and Patty Levine cut through downtown Jacksonville from the Thomas School on their way to the Tischler house near the beach, Patty closed her cell phone and said, "The housekeeper told me Mrs. Tischler won't be home for another forty minutes. I think we should talk to her before the husband gets home."

"Should we try to meet her while she's away from the house?"

"I don't want to scare her with a call, and this is something we should handle face-to-face."

Stallings nodded his agreement. His mind was whistling through the information they'd learned today, as well as a very cold phone conversation he'd had with Maria when he called to inquire about the kids. That made him think of a pleasant conversation he'd had with Liz Dubeck at her small hotel not far from where they were right now.

Stallings said, "Let's go by and see if the lady at the hotel remembered anything more about her brief conversation with Leah."

"You mean the pretty lady at the hotel near Davis Street?"

"That's exactly who I mean. And I would appreciate it if you didn't give me any shit about it."

"For how long?"

"Until tomorrow morning?"

Patty smiled and said, "Done."

A few minutes later Stallings was looking into the dark eyes of Liz Dubeck while Patty politely waited in the car and made a few phone calls.

Liz said, "Any luck on finding the girl?"

He shook his head. "That's why I'm here. See if you remembered anything."

"Nothing new, but I could ask around. People might be more inclined to talk to me than a big, scary cop."

"You think I'm scary?"

"I don't, but others might. I've gotten to know a lot of people in the neighborhood and can ask without raising any eyebrows."

"That'd be great. I'll be on my cell."

Liz paused, smiled, and said, "Why don't we discuss it over coffee? Maybe tomorrow morning."

He froze, surprised by the offer.

"I'll come over near the sheriff's office. Is there someplace you like in particular?"

He stared at her, unable to speak.

Liz said, "How about Junior's by the Mobis Tower? Everyone seems to like it and it's far enough away from your office that we won't run into anyone if that makes you more comfortable."

He slowly nodded.

"Maybe you'll regain your power of speech by then."

He nodded again and headed out to Patty in the car.

It was late afternoon and he finally had the good luck to see Cheryl in the fancy new Chrysler 300 her mother had bought her. He'd stayed well back on the long ride west and north of the beach at Ponte Vedra toward Jacksonville. Even with no commercial lettering on his white van it was taller than most vehicles and stuck out in traffic. On the bright side, he sat up high and could see a good distance. He realized he was distracted thinking about meeting Mary tomorrow night at the cozy café not far from his apartment. He wasn't sure exactly what he was going to do but knew it was the perfect window because of her cruise. She had already told him how she was going to park in extended parking at the airport and catch the quick flight to Fort Lauderdale, where she'd board the cruise.

It'd be at least four days before anyone even came close to realizing she was missing, and her friends might not even report it right away. If he played his cards right, he'd have one more piece of this work of art completed without any risk whatsoever.

But now he was planning ahead. Planning something that might be satisfying, as well as necessary. If he had to be honest with himself, he was curious what it would feel like to plunge his razor-sharp knife into Cheryl's heart. See how long she twitched at the end of the metal blade. Every time he thought about her snide comments, sneers, and generally smug demeanor, he got so mad he could feel his face flush. And that made him believe he'd enjoy sticking her like a marshmallow about to go over a campfire.

He had no idea where Cheryl was going, but was surprised when she pulled over quickly into a large strip mall with a Home Depot at one end and a Sports Authority at the other. He eased into the parking lot and caught a glimpse of her walking near the Sports Authority. All he was really trying to accomplish today was to get an idea of where he could deal with her since he knew he couldn't do it at her house or his apartment. Maybe his best bet was to follow her out of her parents' development like he had today.

He pulled the van into a spot where he could see her walk from her car toward Sports Authority. She was wearing jeans and a tight blouse showing off the big, fake boobs she was so proud of. Then, as she pushed through the front door, she stopped and looked back like she was checking to see if anyone was watching her. She didn't look directly back at the van, but her suspicious movements made him very uncomfortable.

The sooner she was dead the better off he would be.

SEVENTEEN

Patty Levine and John Stallings waited in the car at the end of the long driveway to the Tischler house. As soon as Mrs. Tischler pulled in and parked her Jag, they were out of the car and meeting her at the front door.

Just the sight of the two police officers approaching her made Mrs. Tischler gasp and start to cry.

Patty knew Stallings had been through this and was amazed how quickly he got to her to say, "We don't have any news, Mrs. Tischler. Just a few more questions." He firmly grasped both of Mrs. Tischler's arms until she looked at him and seemed to acknowledge his comment.

Stallings said, "Do you understand me? We don't have any information about Leah yet. I promise you we're looking very hard."

Mrs. Tischler nodded her head and ushered the detectives inside the opulent home.

Patty noticed the two younger boys nestled in front of the TV watching an older Jackie Chan movie. When they settled in the den, Patty sat close to Mrs. Tischler.

That's when she noticed the telltale signs of someone strung out on prescription drugs. It looked like she was moving in slow motion, she was clearly lethargic, her tongue worked its way around her lips as if she was thirsty, and her pupils looked like pinpricks even in the low light.

Patty said, "Have you heard anything at all about Leah from anyone else since we spoke?" It was more a habit than a real question.

Mrs. Tischler shook her head.

Patty asked a couple more questions, all of them receiving slow, negative responses. She paused and said, "I have one question that, um, could be a little sensitive."

Mrs. Tischler looked at her with those pale eyes, waiting for the question.

"Did you or your husband have any intense discussions with Leah last week before she disappeared?"

"I told you we hadn't really had a serious fight."

"I'm not talking about an argument, so much as a disclosure. Perhaps Leah told you something that upset you or your husband. Anything like that at all?"

Mrs. Tischler's eyes seemed to focus all at once; then in a low voice she said, "Who have you been talking to?"

"Everyone."

"Leah . . ." Mrs. Tischler took a very long pause, using the time to breathe deeply several times. ". . . said that she and another girl at the school had a relationship."

Patty was very careful when she said, "A romantic relationship?"

Mrs. Tischler nodded her head and mumbled, "Why would that matter?"

"What matters is how Leah perceived your response to her admission. It matters because it's very important to know whether she ran away or if something else happened. It's important because we need to know the whole truth."

Mrs. Tischler started to cry and reached for a Kleenex.

Patty said, "Do you have any idea where she might've gone?"

She shook her head.

"Did she ever mention a girl from Tennessee?"

Mrs. Tischler shook her head.

Mrs. Tischler murmured, "She was just so confused."

Patty didn't know how many times she'd heard that exact phrase the past two years and knew that in this case it really meant *we were appalled*. But it answered one question: Leah had definitely run away. Patty wondered if that made any difference to Stallings or if it hit home a little too hard.

Patty said, "So she did run away."

Mrs. Tischler nodded her head and a barely audible "Yes" escaped her.

"It's nothing to be ashamed of."

"It was Bob. He was the one who couldn't take it. He was being so unreasonable and he didn't even realize it. He drove her away from us." The woman started to cry uncontrollably.

Patty sat there for a second, looked at her partner, and could see in his face he was wondering if he had somehow chased away Jeanie.

* * *

Stallings was shaken by the meeting with Leah Tischler's mother. After he dropped Patty off at the PMB so she could check with the computer techs to see if they had any e-mails or indicators pointing toward Tennessee, he swung by the community center where his father would be working on a Thursday evening. As always, he was careful to park his car across the street in the church parking lot so as not to scare anyone participating in any of the classes or support groups in the giant community center.

He was surprised when he walked in the front door and saw how many people were making use of the facility. In the far corner, the single basketball court was being used by a dozen young men. Scattered in front of the court were eight tables, each filled to capacity with people in support groups or learning some new craft.

There were three priests from the church across the street who supervised the busy community center and wandered around with their collars on more casual, short-sleeved shirts.

After Stallings had been standing there a few minutes, one of the priests approached him. He looked to be about Stallings's age or maybe a little younger, like his late thirties, but he still had a paternal air about him.

"Can I help you with something?"

Stallings pointed at the table where he saw his father was leading a discussion and said, "I'm James Stallings's son."

A smile spread across the priest's face as he said, "You must be the policeman, Johnny. I've heard a great deal about you and your wonderful family."

Stallings didn't know what to say so he smiled and nodded.

The priest said, "You should be very proud of your father. Not only has he been able to overcome his alcoholism, but he's obviously working hard to help others. He and I have gotten very close over the last few years as he's worked more and more around here."

Stallings nodded again, realizing he didn't have to go into the history he had with his father. There was no need to detail the beatings or the rantings that had driven his sister to run away, then come back, never quite the same. He let the priest have his saintly view of his imperfect father.

The group sitting around his father's table broke up and the priest led Stallings over. He could hear his father say good night to each of the men by name, offering them some little encouragement.

His father looked over, smiled, and stood, saying, "Hello, Johnny, what a nice surprise to see you over here." He looked at the priest, whom he'd known for several years, then back to Stallings. "Are you going to introduce me to your friend, Johnny?"

Now Stallings knew there was a problem.

EIGHTEEN

It was too early in the morning for Stallings to have so much on his mind. He got into the coffee shop where he was supposed to meet Liz Dubeck early and was sipping on a cup of unsweetened black coffee. He felt a pang of guilt meeting a woman for coffee. It didn't matter that she was a witness. He was meeting her because he liked talking to her. In addition, he was troubled by his father's confusion last night. He had talked it over with the priest, who said he hadn't noticed any previous memory lapses. He promised to keep an eye on Stallings's father and note any similar incidents. Stallings silently pledged to visit more frequently to make sure it wasn't anything more than a man who had had a hard life and was getting older.

Liz came through the front door, looking cute, like a suburban mom with a slight edge. He got her a cup of coffee and they sat and chatted, first about her work at the motel, which was funded by grants through the city and the federal government, then about her personal life. Stallings wasn't surprised she'd been married and had no children of her own. He could see a woman like this spending so much time working with the runaways that her husband had found other ways to occupy his time. He found himself confiding in her about his separation and gave her some details about his kids and how he hadn't seen Jeanie in three years.

Stallings said, "What's your plan now?"

"What'd you mean? Like my plan on convincing you to have dinner with me?"

He smiled. "I meant your long-term plan with your job and those sorts of things. You made it sound like you were looking around."

"Does that mean you won't have dinner with me?"

This time he even laughed. He could think of nothing he'd like to do more than have dinner with her. Instead he said, "Things are complicated right now. Can I have a little time to answer you?"

"That's a refreshing attitude from a man separated from his wife. You can have all the time you need."

He felt like leaning across the table and kissing her on the cheek, but before he could, she gave him a kiss on the lips.

He said, "What was that for?"

"For not realizing what a sweet guy you are." She stood, straightened her blouse, and said, "When things are less complicated, please give me a call."

Like the night before, he couldn't speak. Instead he smiled, nodded his head, and watched her as she turned quickly and walked out of the café. He thought about running after her but realized she wanted to exit on her own terms. Instead, he leaned back in his chair and took another sip of coffee as he dug in his pocket for a ten-dollar bill to lay on the table.

As he looked up, a face caught his attention. Staring at him from across the room was his wife, Maria.

* * *

It was quiet in the office so Patty used the opportunity to casually take a seat next to Tony Mazzetti's desk. She knew John was having coffee with Liz Dubeck. She fully approved of Stallings's informal meeting, hoping it might get the guy's head out of his family situation. It seemed clear to everyone but him that Maria intended to move forward with the divorce. But poor John could never let anything go easily. It broke Patty's heart to see someone she cared so much about experience the kind of problems John Stallings had.

Her eyes made an involuntary sweep of the detective bureau. That's what her secret relationship with Tony Mazzetti had done to her. But the Land That Time Forgot was almost devoid of people except for Yvonne Zuni, working quietly at her desk in her office, and a team of crime scene people collecting any possible evidence left from the fight the day before. It seemed odd to her that they were so worried about errant DNA and fingerprints, but one of the crime scene techs had explained that the state attorney's office was considering additional charges, which could include attempted murder if the injured detective did not recover fully. She noted that there were no detectives supervising the crime-scene geeks and thought it was a little unusual. But in cost-cutting times like this there was no telling what was important enough to warrant a detective and what wasn't.

She focused her attention on Tony Mazzetti's handsome, smiling face. He had a strong chin and his nose had been broken one too many times, but he still had a cute quality to his looks. If Patty could correct anything about her boyfriend's appearance it'd be his crooked bottom teeth. He definitely would have bene-fited from a couple of years in braces as a teenager, but it was nothing she'd ever mention.

She even liked the neat mustache he spent so much time trimming and loved to show off on TV.

Mazzetti said, "You okay? You look tired."

Patty shrugged. "Just a few aches and pains."

"Maybe you should take a day off and rest up."

She was shaking her head before he even finished the sentence. "No. No way. Not until we find out what happened to Leah Tischler or find the killer. I think Stall believes there's a chance she's alive."

"Even after finding the belt?"

"He says she could've discarded it."

"Keep dreamin'." Mazzetti took a moment to really look at his girlfriend. He said in a quiet voice, "You look beat. You sure you're okay?"

"I've been tired before."

"Fair enough. You have any plans for this evening?"

"I haven't checked my datebook or any messages on my phone. But I can assume I'm relatively open. What'd you have in mind?"

"I have to check a couple of construction sites down in the south and near Dearwood Park. There's an Italian place named Gi-Gi's off J. Turner Butler Boulevard. I thought it might be nice if we ran into each other there about eight o'clock."

"I'm assuming you visiting the construction sites has something to do with your homicide investigation."

Mazzetti nodded quietly.

"What if you get hung up and I'm waiting all alone in a nice Italian restaurant? Maybe I'll wear my tiny black dress and other patrons can hit on me if you don't show." She gave him her best mischievous smile.

Mazzetti said, "I really don't expect to find our man at this construction site. It's more of a process of elimination. But if he turns out to be there and I make an arrest, I feel pretty confident I can call you, explain what happened, and you'll fully understand. Then I'll deal with anyone who tried to hit on you."

Patty leaned in close and let her hand drift over to his leg. "You have no idea how much I wish I could kiss you right now."

Yvonne Zuni had a good sense of what was going on in the squad's homicide case. She'd finally finished reading and approving the reports from the night before and felt confident they were doing everything they could to find the killer. She didn't react to the parents' sorrow like Stallings did. She felt her strength was in the cool and rational deployment of the resources. The thing that bothered her now was Ronald Bell's disclosure that someone in the detective bureau was a suspect in the theft of evidence.

As this thought occurred to her the phone rang. A male voice said, "How is the most beautiful sergeant in all of JSO doing this morning?"

Sergeant Zuni couldn't help but smile. "I'd be doing better if I didn't have a covert IA crime scene in my squad bay."

"Would you rather have a full-blown investigation airing out everyone's dirty laundry?"

"No, I think this is disruptive enough."

"That was one of the reasons I was calling. I wanted to make sure everything was going smoothly. I have no idea what they might pick up, but we need to have as much information as possible before we go public."

"It's quiet in here this morning. Everyone's out running leads or taking comp time so they can work on the weekend. I hate being sneaky about anything with my detectives."

"Please don't make it sound like I want to be sneaky. This is the best way to handle it."

"I agree. But it doesn't make me feel any better."

There was a short pause on the phone line until Bell said, "The other reason I was calling was to see if you might be available for dinner tonight."

"I thought it was too dangerous to eat out in public."

"Not if we pick some out-of-the-way place. What'd you feel like eating?"

"I love a good Italian place. Any ideas?"

Bell said, "I have just the place. It's down in Deerwood Park. It's called Gi-Gi's. How does eight o'clock sound?"

"Like a date."

NINETEEN

John Stallings was surprised Maria wasn't bent out of shape. He sat across from her at the small table in the same café where he'd met Liz Dubeck. As soon as he'd noticed her, he'd walked over and tried to explain why he was sitting with another woman, but Maria had showed no real emotion. His first concern was she'd fallen off the wagon, but as he sat there quietly talking to her, he realized it might be a worse problem. She just didn't care.

Maria shook her head and said for the third time, "You don't have to explain anything to me. We're separated. As I recall, I'm the one who asked you to move out. You can have coffee with anyone you want."

Somehow her calm and rational response was even more unsettling than if she'd yelled and cursed. But Maria had never been prone to emotional fits. Even her choice of drugs, prescription narcotics and other depressants, mirrored her personality. She was quiet and thoughtful rather than fiery and vengeful. Right now the quiet, thoughtful approach seemed much harsher to Stallings.

Stallings said, "What're you doing over here, Maria?"

"Like I said, we don't have to explain ourselves to each other."

"I'm just curious. It's not near the house and there's no reason for you to be downtown."

"What if I told you I was headed down to the football stadium?"

"I'd say there's no reason to be sarcastic. I worry about you. I worry about the kids too. Some days you guys are all I can think about."

"But apparently not today."

That hurt Stallings more than about anything she'd ever said.

It was midmorning and Mazzetti felt like he had to get out and do some work on the case rather than read other people's reports about the work they'd done. But there were a lot of aspects to Kathy Mizell's murder and it required a lot of detectives. That's why he and Sparky Taylor were now at the Jacksonville Medical Examiner's Office on North Jefferson Street. The modern, two-story, white building looked more like a middle school than the last place the residents of Duval County visited.

Mazzetti gawked at the young, pretty assistant medical examiner. Goggles covered her blue eyes as she perched on a stool, working on a body of a seventy-eight-year-old drowning victim. It was not uncommon for Mazzetti to discuss cases with her while she continued her work. He was amazed at how the young Syracuse graduate could do so many things at once and still get it all right.

She used a scalpel to slice the skin along the crown

of the man's head as she said, "The one thing I'd say is our killer is strong. He didn't use the belt as tourniquet; he pulled it manually with his hands. That makes me believe he's probably large with some muscle mass."

Mazzetti said, "But there's nothing to link Kathy Mizell to the Pamela Kimble murder in Rolling Hills, is there?"

"Not that I can see." She paused for a moment as she peeled back the skin and hair of the elderly man's head. "Kimble was a manual strangulation where the killer used his hands. There are no links. No decent DNA or fingerprints or other organic material. Aside from asphyxiation, even the mode of death is different. One killer used a belt and the other his bare hands. It's very uncommon to see a strangler change details like that between two different murders."

Mazzetti wanted to tell the young assistant medical examiner to stick to the medical aspects of the case and leave the other forensics and profiling to the detectives. He knew she also had a background in psychiatry and kept up with all the medical journals about deviant behavior so he kept his mouth shut. He had learned a long time ago it was easier to let people run their mouths and ignore them than it was to tell them to stick to their fields. He'd need a good working relationship with this woman for a long time to come.

The assistant medical examiner said, "Any idea where the belt came from?"

Mazzetti looked at Sparky Taylor to involve him in the conversation. The rotund detective took the hint and said, "We've identified it as a part of the Thomas School uniform. There's a girl named Leah Tischler missing from the school and it's a good bet the belt was hers. The only question now is, did she discard it when she ran away or is she another victim of the same killer, who took the belt from her?"

The woman looked at Sparky and said, "The Thomas School. That's big-time. I bet you boys are under some pressure to solve this one quick."

Mazzetti cut in and said, "We're under pressure to solve every murder quickly."

The assistant medical examiner stood from the stool and stretched, removed her glasses, focused those drop-dead-gorgeous blue eyes on Mazzetti, and said, "You look like you handle it pretty well. Wish I could stay in shape as well as you." She smiled at him.

Mazzetti felt like he'd stumbled into a robbery the way his heart raced and his face flushed. He wondered if he was misreading the cute assistant medical examiner when she added, "We should meet at the gym over at the PMB sometime."

No, he was reading it right.

Patty Levine knew when to ask her partner personal questions and when to keep her mouth shut. She didn't know what had happened earlier in the morning, but John Stallings was in a silent, brooding mood.

She casually asked, "How was coffee?"

"Look, I'm married. Nothing happened."

She couldn't remember her partner ever speaking so sharply to her and, although it was hard for a moment, she knew he wasn't mad at her. Something else was eating at him. They rode along in silence as she checked her list of safe houses that runaways used on occasion. The runaway population in Jacksonville had its own underground railroad of sorts. It also had a communications network rivaling AT&T. The runaways seemed to know where they could congregate safely, eat, and sleep with a roof over their head. The county government provided very few services for runaways compared to the problem, but there were a number of alternatives like the cheap hotels decent people like Liz Dubeck ran or houses that rented rooms cheaply.

Patty and Stallings had already checked three safe houses Stallings had a very good relationship with. No one had seen any sign of Leah Tischler or knew anyone who had had any contact with her. A common response during one of these investigations.

Stallings pulled his Impala to the curb in front of an old Florida, flat-roofed, cement-block house. Two men in their early twenties sat on the porch with their feet dangling off. They started to get up when they saw the car stop but relaxed once they realized it was Stallings.

Patty was always amazed how calm her partner was as he approached people and situations like this. He nodded and said, "Hey, boys. Darryl inside?"

One of them said, "Watching *Family Guy* in the main room. He got himself a DVR and hasn't left his TV chair in four days."

Stallings chuckled. "Everyone needs a goal in life."

Patty followed him through the open door, aware of the gun on her hip covered by a loose shirt. She knew Stallings and Darryl Paluk had a long history, which included a broken nose and several broken fingers before Darryl realized he should never hold back information from Stallings about missing girls. For his part Stallings had never hassled Darryl about his pot dealing and constant use of the drug inside the house. Even now, late in the morning, Patty navigated through the thick haze of marijuana smoke.

The big, hairy, shirtless man sat in an oversized La-Z-Boy recliner, laughing wildly at an episode of the animated show *Family Guy.*

Stallings stood in the doorway to the main room until one of the men on the couch looked up and gave a little shout of surprise. Darryl turned his massive head, chuckled loudly, and said, "Stall, my brother. What brings you by this bright, sunny day?"

Stallings stepped into the room, and Patty automatically slid to the other side of the doorway so that between them they could cover the entire room.

Stallings said, "Have you met my partner, Patty Levine?"

Darryl Paluk struggled to his feet, pulling his shorts all the way to his gigantic waist. "I have not had the pleasure." He extended his hand. "I can't believe the local police agency would have the good taste to hire a babe like you."

Patty gave him a short glare as Stallings said, "This babe will crack you in your head with her ASP and not think about it again today."

Darryl looked at Patty and said, "Is this true?"

Patty knew actions spoke louder than words with guys like this so she reached behind her loose shirt, grasped her ASP tucked in the small of her back, yanked it out with her right hand, and flicked it open over her right shoulder so it made a sound like a shotgun racking. The metal baton expanded from eight inches to thirty inches in the blink of an eye and had caused more than one street thug to poop in his pants. The action brought a stunned silence to everyone in the room except Stallings, who used it as a chance to produce a photo of Leah Tischler and ask Darryl and his friends if any of them had seen her. It was a perfect example of how well they worked together as partners. They always wanted the element of surprise but never wanted to surprise each other.

A tall, thin youth leaned up from the couch, his long greasy hair dangling over his shoulder. He took a good look at the photo, then faced both Stallings and Patty. This was usually a sign someone had some information. The young man looked at Leah's photo again and said, "I think I saw her. She was in some kind of school uniform over near Davis."

Patty didn't say anything and she felt her heart skip a beat.

"She's a rich girl. I can tell by the professional photograph. And that's one of the reasons I noticed her. She got into a white van, I think. I remember the uniform and her pretty dark hair. If you give me some time I might be able to come up with a few more details."

Stallings said, "Could it have been a construction van?"

"There was no sign I remember, but it could've been,"

They had another lead.

TWENTY

Tony Mazzetti sat across the table from Sparky Taylor at a local sandwich shop. Sometimes detectives new to homicide and not used to visiting the medical examiner's office had a problem eating after witnessing an autopsy, especially the autopsy of an elderly man who had nothing to do with your case. The way Sparky Taylor wolfed down his ham sandwich and extra-large bag of Doritos told Mazzetti he didn't suffer from that kind of problem.

Mazzetti said, "I got a line on five possible people of interest. It's a long shot, but the names my snitch, Joey Big Balls, came up with work at a couple of construction sites he manages down in Deerwood Park."

"That *is* a long shot. Don't you think there are better ways to utilize our time?"

"There're always better ways to use our time, but sometimes it's a weird lead that breaks things wide open. This isn't tech services where we know how long it takes to install a hidden camera or copy a couple of tapes. This is homicide, which is part science, part luck, and all hard work."

"I wasn't questioning your methods, Tony. I was analyzing them. When are we gonna visit the construction sites?"

Mazzetti felt bad for snapping at his new partner. The guy had proved to be hardworking and insightful and was merely bringing up something he thought was important. "I was going to try and hit the swing shift tonight about seven o'clock. There's one guy I'll focus on first."

Sparky paused while he swallowed a tremendous bite of the Reuben sandwich. He wiped his mouth from left to right like he did after every single bite. He wadded up the napkin and added it to the growing pile at the end of the table. Mazzetti had wondered why his partner grabbed the huge stack of napkins as they walked past the counter. Now he realized the quirky detective used a brand-new napkin after every bite. Finally, Sparky swallowed and said, "My son is in the academic games tonight over at the community college. Twice a year they take the winners of the local elementary school academic games and host the finals at the college."

Mazzetti waved his hand and said, "Don't sweat it. I got this covered."

"Policy says at least two officers should be present during any potentially confrontational interview. I'll go with you."

"That's crazy. If we chased every kooky lead and ignored our families on everything that came up at the office, no one would be married and kids would be running wild in the streets. I'll get Patty to go with me." He watched his partner carefully until he was certain Sparky was satisfied. Mazzetti had no intention of asking Patty to go out on a lead prior to a romantic dinner.

She already looked tired and he didn't want to add to her workload. It would only take a few minutes to talk to these mopes at the construction sites; then he could meet Patty at Gi-Gi's and maybe even consider taking Saturday off.

John Stallings never liked to think of himself as the brooding type, but as he sat at his desk in the Land That Time Forgot he did feel down and maybe even depressed. The whole day had worn on him from his awkward and uncomfortable encounter with Maria to some unknown anxiety that had been creeping up on him for several days. A least the guy who gave him a lead at Darryl Paluk's house had been encouraging. Not encouraging in a way that meant Leah Tischler might still be alive, but any information, anything he could use at all, was helpful.

He'd made dozens of phone calls to missing persons detectives he knew across the Southeast from Atlanta to Daytona. Each of the detectives knew him well from three years of inquiries about Jeanie. Usually he was careful to make contact with them off-duty so no one would ever accuse him of searching for his own daughter—a case that was not even assigned to him—while he was on duty at the Jacksonville Sheriff's Office. He had an official reason to call them today. Leah Tischler's disappearance was assigned to him and Patty. He didn't think anyone would care if he happened to mention Jeanie while was talking about Leah Tischler.

He often limited his initial search for a missing person to Atlanta in the north to Daytona in the south. It was amazing how people from the Jacksonville area didn't drift much farther than either of those two cities.

Atlanta had a certain mystique and held an allure to people hoping to get rich. Whether it was large corporations that seemed to always be hiring or the lucrative drug market, young people from Jacksonville often thought their fortune lay in Atlanta. On the flipside, Daytona had a reputation as being a laid-back surfer community where young people thought they could draw caricatures of the tourists or some other fun activity to make a few bucks while they lived a relaxed lifestyle.

Stallings didn't know which image of the cities was more incorrect. Atlanta was a sprawling urban metropolis with a horrendous crime rate. A young woman without any skills or family could likely find herself in the stable of an industrious and vicious pimp. While Daytona was smaller, the opportunities for legitimate employment were grim.

Stallings made it a point to stay on close terms with detectives from each of the cities, as well as the other points of interest as far west as Tampa, and definitely to include Orlando. Oddly, it was the tourist capital of Florida that offered the best opportunity for people fleeing their lives in Jacksonville. There really were a number of legitimate job opportunities at the incredible number of hotels and restaurants in the landlocked tourist haven.

Stallings called the detectives he knew best, then a contact at the National Center for Missing and Exploited Children in Washington, D.C., a public and privately funded agency that grew from the efforts of John Walsh, the father of a young boy who was kidnapped and murdered in South Florida in 1981. Most people knew John Walsh as the host of *America's Most Wanted*, but he was one TV commentator who had earned his credibility the hard way. He'd been relentless and utterly honest about all aspects of his son's disappearance and what it did to his family. He had turned his own anguish into a national crusade, and as a result thousands of children had been reunited with their families.

The analysts and supervisors at NCMEC always gave Stallings their utmost attention and followed up on every request. He was that rare hybrid of mourning parent and devoted cop. One thing the people at NCMEC appreciated was a hard-charging missing persons detective. They recognized that there were other assignments cops often preferred, including homicide or narcotics. So they cherished a cop who put his entire efforts into finding missing children. They didn't care what the cop's motivation was. They understood that it was a special breed of cop who had the determination of Stallings. This was forged through personal desire and loss. Some detectives just understood the issue and the mind-set of other cops. It was hard to convince an old-time road patrolman that a runaway was anything more than a spoiled kid looking to get out of punishment. And the National Center for Missing and Exploited Children was always there to help.

Today Stallings checked to see if they had any new information developed from what he'd provided about Leah Tischler. It didn't hurt to throw in a quick query on Jeanie.

At least now he felt like he was accomplishing something and, for whatever reason, just the ritual of talking to the same people and going through the same tasks made him feel much better

*   *   *

He was enjoying himself sitting on the balcony of the seafood restaurant on the second floor of Jacksonville Landing. The Landing was Jacksonville's desperate effort to provide a convenient, clean, safe tourist area. Like most restaurants and big commercial facilities, it was sort of bland and geared toward general tastes. But he enjoyed a moderate breeze and watching Mary try to eat an oyster in a ladylike manner. He soaked in every detail of her pretty face and perfect smile. Although his recent spate of activity had left him tired, he was revitalized knowing he could honor someone like Mary for all eternity.

She did most of the talking, telling him all about her cruise and how she was a little nervous about her flight to Fort Lauderdale to board the ship. She showed him her bottle of Xanax she claimed would keep her calm during the fifty-minute flight.

He said, "What time do you have to be at the airport?"

"My flight's at nine fifteen, so I'll get to the airport about eight o'clock." Mary looked at him and said, "Did you say your apartment is in this part of the city?"

"Yeah, not too far from here. About ten minutes from the airport."

"Maybe I won't have as far to ride in the morning as I usually would." She gave him a sly smile and a wink.

He was surprised by her aggressiveness and couldn't think of anything witty to say in reply. He was also disappointed she'd be so obvious on their first date. On the bright side, it sounded like it wouldn't be difficult for him to get her over to his apartment.

"I'd love to show you one of the pieces of art I made through blowing glass. I keep it in my apartment above my workshop."

She gave him the smile her employer should use as an advertisement and said, "I'm dying to see it."

Although Patty liked to think of herself as a tough, educated, experienced cop, right at this moment, on a Friday evening, checking herself in the mirror of the ladies' bathroom next to the Land That Time Forgot, she felt more like a schoolgirl. After the wild week and her increasing pain in her back and lack of sleep, she was really looking forward to an honest-to-goodness date with her boyfriend, Tony Mazzetti. She'd gone so far as to look at the restaurant's website and dream about sipping good pinot noir and eating clams oreganata. She wished she could talk about her date to other people in the squad, but that seemed minor compared to the date itself. She felt confident things would work out and she and Tony could talk about the relationship openly. It might be a good time for her to move forward with her plans to take the sergeant's exam. If she left the unit as a sergeant, she'd not only be advancing her career, she'd be opening herself to a serious, normal relationship. But before she could think about anything like that she had to make sure her prescription-drug habit was under control. At least under better control than it was now. The Xanax she'd taken earlier in the afternoon still had her on an even keel as she got ready to meet Tony down in Deerwood Creek.

Sergeant Zuni's voice surprised her, "What are you doing here so late? I thought you and Stall were in pretty good shape on your leads."

"I was killing time before I meet . . . before I meet

someone for dinner. I didn't want to run back to my condo and out again."

The sergeant smiled. "I'm glad you have plans tonight. I worry about you guys working too hard. Especially about Stallings. He always seems to be involved in stuff after hours. I never met a cop who got so fixated on a case."

"I worry about him too. He's under a lot of stress with his kids and he's trying to keep better track of his father and his health. I keep a pretty good eye on him."

Sergeant Zuni gave a short laugh. Patty realized it was because the sergeant knew no one controlled Stallings for very long.

Patty said, "What about you? Anything exciting on the agenda?" Patty often wondered if the beautiful sergeant got out much. She seemed very private and quiet.

Sergeant Zuni said, "I might manage to grab a bite to eat tonight."

Patty smiled as the sergeant walked away. There was something in the way she'd said she might grab a bite to eat that led Patty to believe she had a romantic evening planned.

Mary couldn't believe how lucky she was to meet a guy like this before her cruise. It gave her something to look forward to as well as an easy way to get to the airport. She liked him a lot. He was sweet and polite and a really good listener. That was hard to find in Jacksonville. It seemed like the men were either hotshot attorneys who felt the world revolved around them or underemployed high school dropouts who still lived with their mothers. She'd been burned too many times and had a tendency to take the all-or-nothing bet on men. She rarely waited to see how things would evolve because it was outside her control. Instead, she liked to commit early and completely. That either scared men away or hooked them so solidly she had to get a court order to get rid of them if things went south.

But this guy really did seem nice as he drove her to the long-term parking lot near the airport. She'd already decided to do something special to show her appreciation. But it also gave her a chance to see that lovely smile with the cute dimples. She couldn't decide if she had gone into dental hygiene because she liked teeth or if she noticed teeth because she was a dental hygienist. Either way this guy had a great smile.

She hadn't dated a guy she'd wanted to sleep with in months. Her last boyfriend, Troy, showed up occasionally to keep her satisfied. She knew he told his friends it was just a booty call, but it worked both ways. The problem with Troy was he was only twenty-three years old and not mature enough to realize how great he'd had it when he was with her. She missed those washboard abs as well as some of his grander attributes. But tonight she was going to let loose with someone else. She hoped he felt the same way. The same fire. She recognized this as one of the special nights in her life as she started an exciting vacation by having a rendezvous with a man she thought might be something exceptional. She loved to look at her life that way.

He had a quiet, calm quality she found irresistible. Too many guys wanted to sit around and talk about themselves or sports or the damn Jaguars. He seemed much deeper than all that. And she had a scary thought. What if she didn't like his art he'd been talking about? She knew she'd suck it up and play along. She'd tell him it was so beautiful she wished she'd inspired it. Or some kind of shit like that.

Tony Mazzetti had already visited the first construction site and talked to two of the names Joey Big Balls had given him. One of the men had given him the names of two others. But Mazzetti had questioned him ruthlessly about his whereabouts the night Kathy Mizell was killed. He had a foolproof alibi. He'd been in jail for the night after being arrested that afternoon on a probation violation. The arrests and even the probation had not made their way through the computer yet to show up on his criminal history. Such was the life of a cop in modern times. Mazzetti tended to depend on computer printouts so much that he was surprised when someone had an excuse not shown on one.

The other man had been much tougher to talk to. Sour and holding a serious chip on his shoulder, the convicted car thief had felt as if he was being harassed for a crime he had already served two years in prison for. Now he worked as a carpenter and kept pretty steady hours. Mazzetti didn't want the guy to feel persecuted, but he needed some questions answered and it took a little pressure to get the guy to talk. All Mazzetti did was mention that he could be forced to look into the disappearance of two trucks near the worksite. He had no idea whether this guy was involved in the theft of the trucks, but there were reports in the system and it seemed to make him much more talkative. He claimed he'd been at home and his wife and at least one neighbor could verify his story. But Mazzetti really didn't even need to talk to the wife because he could read people pretty well and this guy wasn't pulling his chain.

So now he was at the last site and had forty minutes to find his man, talk to him, and drive the 3.2 miles to the restaurant to meet Patty about eight o'clock. It seemed like a good plan and a decent end to a hard week. He hoped to take tomorrow off to recharge his batteries and maybe even Sunday too. The sergeant had been very easy about the progress of the case. She knew all the detectives were working as hard as they could and they really needed a break in the case and in their workweek. That was a good fucking sergeant.

Mazzetti calmly walked onto the construction site and looked at the five-story building, which only had the walls and bare cement floors built. There were wide, gaping holes for the windows and doors. Joey Big Balls had said the crew was behind schedule on this building and worked two full shifts from 6 A.M. until 10 P.M. This seemed like the perfect time to catch as many workers as possible at the site.

He knew he stood out in his Brooks Brothers suit and silk striped tie, but this wasn't a mission of secrecy. He paused in the dusty gravel in front of the main open door to the building and cringed as he looked down at the dust on his new leather shoes. He looked up and mumbled, "Motherfucker." As his eyes scanned the building he saw a man lean out one of the windows and look down at him. It was only a short glance, but he recognized the man as Eldon Kozer. To be sure, he looked back down at his info sheet with Kozer's driver's license photo, identifiers, and criminal history. This was his man, there was no doubt.

Mazzetti stepped into the building, moving quickly

to avoid a man with a wheelbarrow full of jagged metal debris. He saw several ladders strapped to the ironwork inside the building and one set of temporary stairs. He took a deep breath to cleanse his lungs before tromping up the stairs. So far no one had even bothered to ask him who he was or what he was doing on the site, and that was fine with him.

About halfway up the stairs, Mazzetti glanced to his right and saw someone easing down the ladder secured to the next wall. His eyes met the man coming down the ladder. It was Eldon Kozer. Kozer looked Mazzetti up and down but didn't move.

Mazzetti said, "I need to talk to you for a minute."

"Me?"

"You're Eldon Kozer, aren't you?"

The man scowled and said, "Who are you?"

"JSO."

Without another word Kozer pulled his feet out of the rungs of the ladder and clamped them on to the outside edge and used his heavily gloved hands to slide down the ladder like it was amusement ride.

Mazzetti could hear Kozer shouting something to his buddies as he smacked the ground and started to run. Mazzetti turned to race down the stairs.

The chase was on.

TWENTY-ONE

He couldn't believe how lucky he'd gotten convincing Mary to leave her car at the airport parking tonight. He'd said it'd be easier to drop her off directly at the terminal. When she'd asked why she couldn't leave her car at his place for the week she was gone, he'd told her he wasn't going to be around to pick her up and he didn't think it was a safe enough neighborhood. She'd bought it. And now he had no worries whatsoever.

He'd spent a few minutes showing her his warehouse before they walked up the loud wooden stairs to his apartment. Over the years he'd put in nice hardwood floors and tile and bought decent furniture so the apartment didn't feel like a place above a dingy workspace. The two bedrooms were for him and guests, which he had never hosted. The main living room had a big-screen TV and a leather sectional couch. The kitchen was attached to the living room and at the far end, past the hallway to the bedrooms, he had his private workshop with his main work of art hidden under a clean padded moving blanket. He knew once he showed it to her she'd be in such awe of his talent that he could probably tell her what was going to happen and she wouldn't be upset.

As soon as they walked in the door Mary wrapped a hand around his neck and pulled him in for a long, deep kiss. She'd done this a couple times and it made him a little uncomfortable. Her soft lips did feel like satin against his. It was her long, probing tongue that startled him.

She said, "I hope you don't have a water bed because the way I feel tonight I might cause a tsunami."

He looked at her, thinking how a comment like that was not the way he'd pictured her. Not with the angelic face and wholesome smile.

Then she said, "I got some decent grass with me if you want to get high."

What'd she say? Drugs? Angels didn't use drugs.

As she flopped onto the corner of the couch, he started to realize she had some serious flaws. He looked closely and realized for the first time how much eyeliner she had on. She had a lot of makeup on in general. Maybe her dazzling smile had blinded him or maybe he was seeing her in a new light.

As he stepped closer she leaned forward and acted like she was going to playfully bite at his crotch. He jumped back partially out of reflex but mainly from repulsion. Who was this? Is this the kind of behavior that should be rewarded with eternal remembrance?

He wondered if he shouldn't move forward quickly before he changed his mind; otherwise he might be stuck with her for the night. He watched as she nestled herself on the couch and he mumbled he needed a second. He knew what he wanted to use, a heavy braided cord from a shipment of cut glass. He had taken the storage hooks off each end of the cord and tested it several times for strength and elasticity. He retrieved it from the drawer near his work of art.

He heard her belch from the couch and turned to see she'd unbuckled her pants and unbuttoned the last three buttons of her blouse. She looked at him and smiled, saying, "I might've had too much to eat." She belched again and giggled.

He turned away from her, wrapped the ends of the strap in each hand, and pulled out one last time to make sure it was strong.

Tony Mazzetti had never been much for foot chases. Of course as a uniformed officer with the Jacksonville Sheriff's Office he'd been in several. One fact he tried to forget and certainly never mentioned to anyone was that in his entire law-enforcement career he'd never actually caught someone by running after them. That's not to say he'd never made an arrest of someone running from him. Once, the year he started with JSO, he'd chased a burglar on foot behind a row of houses for more than ten minutes. He remembered gasping for breath as he shouted into his handheld radio for help. He'd lost the fleet runner and walked back to his car feeling like a failure. As he drove away from the scene, just before he went ten-eight, or in-service, on the radio, Mazzetti had taken one last look over his shoulder to the area where he'd lost the runner, taking his eyes off the road. In that instant he'd felt a sickening thud of a body crumple against his hood. He'd popped out of his cruiser, sick to his stomach with fear, and been shocked to see he had hit the man he'd been chasing. Two months later he'd received a commendation for not giving up the chase. He'd never told anyone exactly what had happened.

His last foot chase had been two years ago during a homicide investigation involving gang members. The suspect had run from Mazzetti, who lost him in two blocks. Luckily for Mazzetti but not so lucky for the suspect, he'd run into a rival gang area and been gunned down twenty minutes later.

Mazzetti's wide body was built for lifting weights, not running after criminals.

He kept all that in mind as he raced down the stairs and landed on the cement floor with an ungraceful thud. All he caught was a glimpse of the man's white T-shirt and fast-moving legs racing through one of the interior doors of the unfinished building. Mazzetti stayed on the trail and caught several more quick looks at the man, who seemed to be running in a circle around the construction site. Then he raced out the rear door to the building with Mazzetti relatively close behind him.

Mazzetti was constrained by a suit and hadn't reached for his gun yet. As he popped through the doorway, he took about ten steps before he froze. He felt his arms seized from both sides. Someone said, "No one chases down a worker on this crew. You must be crazy."

Mazzetti realized the grip on him was too strong to struggle out of so he let his eyes track the voice that had spoken to him. It was Eldon Kozer. He had the thin, hard look of a local redneck who'd done time.

Kozer said, "Out in the world you may be important, but here on our work site you're just a visitor and we don't like how you're behaving." He had a twang from Southern Georgia. Mazzetti had heard the accent all over town.

"I'm a cop. All I need is to talk to you."

That brought the stubby redneck up short. But he looked to each of his friends for support and maintained a tough attitude. "What if I don't wanna talk?" He slapped his lean, hard fist into his left hand.

Mazzetti knew he was in a tight spot.

Mary wanted to make sure she got her message across. She was ready. She unbuttoned her jeans and lifted the bottom of her blouse to show off her solid abs, which had taken her hours in the gym and a two-month contract at the Quick Weight Loss clinic that cost her almost eleven hundred dollars. It would've been more, but she had agreed to give the three saleswomen free cleanings after hours at the dentist's office.

But this guy seemed preoccupied and wasn't even facing her. He hadn't liked her little playful act either. Mary wasn't used to working this hard. She may not have been a tight teenager anymore, but she was hardly past her expiration date. Besides, now she knew what she was doing and enjoyed it rather than enduring it like she had for over a year after she started having sex.

And this guy had a quality she loved: he was shy. Didn't say much, didn't show off, and now he was avoiding her obvious advances.

Mary had already done a good scan of the apartment. On their way up the wooden stairs she'd been disappointed. The idea of an apartment above a warehouse was romantic in New York but a little on the redneck side in Jacksonville. The glass company looked prosperous enough, but the stairs gave the living area a second-rate vibe. She was pleasantly surprised when she finally saw the inside. Granite countertops in the kitchen. Hardwood flooring with nice, contemporary furniture. This guy might well be one to bring over for her parents' inspection. At least it might shut them up for a while. She didn't know how much longer she could take the third degree about when her mom could expect grandchildren.

Here was this nice, cute, employed guy who happened to be a little shy.

She started to think of ways to bring him out of his shell.

John Stallings felt slightly drained from his day. The one bright spot was the lead that someone had seen Leah Tischler get into a white, unmarked van downtown near the hotel where she'd looked for a room. Clearly the big anchor around his neck today was his conversation with Maria. It wasn't that she'd seen him having coffee with another woman. What bothered Stallings most was Maria didn't care one bit. He knew if she'd given him the chance he could explain everything and he hoped his years of predictable behavior would back up the veracity of his claim, but she never really asked for any explanation. In fact, she had specifically told him she didn't have to explain herself and he didn't have to explain himself. That was the knife stuck in his heart right now.

He acknowledged, at least to himself, that Liz Dubeck fascinated him. She was attractive and had ideas about helping people that were very similar to his. Her pretty face stuck in his mind and he'd definitely enjoyed their time chatting over coffee this morning. But he had no plans other than coffee. Despite what Maria had told him, he still considered himself married and had not given up on the chance he might move back into the house one day. Family was the most important thing to him. He was sorry it'd taken Jeanie leaving the family for him to realize it. But now he was trying to make up for the time he had spent away from Maria and the kids. He was even extending his family by reconnecting with his father.

He parked his county-issued Impala in front of the rooming house where his father lived. He was concerned about the confusion his father had displayed over the past weeks and wanted to keep a closer eye on the elder Stallings.

He walked along the brick walkway, looking up at the porch as he approached the building. Two elderly men played backgammon at the far end of the porch and the woman who ran the place sat in a rocking chair near the front door.

She smiled at him as Stallings climbed the front stairs and said, "Johnny Stallings, what a pleasant surprise."

Stallings nodded. "How are you, Ms. Williams?"

"I'm fine, sweetheart. Are you looking for your father?"

"Thought I'd surprise him. Maybe take him out to dinner."

"You're a thoughtful son. But I haven't seen your dad since early this morning when he left to help out at the community center. I hadn't really noticed until now. He usually comes back a couple times during the day."

Stallings's police sense tingled, and he didn't like it one bit.

TWENTY-TWO

He stood facing away from Mary with the cord in his hand when he smelled an odd odor. He turned quickly to see Mary puffing on a marijuana cigarette. He stared at her, shocked, and watched as she held her breath and offered the joint to him.

He shook his head as she let out a long exhalation and smoke filled the room.

Mary said, "Come on, don't be a pussy. Come take a hit." When he didn't move she turned on the sofa, her pants still unbuttoned, patted the cushion next to her, and said, "Come over here and relax, take a toke, while I give you the best blow job you ever had."

He felt the muscles in his arm tighten as he pulled the cord once more. But did he really want to infect his work of art with something short of perfection? Did he want to taint it with a drug like marijuana throughout eternity? This was a turn of events he never would've imagined. He hadn't even realized there were women who could look like Mary and act the way she was acting. This was no angel. As he stood there trying to decide what course of action to take, he heard something.

It took him a second to recognize the familiar sound. He froze and felt his stomach turn as he realized someone was coming up the rickety wooden stairs leading to his front door.

Mazzetti tried to stay calm in the face of the threat. The last thing he wanted to do was have to arrest some of these assholes for obstruction. He really did just want to talk. An arrest had not been in the front of his mind. He didn't want to divulge where he'd gotten Kozer's name. He'd promised Joey Big Balls he wouldn't give him up and he intended to keep that promise.

Mazzetti said in a low voice, trying to avoid any sort of menacing tone, "Let me go right now and there won't be an issue. I'm a detective with the Jacksonville Sheriff's Office. I want to ask you some questions." He couldn't help adding, "You fucking dipshit."

"You got a warrant?" asked Kozer.

"I don't need a warrant to come and talk to someone, and that's all I was trying to do."

"Looks like you're trying to do more than talk. You see, I just appealed my case to my friends and we are going to decide what sort of verdict to give you. How do you like that kind of crazy change?"

Mazzetti could tell no one had taken his gun from its holster. They weren't that stupid. But he did know he was about to suffer some sort of unpleasantness. He made one quick struggle to get free of the men holding his arms, but they were too strong. Kozer stepped closer to him, slapping his fist into his open palm. Mazzetti looked around and determined there were five men total: two holding his arms, Kozer, and two more standing to the left of Kozer. There was no way to overcome them physically, and no one seemed to want to hear him explain himself. As he was about to bring up the issue of assault on a police officer, he saw movement out of the corner of his right eye. At almost the same time he heard a loud noise and felt the man holding his right arm relax his grip.

He could see the look on Kozer's face and heard him say, "What the fuck?"

Suddenly someone stepped from behind him and struck the redneck in the leg with a nightstick-like weapon.

After that it was all movement and screams.

He ignored the jabbering Mary and walked directly to the front door in an effort to intercept whoever was coming up the steps. He opened the door, slipped out onto the landing, and closed the door behind him in time to see Cheryl stop right in front of him.

Cheryl said, "There's no way I'm going to let you stay here and screw up our chance to make some real money. I can't have my sister mooning over you either."

He could've gotten angry, but he knew that in the very near future Cheryl wouldn't be causing him any more problems. If Mary hadn't been in the apartment already he might've handled this issue right now. Instead he looked at her and said, "I've already told you I like it here. If you keep coming here and harassing me I'm going to get a restraining order."

Then she surprised him. Over the years she'd been many things—nasty, shrill, degrading, sarcastic, and vicious—but she'd never been surprising. In fact, she was one of the most predictable people he'd ever met.

That's why he knew it was better to kill her than expect her to change her tune and leave him in peace. But now, standing two steps below him, she surprised him by pulling out a small revolver. She held it in her right hand and pointed it directly at his face. The black hole in the center of the barrel mesmerized him, but he could also see she was shaking badly by the way it darted left and right, then up and down.

He couldn't help himself when he said, "You picked this up at the Sports Authority, didn't you?"

That shocked her. "How the hell did you know that?"

He gave her a smirk and said, "You have no idea how much I know. Put the gun back in your purse and we'll forget this ever happened."

He wasn't sure what was more disconcerting—seeing her finger tighten on the trigger, watching the barrel veer wildly in her shaking hand, hearing the deafening sound of the gun being fired, or seeing a blinding flash as the gun erupted a few feet in front of his nose.

John Stallings pulled into the driveway of his former home, still concerned about the whereabouts of his father. There was nothing else he could do right now. There was nothing unusual about his father's absence from the rooming house, and his history of being a street person would not spur the sheriff's office into action. The chances were James Stallings was running errands or helping out at some soup kitchen. He decided to give it a couple hours before he ran by the rooming house to check on him again.

Now he readjusted his mind to dealing with the family he'd raised instead of the man who had raised him.

As he crossed the yard a soccer ball popped out from over the rear fence and Stallings was able to use his head to knock it back into the air.

He heard his son, Charlie, say, "Cool." The seven-year-old tried to do the same thing; instead the ball bounced off his forehead and struck Stallings right in the face. The boy said, "Sorry, Dad."

Stallings waved him off to assure the boy there was no problem, in fact, considering the conversation he was probably going to have with Maria, the ball in the face might be the most pleasant thing that happened to him during the entire visit.

After he recovered from the blow and kicked the ball with Charlie for a few minutes he wandered into the house. Instead of being confronted by Maria he found his daughter Lauren sitting on the couch in the living room reading one of the *Twilight* books.

He said, "What's up?" He knew better than to try to seem cool or make some crack about vampires.

Lauren looked over the edge of the book, her dark eyes refocusing on her father, and surprised him by smiling and saying, "Nothing, Dad. I told Mom I'd watch Charlie for a couple of hours."

"Where's your mom?"

"I don't ask where she goes, I just try to help out around here. Isn't that what you're always telling me to do?"

He nodded. "I appreciate it. But I wouldn't mind if you kept track of your mother for me too. You know the issues she's had in the past."

"I don't think she's at any meetings. She seems to be doing pretty well. But there's something going on in town she wanted to go see, so I'm hanging out with Charlie."

Stallings was content to sit across from her in his old chair and just look at his daughter for a few minutes before he ventured back out in the world. He couldn't believe how much he missed this place.

As soon as his right arm was free, Tony Mazzetti swung his whole body and drove his right elbow into the face of the guy holding his left arm. Once he was free all he saw were the other four men on the ground moaning with Patty Levine standing in the middle of the group. The ASP was in her right hand and it didn't look like she was even breathing hard.

Mazzetti stared at his beautiful girlfriend, who made a quick scan of the men lying around her to ensure no one was a threat, kneeled down, and slammed the top of the ASP into the hard ground to close it. Just like they had been taught in defensive tactics class.

Mazzetti said, "How'd you know where I was?"

She casually looked at him and said, "You told me you were coming down to some construction sites and Deerwood Park isn't that big. I was running early and came by to see if I could speed things along. And I guess I did." She winked at him.

Mazzetti thought about the benefits of charging these guys with obstruction and assault. He considered the time it'd take away from his homicide investigations to give a statement and follow up with court testimony. Each man grasped a damaged extremity. Mazzetti made the assessment this was punishment enough, but he didn't let them know that. Instead, he walked over and grabbed Kozer by his right ear and pulled until he sprang to his feet. He gave Patty a quick look to make sure she realized he wanted her to watch the other, injured men.

Once back inside the building and alone, Mazzetti said, "You want to be charged with assault on a police officer?"

Kozer had to stand with his left leg in the air to relieve the pressure where Patty had struck him in the thigh. He shook his head, wiping the sweat pouring from his forehead.

"Why'd you run from me, you little shit?" Mazzetti raised his hand as if he was going to slap him. He wanted to but restrained himself.

"I, um, I don't know. You spooked me."

"Where were you Monday afternoon and evening?"

"What?"

"You fucking heard me."

"I was here. I work Monday through Friday three to eleven."

"Any witnesses?"

"There are four of them lying on the ground back there."

Mazzetti believed him but would check before he left. As he thought about his next question, Kozer said, "I ain't done nothin' illegal in a few years. Whoever you're looking for it ain't me."

Mazzetti said, "There's one way you and your buddies can avoid a lengthy and costly criminal record for the shit you pulled back there."

"What do I gotta do? Tell me and I'll do it."

Mazzetti had the man just where he wanted him. "I'm looking into a girl's death. The killer might be a construction guy. I need eyes and ears at the sites looking around."

"Looking for what?"

"Anyone acting strange. Anyone who has issues with women. Anything odd. We need a break."

Kozer kept staring at Mazzetti as the larger cop released him. He said, "I been wonderin' who I could talk to about a guy who works at a few different sites. He's not a construction worker, he's a finisher."

"What's a finisher?"

"Guys who lay in decorative floors, or crown molding or windows or special doors. They don't build nothin', just make it prettier."

"Why'd you want to talk about this guy?

"He came in late one day, all hungover and wearing makeup. I mean eye shadow and stuff."

"That doesn't make him a killer."

"You said something odd. That was way odd. Then we caught him watching women through a bathroom window that was supposed to be covered. He uncovered it and hid to watch."

Mazzetti was interested now. "Where was he doin' this?"

"A couple of months ago over by the new health building for the university nursing center."

That made Mazzetti snap his head up and stare at the greasy redneck with more intensity.

"What's the guy's name?"

"Daniel Byrd."

That was a name Joey Big Balls had given him too.

Mazzetti wrote down the limited information Kozer had on Daniel Byrd.

Kozer said, "I know you said you won't charge us, but do you have to tell anyone what happened?"

"Why?"

"Because I don't want it getting around that a cute little girl like that kicked our asses."

TWENTY-THREE

The shock of the gun exploding right in front of his face caused him to fall back hard against the door. He desperately reached with his right hand and felt for the knob, twisting it and causing the door to burst open and him to flop onto the floor. He took only a second to check his face but felt no blood. The gun had jumped. He looked up and noticed a hole in the door. But now was not the time to rejoice at not being shot because Cheryl was regaining her composure and still had the gun in her hand.

He was vaguely aware Mary was screaming from the couch and had jumped to her feet. He scrambled backwards, turning so he could spring to his feet and dive into the kitchen. But Cheryl had come into the apartment right behind him with the gun in her hand.

He crouched behind the cabinets in the kitchen, trying to think what he should do; then Cheryl screamed at Mary to shut up. He pulled one of the drawers hard off its track and dumped all the utensils on the floor. He quickly grabbed the first knife he could find and was surprised to see it was one of the heaviest butcher knives he owned. He wrapped his right hand around the plastic laminate handle and crouched at the edge of the cabinets waiting for his chance to spring.

As soon as he saw Cheryl's foot slide onto the kitchen's new tile floor he sprang up, swinging wildly with his left hand in a wide arc to knock the gun away. Once again the gun boomed as Cheryl jerked the trigger. This time he didn't wait and threw his entire body into her, driving the knife hard into her solar plexus. The force of his body behind the thrust of the knife drove it even farther into her torso and he turned his wrist to make sure the blade worked deeper under her rib cage. He felt the blade bounce off bones and sinew on its path to her beating heart. He kept his left hand on her right arm to hold the gun away from him when it went off for a third time. The deafening sound of the gunshot had closed his eardrums.

Now he took a moment to look into Cheryl's face. He could see the shocked expression in the way her eyes wouldn't focus. Considering the force of his knife attack he was surprised she was even breathing. But he clearly felt the power running out of her legs and arm as she dropped the pistol and slowly started to sink to the tile floor. He released his grip on the knife, took a step back, watching in fascination as she slipped onto the floor and rolled to one side. Blood gushed out of the wound below her chest and a red puddle formed around her face with her blond hair sticking to it.

Once again he checked his face and his chest for any wounds. He was shocked she'd fired the pistol three times inside his tiny apartment and had failed to hit him. He was just as shocked his knife attack hadn't immediately stopped her. He had a lot to learn about everyday violence.

Already he started to think how he could explain this to Mary or if it would be easier to go ahead and kill her but not use her for his work of art. Neither of these women were worthy of eternity. He stepped over Cheryl's body as he scanned the living room to see where Mary had ended up.

It only took him one step to see Mary had never made it past the couch as she lay on the carpet staring directly at his ceiling with a bullet hole an inch to the left of her pretty nose.

This was one mess that was going to take a while to clean up.

Patty enjoyed the position she found herself in. She'd been lecturing Tony Mazzetti about his immature stupidity in coming to the construction site without any backup. To his credit, he took full responsibility and admitted he'd made a mistake. Then he said something that truly surprised her.

Mazzetti said, "You saved my ass. You're the best girlfriend anyone ever had."

She wanted to hug him and give him a big kiss, but she was enjoying her position of power and thought she'd make it last longer. It was the closest she had felt to him in a month. She'd parked her car in a lot down the street and climbed into his Crown Vic. She let him sit there and sulk for a few minutes as she occasionally lobbed another recrimination at him, but, in fact, she wasn't really upset. He'd done what many men could never do: he'd accepted responsibility. And the fact that he'd acknowledged she'd saved him and didn't try to make up some story about having the construction workers right where he wanted them had been icing on the cake.

Now Patty said, "You really think this Daniel Byrd could be our killer?"

Mazzetti shook his head, "I doubt it, but I can't discount him as a suspect. By Monday night he'll be spilling his guts to me."

Patty reached over and patted Mazzetti on the head. "That's my bulldog. Now take me to the restaurant. Beating poor defenseless construction workers worked up an appetite."

She caught Mazzetti's smile as he turned toward Gi-Gi's Italian restaurant.

John Stallings used all the tricks he'd learned looking for fugitives to try and locate his own father. So far he'd had no luck. The priest at the community center shared Stallings's concern when he came by and explained that his father had not been by his room all day. They both immediately came to the same conclusion. The confusion James Stallings had been suffering was clearly an indicator of something much more serious. The fact that he had no car made it more ominous he was missing. He was out of the area and no one had seen him. That meant he had walked a long way or could be on public transportation anywhere in the largest city in the country.

From there Stallings stopped at soup kitchens where his father worked and ate. One kitchen was only open on Tuesdays and Thursdays, and no one at the second soup kitchen, located north of the municipal football stadium, had seen Stallings's father all day. The kitchen was jammed with clean-cut young people busy at every section of the room.

A volunteer, older than most of the others, maybe in her early thirties, said, "What do you want?"

"That how you talk to everyone?"

"Only to cops that might scare our diners."

Stallings smiled and held up his hands. "I'm just looking for my dad." He explained the situation. He knew her name was Grace Jackson and she was well known in the Jacksonville area for her work with the homeless and as an outstanding teacher at a charter school in a rough section of the city. She had the determined voice and mannerisms of a woman on a mission.

Grace looked him up and down. "You got a good reputation as a cop."

"You have a good reputation too." He liked the smile on the plump, pretty black woman's face.

"Your dad makes me laugh."

"My dad?"

"I got similar issues with my father. I'm sure he's a riot to people whose childhoods he didn't screw up."

Stallings laughed and realized why this woman was so effective. He slipped onto a stool and took a moment to clear his head.

Yvonne Zuni liked wearing a nice dress for dinner. She spent so much of her time in a profession dominated by men, having to act tough and having to dress professionally but also tactically, she sometimes felt like she was playing dress-up when she was able to actually wear a dress. She raced home, changed, put on some makeup, and brushed out her hair instead of the more drab, simple hairstyle she wore around the office. Now she wore it straight with a few curls on the side.

She didn't even bother to drive her county-issued car; instead she grabbed her BMW M3. She'd been shocked no one had pulled her over on her way to Deerwood Park, with her treating J. Turner Butler Boulevard like the racetrack at Indy. There was definitely a different feel to the BMW from any of the American cars issued by the sheriff's office.

For some reason, the southern end of the county didn't feel like part of JSO's jurisdiction and she started to relax immediately. The idea of a secret, but almost normal, date with a handsome man and no restrictions made her smile. Although the sheriff's office would not approve of their relationship, she was confident no one she knew would possibly run into them at an intimate restaurant like Gi-Gi's.

As she pulled in the parking lot she saw Ronald Bell standing by the valet and couldn't resist squealing the tires when she brought the car to a precision stop. She appreciated his smile at the sight of her and threw caution to the wind as she watched the valet pull away in her car, embracing her date and planting a wet kiss on his lips.

She could sense Bell was a little nervous at the open display of affection.

Bell said, "It'll be two minutes before they set up our table. We can go into the bar or just enjoy the night breeze for a few minutes. The choice is entirely yours."

She loved the idea of not hiding. She also liked the idea she didn't have to answer him. Instead she turned and planted another kiss on his lips.

She was so involved with the kiss she barely noticed the dark Crown Vic as it pulled into the parking lot.

TWENTY-FOUR

Sitting in the passenger seat of Mazzetti's immaculate Ford Crown Victoria, issued by the Jacksonville Sheriff's Office, Patty Levine imagined she was in a limousine taking her on her first date. She couldn't explain the feeling she was experiencing, but it was something near pride. The biggest of the seven sins. The one that brought down Lucifer. She didn't really care. She was sitting in the front seat across from her attractive boyfriend, dressed in an expensive if slightly dusty suit, working in an exciting and interesting job, and she'd just kicked four guys' asses. The University of Florida could not have prepared her for such an accomplishment. No drug could give her the kind of rush she had felt wading into the construction workers who had threatened her boyfriend. She'd felt her entire body get into each swing of her ASP and hadn't been afraid to enjoy connecting with the beefy legs and bony arms. The way she felt right now, looking at Tony, she could skip dinner and drag him right to bed. Maybe this was the primal feeling that made men act the way they did around women.

Tony had recognized he'd been in deep shit and had liked having a tough girlfriend who could rescue him. Looking across at him now, Patty wondered how many women hit on him in the course of a normal day. She knew from her long professional association with cops that a certain type of woman was attracted to the excitement and mystery of police. Sometimes it was the uniform. Sometimes it was the plainclothes narcotics agent who could lay down a line of shit. Sometimes it was the romanticized image of the dogged homicide detective. Whatever the reason, there were women who were attracted to police officers. And her boyfriend was an educated, well-spoken, and good-looking police officer. Patty wasn't prone to jealousy but a thought crossed her mind: maybe they were ready to move to the next level.

The outside of Gi-Gi's Italian restaurant was ornate and busy. Cars were parked up and down the street as well as jammed into the small parking lot on the west side of the building. There was a circular drive with an overhang where well-dressed people were waiting for their fancy cars to be brought from the valet lot. Tony didn't hesitate to pull in his county-issued Ford.

When the valet approached him, Tony didn't pull out his sheriff's ID. He gave him a good police look and said, "Sorry, pal, I can't let you drive it, it's a police car. Let me pull it in where it won't be in the way." He slapped five dollars into the valet's hand and turned to Patty. "You get out and I'll be back in one minute."

Patty leaned across, kissed him on the cheek, and slipped out of the car. She watched him pull away slowly to where the valet was pointing at an empty space. Patty turned around and was shocked to see Sergeant Yvonne Zuni in a beautiful dress with her hair down in a much sexier style than she wore to work every day. Even more surprising was seeing the tough sergeant kiss Ronald Bell squarely on the lips. When Sergeant Zuni turned and saw Patty, she immediately whispered something to Bell, who quickly walked inside the restaurant.

Patty said, "Wasn't that . . . ?" She could read a slight appearance of panic on the sergeant's face.

"Who was driving the Crown Vic?"

Patty let a slight smile wash across her face and saw the sergeant smile at the same time. They were two women bonded together in a profession dominated by men. Now they had a secret. There was no promise or oath. They each knew the other would keep her mouth shut.

Then she remembered Tony was walking toward them from the valet lot. She nodded good-bye to the sergeant and hustled down the sloped parking lot to intercept Tony Mazzetti before he could see anyone standing near the front door.

Patty grabbed his arm by the elbow and interlocked her own, spinning him back toward the car and walking at a fast pace.

Mazzetti looked at her and said, "What's wrong?"

Patty only had to think for a minute when she looked into his handsome face. She smiled and said, "I need to fuck you right now."

She knew no man would ever argue with that statement.

Buddy liked the way Cheryl's Chrysler handled. He was so used to his van he had forgotten what driving a decent car felt like. The music from the radio speakers filled the car nicely with the sounds of Nirvana. There was just something about "Smells Like Teen Spirit" that got his motor running and his head rocking. He suspected the excitement of the evening added to his feelings of euphoria. The two dead women crammed on the floor of the backseat didn't put any damper at all on his good mood. The only downside was that he had not moved his work of art forward in any way. In hindsight it was better to take a step back than to force someone who wasn't worthy of eternity into his dreams. At least he didn't have to worry about that harpy Cheryl anymore.

The steering wheel felt a little awkward with his heavy canvas work gloves, but it was still better than leaving his fingerprints and DNA all over the car. He had slipped a plastic bag over Mary's head to catch any blood that seeped out of the deep hole in her face. Cheryl was another story. He didn't realize a relatively small human body could hold so much blood. He'd used three towels to sop up the bloody kitchen tile. He'd burn them up in his glass furnace later.

He had only a rough plan in his head and liked going with the flow for a change. He intended to leave Cheryl in her car somewhere. It was Mary who was causing him concern. He could take her back to her car at the airport, but someone would notice her and Buddy wanted to take advantage of the fact that she had told people she'd be away on a cruise for a full week. That was a lot of time to distance himself from anything to do with the pretty dental hygienist.

He needed a few minutes to consider his options and pulled into an older, off-brand gas station next to the interstate on Tallulah Avenue. He had often used the convenience store at the station to grab a soda on his jobs the northern part of Jacksonville. A semi truck with an open trailer blocked the northern side of the gas station. Buddy pulled to the rear of the truck, out of sight of everyone, and thought about buying a sixty-four-ounce Sprite. He noticed the burly truck driver hop down from the high cab and waddle into the store. That got Buddy thinking and he slipped out of the Charger and jumped up on the rear bumper to peek into the tractor, under a tarp covering the load. It was some kind of agricultural fertilizer or construction material he wasn't familiar with. It had a musty smell and was dark green, filling more than half the trailer. Then Buddy had an idea.

As soon as it popped into his head, he knew he had to act. This was a now-or-never move and he didn't intend to screw it up. He hopped off the trailer and grabbed Mary from the back of the car. She felt like a heavy doll as he lifted her onto his shoulder and hopped up onto the bumper. He saw the driver still inside the store chatting with the clerk at the cash register. Buddy had to be fast.

He slipped the plastic bag off Mary's head and tossed her into the corner of the trailer. Her body naturally sunk into the soft fertilizer like it was quicksand and he was able to reach down and scoop a little more over her head until she was almost completely covered. He jammed the bloody plastic bag into his pocket. She had no identification and nothing that stood out in her clothing. If he caught a few breaks and the truck headed north, they may not have any clue where she came from.

Buddy hopped down off the trailer, slipped back into the Chrysler, and headed east from the interstate. He slowed a few blocks away and pulled to the side of the street. He intended to wait until he saw the tractor trailer pull onto the highway and, he hoped, drive north on the interstate.

Considering that it had appeared the driver was ready to leave the store, it took a surprisingly long time for the truck to move. Buddy glanced over to see the lifeless form of Cheryl sprawled on the floor. He said, "Why couldn't you have been more like your sister? You had to play hardball. I'm an artist. I shouldn't be pushed to do things like this. Now where should I leave you?" He thought about her abrasive manner and gaudy fake boobs. He wasn't worried about her being linked to Mary now.

A smile washed over his face as he said, "Jacksonville Landing."

It was perfect. He'd already been there this evening and knew that it would still be hopping at this time of night. No one would ever notice him slip in and slip out. A few minutes later he saw the trailer pull out of the gas station and onto the northbound ramp up I-95.

Being lucky had its rewards.

TWENTY-FIVE

Grace Jackson had talked to Stallings's father the night before. She explained the current excess of volunteers to Stallings. There was an ongoing Christian revival in the area and the participants had flooded into the kitchen to help. Stallings's father could've seen the crowd and decided not to stop.

Several times Stallings waited patiently while young Christian revivalists came in and asked Grace questions. She was never short or harsh with any of the well-intentioned young people but offered direct and simple advice or orders. Stallings thought she'd make a good cop. Finally he said to her, "Did he say anything at all about being busy today or visiting someone in another part of the city?"

Grace shook her head, keeping her intense brown eyes on him. "He always chats with me about his grandchildren and once he told me about being in the Navy. He really didn't go over his schedule with me." She placed a comforting hand on his shoulder, then surprised him by wrapping her arms around him and giving him a loving hug. "It's hard looking after parents and kids at the same time. I appreciate what you're doing. I love your dad. I love hearing about his friends and family and the groups that he moderates. He once told me he wished he had the courage to do it when he was drinking and regrets what it did to his family."

Stallings couldn't imagine his father saying something like that, but he couldn't imagine this lovely, caring woman making something up.

Grace said, "He's very proud of the man you turned into and says you're better than him. He says he would've held a grudge if his father had treated him like that as a child."

"I still hold a pretty good grudge."

"But you're out here looking for him. I'll pray for him and for you."

Stallings nodded his thanks, barely able to speak. Finally he managed to say, "Did he seem all right to you when you spoke yesterday?"

Grace said, "He did do one odd thing."

"What's that?"

"He kept calling me 'Jeanie.' Even after I corrected him. After a while I just went with it."

Now Stallings was really worried.

Buddy only took one pass in front of the tall parking garage at Jacksonville Landing. The trick was slipping inside the lot without being noticed. He waited until he saw the line of cars exiting grow and knew the attendant would be focusing on them. He drove the Chrysler through the second lane and snatched the parking ticket from the machine. Pulling onto the fourth floor, he found a spot in the middle of the row facing the St. Johns River.

Buddy did not hesitate to park the car, take the keys, make sure it was locked, and look around to be certain no one noticed him as he took the stairway down to the ground floor. He walked at a leisurely pace and took a right on the scenic walkway along the river. He heard a reggae band playing from the balcony of one of the restaurants and let his feet fall into rhythm with the music. Once he was past the main buildings that made up the touristy, commercial property, he crossed the street and walked past some of the smaller, locally owned establishments. His stomach rumbled slightly and he suddenly realized he was thirsty as well. The first place he saw that looked appealing was called Sal's Smoothie Shack.

As he stepped through the door he noticed there were no customers and the young woman behind the counter looked up with a surprised expression. She started to say, "I'm sorry, we're . . ." Then she looked at Buddy and smiled. This time she said, "If you flip the closed sign on the door behind you, I'll give you the last of our fresh strawberry smoothies in a giant cup."

Buddy didn't hesitate. He turned and eased up to the counter and said, "Only if you have one with me." He was dazzled by the girl's smile, which was accompanied by dimples in her pretty face. He said, "My name is Buddy. What's yours?"

The girl handed him his smoothie, then stepped from behind the counter with a smaller smoothie in her hand. She said, "I'm Lexie."

Angela Lusk leaned back on the hard park bench and almost wished she could vomit up all the stuff that had upset her stomach. Her head pounded with a hangover that would've slowed down the most hardcore alcoholic. She had not bothered to do anything with her hair, deciding instead to tie it back in a ponytail. Last night, on the dance floor—and for a little while on top of the bar—she had her long bleached locks loose and flowing. Now each strand seemed to throb after all the margaritas and shots. Damn tequila night. Rum night seemed to go easier the next day. The early-morning sun didn't help any part of her body right now.

Angela looked around at the other two quiet mothers watching their kids at the playground located inside Pine Forest Park. They may not have had as much to drink, but they seemed no happier to be out on a bright Saturday morning. It wasn't even 7:15 yet. Shit.

Taylor had wanted to visit the park and Angela had promised they would if Taylor used the "big-girl potty." There were no dirty diapers this week, so they were at the park. Angela had thought that once she had to pay for babysitters she'd slow her personal night life down. Instead she crammed more into fewer hours. She threw down too many shots between eleven and midnight when she knew she had to head home. She couldn't even bring a guy with her because the snotty sitter would blab to her mom and others in the River's End apartment complex. She didn't like guys to meet Taylor right away anyhow. She preferred to hook them solidly first. That's how she intended to approach the cute young lawyer from Arlington who spent a small fortune on Patrón Silver for her last night.

Angela looked up to see Taylor and a cute little black girl move from the slide to play in the soft sand of the playground. She didn't care if the girls dug; she and Taylor would take a dip in the complex's pool as soon as they got home.

After a few minutes the girls stopped digging and the little black girl scurried back to her mom, squealing. Angela watched as Taylor slid away from the hole the girls had dug. Something tugged on her "mother" string and she stood and started to trot toward her daughter.

The sun slapped her in the face as she approached the mini-excavation. She looked over Taylor's shoulder. The first thing she made out was cloth; then she saw fingers. It was a hand. It was a body.

They both started to scream.

TWENTY-SIX

John Stallings rolled over and let his eyes adjust to the sun rising above the windowsill. He had no blinds on his bedroom window and knew that when the sun came into view it was just about eight o'clock. He estimated, with the shifts and turns, he'd gotten about three hours' sleep. This kind of night seemed to last forever, when he was lying in bed worrying about everything from where his father was to if the kids were eating right. He always included Jeanie in those same concerns. Wherever she was, he hoped she was eating right. But now, with his eyes open, his immediate problem was telling his mother that his father was missing.

He dressed quickly in jeans and a short-sleeved, button-down shirt he could leave untucked to conceal his Glock in the waistband of his pants. Just because he wasn't on duty didn't mean he might not have to take action sometime today.

His first stop was his father's rooming house. As he walked up the path in front of the two-story house he was surprised no one was on the porch on such a nice Saturday morning. The wooden planks of the porch creaked under his careful steps to the front door. He didn't bother to knock, not wanting to wake anyone. Instead, he turned the knob slowly, poked his head into the entryway, and called out, "Hello?"

The woman who ran the house poked her head from the doorway down the hall. She smiled and said, "Come on down here, Johnny. I'm getting breakfast together for everyone."

He followed her into the kitchen, where she worked a big griddle with ten eggs frying and four pancakes cooking on the hot surface. A small smile crept across his face as he watched the older woman hustle around the kitchen, keeping everything in motion.

He didn't even have to ask the question. She looked up and said, "I checked the room ten minutes ago and your father hasn't been home since we talked. Now I'm worried too. This isn't like James at all. He's usually so responsible and good about letting us know where he's going and when he'll be back. It's almost like we're all one big, odd, former alcoholics, not-too-sharp-on-hygiene family."

Stallings let out a little laugh at that comment and appreciated that this woman stayed sane while doing so much for so many. He quickly lost the smile when he thought about talking to his mother.

Tony Mazzetti had not slept well. It often happened in the middle of a homicide investigation. But this time it had more to do with an awkwardness that had developed between him and Patty. Not only in bed, but last night, that was the focus, it seemed like it had crept into their relationship too. How many super exciting rescues could either of them have to keep things interesting? Last night he had realized Patty felt it too. Maybe it was just the freshness of the relationship wearing off. He didn't have enough experience to know for sure.

Now he was having a dream he couldn't quite figure out when the same sound kept occurring in his head. His eyes snapped open. His cell phone was ringing on the nightstand next to Patty's bed. He reached across and fumbled with the Nextel phone, squinting in the dim light trying to pick up the name of the caller before he flipped it open. Finally he gave up and answered with his usual abrupt greeting, "Mazzetti."

"Tony, it's Francine over at the SO. We got a report of a body buried in a park east of the river. Yvonne the Terrible told me to get you moving over there as soon as possible."

"Have we ID'd the body? Is there someone maintaining the scene? Are there any witnesses?"

The flat nasal voice of the dispatcher said, "All I know is what I've told you. Sergeant Zuni wanted me to call her back when I got you and crime scene on the phone. You want me to tell her you're headed that way, or do you have a different message?" She explained exactly where the body was found.

Mazzetti took a moment to clear his head and said, "I'll be there as quick as I can. Call crime scene and get their fat asses rolling." He slammed the phone shut and sat up in bed. Through his entire conversation, Patty had not moved one inch. He placed two fingers on her exposed throat to make sure she had a pulse. Maybe he'd been in homicide too long. Then he gently rubbed her hair trying to wake her. When that failed, he shook her head and still barely got a response.

He climbed out of the queen-sized bed and padded to the bathroom. A few minutes later he came out, dressed in his clothes from the night before. He finally managed to get Patty to grunt in acknowledgment. When he told her what had happened she slowly sat up in bed and in a sleepy voice said, "I'll come with you."

Mazzetti said, "Meet me at the park. I have to go by my house and pick some stuff up."

"What'd you have there, you don't have here?"

"Clean clothes and the gel I use on my hair. This is probably gonna attract media attention before the day is over."

A few minutes later, as he drove away in his Crown Vic, Tony Mazzetti had a fresh wave of concern about his girlfriend and what sort of things she was doing to make her so groggy in the morning.

Stallings rehearsed some of the ways he might phrase things to his mother. One lesson he'd learned on the job was to not provide false hope or unrealistic expectations. On the other hand, he didn't want to alarm her either. Even with his father's history, Stallings could find no explanation for his disappearance other than something bad. He had done the whole routine of checking with hospitals to make sure nobody matching his father's description had been checked in. He imagined the multitude of car crashes and hit-and-run accidents, cardiac arrests, strokes, and violent crimes or anything else that could happen to a sixty-five-year-old man with a shoddy memory running around Jacksonville completely unsupervised. When he thought of it in those terms he felt like a bad son. But considering the life his father had provided him, he felt like he was doing the best he could.

He parked and took the three stairs in one leap to the

porch of the three-bedroom house a block from the St. Johns River. He hesitated outside the door, trying to come up with something that might cushion the news his father was missing. In all honesty, he didn't know how close his mother and father were, but knew that she had stayed in touch with him after the rest of the family had completely blocked him and the memories. He also knew that his mother tended to be lonely and that was one of the reasons his sister, Helen, still lived with her.

He knocked gently on the door and stepped back, waiting see his mother's usual smiling face. He could hear footsteps coming toward the door as the knob slowly turned and the door opened out. He was about to greet his mother when he was shocked to see who had opened the door.

It was his father.

TWENTY-SEVEN

Tony Mazzetti prowled inside the crime scene like an anxious tiger. The crime scene investigators had decided to rope off the entire fenced-in playground. It made for a very wide scene because no one had any idea how far away from the body they would have to search for evidence. That also gave Mazzetti a reason to close down the larger surrounding park with its open soccer fields and running trail. That kept the two news trucks almost two hundred yards away from where the crime scene techs were now excavating the body.

God bless the crime scene techs. Mazzetti would never let them know how important they were, but he needed them. They had the patience, concentration and determination to do what almost no detective could: lay out a detailed map of the evidence. It always took hours and sometimes the better part of the day. It was time that Mazzetti spent formulating theories and deciding who needed to be interviewed on any specific case. Right now he was anxious to see if there was anything to identify the body or if he'd have to rely on the medical examiner and hope there was a matching record of fingerprints or dental records. He'd seen her T-shirt used to be white and had a logo of a sun rising. He couldn't make out the lettering yet. Someone would clean it up so he'd see it later. The decomposition around her face would make identification of her by sight much less certain. He hoped there was enough flesh to get fingerprints. There were a number of lab tests to confirm an identity, but there was still something about recognizing a face, even in death, that made a homicide detective feel more competent.

Inside the crime scene there were only two detectives, Mazzetti and Sparky Taylor, and a four-person crime scene team. This remained standard at almost every homicide crime scene investigation. Occasionally, if circumstances required it, another detective might come into the area. But the rule of thumb—and, as Sparky had pointed out, the policy of the Jacksonville Sheriff's Office—was to limit the number of people who might come in contact with evidence relating to a homicide.

Outside of the scene, on a picnic bench under a tree, Patty Levine comforted a clearly upset young mother and her little girl. She had arrived at the scene about fifteen minutes after Mazzetti and he was pleasantly surprised to see how alert she looked.

Sergeant Zuni motioned him over to the edge of the fence. She was dressed more casually than during the week but still had a professional and direct air about her. She was a good sergeant who managed the scene without interfering. She didn't even try to enter the immediate scene around the body. Her job was to keep the perimeter secure with uniformed patrol officers, figure out what needed to be done right now, and keep the command staff informed of developments. She also talked to the media. Mazzetti didn't like that so much. Before the squad had a regular sergeant, he'd gotten to like talking in front of the cameras. It made him feel important and gave his mother something to brag about. It was tough to compete with a sister who was a judge in Westchester County. The TV interviews aside, he'd found that Sergeant Zuni made life easier for him and that's what a sergeant was supposed to do.

He stopped at the fence and leaned down on the top tube that ran the perimeter.

The sergeant said, "How's it going?"

"Female, dressed like she was in her late teens." He looked over his shoulder at the team working around the body with Sparky Taylor hovering right over them. "We'll know more soon."

Sergeant Zuni said, "I couldn't work with someone over my shoulder like that."

"That's his interpretation of the policy that says a detective must supervise evidence collection."

The sergeant laughed. "He follows policy like a religion."

"And he's trying to convert me."

"Need anything else?"

"Where's Stall? He's usually good for some theories."

"I didn't call him out yet. I have to manage man power. As it is you're not going to get a day off today or tomorrow. I had to send another team over to the Landing because someone found a body in a car parked in the garage."

"Please tell me the mode of death wasn't strangulation."

"Relax, Tony. Knifing. Lots of blood."

"Thank God. I got enough to worry about." He didn't

even bother to ask who was going to be assigned; as long as it didn't take Sparky or his crime scene away he didn't care.

The sergeant looked at him and said, "I didn't call out Patty, either. How'd she find out about it?"

Mazzetti paused, considering what he should say. She kept those sharp, green eyes on him and he understood why so many dopers confessed to her. "I called her."

"May I ask why?"

"I heard kids had found the body and she's better at keeping people calm."

The sergeant eyed him a moment more, then nodded as she turned away.

Tony Mazzetti joined Sparky by the shallow grave and looked at the body. He thought about this girl's family and felt something resembling pity. He wondered if he was getting soft. He thought back to the conversation he'd had with the construction worker last night. He'd been hoping to get a chance to track down this Daniel Byrd. Something in his gut said this was a suspect he needed to look at. Mazzetti had broken bigger cases with weirder hunches over the years and had learned to rely on his sixth sense. It was not something he could put into a PC affidavit or even something he could explain to the sergeant without a snicker or being dismissed altogether. But he knew he needed to find this Daniel Byrd.

John Stallings sat on the couch in his mother's living room while his father straightened up the kitchen. It had been an odd experience chatting with both of them for the last twenty minutes. He didn't come to terms with it immediately because it was something that had never happened, not even once, during his childhood.

Stallings looked at his mother said, "It creeps me out a little bit you guys are here in the same house."

"I told you that I saw your father occasionally."

"You made it sound much more casual and you didn't tell me until recently."

His mother smiled, making him realize that even at sixty-two years old, she was a very attractive woman. "If you think you're freaked out by it, imagine how your sister felt. When he showed up yesterday, confused, she refused to stay in the same house with him."

"I'm surprised that she didn't call me. It would have saved me a lot of worry and time yesterday."

"She went up to Fernandina Beach to see her friend Mario."

Stallings raised an eyebrow in mock outrage.

But his mother seemed more disappointed as she shook her head and said, "He's just a friend. I've met the young man and I doubt that Helen will be able to convince him he has mistakenly believed he's a homosexual. My hopes for her providing me with any grandchildren are fading faster than your father's memory."

"So you've noticed it too?"

"Noticed it? I've documented it over the past two years. But he manages his bus schedules okay and rarely confuses anything important. For a long time I thought it was a side effect of his alcohol use. I did notice that he started to refer to Jeanie as Kelly when he talked about her. For a while he even thought that she had visited him on occasion. I have no idea where he got that from."

Stallings looked over his mother's shoulder at his father, who seemed to be happy scrubbing a pan and whistling some unknown tune. "I didn't realize he thought she had visited him."

"He was never clear about it and I'm afraid I just dismissed the whole idea as part of his memory problem."

"Is he always like this?"

"Keep in mind our visits could be sporadic. I dated on and off when he first tried to get back in touch with me and I had a regular boyfriend for a while last year. You remember Ralph. Your father didn't come by at all when he was here. Unfortunately I haven't had a chance at many dates recently so your father's visits have been more welcomed."

"What are you talking about?"

She gave him a look. "Your need for sex doesn't diminish with age. And it's hard for me to find a man able to participate at the level I want."

"C'mon, Mom." He cringed and couldn't look at her for a moment.

"Just because I'm a mother doesn't mean I don't need sex."

"But because you're *my* mother, I don't need to hear about it."

"I guess we should have your father evaluated by a doctor."

"That would probably be a good idea."

"I didn't like the way your sister stormed out of here when he showed up."

Stallings was starting to feel like he was living his childhood all over again.

It was a beautiful Saturday afternoon, and already Buddy had heard more on the news that interested him than he had in the past year. There had been several blurbs on the radio and TV about a body being found buried in Pine Forest Park. That would be Jessie. He'd hoped she wouldn't be discovered for several more weeks, if at all. He'd chosen that spot because he was able to park his van without anyone noticing it and the whole playground area was soft sand. It'd only taken him about ten minutes to dig what he'd thought was a good, deep hole and dump the warm body of the cute girl from Ocala into it. His reasoning also included a sort of "hide in plain sight" mentality. He thought because of the public nature of the park, there would be no reason for anyone to search for her there. But it didn't matter because there was nothing to tie him to her.

About an hour later he heard the first report of a body being found in the parking garage of Jacksonville Landing. That was the report he had been waiting for. The big news there was not necessarily the body but the fact that the police had shut down the entire parking garage and commercial tenants of Jacksonville Landing were screaming for them to reopen. Bars and restaurants remained open, but empty, on what should be the busiest day of the week.

The only thing he regretted about his busy Friday night was that he was forced to expend the effort to get rid of two bodies but was unable to advance his project in any way. Mary was the one who was a real disappointment. Considering the way she had died, he wouldn't have been able to capture her last breath anyway.

During his restless fit of sleep he dreamed of plunging the knife over and over again into Cheryl's heart. In his dream, a little like in real life, she just wouldn't die. But now, in the light of day, he felt a certain satisfaction and excitement at the thought of eliminating one of the big pains in his ass. But he had his story straight in his head for when cops came to ask when the last time he'd seen her was. He'd even practiced acting surprised, but not too surprised. He knew the cops were pretty sharp when interviewing people so he was prepared not to be shaken.

Right now he was in the northern part of the city, where a row of small cafés offered privacy and intimacy. He even had a small bouquet of flowers in his hand as he slipped into the front courtyard of the modest café. He saw her sitting under an umbrella waving to him.

He appreciated the beautiful smile and bright eyes as he said, "Hello, Lexie."

TWENTY-EIGHT

Tony Mazzetti was afraid he'd missed something by moving at such a fast pace, but the sergeant had only approved a half day for this Sunday and he wanted to use it wisely. In this case she wasn't being cheap and withholding overtime. She was actually showing some supervisory sense and encouraging him to get some rest and clear his head for the busy week ahead. She even told him she wanted him home and in bed by nine o'clock. Imagine someone imposing a curfew on a thirty-nine-year-old cop. Normally, he'd have balked at an order like that, but she scared the holy shit out of him and he had no doubt she'd kick his ass if he wasn't in bed by nine. That was truly the mark of an outstanding sergeant.

He'd told Sparky Taylor to spend some time with his kids today and had a hard time telling Patty Levine to take the day off as well. She even told him she wanted to come as his girlfriend, not as another detective on the squad, while he went into the office and organized the most important tasks, then went to the medical examiner's office to witness the autopsy. Mazzetti really did want Patty to rest, but some part of him didn't want her in the same room with the cute, female medical examiner who'd asked him about working out earlier in the week. He knew it wasn't right and it didn't make him feel good, but it did keep him thinking about the medical examiner's offer.

It was going to be a hell of a week.

Lauren Stallings loved these Sunday afternoon lunches with her grandfather. Not that she'd ever admit it. She liked playing the role of super-cool teenager. Today was even better because her grandmother sat next to her grandfather at the long table in the Pizza Kitchen on Atlantic Boulevard near the beach. She'd never seen her grandparents together and it felt like a party.

The shocking thing was that her mother had joined them and sat silently at the end of the table with Charlie on one side of her and Grandmother on the other side. Lauren's father sat next to her and didn't say much either.

Her grandfather was in the middle of one of his stories about life in the Navy. She studied his face, noting the small blemishes and scars. She knew he was an alcoholic and had spent a long time living in homeless shelters. The issue of alcohol and drug abuse on both her mother's and father's sides of the family made her worry about herself and her sister Jeanie. Were they genetically disposed to abuse issues? She missed her sister, especially on days like this when everyone was together. The gathered family made her loss more acute, as if Jeanie had disappeared last week instead of three years ago.

Now she looked at her father and saw the resemblance with her grandfather. Her father looked rugged and put on a tough façade, but he was actually fragile since Jeanie had disappeared. She'd caught him crying more than once and knew he prowled the Internet for any clues about her missing sister. Lauren realized her mother was almost the opposite. She looked frail emotionally, but she had proved to be tough. She'd asked her father to move out because of his obsession with his job and Jeanie. Lauren knew she wasn't supposed to know any of that, but it was hard to keep secrets in a house. She didn't think her father was hurting the family, but she wasn't in her mother's shoes. Marriage was complicated and she wasn't sure it was something she wanted to try. Not based on what two decent people like her parents had gone through.

She leaned in close to her father and said, "Why don't you go sit down near Mom?"

Her father turned and looked at her, a small smile spreading across his face. "I wish she wanted me to, but I like sitting here with you."

"Will you ever be sitting next to her again?"

"I hope so."

"Me too."

Lauren decided to relax and enjoy the time she had with her family. She'd have plenty of time to worry about things later. She always did. This was a special day, she could feel it.

But she still missed Jeanie.

* * *

John Stallings felt a deep sense of satisfaction sitting at the table with most of his family. The tension he felt with Maria didn't interfere with his enjoyment of having his mother, father, and both of his kids devour a gigantic vegetable pizza. He paid special attention to his father since his latest episode. He noticed the old man drank glass after glass of water and seemed to be tuned in at the moment, keeping everyone straight in his mind.

He also appreciated the broad smile on his mother's face. She had raised him and his sister, Helen, almost as a single mother but didn't get the credit. Between his long hours in the Navy yard at Mayport and his long nights drinking with his buddies, Stallings's father had not been the ideal husband. But at this moment his mother didn't seem to hold any grudges and neither would he.

James Stallings set down his tall glass of water and made some joke that caused Charlie to snort with laughter. Lauren started to cackle as well. She said, "I guess Dad didn't inherit a sense of humor from you."

The whole table erupted at that comment. Stallings's father pounded the tabletop and said, "Your voice is very similar to Jeanie's."

That brought an immediate dead silence to their end of the restaurant.

Stallings said, "How do you know what she sounded like?"

"I remember. Even if she only visited me the two times."

"I never brought her to see you. You and I didn't speak during her entire life with us."

"She came on her own. Two different times, about a week apart. Must've been a little over two years ago."

Now everyone was staring at the elder Stallings. The old man seemed confused by the attention. Then he said, "The first time she came she was Jeanie, the second time she came as Kelly."

"Who?"

"Kelly."

"Who's Kelly?"

The old man looked from Stallings to the kids and now seemed confused. "I don't know anyone named Kelly. Why, is she supposed to meet us?"

Stallings didn't know what to do. His instinct was to grill the old man, but he didn't want to do it in front of the kids. But somewhere inside of him, he had the sense that his father was not confused or making up the story. Had he, in fact, had contact with Jeanie? Finally Stallings said, "Why haven't you ever said anything about seeing Jeanie?"

The old man hesitated and scratched the short gray bristle on the top of his head "She promised to come back and visit me if I didn't say anything. She was scared and so was I. The whole thing slipped my mind. That happens to me sometimes. I forget a lot of things. You may not notice it yet, but I get confused easily."

Stallings's mother patted his father on the back and gave him a hug from behind. Lauren reached across the table and grasped his hand.

Then James Stallings wept silently.

Patty Levine didn't think of her quiet Sunday afternoon as sulking; she considered it recharging. But as she sprawled on her couch, watching an old, sappy Meg Ryan movie, she had to admit it felt like sulking. The more accurate word might be *depressed*. She couldn't point to anything in her life that would depress her except the total failure she had suffered kicking her prescription-drug habit.

The sergeant had made it clear she wanted a rested crew ready to kick ass on Monday morning, so Patty was confident she wouldn't be called out today. That was how she justified swallowing a Xanax earlier and now used a couple of painkillers to ease the throbbing in her lower back. She felt some guilt about the painkillers because she'd thought she'd gotten past them and could make it without the subtle fog the long, light blue pills put her in.

The long hours of the afternoon gave Patty a chance to contemplate her entire life. She wondered if she was like an alcoholic who, after an absence of drinking, started right back where she was when she had stopped.

Despite the guilt about using again, she considered the advantages of using a prescription antidepressant to pull her out of her funk. Maybe she needed someone to talk to. Despite her feelings about John Stallings or even Tony Mazzetti, she didn't want to put them in an awkward position of knowing she had a problem and not telling a supervisor. If something happened and it was discovered that they had known she had a problem, they could face discipline as well.

No, she'd been too good at keeping her issues private for too long. There was no reason to yak about them now. Her issues would be hard for a man to understand. They might treat her like one of the boys, but she wasn't. Some cops just looked at her like a cute chick who had lucked into a job or slept her way into the detective bureau. That was another reason why she didn't really want to go public with her relationship with Tony.

She'd continue to keep it quiet a while longer. She had to.

TWENTY-NINE

John Stallings intended to attack the day. He'd appreciated the rare Sunday afternoon with his family. His father's odd comment about Jeanie haunted him. That's why he was glad he was taking the old man to the doctor this afternoon.

This morning was about work. It was about finding the asshole who'd killed the girl found in the shallow grave at Pine Forest Park. He was learning all he could about what might happen to a runaway in Jacksonville who just disappeared one day. He couldn't stop thinking about the girl found buried in the park. He wanted the man responsible. It burned in him like the start of an ulcer. Which Stallings realized really could be the source of the feeling.

Tony Mazzetti was welcome to make a case, to talk to the media, and to advance his career, but Stallings was going to catch the killer. He didn't care who took the credit. He just wanted this creep.

He couldn't help but consider Jeanie when he thought about Leah Tischler. Stop at the wrong bus stop, at the wrong time, and God only knew what could happen. A life could be gone like a wisp of smoke. He knew from experience that some of the killers who roamed the streets felt about as much from taking a life as they did from blowing out a candle. He hated trying to think like them, but sometimes it was the only way to catch them. That's all Stallings wanted to do: stop assholes like the one who had killed the girl found at the park and the nursing student at the bus stop.

He wanted to punish the killer not just for the girl in the park or Kathy Mizell, but for all the Jeanies in the world too.

Tony Mazzetti was waiting at the parole and probation office in downtown Jacksonville when the portly parole officer strolled in with a bag of doughnuts in one hand and a giant container of Dunkin' Donuts coffee in the other.

Mazzetti sprang from the uncomfortable plastic chair he'd been sitting in for thirty minutes while he waited. "Tom Laider?"

"Who's askin'?"

Mazzetti had his ID out and open in a flash. "JSO. I need to talk to you right now."

Mazzetti nodded to Sparky Taylor, who calmly closed his *Popular Mechanics* magazine and followed.

The heavyset parole officer led them down a series of narrow hallways. One was so tight the fat man's sides brushed booth walls. Mazzetti worried that Sparky might be having the same problem behind him so he was careful not to turn around.

Once they were sitting in the miniscule, windowless office with drab, blank walls and the parole officer had wedged himself behind the desk, he said, "What can I do for JSO this morning?

"We need to talk to Daniel Byrd."

"So do I."

"What's that mean?"

The fat man sighed and rubbed his face like it was 3:30 in the afternoon instead of nine o'clock in the morning. "It means I haven't seen Mr. Byrd in two months. He's never at the construction site where he tells me he'll be. He switches apartments like most people switch underwear and misses every appointment I've ever set for him in this office."

Mazzetti stared at the ineffective parole officer. "Why don't you violate him? Send his ass back to prison."

The parole officer shook his head. "Do you have any idea how much paperwork that'd be? Besides, you've seen the state budget. We can't afford to house inmates anymore. The only way anyone gets violated is if they commit a new, violent felony."

"What if I told you he was a suspect in a murder?"

"I'd say call me after you convict him." The fat officer munched happily on an iced chocolate doughnut, then washed it down with a huge swallow of coffee. "Now if you gentlemen will excuse me, I'm very busy."

"Busy! What do you have to do to keep busy? You're not seeing anyone, not violating anyone, you don't even get in the goddamn office until after nine o'clock. How can you be busy?"

The parole officer didn't bother to acknowledge Mazzetti's outrage.

Mazzetti looked at the parole officer, at his partner, and finally at the folder containing Daniel Byrd's photograph and criminal history. He considered the few options he had to track the construction worker down. As much as he hated to admit it, this sounded like a job that Stallings could handle better than anyone else.

Lexie Hanover liked her independence. She worked evenings at Sal's Smoothie Shack to earn extra money, but she really enjoyed working at a vet's office during the day. The poor veterinarian was so busy in his personal life and made so little money at his beachside office that he relinquished much of the regular duties to Lexie. That's why she knew that one day she'd make a great veterinarian herself. She had two more courses at a community college before she could transfer to the University of Florida and start the real competition for the limited number of spots in their veterinary medicine program. She knew she could do it.

Lexie rushed around her small apartment because she liked to make a good impression on people when they stepped inside. She recognized the building wasn't new and didn't look historical or anything like that. Not in an industrial section west of the interstate. Her apartment was tiny and therefore easy to keep clean, and her two cats didn't leave much of a mess.

She'd been thinking about the guy she'd met Friday night. He had been very interested in her life, asking her all about her hobbies and family. Eventually he had gotten her talking about her hygiene, drinking habits, and the fact that she had never smoked a cigarette in her whole life. He had really liked that and had complimented her about her smile instead of her body the way most guys did. He had also been interested in her dreams and hopes and had told her that being a veterinarian was something noble to aspire to. He'd said he really admired people in the medical field and that his most recent girlfriend had worked at a dentist's office. Lexie had a feeling that he was truly interested in her and she liked the way he told her she had the face of an angel. He seemed sweet and deeper than the average jerk who rolled out of Jacksonville Landing half drunk and completely immature. He had already talked philosophy with her and told her how he often contemplated eternity. Most guys talk about themselves. She definitely liked this change.

Stallings had already told Mazzetti and Sergeant Zuni he was splitting his day. He'd run down several leads in the morning and wasn't looking forward to the afternoon. He was taking his father to the doctor for a real evaluation of his memory issues. He intended to come back and work in the early evening before he navigated to his little house and collapsed on the lumpy bed.

Right now he had a few minutes to take a risk and swing by his old house. He wanted to see Maria; something inside him said he needed to hear her voice. Even if all the voice did was tell him to get lost and leave her alone.

As he knocked on the front door he realized his attitude was dangerously close to a stalker's. His stomach tightened and he considered chanting his mantra from work, *Is today the day that changes my life?* Standing at the door he felt somewhat like he did before executing a search warrant, nervous and apprehensive. The TV cops always looked cool, but they had never been shot at with live ammo.

The door opened a few inches and Maria's beautiful face appeared. After a moment's hesitation, she opened the door wide and said in a pleasant voice, "This is a surprise. Is everything all right?"

"I needed to talk to you for a few minutes." He didn't think it was a good idea to tell her he had wanted to hear her voice.

"I told you that we don't need to explain ourselves to each other. You can have coffee with whoever you want to."

"That's not what I'm talking about." Although now that she mentioned it, he still wanted to clear that up. "I wanted to talk about what my dad said yesterday about seeing Jeanie."

Maria's bottom left lip quivered, and she burst into tears.

THIRTY

Buddy parked his van more than three blocks from Lexie's rat-hole apartment just west of I-95 in an odd neighborhood of apartment buildings and industrial warehouses. He knew the whole city pretty well and there was an antique hardware store he occasionally used for brackets and frames on the street. If for some reason someone asked why his van was parked in the area he could legitimately say he was going by the hardware store. The only thing that bothered him was walking three blocks in the heat of Jacksonville.

Lexie was an excellent candidate for eternity. Since their lunch, he'd been on fire with the idea of placing her last breath in the jar he'd finished the night before. He'd made this one especially for Lexie and her smooth, white skin. The glass he had blown had a light, creamy texture and was unlike anything he'd ever placed in his work of art. It fit Lexie perfectly. The jar was wrapped in tissue paper inside a Publix grocery store plastic bag along with a bouquet of flowers. He knew she'd immediately assume the decorative jar was some kind of vase for the flowers. And that's what he wanted her to think. He wanted her to stay calm right up until the very end. He remembered hearing a farmer say at career day in sixth grade that he never let his pigs get frightened before they were slaughtered because it ruined the meat. Buddy had had all kinds of questions he wanted to ask before the teacher rushed the bewildered farmer out of the room. All the man had done was tell the truth. He had been honest enough to say that if the pigs didn't know they were about to be shot in the back of the head it was a good thing. Buddy definitely saw the logic in that.

He turned the corner and instinctively looked in every direction. It was the middle of a workday and there was no one wandering the streets. Lexie had the day off from the animal hospital and didn't have to work at Sal's Smoothie Shack tonight. He had no pressing jobs to complete and felt like the stars had aligned to provide him with this chance to complete another section his work of art. He loved that Lexie cared so much about animals. Along with her angelic face, it was the quality he'd latched onto. He wouldn't tell her anything about his experiments with his mother's cats.

John Stallings sat on the couch of his former residence with his arm around his wife's shoulder. Her sobbing had decreased to a sniffle. She turned to face Stallings, cleared her throat, and said, "I'm sorry I lost it. I just miss her so much. When your dad said he'd seen her, he got me thinking about so many things."

Stallings didn't say anything as he gave her a squeeze with his arm.

"And this week is the anniversary of her disappearance."

He said, "I know."

"It must be hard on you too. I never seem to remember that until it's too late."

"It's never too late."

Maria didn't answer his comment as she stood, crossed the room, and snatched a tissue from a decorative wicker dispenser. She tried to remain ladylike wiping her tears, but finally gave up and blew her nose like a lumberjack.

Fifteen minutes later he found himself at the kitchen table eating a ham sandwich and chatting quietly with Maria. It was the first time in months he'd done anything like this. He missed the domestic life. The last few years he'd spent many lunch hours right at this table, doing the same thing he was doing now. It was his time in homicide that had screwed everything up. There were fewer lunch hours, then fewer dinner breaks. He'd almost forgotten what it was like to come home to three cheerful, screaming kids. He could remember holding an infant Charlie like a receiver with a football while Lauren and Jeanie vied for his attention. Jeanie, with her light hair and a smile that was infectious. Customers at restaurants would often comment about her brilliant and charming smile.

After several awkward silences, Stallings finally worked up the nerve to say to Maria, "I really wanted to talk to you about the woman I had coffee with last Friday."

"John, I told you, you're free to do as you wish. We don't owe each other any explanations at all."

"Does that mean we're through?"

She took a moment to answer, making him feel like he was waiting to hear the results of a biopsy.

Finally Maria shook her head and said, "No, not necessarily. But I need some more time."

Since he had her in a talkative position, he said, "What were you doing downtown anyway?"

"It's personal."

Somehow Stallings hadn't realized that simple phrase could sting so much.

Lexie was thrilled to have someone in her miniscule apartment, interested in her and her life. She'd never admit to her parents how sad she got or how shallow most of the men she met were. Buddy seemed perfectly content to listen to her chatter on about animals or classes or working at the stupid frozen-yogurt shack. She never had the feeling he was just interested in her for her body. And that was such a nice change here in Jacksonville. Maybe it was like that in every big city, but she had really only lived in Jacksonville her whole life.

The bouquet of flowers he'd brought was as pretty as the first. He'd also brought her one of his homemade jars, which was too short to put the flowers in. She did like the milky-colored glass with bubbles rippling through it. She also liked how original it looked and felt. It had a thin, sticky film around it. Buddy told her it was from the glassblowing process. There was something decidedly uncommercial looking about the jar, and she was happy he wanted to share the artistic part of his life with her.

She set the glass jar on the windowsill between them, then leaned over and kissed him gently on the lips. Not a flirty or sexual move, but a gesture of how much she appreciated his present.

Buddy had already quizzed her about how much she loved animals. Now, out of the blue, he said, "Do you believe in God?"

"Sure. I was raised in a Baptist church and now I go to a nondenominational service a few blocks away. I don't go every week, but I make it more than I miss it."

"That's nice. You don't see that much with people anymore. Everyone wants to live for the day and gives no thought to eternity. If you think about it, we'll spend a lot more time in eternity than we do shuffling around on Earth."

"That's a nice way to put it."

"I was hoping you'd think that way." He scooted the bamboo chair closer to her and coughed loudly in his hands.

"Are you okay?"

"One of the dangers blowing glass. Sometimes your lungs can be coated with film just like that jar. A small price to pay."

Lexie liked the way he looked deep into her eyes as he gently stroked her cheek and then ran his fingers through her hair. She closed her eyes as he tilted her head back slightly and started to caress her throat.

Tony Mazzetti and Sparky Taylor stood on the opposite side of the procedure table watching the autopsy of the girl found buried in the playground at Pine Forest Park. Mazzetti went through his long list of tasks to accomplish on this case as he watched the assistant medical examiner go through her preliminary steps. He was a little annoyed at John Stallings taking off the afternoon for personal business. Mazzetti didn't know what the personal business could be, but from his point of view there was nothing more important than an unsolved homicide.

Sparky made notes as he looked closely at the girl's shirt and then her hands and wrists. He said, "One mark on her wrist here is from a crime scene tech's trowel."

Mazzetti said, "The goddamn rednecks we hire should be working for a landscape company like their DNA compels them to."

Sparky shook his head. "The constant insults to Southerners in general and Floridians in particular are not helpful. It doesn't make you, as a New Yorker, sound like you're trying to fit in."

"I'm just saying sometimes backwards rednecks down here annoy me."

Sparky gave him a thoughtful look and said, "You know, Tony, the average New Yorker who moves here is less educated than the general population already here."

"Then they're getting a shitty education if they're too stupid to dig out a body without destroying evidence." He didn't have time to waste arguing with a guy like this about a topic that meant nothing. But he found it hard to concentrate on the task at hand.

No matter how hard he tried, Tony Mazzetti couldn't keep his eyes from the pretty assistant medical examiner. He liked the way her long curly, red hair was tied in a neat ponytail and tucked under a sanitary, Mylar cap. He normally didn't go for redheads, but this girl's features were pretty and her skin so creamy looking that he made an exception. He shuffled around for a better view of what she was looking at.

She caught his movements and explained that she was interested in where the clothes touched the victim's body as well as all the marks. She said, "There was a chemical residue of some kind on the seat of her shorts. I'd like to see if it touched her skin and what effect it had."

Mazzetti said, "We won't know what the chemical is for a while. The lab has all that information now. We were able to identify her through fingerprints. Her name is Jessie Kalb and she taught preschool last summer so they were required to fingerprint her and run the prints through FDLE. She's twenty years old and told her parents she wanted to travel the world before she got serious about school."

The medical examiner looked up and let her blue eyes focus on Mazzetti. "See these bruises?" She pointed to the girl's throat. "There is a faint pattern that shows a ligature strangulation. It was a decorative belt or strap. The other girl, Kathy Mizell, was killed the same way." She straightened her lithe frame and stretched. "Based on the marks around her throat I'd say you boys have a real live serial killer."

Mazzetti thought to himself. *Tell me something I don't know.*

THIRTY-ONE

Buddy felt quite satisfied with himself. He'd planned things out and so far everything had fallen into place. Lexie was relaxed and giggling on the chair. He had the cord in his belt line and pulled it out. The jar was between them on the windowsill. It was like lining up a great golf shot. He had his left hand near her throat and right hand closest to the jar. After he was done using the heavy cord around her neck he'd be able to slip the jar in front of her face very easily. After his last few attempts he needed one that went smoothly and didn't scare a month off his already sketchy life.

In his head he started the countdown. He flexed his shoulders and arms, knowing they could be in for a workout, his heartbeat revved to the point that it sounded like a hammer in his chest. Lexie felt hot to the touch. Her pupils were dilated. She was definitely an angel worthy of worship.

He gently tilted her head back as he stroked her graceful neck. Her eyes closed. Then he committed. He wrapped the cord around her throat and pulled with all of his might. It was important the first contact with the cord was shocking.

This was a very odd situation for Yvonne Zuni. She was seated in front of Lieutenant Rita Hester with senior IA investigator Ronald Bell sitting across from her. Lieutenant Hester leaned back in her massive padded leather chair, her dark eyes shifting between them, her poker face never gave a hint of what she was thinking. Sergeant Zuni realized it was the lieutenant's years on road patrol and actual, practical experience that gave her the ability to intimidate someone without saying a word or, in this case, even moving a muscle.

Sergeant Zuni, like many of the female members of the Jacksonville Sheriff's Office, looked up to Lieutenant Hester as a role model. On the street she'd cracked so many heads with a nightstick she'd been given the nickname *The Brown Bomber*. As an administrator, she got the most out of her people while developing a reputation for protecting them. She had also been John Stallings's partner many years ago in road patrol. That was an important tidbit to keep in mind.

Every time Sergeant Zuni looked across at Ronald Bell she couldn't help but think of their fantastic weekend together. He'd stayed over Friday night after their wonderful meal at Gi-Gi's, then met her again Saturday night when she was done at the crime scene at Pine Forest Park. After drinks at an island-flavored bar near Jacksonville Landing, they'd gone dancing and ended up at his lovely riverfront home. It was only three blocks from her parents' house. She didn't bother to mention that to Ronald.

He made her feel like a princess, catering to her every desire, and as a result, it had been the best weekend she'd had in years.

Right now, midday on Monday, Sergeant Zuni was seeing a different side of Ronald Bell. Sure, he was devastatingly handsome and dapper in a sharp Armani suit. But she didn't like what he was saying, even though she realized he had a different job from hers.

Bell looked at the lieutenant and said, "We've gone as far as we can go on the investigation without being overt. We're gonna need to start interviewing people and seeing if anyone talked or tried to sell the drugs on the street."

Sergeant Zuni said, "Are you trying to say you think one of my detectives not only stole the pills but then tried to sell them for profit?"

Bell gave her a smile, but it was not like the ones she had seen over the last few days. "So you think it's possible that one of your detectives took the drugs for personal use?"

"That's not what I said."

"But is it a possibility?"

The sergeant didn't know what to say or how she should feel toward this man who only yesterday she had thought was something special.

Bell said, "I could narrow down the suspects."

At the same time both the sergeant and lieutenant said, "How?"

"I checked the JSO medical records for everyone who was present in the squad bay."

Sergeant Zuni interrupted him. "Wait a minute. You can't check personal medical records for just any reason."

"No, but I can check the records of JSO employees

who have to go through a physical every two years. And I have a very good reason. A bundle of diverted prescription narcotics worth a small fortune is missing. That's not just any reason."

Sergeant Zuni caught a glimpse of the smugness that rubbed John Stallings and many of the other detectives the wrong way. Right now she didn't much care for it either. She kept her mouth shut. She had to trust Lieutenant Hester to come to her aid before this got out of hand.

The lieutenant said in a very even tone, "What'd you find, Ronald?"

"I think Patty Levine is a plausible suspect in this theft."

Sergeant Zuni almost sprang to her feet. "How in the hell did you reach that crazy conclusion?"

This time it was Bell who kept a very even tone. "At her last physical, Detective Levine listed the prescriptions she was currently taking. Those include Ambien and hydrocodone."

The lieutenant said, "What is hydrocodone?"

"The most common drug you'd recognize from that generic name is Vicodin."

Sergeant Zuni said, "So you're telling me because she followed the rules and admitted to exactly which drugs she was legally prescribed, now you're going to drag her name through the mud. That seems like pretty thin evidence to skewer a good cop on."

"Another way to look at is that she knew there was a drug screen and decided that no one would check if she admitted it. She wrote on her own form that she only used the painkiller occasionally for back pain and never on duty. But that was more than two years ago. There's no telling what her drug problem's like now."

Sergeant Zuni kept her mouth shut. Like a mother tiger, her first instinct was to protect her cub. She needed time to know how to go about that the best way. Finally she said, "So what happens now?"

Bell gave her that smug smile and said, "Think she'll talk to me?"

Sergeant Zuni knew she'd wasted her entire weekend.

Lexie Hanover was excited and nervous. She'd only had two serious boyfriends in her entire life. Her first boyfriend, Elby Harris, had stayed with her three years until he graduated and went off to Auburn. She'd loved him and was not unhappy that she had lost her virginity to him. In the big scheme of things, losing your virginity on a king-size bed while his parents were out of town was not such a bad thing. It certainly wasn't romantic, or at least how she had fantasized losing her virginity, but it was much better than the backseat of a Trans-Am or the bed of a pickup truck.

Lexie's only other boyfriend was a guy named Chuck who had an adorable miniature Doberman he brought by the clinic. He was older than her, about twenty-seven, and had led her to believe he was crazy about her. He took her on a weekend to Savannah and out to dinner four different times. Somehow it had shocked Lexie to learn he was married and that was the reason he never took her back to his place. She tried not to let the experience jade her toward men. Lexie focused on how experienced he had been and how much she had enjoyed the things he did to her. It opened her eyes to the advantage of dating a man who was perhaps a little older and more mature. Maybe that's why she was attracted to Buddy. So when he suggested she close her eyes while he stroked her neck, she listened

It was almost like a dream. Her whole body relaxed. She could drift off to sleep or turn into a wildcat on a second's notice. She felt something on her throat. It was soft like cloth but heavier, but it wasn't jewelry, it was too soon for extravagant gifts. As she drifted deeper into this wonderful state, she wondered what delightful trick he had in store for her.

She could feel his breath near her neck and it smelled fruity and fresh. Her whole body tingled with excitement and expectation.

Then something went drastically wrong. For a split second she thought she'd swallowed wrong. Lexie became disoriented and a violent jerk snapped her head. She was choking. She had no air at all.

As fast as it started, she could breathe again. She'd sucked in one breath and opened her eyes. Buddy was right next to her face with the homemade jar in his hand. Maybe he thought it would help funnel oxygen into her. Her mind raced with all the dreadful possibilities. Had she had a stroke? A brain hemorrhage? Some kind of heart attack?

Lexie tried to take another breath, but another sharp jerk cut off her wind. She realized it was a strap around her throat. It was Buddy. He was doing this.

Lexie saw him set the jar down on the ground. Then the pressure around her throat increased drastically and she realized he was using both hands on the strap to choke her. Why?

She struggled to stay conscious, her arms uselessly flailing against his; then she tried to dig her fingers under the cord around her neck. She didn't know what to do or what she had done to cause this. She felt her consciousness slip away faster and faster as the room grew dim. The last thing she saw was Buddy's pleasant smile.

THIRTY-TWO

John Stallings sat in the doctor's office next to his mother on a small couch while his father reclined in a chair next to the wide, dark oak desk. He felt his mother's small, trembling hand reach across the short gap between them to grab his. As soon as the doctor bustled into his office, Stallings knew what he was going to say. This was obviously not one of those doctors who could detach himself from the patient.

The middle-aged doctor, wearing almost comically thick glasses, tried to buy some time while looking through several pages of a lab report. Finally he looked, first at James Stallings, then over to John on the couch. He started to speak slowly, but it didn't hide his New York accent.

"I'm afraid I have some very bad news. And I don't believe in providing false hope. All the tests seemed to indicate . . ."

All Stallings heard was *Blah, blah, blah, blah—Alzheimer's*. Then another phrase he didn't want to hear: *Prepare for the worst*.

* * *

Buddy had held the limp body of Lexie in his arms until he felt a change in her body temperature. He was comfortable on the floor of her tiny apartment with her head in his lap and her smooth arms neatly at her sides. He had done nothing lewd or inappropriate as he tried to reassure her that this was for the best and she'd now be recognized for all eternity.

He looked over to the small glass jar he'd set back on a windowsill and smiled, knowing he had another piece of his work of art completed. He'd been careful not to move from this area of the apartment and slid away from her like he was trying to keep from waking her up. He took the jar and glanced around. There was nothing that indicated he'd been in the apartment. He knew the cops had a way of picking up flecks of skin or strands of hair, but he wasn't that concerned about it anymore.

Buddy leaned down, lifted Lexie into his arms, and carried her across the room to the old, ratty couch. He laid her out gently and placed a pillow under her head. He turned the TV on and put the volume high enough that someone might hear it if he leaned against the door. Buddy figured that would buy him a day or two.

He picked up the jar and made one more scan of the room, then looked at the peaceful image of Lexie. That's how she'd be remembered until time itself ended.

It wasn't dark outside yet, but Stallings had the impression it was late. The office was completely empty and he appreciated the few minutes of silence while he sat at his desk and stared at the framed photo of Jeanie.

He picked up a photo of Leah Tischler and stared at it for a few minutes. What had happened to the teenager from the wealthy family who lived near the beach? Would they be torn apart by this like his family was torn apart by Jeanie's disappearance? Had his father really seen his granddaughter, or was it the wishful thinking of a sick old man?

The doctor couldn't have been less encouraging and his father couldn't have been less interested in the diagnosis. Maybe it was his career in the military or his time on the streets, knowing that life was short and you shouldn't have any regrets. Either way, his father's Alzheimer's seem to be taking more of a toll on Stallings than the old man.

Stallings looked across his desk at all the information on the Leah Tischler case. He played an MP3 of the girl singing in the choir of the Thomas School. Her mother had provided it, thinking it might motivate him more. She had no idea how much he was motivated on his own. Even with the computer's small speakers he could appreciate the girl's soft, sweet voice. Definitely fit her innocent face.

His desk phone's loud, ancient ringer jolted him out of his trance.

He snatched the receiver, simply saying, "Stallings."

The bored-sounding receptionist from the main lobby said, "Stall, we got someone down here to see you." She hung up the phone before he could ask questions.

He trudged down the main stairwell that opened into the lobby. As soon as he opened the door he was shocked to see his visitor.

Liz Dubeck stood up from the hard plastic chair and gave him a tentative, hopeful smile.

* * *

Patty Levine felt as if she was operating at half speed all day, as though a fog had fallen over her. A day to recharge felt more like it had sapped her of any energy at all. The minor contact she'd had with the other people in her squad had proved to be disconcerting at best. Tony Mazzetti had virtually ignored her after he got back from the medical examiner's office. She chalked it up to the stress of running a serial-killer investigation. The media had started to talk about the bloody weekend Jacksonville had suffered. The news coverage focused on the discovery of a wealthy local woman's body in the backseat of her Chrysler at Jacksonville Landing.

Patty had heard Luis Martinez, one of the detectives on the case, mention that the big mystery of the crime scene was two different sources of blood. Right now the assumption was the other blood was the killer's. Patty knew the media had latched on to the murder because the victim was extremely attractive and lived in Ponte Vedra Beach. The local news stations rarely covered the story of a murder of a black prostitute or crack addict from Arlington.

Stepping out of the Land That Time Forgot, Patty was surprised to run into Sergeant Zuni and Ronald Bell leaving the lieutenant's office. All three of them stood, frozen, assessing each other. Patty assumed they were uncomfortable after the chance encounter at Gi-Gi's restaurant down in Deerwood Park. But she got an odd vibe and a sharp look from Ronald Bell.

Patty said, "Hey, guys. How's it going?"

There was an awkward silence until Sergeant Zuni cleared her throat and said, "Busy. How about you? You have a good weekend?"

"Not bad. What about you?"

Sergeant Zuni glared over at Ronald Bell, then back to Patty, and said, "Weekend was good, it's today that sucks."

Patty couldn't miss the murderous stare Sergeant Zuni gave the senior IA investigator.

John Stallings had to admit he liked sitting at the picnic table, staring into Liz Dubeck's beautiful face. The table sat under a small stand of willow trees that overlooked the St. Johns River. Technically it was owned by the condo next to it, but the manager of the condo, a retired NYPD sergeant, opened the beautiful spot to any cop who wanted to walk across the street from the PMB and welcomed them to think of it as their office away from the office. During the day it was rare the table did not have some frustrated detective jabbering on his cell phone. But this time of the evening Stallings and Liz had complete privacy.

Liz reached across a wooden table and took both Stallings's hands in hers. "I thought you might call. I know I'm acting like a schoolgirl, but I felt the chemistry between us."

"Sorry, I . . ." He couldn't come up the combination of words that would explain how he felt about her or why he couldn't do anything about it. He'd never been a very good liar, even if it was to spare someone's feelings. Instead, he sat there and stared at her.

"You're stuck on your ex-wife, aren't you?"

"Not ex, yet."

Liz looked down and nodded her head. "I can respect that. Probably the reason I hoped you'd call me.

You know how hard it is to find a guy who's loyal and honest?"

Stallings shook his head, trying to keep eye contact.

"I don't want to screw anything up between you and her. But I don't want to walk away either. Maybe this would be a good time to wait and see what happens."

Stallings nodded, feeling the connection but knowing he had to walk away. "We could be friends."

Liz let loose a tired smile and said, "That's usually my line." She stood and stepped away from the bench, motioning for him to stay. As she walked away she turned and said, "You'll keep me informed about Leah?"

"As soon as I know anything, I'll let you know." He felt a sharp pain in his chest as he watched her slowly leave. He wished it was just a heart attack.

THIRTY-THREE

This was exactly the type of activity John Stallings needed to get his head out of his own personal problems. He was a cop and this was one of the most satisfying aspects of police work: looking for a specific suspect.

Stallings hadn't cared much about the details when Tony Mazzetti approached him an hour ago to go to the apartment of some guy named Daniel Byrd. Mazzetti had laid out a few pieces of information that sounded interesting but did not necessarily make Byrd a prime suspect in the recent strangulations.

Generally a car with three detectives in it was full of chatter and smart-ass remarks. Tony Mazzetti was preoccupied while he drove, and Sparky Taylor was working on one of his complex Sudoku puzzles in the front passenger seat. That was fine with Stallings, who was content to sit in the backseat and hope that this was the guy who could provide some answers about Leah Tischler and any other girl who might've gone missing in the area. Although the more he considered his father's comments, the more likely it seemed that Jeanie had escaped harm at the hands of a man who strangled young women.

The apartment was in the north end of the city not far off U.S. 1. The kind of place construction workers and rodeo riders might rent. Cheap and not opposed to loud music or parties. Toby Keith blared from a window on the side facing the road, competing with loud hard rock from an upper window on the side. The three detectives took a moment to assess the entrances and exits as well as how crowded the apartment building looked.

Sparky Taylor said, "Policy dictates that if there is a chance for violent confrontation we should at least consult the tactical team."

Mazzetti said, "If we called those dildos every time we thought we might have a confrontation nothing would ever get done. Last I checked we were all authorized to carry a gun and make an arrest. I think policy will back me up on that, won't it, Spark?"

Stallings could see Mazzetti getting a handle on his new partner and understanding how to manipulate him. It didn't matter one way or the other. Stallings was in a mood for results, and smacking someone in the head might make him feel better. He kept his mouth shut and followed the two partners through the front door of the apartment building, then up one flight of sketchy wooden stairs. Even stepping slowly and carefully Stallings knew they were broadcasting their presence to the entire floor.

Mazzetti said, "There's only one way in and out of this place, so we don't have to worry about covering any back doors. No matter what, we don't want to have to chase this guy on foot. As soon as he opens the door, we grab him."

As he approached apartment 2-C, the third door on the right-hand side of the hallway, Stallings quickly and silently went through his personal rituals. First he placed his right hand on the grip of his Glock .40-caliber pistol. He liked the feeling of knowing it was on his hip as he muttered his mantra, "Is today the day that changes the rest of my life?" He knew Mazzetti had heard it, but he didn't turn or acknowledge Stallings. The same instructor had taught the phrase at the police academy for twenty years as a way to keep cops sharp and focused every time they stepped into an unknown or dangerous situation.

Mazzetti stood to the left of the door with Sparky Taylor behind him, while Stallings stood to the right. No one had his gun drawn because, in theory, this was just a simple interview. Ask the guy a few questions and see what kind of a read they could get from him. Simple.

Despite his years of experience, both as a road patrolman and as a detective, Stallings's heart rate started to increase and he felt the excitement of the unknown. It was a thrill most cops appreciated on some level. It was the reason for the thrill that caused so much grief and sorrow. It was a one in one thousand chance that whoever opened the door would have a gun in his hand.

Stallings tensed when Mazzetti banged on the door.

Sergeant Zuni sat at her desk getting ready to leave for the evening.

Ronald Bell, sitting across from her, said, "You got to be kidding me. That was business. I'm just doing my job. I thought we were going to separate work and personal business."

The sergeant flashed her dark eyes at him. "Look, Ronald, I agreed not to say anything and you agreed to keep this quiet as long as possible. But the way you seemed to relish trashing a good cop and sneaking through medical records has left a bad taste in my mouth. I can't hide the fact that I don't like how you did your job. And I can't change who I am."

"What does that mean?"

"It means you're a douche bag and you will not be seeing me naked again."

THIRTY-FOUR

John Stallings leaned against the wall as several residents peeked out their doors at the sound of Mazzetti's incessant pounding. There was no turning back now. Even if Daniel Byrd wasn't home, the neighbors would drop a dime that the cops had been here looking for him.

Mazzetti glanced at Sparky briefly, then over at Stallings. "What do you think, fellas? Simply go in to take a look around?"

Sparky Taylor appeared outraged at the suggestion. He didn't have the most forceful voice, but he got his point across. "We do not have nearly enough PC for a warrant and there are no exigent circumstances. We have no more right to walk into this apartment than we do to walk into any other room in this building."

Stallings said, "Most of the other rooms don't house a potential murder suspect." When he looked down the hall at a couple of the residents gawking out their doors, he wondered how accurate that statement was.

"We don't know that this apartment does either. This

doesn't just go against policy, it goes against the Constitution."

Stallings said, "Look at the totality of the circumstances for the probable cause. With his failure to report to his parole officer, and the comments from the other construction workers, we have enough. Citizens get jumpy when young people in the community end up strangled. I feel confident that a judge will cut us some slack."

"Is that what you want to base our court case on? Slack? Gentlemen, there's a reason we have policies and rules, and neither of you are such legal scholars that I trust your reasoning about why we should enter this private apartment without court authorization."

Stallings recognized that Mazzetti was sitting back and letting him make the argument. If they made some massive fuck-up, Mazzetti would claim he was just following Stallings and trying to keep him out of trouble. At this point it didn't matter. They had at least two dead girls and Stallings didn't want to go to three. He briefly looked at Sparky Taylor, saying, "If this makes you uncomfortable, I suggest you head back to the PMB." Without another word or glance, Stallings threw his shoulder into the door and popped it off the lock instantly, tumbling into a cramped, cluttered apartment.

Sparky Taylor refused to step past the doorway and stood there, shaking his head.

Mazzetti chimed in, "Spark, we can't have an unsolved homicide our first case together. We gotta take a few risks to find this guy."

Stallings scanned the small apartment, then turned to Sparky at the doorway. "What happens if he kills again while we're building a case? Or, if this guy Byrd turns out to not be the killer, we can't let him distract us from our mission for very long. Homicide works a little differently than narcotics or tech. There's a bit of art involved with the science." Stallings could see his comments had no effect on the portly black man, who refused to cross the threshold of the nasty apartment.

There was a tiny bathroom that had no door and only a filthy toilet and sink. On the single bed, a sleeping bag was laid out on one side with no sheets or pillow.

Stallings didn't want to touch anything, let alone search, but he knew it had to be done.

Mazzetti stepped to the other side of the small room, muttering, "Maybe Sparky's right. This is bullshit." Then he slid open the single walk-in closet door and froze.

Stallings glanced from the pile of clothes on the bed and saw what was in the closet. Even Sparky had fallen silent.

Patty Levine had given up on being productive today, shut down her computer, gathered a few notes, and headed down to her car. She didn't speak to anyone as she plodded down the stairs. She felt like the new girl in high school who wanted to be alone but didn't like being lonely. The walk through the rear lot seemed to take forever, but at least it wasn't raining for a change.

She slipped into her county-issued Ford Freestyle and plopped her notebook and purse onto the front passenger seat. She felt like calling Tony Mazzetti and finding out if he had some time to see her later, but she knew he and Sparky Taylor had gone out on a lead. She'd also felt some underlying tension between she and Tony and wondered if it was her reticence to move in with him. Patty didn't feel like it was the right time and the fact that she had spent Sunday afternoon in a comfortable, drug-induced haze supported her idea that she should get a better handle on her drug use before she tried to make someone else happy. Her sour mood and lack of focus today were a direct result of the pills she had taken yesterday. She in no way felt recharged or rested, which was the only reason they were all given Sunday off in the midst of a big homicide investigation.

Patty pulled through the lot, twice braking hard to avoid patrol cars coming and going. Each time she mumbled some swear or curse, when, in truth, she didn't know if it was more her fault or theirs.

The rear gate moved in slow motion. As always there were several day laborers and homeless people wandering on the sidewalk behind the building. Two young black men hurried down the street on the opposite side; their quick strides and confident manner told her that they weren't homeless people. An elderly woman pushed a tiny shopping cart along the sidewalk toward the young men, who politely stepped to the side and allowed the old woman the full width of the sidewalk. On Patty's side of the street a middle-aged Hispanic man wobbled toward her. At first she thought he might be drunk; then she realized he had one bad leg and he compensated for it with a lively swing of his arms.

Finally the gate locked open and Patty pulled through onto the street only to have to mash her brakes again. There was never traffic on this side street behind the PMB. The jackass in a pickup truck coming toward her wouldn't swerve around. Instead, he stopped and stared until she threw her Freestyle into reverse and started to back into the lot.

Before she was out of the way of the pickup truck, still moving in reverse, she felt a thump and heard a sickening shriek.

Maria Stallings had spent many evenings wondering what went wrong in her life. One thing the Narcotics Anonymous meetings had taught her was not to dwell on the bad things but think about the good things in her life. The easiest way to do that was to think about her two children still at home.

Tonight she wasn't contemplating anything; she was taking action. She'd been doing a lot of that lately. No matter how hard it was for her to send her husband away, Maria felt like it'd given her room to look at her life and hopefully make him realize how important the family was. No matter how many people he arrested, it wasn't going to change what happened to Jeanie. Tonight's activity had Maria in Jeanie's room. It was largely the same way it had been the day she disappeared. Maria made it a point to vacuum and clean in the room just like she did the rest of the house. It made her feel better, and if Jeanie did come home she'd realize that no one had ever given up on her.

There were a number of things stored neatly in boxes stacked in Jeanie's walk-in closet. This was where Maria had started her search. She had questions that needed answers, and she liked the idea she was the one who was going to find them.

* * *

Tony Mazzetti had not said a word. Now he, Stallings, and Sparky were inside Daniel Byrd's apartment in front of the walk-in closet. In addition to a work shirt and a pair of men's pants, there were five dresses hanging in the closet.

Mazzetti had a feeling this could be their man. Something about dresses in the shitty apartment didn't fit. He looked around the apartment and said, "I'd bet my left nut that no woman lived in this apartment."

"At least not willingly," mumbled Stallings.

Mazzetti and Stallings turned to Sparky at the same time.

The portly detective looked at each of them and said, "No matter what we found, it doesn't make breaking into this apartment right." He checked the labels on each of the dresses quickly and said, "All big sizes. But this doesn't mean anything."

Mazzetti shook his head, "Come on, Spark, the totality of the circumstances, man. We get more and more information about this creep and it's starting to add up. It may be that he likes to keep a dress from each of his victims. It may be something weirder. I know we need to snap some photos and decide what to take with us."

Sparky said, "Now we're gonna include theft with our burglary?"

Mazzetti knew he was in an odd position. He had no idea what could be evidence. Anything they took now would be thrown out if they made a case. At the very least he needed some DNA samples. He glanced around the room and saw an ashtray overflowing with Marlboro Light cigarette butts. He hesitated, not wanting Sparky to see what he was about to do.

Mazzetti pulled several small Baggies from his inside coat pocket. He always threw a couple in when he was going to do an interview of a suspect or be in a place where he might need to store something for DNA testing later. These were all hard lessons learned through experience. He let Stallings see the bags in his hand and then cut his eyes to the ashtray. He thought Stallings was an asshole, but he was an asshole Mazzetti could trust. Mazzetti knew Stallings wanted this guy captured more than anyone.

Stallings took the cue and knew exactly what to do. He said to Sparky, "Come into the hallway and let's discuss this."

Mazzetti heard the other detectives' voices raise as Sparky stuck to his position and Stallings tried to get him to look at the other, less legal aspects of the investigation.

That was all Mazzetti needed to reach down and pick up four of the cigarette butts. He shuddered at the thought of touching something that had been in a convicted felon's mouth, but sometimes he had to do what he had to.

Mazzetti heard Sparky make a final comment on his stance that everything in the apartment was off limits. But he had all he needed.

Now Mazzetti had to worry about this apartment along with everything else. They had to put a full-court press on to find Daniel Byrd and get some questions answered.

THIRTY-FIVE

Patty Levine froze behind the wheel and felt her blood turn to ice. She didn't want to look into the rearview mirror, but when she did there was nothing to see. The pickup truck scooted around her, the redneck flipping her off as he drove past. None of the pedestrians on the other side of the street turned to look at her way. She pulled the car forward a few feet, threw it into park, and bailed out like she was about to chase a suspect. Instead she ran directly to the rear bumper and her worst fears were realized when she saw the man lying flat on his back with his one good eye focusing on her.

She put both her hands to her cheeks and said, "Oh my God." She dropped to her knees and put her hand gently on the man's shoulder. "Can you understand me, sir?"

The man just moaned.

"I'm going to get help. Don't move." But when Patty started to stand up he gripped her wrist firmly. She turned back to him.

The man said, "No, no. I okay."

Patty stared at the man carefully. Even in those few words she heard his Spanish accent. Patty didn't want the man's immigration concerns to keep him from getting medical treatment. "It's all right. We have to make sure you're not injured." But he wouldn't let go of her wrist.

The man slowly sat up and twisted his head around in every direction. "See, I not hurt." He braced himself on her and slowly worked his way to his feet. Then he spent another thirty seconds shaking his limbs, even though one leg had been hurt by some earlier injury.

Patty kept her hand on the man's shoulder to make sure he was steady. Finally she said, "Are you sure you're okay?"

The man gave her a smile that revealed crooked and broken teeth. He nodded his head vigorously and started to walk the way he had been headed originally.

Patty looked in every direction and saw that no one had even noticed her accident. Her stomach burned and her hands were so shaky she wondered if she'd be able to drive.

The man turned and gave her a brief, cheerful wave.

Patty smiled and waved back. She had to get home and swallow something that would calm her down.

John Stallings almost bolted from Tony Mazzetti's car as he parked behind the PMB.

Mazzetti said, "Where you headed in such a hurry?"

"I'm gonna sit on Byrd's apartment."

"You need some sleep. We'll get out and hit it hard tomorrow and find the shithead. Believe me, we got plenty to do without wasting our time sitting on an empty apartment."

"I got nothing to do anyway. I wouldn't be able to sleep if I went to bed now. I'm gonna give it an hour or two."

Mazzetti shrugged. "Suit yourself."

Stallings noticed Sparky Taylor wasn't speaking to either of them and was giving Stallings a dirty look as he hustled to his county-issued Impala.

Stallings found a place a block down from Byrd's apartment where his silver Impala didn't stand out too much. He could see the entrance to the apartment building and the street in each direction for a couple of blocks. He had Mazzetti's information sheet on Daniel Byrd, which included several photos from over the years. The guy had been in and out of jails since he was sixteen. He went by a number of aliases and one narcotics report noted Byrd always maintained more than one residence. Sometimes it was a small apartment he could run to in addition to a house in a residential area. That got Stallings thinking about how long it'd been since someone had slept in the dingy apartment. It dawned on him that this place was probably a safe house where Byrd only came if he was in trouble. He wanted to talk to some of the neighbors, but it was too late and that was something he needed to talk over with Mazzetti.

As he was about to start the car and head back to his lonely house, his phone rang.

He flipped open the Motorola phone and said, "Stallings here."

He instantly recognized Maria's voice. "John, come to the house right away. I've got to show you something."

The line went dead, but Stallings didn't need any explanation. If Maria needed him, no matter what time of the night, he was going to be there as fast as possible.

Patty Levine lay on top of the covers of her bed ferociously stroking her cat, Cornelia. She'd been practicing deep, cleansing breaths she'd learned in yoga, trying to calm down from the anxiety built up since earlier in the evening. It was not only backing over the homeless man that had upset her. She realized things were unraveling with Tony Mazzetti. She had no idea where he was or what he was doing, just like he had no idea where she was or what she was doing. If that wasn't a sign of a dying relationship, she didn't know what was.

Her big concern was that her drug use had bled over into her daily life. She used to think that she'd confined it mainly to the evenings in the privacy of her own house. But she wondered if the effects of Sunday's prescription-drug binge hadn't lingered and made her less attentive than usual. She should've known the older homeless man would walk behind the car when she pulled out. She should've checked before she put the car into reverse. There were one hundred little things she should've done, but she had not. It scared her.

The irony of it was that her solution was to down another Xanax, and now, as she lay on her bed, she popped two Ambien as well. This was not the first time she'd faced irony in her drug use. It was, in fact, her overuse of the sleeping drug Ambien that had saved her life less than a year ago. While working on her first serial-killer case with John Stallings she'd allowed herself to be captured by the killer, dubbed the Bag Man, for his penchant for leaving bodies in suitcases. He'd thought he'd knocked her unconscious with two Ambien and a cocktail of painkillers, but the tolerance she'd built up through overuse allowed her to maintain her consciousness, escape, and save the girl she'd been imprisoned with.

It was also one of the reasons she cared so much about John Stallings. He was the only one who seemed to understand what she'd gone through, yet he hadn't made a big deal out of it once she came back to work. He treated her like he always had, as an equal and true partner.

The incident also solidified her relationship with Tony Mazzetti. He'd shown that he cared about things other than police work by opting to stay with her at the hospital instead of traipsing off with Stallings to find the killer who'd escaped from the scene. She wondered if he'd do the same thing today.

All that seemed like a lot to deal with for a young woman who graduated from University of Florida with a degree in psychology. That should be reason enough for Patty to keep using a few anxiety drugs now and then.

Buddy was awake late, partially on an adrenaline high from his afternoon with Lexie and partly because he was in the mood to get some work done. That was the true beauty of living above his shop. He'd always kept a small apartment downtown as a place to hide if things ever got too hot. The rent was cheap and he rarely even visited the place anymore. And it was times like this he realized how lucky he was to have a large workspace near his sleeping quarters. Glassblowing wasn't like any other art. It took space and could be very dangerous. He needed a place for his furnace, as well as plenty of space for the raw material.

The furnace got as hot as two thousand four hundred degrees and radiated heat in all directions. Buddy often used potash and soda ash as an added fuel, which vaporized almost immediately but was easy to get off the final product with a spritz of industrial cleaner. He used a cleaner the consistency of jelly. It looked like a tub of K-Y Jelly but was a hell of a lot cheaper.

He used a mold for the jar so all the jars would be very consistent in size and shape. They had to be to fit into the glass wall he had made.

Next to the furnace was the steel marver, a flat table used to work the glass and form a cool skin on the exterior of the glass.

Buddy liked the idea of practicing an art developed before the birth of Christ. Sure, it had been refined, the equipment updated, but the craft was roughly the same.

After he'd made a jar and cleaned up his workstation, Buddy carefully carried the jar containing Lexie's last breath to his apartment, where he kept his work of art safely stored behind a padded moving blanket. Once inside he carefully removed the blanket and started the simple ceremony he'd created over the years. It was very personal and, for the first few years, short. All it involved was placing his hand over each jar that contained the final breath of one of his subjects. He took a second to recall them in as much detail possible. How they had looked when he first met them, how long he had talked to them, how easily they had made the transfer to eternity.

In his first three years of this project he'd only had two jars. Then he settled in to about a jar a year until the last three years when he knew things were moving far too slowly. Back then he wouldn't have believed the pace he kept now.

He rushed the ceremony as he slipped his hand past the jars in the top, then moved onto the next row, pausing only on the jar in the middle. He remembered Alice. She had been so sweet and young. Maybe too young. It was only through the news that he had learned she was fourteen years old. She had those big blue eyes and blond hair and that thin, graceful neck that his left hand was able to envelop completely. He remembered that stunned look on her face. He'd only known her a few minutes. It was entirely a wild opportunity that he took without any hesitation.

During the lunch hour on a job in northern Flagler County she'd sat down next to him on a bench near the Intracoastal Waterway. They chatted for a few minutes. He excused himself and walked back to his van, picked out a jar he'd made only the day before, walked back, and sat next to her like he was about to finish his lunch. Instead, he casually reached across and clamped down on her windpipe like a vise. She let out a little squeak. Her legs thrashed, but he'd used so much pressure he almost didn't get her final breath. He had never heard for sure, but he thought he might have broken her neck because he'd moved so quickly and she was so fragile. For some reason during the ceremony he always paused over Alice.

He also let his hand linger over Rhonda. She'd been a few years older than most of his subjects. Classy and beautiful in her own way. He remembered seeing her eighteen-year-old daughter on the news afterwards and wondered if there was a place in his art for her too. How old would she be now? Twenty-six?

Overall he was well satisfied with his efforts and knew, given the expanse of time to look back, each of the women would appreciate how much care he had taken to save them for eternity.

Stallings arrived at his former residence, darted up the driveway, and knocked once before bursting in. Maria had sounded serious enough for him to not waste time and knock. Maria sat alone on the living-room couch, and when she looked up he could see she'd been crying. Her eyes were red and puffy and a pile of tissues sat on the coffee table they'd bought together the week after they moved into the house. She had a notebook in her lap as she slowly turned her head to Stallings with that sad face.

Stallings did a quick scan of both downstairs rooms to see if either of the kids were around. He stepped forward and said, "What's wrong? What do you have to show me?" He eased down on the couch next to her and she immediately grasped his hand. He asked one more question, "Where're the kids?"

Maria sniffled, then said, "Charlie's already asleep and Lauren's in her room studying." She held up a small leather notebook and turned it so he could see Jeanie's name on the small brass plate in the front. "This is the diary I gave Jeanie on her tenth birthday. The detectives with JSO took it for a couple of weeks after she disappeared, but because her last entry was more than two years before she disappeared they returned it to us."

Stallings couldn't recall the exact details of what they had taken from his daughter's room. It sounded about right. That was sort of thing Patty Levine would look into. Stallings was more of an interviewer and hunter.

Stallings gave Maria plenty of time. No pressure, just a gentle arm around her shoulder while she started to cry again. Finally she sniffled and wiped her eyes with a Kleenex before blowing her nose. "I never looked at the diary. It felt like an invasion of Jeanie's privacy. It was like I didn't want her to be angry when she came home. But tonight I searched through her closet and pulled this out of storage." She tapped the leather cover of the diary. "And I found an entry that might lend credence to your father's comment that he saw Jamie after she disappeared." Maria carefully opened the diary and read a passage. *"I learned more about my grandfather. My dad saw him today and thinks he lives in a rooming house on Davis Street. My mom encouraged Dad to visit him. But my dad said there was no way he would go see him."* Maria closed the diary and looked up at her husband. "That's the only entry that mentions it. I searched the whole diary a couple of times."

Stallings had looked through the diary himself when it was returned. He'd jumped to the same conclusion as the JSO detectives. He had been so frantic to find a fresh clue that he hadn't read back into the diary two years before she disappeared.

Stallings was stunned into silence, unable to do anything but stare straight ahead as a thousand possibilities raced through his brain. He clearly remembered the evening he'd come home and told Maria he'd seen his father shambling along the sidewalk on Davis. Stallings had been working the homicide of a homeless man not far away and had canvassed the entire neighborhood for witnesses. He'd slowed his car and stared at the old man but couldn't work up the nerve to stop and actually speak with him. It was one of only a few times he'd seen the man during their long period of estrangement. Stallings had seen him in lockup after he'd been arrested for drunk and disorderly. And he'd seen him on the street now and then but never anything regular. Maybe only three times in the last ten years. He remembered this time and how he'd come home and told Maria all about it after he'd thought the kids had gone to bed. It wasn't hard to extrapolate what had happened. Jeanie was a very bright girl and she would've found a way to narrow down where his father was living. The only question was if she'd purposely planned to visit him after she ran away.

So it came down to the fact that she did know how to find his father and the old man had not had a hallucination and his recollection of the visit wasn't a component of his memory problems. Stallings had a lot to talk to the old man about.

He laid his head on the back of the couch and put his feet on the coffee table. Maria nudged closer to him, then looked him in the face.

Hope flashed in Maria's dark eyes.

THIRTY-SIX

John Stallings woke to sunlight streaming in from all the windows. He'd slept through the night for the first time in months. It took him a few seconds to realize where he was and why he slept so soundly. He was on the couch in this old house and Maria was snug against his chest, snoring softly.

He worked his arm out from under Maria, who was sleeping comfortably on the couch. He would've enjoyed staying and spending a few moments with his wife in the setting he missed so desperately. Instead, he had a burning desire to speak with his father. Stallings didn't know what he could say or do to help the old man's memory, but he could try.

Stallings covered Maria with a small blanket that was always stored in the window seat of the front room.

He stepped into the bathroom, washed, and got ready to leave. He stepped out and closed the door quietly and looked up and saw Lauren. She was already dressed for school and gave him a sly smile and nod.

Stallings didn't know what to say or do, so he set out on his day.

Buddy sat at his usual Starbucks table like he did almost every Tuesday and completed his downloaded version of the *New York Times* crossword. Ever since seeing the nurse he always sat in the same place. During a lull in the constant flow of customers seeking overpriced, flavored coffee drinks, he looked up and saw her standing one person back in line. She flashed a brilliant smile and gave a cute wave. It was enough to set his heart on fire.

This time he made room at his own table for her and she didn't hesitate to sit with him.

The pretty nurse said, "I was hoping I might run into you."

Buddy was truly surprised and blurted out, "Really?"

He settled into a pleasant conversation with her and she did most of the talking. That was one thing Buddy realized a long time ago: Who wouldn't want to talk about themselves? It wasn't just that women liked to talk about themselves but also that there were very few men willing to listen. He loved to listen to women, especially pretty ones. And the more he listened to this one, the more he realized she really was a possible candidate for eternity.

Her name was Katie Massa, a divorced mother of a four-year-old boy named Tyler.

Buddy said, "How do you work the late shift at the hospital if you have a four-year-old?"

Her face lit up and she reached across and placed her hand on top of his. He could tell she liked questions like this. She liked to explain how industrious and intelligent she was. "I work three twelve-hour shifts in a row from eight p.m. to eight a.m., then I'm off for days. My mom comes over and spends the night for the three nights I have to work and I get to spend the rest of the time with Tyler. We have a great time."

"Where's his father?"

She hesitated, then said, "He works as a security agent for Blackwater. He's off in Iraq or some other place like that protecting executives and Halliburton contract workers. He's listed his official residence as Switzerland and gets away without paying any child support whatsoever."

Buddy said, "It's his loss to miss out on his son and someone as bright as you."

Katie smiled and it was dazzling.

John Stallings found his father working in the community center across the street from the house where he lived. He hung back to watch with an unmistakable pride as his father patiently supervised three younger homeless men while they worked on out-of-date computers with huge, green-screen CRTs. When it looked like he was done with his lesson, Stallings started across the floor.

The old man's face brightened, and he said, "Johnny, what are you doing here?"

"Came by to check on you, Dad."

"How'd you know I was here?"

"Your landlady told me."

James Stallings sighed and looked off into the distance. "She is a fine woman. Almost as great as your mom."

Stallings smiled.

His father looked at him and said, "Everything all right?

"Why wouldn't it be?"

"I'm a drunk and a shitty father, but I know when someone's preoccupied. Spill it and tell me what's going on."

"I worry about you, Dad."

"What are you worried about me for?"

"Your memory problem, for one thing."

"What memory problem?"

Stallings stared at his father and was about to explain some of the problems he'd been having when the old man grinned.

James Stallings said, "You can't even take a joke anymore. Oh wait, I forgot, you never had a sense of humor."

Stallings had to give his father a chuckle for that one. He led the older man over to a set of chairs and they sat, facing each other. "There's something I'd like to talk to you about, Dad."

"Fire away."

"I think Jeanie did know where you were living and would've been able to find you. What I need you to do is think real hard about your visit with her. Try and remember if she said anything that might give you a clue as to where she was going or if she was in real trouble."

The old man looked off in space and seemed to concentrate as his face clouded and his eyes began to water. Finally James Stallings said, "I'm sorry, son. I'm not even sure I know what you're talking about. I remember enough to know that I'm causing a lot of pain when I didn't mean to."

Stallings put his hand on his father's shoulder. "Don't worry about it, Dad. I want you to think about it and maybe write some notes." He knew he wouldn't get anywhere with the old man today, but he wasn't going to give up either.

Then his phone beeped into the text message from Sergeant Zuni: COME BACK TO THE OFFICE RIGHT NOW—YZ.

Tony Mazzetti heard the sergeant's voice when she called out for Stallings. It had an edge similar to the voice of his second-grade teacher, Sister Teresa, when she'd yell at him for not paying attention in geography class. Mazzetti had a similar reaction to the sergeant's call for Stallings. He almost giggled out loud thinking of all the things Stallings could have done to rate the sergeant's ire. Knowing Stallings, he probably punched a city commissioner or roughed up a doctor who didn't tell him everything he knew right that second. Whatever it was, aside from providing temporary amusement, it was not Mazzetti's business.

Then Mazzetti heard his name in the same tone. He looked around and saw Stallings hustling in from the hallway and realized she must've already sent him a summons over his cell phone. The two detectives slipped into the small office and stood silently for a moment until Yvonne the Terrible stared up at them and said in a brusque voice, "Shut the door."

Both detectives were so big that Mazzetti had to step to one side while Stallings carefully shut the door.

Then the sergeant said, "Sit." Both detectives com-

plied immediately. Then she did what all good sergeants did when they wanted to make a point: she let
them stew in silence for a few seconds. Finally she cut
her dark eyes back to them and said, "What the hell
were you two thinking?"

Neither detective answered. Mazzetti didn't want to
be the one who had to ask what she was talking about.

Then the sergeant said, "It's bad enough you're out
searching for a suspect no one even told me about, but
you broke into an apartment with no warrant or authorization. Shit, you didn't even have any probable
cause." She kept her green eyes on them like they were
bright lights and she was giving them the old third degree.

Mazzetti stuttered as he began to answer. Nothing
he said seemed to make any sense with the long pauses
and clearing his throat. Finally he said, "I'm not sure
how to answer that, boss."

Stallings got right to the point. "Sparky ratted us
out, right?"

"Sparky followed policy. He could've gone to IA.
He could've done a lot of things. Instead, he came to
me to handle it as quietly as possible because he didn't
want to go to jail if things went bad. I don't call that
ratting someone out. I call that showing some good
common sense. Something neither of you have shown."

Mazzetti was amazed how calm Stallings appeared.
Stallings looked at the sergeant and said, "Let me ask
you one question?"

"What?"

Stallings took a moment and then said in an even
voice, "Do you want us to start acting like Sparky,

strictly by the book, or do you want us to catch this goddamn killer?" He kept his eyes solid on the sergeant.

Mazzetti was impressed by Stallings.

Yvonne Zuni said, "Catch the goddamn killer, but use common sense when others are around."

THIRTY-SEVEN

After the meeting with the Yvonne the Terrible, things had happened so quickly John Stallings's head was spinning by the time he arrived at the crime scene west of U.S. 1, in a northern industrial section of Jacksonville. When a veterinary tech named Lexie Hanover had not shown up for work and her employer was unable to reach her, he got worried. After he contacted her parents, they got worried too and their first stop was her tiny apartment wedged between industrial buildings. They found their little girl lying so peacefully on the couch with the TV on that at first, they thought she'd died of some natural cause like a stroke or an embolism. It was the paramedics who realized she'd been the victim of violent crime and had the patrolman at the scene call in the body to JSO homicide.

Stallings wasn't even sure why he'd come all the way here. The crime scene investigators were doing their job efficiently and didn't need an old-time detective interfering. Mazzetti, as the lead investigator, was running things along with Sergeant Zuni. Sparky Taylor was right on top of the crime scene investigators, watching their every move. Stallings wondered if Sparky felt differently about how they handled Daniel Byrd's apartment the night before now that he was looking at another victim.

Mazzetti stepped out of the apartment and chatted with Stallings at the end of the hallway. He said, "Gotta be the same shithead. She was strangled with a ligature that left very similar marks to the girl we found over at Pine Forest Park. This shit is getting way out of hand."

"What d'you want to do?"

"We're gonna be stuck here for a long time. They've already started the canvass of the neighborhood, but so far no one saw anyone or anything suspicious. We've gotta either shit or get off the pot with Daniel Byrd. You go out there and beat the bushes. I guarantee you no one will care how you find him or what you have to do."

Stallings said, "You thought about putting it out to road patrol?"

Mazzetti shook his head. "We can't risk it getting to the media and causing him to flee to another city where they'd have to start an investigation all over again. We gotta find him." Mazzetti flipped several pages of notes and said, "I looked up some old reports in narcotics. Narcotics boys say Byrd used to be a mid-level meth dealer in the city. He always kept more than one residence. That place we checked out last night might not be his only pad. Keep that in mind."

"Got any ideas?"

"Construction sites. Even if the asshole is dealing dope again, he's dealing to construction workers. I got a couple of snitches in the construction sites and I'll see what they say.

"You got a lot to do here, Tony. Don't sweat Daniel Byrd. I'll find him."

Stallings was surprised by Mazzetti's response.

"I know you will. That's why I'll keep Sparky Taylor busy here with me."

Buddy enjoyed his afternoon. He had a couple of jobs around town but nothing big. He had messages on his phone he hadn't bothered to check. It was always someone with a cracked bay window or foggy entrance-way etching. That was not how he wanted to spend the rest of his life. There was art to create. More important, there was art to finish.

He didn't want to make the same mistakes, so instead of taking the pretty nurse, Katie Massa, at her word, he was doing a little checking on Facebook and other Internet sites. If he had done the same with the dental hygienist, he would've saved a lot of time and she might even be alive today. It made him think about how he hadn't heard anything about her body being found. He'd searched the online newspapers across the Southeast and had seen no mention of a body found in the trailer of a big rig. He supposed it was possible that the driver had dumped the load and she ended up buried at the bottom of it. Of course telling everyone she was going on a cruise for a week didn't help her chances of being missed.

Now he concentrated on Katie Massa, searching through Duval County court records as well as the county tax assessor. He saw that she'd been divorced for three years and bought a small house east of the hospital five years ago. There were a few images of her from Facebook and all of them showed what a fun-loving and vivacious girl she was, but nothing too risqué. He liked that.

Maybe he'd pay Katie Massa a visit tomorrow night. That was the next time she worked.

Tony Mazzetti was getting impatient with the crime scene team. He knew it was vital that they got any information they could from Lexie Hanover's apartment, but there was too much going on for him to wait at the apartment any longer. As he had gotten everyone moving and cleaning up their equipment, Sparky Taylor spoke.

The rotund black detective said, "Tony, you and I need to do a final sweep of the apartment."

"Says who?"

"Says policy. The lead detective, the de facto supervisor on the scene, must do a final inspection of all crime scenes to ensure nothing of value was overlooked."

Mazzetti looked at his partner and said in a much quieter tone, "Did you just read that or did you know it off the top of your head?"

Sparky was apparently starting to catch on to sarcasm and opted not to answer.

Mazzetti said, "Sparky, these are professionals. Their entire fucking job is crime scene investigation. I think we can depend on them to do a good job. Haven't you seen the TV show?"

With a straight face Sparky said, "Yes, I have and I don't care for it much. I think it's very unrealistic."

Mazzetti had plenty to do himself so he growled at Sparky, "Do the check and let me know how it goes." Mazzetti went about his business, ensuring all the neighbors were interviewed and sending someone out to check if there were any commercial surveillance cameras in the area that might pick up a car or someone walking into the building. About twenty minutes later he noticed several of the crime scene people gathered around Sparky Taylor at the main window in the small living room.

Mazzetti headed over to the group and said, "Anything important?"

Sparky said, "There's a substance here on the windowsill we should take a sample of."

A belligerent, middle-aged crime scene investigator said, "It's nothing. It's just sugar or something off a drinking glass."

Mazzetti said, "Take it." As he turned away he had to add, "Asshole."

THIRTY-EIGHT

John Stallings had worked almost nonstop after leaving the crime scene at Lexie Hanover's apartment the day before. He'd taken a few hours to go home and grab something to eat and sleep. He called Maria, hoping she might invite him to spend the night back at the family's house, but when he reached her she was back to being aloof. When he called the house earlier in the day, Lauren answered and said her mom was "out." His daughter didn't elaborate on the statement and didn't sound happy to be delivering the message. Stallings didn't have time right now to dissect his wife's emotions.

Right now Stallings had to focus on finding Daniel Byrd. The rest of the squad was busy with the standard post-homicide tasks. Sergeant Zuni had a knack for using everyone according to their strengths. Patty was trying to find any link among the victims on the Internet or through employment. Other detectives were conducting wide canvasses of the neighborhoods around the homicides. Tony Mazzetti was dealing with the medical examiner and coordinating the tremendous amount of information that came in from a group effort like this. And Sparky Taylor did the things that required cold, objective analysis or anything that kept him away from Tony Mazzetti.

Stallings had already gotten over Sparky's visit to the sergeant. These were the times and not every cop thought like him. Now Sparky was basking in the glow of finding a chemical on the windowsill of Lexie Hanover's apartment that an entire crime scene team had missed. Stallings understood how something like that could happen. This was not some clean Hollywood soundstage; this was real life. Police and crime scene investigators were human beings subject to all the failings of any human being.

When he thought of things like this, Stallings wondered if he had attended one too many Narcotics Anonymous meetings with Maria. But it was true. Cops made mistakes. The thing no one ever considered was just how few mistakes they made in the big scheme of things. Every time a convicted criminal was exonerated through DNA or some other means, it made headlines across the country. But those headlines failed to mention anything about the millions upon millions of arrests that helped protect the community and keep criminals off the streets. In this case, Sparky's hyperattention to policy had proved to be extremely beneficial.

Sergeant Zuni had given Stallings the quiet okay to do what he had to do in order to find Daniel Byrd. She wasn't like some supervisors who wanted plausible deniability. If he screwed up in some incredible way she was the kind of supervisor who wouldn't leave him out to dry. The last thing he wanted to do was jeopardize someone's career.

So Stallings had spent last evening and all day today checking construction sites and using his veritable army of informants to scour the streets of Jacksonville for one scrawny ex-con. Somehow he knew it'd be his secret weapon, super snitch Peep Moran, who would come through with the information. He had responded to a text message from the diminutive, slightly creepy street hustler asking to meet him near the spot they had first met three years ago.

He found one of the secret holes Peep had created in the hedges to view women urinating. It was amazing how often it happened and more amazing someone wanted to see it. Stallings could put up with almost anything if he could stop this killer.

Stallings leaned against the low wall where Peep was sitting quietly. Neither of them looked at the other, preferring to speak straight ahead in case someone noticed Jacksonville's most feared cop talking to one of Jacksonville's most detested perverts.

"You still staying off your own product?"

"Well, see, it's like this . . ."

"You just told me everything I need to know. When'd you start using again?"

Peep scratched his head and wiped his nose with his fingers. "I think I started using Saturday and never laid off. Monday morning had to go back to work. Things have gotten really hazy for a couple of days. But I've been out asking about your man Daniel Byrd."

"What do you got?"

"He's not real well liked on the street. No one gets very specific. No one has any clue where he stays. Looks like he has cribs all over the city."

Stallings nodded slowly, looking straight ahead.

"That's all stuff I know already, Peep. You have to work a lot harder if you want to earn a living like this."

"Who says I want to earn a living being a snitch? I just want you to leave me alone if I do you a favor now and then."

"You haven't even provided me with enough information to leave you alone."

For the first time he turned and looked at Stallings. A crooked smile crept across his face. "Maybe I haven't told you everything."

Now Stallings faced his informant. "Maybe I left you alone for too long." To make his point Stallings cracked his knuckles so loudly a woman walking by on the sidewalk stopped and stared at him.

Peep said, "Seriously, I have some real information on Daniel Byrd. But it's gonna cost you."

Stallings was not opposed to fair and equitable trade. "It depends on good how the information is, but I'm sure I can come up with something."

"A hundred bucks and a free pass the next time I get caught."

"Get caught doing what?"

"That's the idea of a free pass. You got enough juice at JSO to get me out of almost any trouble I can get into. I'm saying this information is good enough for you to give me out of the jam and pay me a hundred dollars right now."

"I'll get you off of anything that's nonviolent and doesn't involve kids. Basically means you can have any minor drug offenses."

Peep considered the offer. "Daniel Byrd lays low all the time. But he's got to collect his last paycheck at a construction site downtown. He's picking it up tonight before the construction manager leaves the office about nine o'clock." Peep smiled smugly and waited for Stallings's response.

"How on earth did you get all that?"

"A good professional never reveals his methods."

Stallings had to pat the smaller man on the shoulder and say, "If this is good information you earned your pay and a free pass."

"Detective Stallings, this is so good you'll have to take me to a fancy restaurant. I'd like to go to Chili's over near Jacksonville Landing."

Stallings laughed out loud, already thinking about who'd help him tonight at the construction site.

Patty Levine had only one flight of stairs to worry about after being summoned to the Internal Affairs office. There were so many things they could question her about that she couldn't focus or prepare for any one line of questioning. The notice to appear in the Internal Affairs office had been so swift Patty had been unable to find Sergeant Zuni. She had managed to fire off a text message as she stomped up the stairs. This was exactly how these IA guys worked: they caused your anxiety to rise and let you consider every policy infraction you could've possibly violated, hoping you'd confess to some minor violation. Patty didn't have time for this kind of shit this morning. Everyone in the squad was pushing themselves to the limit trying to find the killer of three young women in the city. She hated the idea that someone would distract her from that job.

As soon as she walked through the single, solid wooden door and looked into the spacious, comfortable office of senior IA investigator Ronald Bell she knew exactly what the problem was.

Sitting on a short couch on the back wall was the small Hispanic man Patty had hit with her car two days ago. He had a sling over one arm and a neck brace as he smiled and gave her a little wave. Sitting next to him was a sour-looking young man in an expensive suit with gaudy gold rings and gold Rolex knockoff.

Ronald Bell motioned her into the office and said, "You probably remember Mr. Alvarez, and this is his attorney, Scott Miller."

Patty realized it wasn't going to get any better from this point on.

Buddy was not familiar with this end of the hospital. The Jacksonville branch of the Shands hospital was nothing compared to the main teaching hospital in Gainesville. But it was still a giant and complex building north of the main downtown. He thought he knew his way around most of the hospital, but now he was flirting with the idea of walking past the pediatric endocrinology unit where Katie Massa worked.

It was safe to walk past it now because she didn't get to work for another few hours. Buddy didn't want anyone to recognize his face if there were questions asked later. Mainly he wanted to get a feel for the work that Katie did, to evaluate her worthiness to enter his work of art.

He had a pass that showed the time he had arrived. No one ever checked what time a visitor left. That wouldn't be an issue at all if it came up later. So many people came and went in this medical facility that it would take a lifetime to check each and every one of them out.

Buddy checked his watch and realized he had to hustle down to the main floor. He didn't feel up to taking the stairs three floors so he waited for the painfully slow elevator. As soon as he stepped off on the first floor a young internist dressed sharply in the white coat with a blue University of Florida Gator tie said, "Hey, Buddy."

Buddy smiled and nodded to the young doctor. Maybe an alibi if necessary later on.

His plan was to leave, keep his pass, and come back later tonight when Katie was working. He was certain there were several places they could go to be alone at a facility this size. First he had some jobs to check on and he needed to pick up a check at a site downtown.

He'd definitely be back later.

THIRTY-NINE

John Stallings and Tony Mazzetti had purposely left Sparky Taylor out of the loop. Daniel Byrd was a long shot but one they could take without interrupting the investigation much. He also recruited Patty Levine. Each of them drove their own county-issued cars so they could set up on surveillance at the construction site for a long time. It was the kind of plan Stallings appreciated: short, sweet, simple. He wished life could be as easily defined. Instead, tonight he'd spend long hours alone in his car trying to figure out what his latest offense to Maria was. Since her call after finding Jeanie's diary and spending the night huddled against Stallings's shoulder, she'd barely spoken to him and had been out of the house more than she'd been home. He didn't know what to make of it but couldn't stop thinking about her.

He was also worried about Patty Levine. He knew she'd had a minor accident a couple of days ago and she told him that Ronald Bell had questioned her about not telling anyone what had happened. Patty also said he had asked her a few questions about the fight in the squad bay and if she'd seen what had happened to one of the bundles of pills the detectives were putting into evidence. She said the inquiry was casual, but Stallings didn't trust the son of a bitch any more than he'd trust the president of Iran.

The entire sheriff's office had followed the progress of the detective injured in the fight. He had suffered serious head trauma but appeared to be recovering. Stallings had heard that the detective had large gaps in his memory and drugs were missing from the seizure. The narcotics guys had already been questioned and any moron could see the next step would be interviewing every crime/persons detective who'd been present during the fight. It was nothing that bothered Stallings, but he felt anxiety for Patty. He wasn't quite sure why. She'd seemed distracted over the past month. He had his own problems but always tried to stay tuned in to his partner. God knew she'd been a huge help to him over the last few years.

But now Stallings wanted to focus on finding the jerkweed Daniel Byrd. Nothing indicated that this was a guy who contributed to society in any way. When someone like Peep Moran looks down on you, you're not scoring too high on the social ladder. Stallings didn't care what it would take to catch this guy. He had an idea they'd be successful.

Katie Massa was in a pretty good mood. Often when she left her son with her mother, Tyler would cry as she walked out the door. It drained and distracted her at work when she needed to concentrate on helping the kids on the ward. But tonight Tyler waved a cheerful good-bye and she felt very comfortable leaving him until she was able to roll home about eight o'clock in the morning. This was the first day of her three-day schedule and she knew she'd have plenty of energy to make it through the shift. It was the middle day that caused her problems. On the third and final day of her schedule she was looking forward to four days off to do whatever she wanted. About every three weeks she and Tyler would take the two-and-a-half-hour drive down to Orlando and visit one of the theme parks. She had an annual pass to Disney, MGM, and SeaWorld. Often she'd leave it up to Tyler where he wanted to go as they drove into Orlando. Sometimes he wanted to go see the big fish, Shamu. But sometimes he wanted to see the big mouse, Mickey.

Katie wanted to give Tyler a magical childhood, and she felt like she got a good start on it by taking him on these quick trips. She knew in a few years he wouldn't want to spend as much time with his mother. Katie was determined that the memories Tyler had of spending time with her would be fun and beautiful.

One of the few regrets she had since her divorce was that she would like to have another child close enough in age for Tyler to play with him or her. He'd be a great big brother. But he was already four and she had no real prospects for a man in her life.

She did like Buddy, the guy who had turned her on to the downloaded crosswords from the *New York Times*. He had a very warm smile and friendly manner and she could tell he was intelligent. She wasn't real clear about what he did for a living but knew it was in the construction industry. He'd mentioned that he owned his own glass company, but she wasn't sure if that meant windows or something more artistic like etching. She'd given him her phone number. Something she didn't do very often.

Katie hoped he'd call her. It'd been some time since she'd gone out on a date. She wasn't even necessarily interested in sex, just some adult conversation with a few drinks. It seemed like the last year the only adult conversation she had was hearing about her mother's conflict with her elderly neighbors.

She came in the hospital through the employee entrance in the rear of Shands and said hello to the lone security guard, who rarely got off a specially reinforced stool near the door. She often wondered why the hospital didn't put the security guard in the lobby with the public coming in and out, instead of the elderly female volunteers who seldom asked for identification and could barely hear the requests for the room numbers of patients.

She skipped the elevator altogether and took the rear stairwell to pediatric endocrinology on the fourth floor. There were five babies on the ward tonight under two years old. If she did nothing else but comfort them and make one of them giggle she felt like she had accomplished a lot both as a person and as a nurse.

She wished every day was like today.

Tony Mazzetti was already agitated when they set up a three-car surveillance around the construction site in downtown Jacksonville. Stallings explained that a reliable informant had said Byrd would pick up his paycheck around nine o'clock. That didn't bother Mazzetti; what he was pissed off about was that the man running the finances of the construction site was *his* informant, Joey Big Balls. Joey had known he was looking for Daniel Byrd and hadn't said anything. It was some passive-aggressive bullshit that guys like Joey got off on. Mazzetti lived by a code that included punishing people who double-crossed him. Something terrible would have to happen to Joey Big Balls. Mazzetti wished Joey was still on parole so he could get him violated, if he could get one of the lazy-assed parole officers to fill out the paperwork and go before a judge. With his latest experience at the parole office, he doubted he'd get that to happen.

The other thing bothering Mazzetti was his quickly deteriorating relationship with Patty Levine. She had been cordial and professional as they prepared to go out on surveillance, but when he asked if she would like a ride to his car with she said, "We'll probably need at least three cars after. I'll take my own." It was the professional and right thing to do but not what she would've said two weeks ago. If that wasn't a clear signal that his girlfriend didn't want to spend any more time with him, nothing was.

Mazzetti had told Stallings if they saw Byrd, to allow him to walk into the trailer so that Mazzetti could confront Joey Big Balls too. He recognized Stallings was not one of those detectives you had to explain everything to in great detail. For a jerk and an asshole he was pretty bright.

Mazzetti needed time away from the massive crush of leads and the constant requests for updates by the command staff of JSO. This was a perfect little job for the evening.

*   *   *

Stallings monitored a handheld radio that had been rendered almost obsolete by new, reliable cell phones. But nothing could replace radio's ability to broadcast information to more than one person at a time. When conducting a surveillance or in a chase, it was vital to let every other unit know exactly where you were and what you were doing. It was important to be able to broadcast what kind of threat the suspect posed. If they were armed and dangerous. If there was an active warrant. Or if they were mentally unstable. A cop had to approach each situation differently, and getting the right information was imperative.

Tonight the three detectives from the crimes/persons squad were on a rarely used frequency that was not monitored by dispatch. That meant they could speak more casually and say things they normally wouldn't say over the radio. This included somewhat idle chatter while they waited for Daniel Byrd.

Stallings heard the crackle of static before Mazzetti said, "The second he steps into the trailer we'll move in. Simple, clean, and quick."

Stallings had to chuckle. Experience had taught him nothing was ever clean, quick, or simple. That's why he always tried to stay prepared mentally and said out loud to nobody, "Is today the day that changes the rest of my life?" As he said it, he reached down with his right hand and felt his Glock Model 22 .40-caliber semiautomatic pistol tucked snugly into his Safariland holster on his right hip. He also had an ASP expandable baton in the rear left pocket of his jeans. He was too old to worry about punching people if he had something hard he could strike them with instead. But it was still his hope that Byrd would surrender without an argument. While he was hoping, he wanted Byrd to also confess to three murders and help them find Leah Tischler while he was at it. Those were the kind of wishes Stallings would ask if anyone ever cared.

Over the course of forty-five minutes a number of vehicles had rolled into and out of the lot directly in front of the administration trailer on the site of the renovation of one of Jacksonville's older but more elegant office buildings.

At nine o'clock a truck rumbled to a stop directly in front of the trailer. Stallings caught a glimpse of the driver as he jumped down, leaving the truck running, and entered the trailer without knocking.

Stallings reached for the radio when he heard Mazzetti say, "That's our man, that's our man, let's go." The homicide detective had a tinge more excitement in his voice than normal. He liked to see passion in police officers. Even a jerk-off like Mazzetti.

Stallings didn't rush as he put his Impala in drive and rolled across the parking lot a little faster than a jog. Mazzetti peeled up limestone dust as he skidded across the lot, struggling to maintain control of his big Ford Crown Vic. Patty followed Stallings's lead and did the smartest thing she could've, waited in the lot. Stallings and Mazzetti reached the front door of the trailer at the same time.

Mazzetti drew his gun and said, "I don't care if this is just an interview. This asshole has a long record and has been hard to find."

Stallings agreed but left his gun in his holster as he pulled open the door. Stallings scanned the entire trailer but only saw an older, heavyset man sitting behind a desk.

Mazzetti looked at the man and said, "Where'd he go?"

The man said, "Who?"

Then Stallings heard the truck as it kicked shell and dust into the trailer.

Mazzetti scowled at the man behind the desk and said, "I won't forget this, Joey."

The man just shrugged.

FORTY

Patty suppressed a giggle as Mazzetti's Crown Vic swerved one way then the other in the loose gravel parking lot. John Stallings drove slowly, under control, directly to the front of the trailer. The one look from Stallings told her someone needed to watch the outside of the building. She had already concluded that three detectives inside the filthy trailer was too many. She didn't have to prove herself to anyone. Stallings appreciated her tactical sense and she could've had worse examples set for her.

So she sat in her Ford Freestyle, which was great for surveillance because she looked like a young soccer mom or a junior partner in a law firm downtown. No one gave her a second look until she popped on the hidden red and blue lights or blasted the siren.

Almost as soon as she'd seen Mazzetti and John Stallings step through the front door of the trailer, she noticed someone scurry from the far side of the trailer directly to the truck. It was so fast and unexpected that it took a moment for her to realize it was Daniel Byrd. The truck was pointed toward the exit when he jumped in and he was out of the lot in less than five seconds. Patty knew to stay on him until the others caught on to what had happened.

Patty tried the radio but realized neither of the other detectives had carried one into the trailer. She pulled out onto the street and barely caught a glimpse of the truck turning right at the next corner. Patty didn't want to get into a high-speed chase with someone whom, at this point, they just wanted to interview. The Freestyle wasn't the vehicle to push into a high-speed pursuit anyway. She'd use her natural advantage and wait until Mazzetti and Stallings could catch up to her.

After she made another turn and saw the truck clearly in front of her, she risked a quick call on her cell phone to Stallings.

Stallings answered on the first ring. He said, "I was about to call you on the radio. Did you see him when he came out?"

"Of course. I was where I was supposed to be. Now we're on Myrtle Avenue headed north. He left in a hurry, but his speed dropped back down and there's not much traffic."

"You rock, Patty."

She let a broad smile slide across her face. She needed to hear something like that today. All she could say was, "You bet your ass I do."

Tony Mazzetti was fuming as he raced out to his car and kicked rocks in the air on his way out the exit. Thank God Patty was smart enough to wait outside in case something like this happened. Mazzetti realized that Joey Big Balls would've probably spotted him and Stallings earlier, but he never would've figured the fat man for a double-crosser. He didn't know why Joey had felt like he had to warn Daniel Byrd. Mazzetti knew he'd pay for it one way or another.

He fell in behind Stallings, who was catching up to Patty. There was no way to justify this turning into a high-speed chase, just like there was no way he was gonna let that shithead Byrd give him the slip.

His radio scanned two frequencies. The one he, Patty, and Stallings were using and the main frequency. He'd heard some traffic earlier relating to a search warrant at the north end of the city. Now he noticed several panicked transmissions and realized something had gone terribly wrong. First he heard the dreaded "Shots fired" call; then he heard a narcotics sergeant named Fernandes request fire rescue and any available unit for a perimeter. Fernandes was a cool customer and wouldn't call for the help unless it was needed. It was an unusual call for a slow Wednesday night in Jacksonville and Mazzetti knew every cop in the city was headed that way right now.

Mazzetti used the local frequency to raise Patty. "What's your twenty, Patty?"

"We're north on Moncrief a few miles from U.S. 1. He has no idea I'm behind him."

Mazzetti said, "Excellent. I'm a minute behind you." Mazzetti smiled, thinking about how smart his girlfriend was. If she was still his girlfriend. He'd missed talking to her the past few days, but he didn't want to keep pestering her on the phone. He didn't want her to think he was too needy. She'd made it clear she wasn't ready to move in with him, so he told himself not to crowd her.

He hadn't even heard about her accident until today. She said it was okay, but the IA inquiry had gotten to her. He weighed the benefits of punching that asshole Ronald Bell right in the face. He'd also heard Bell and his IA cronies were looking into some missing pills. They'd interviewed some of the narcotics guys this morning and already the rumor mill churned out all kinds of theories. One of those theories was that the pills had been taken from the crimes/persons squad during the fight with the gangbangers. Mazzetti knew it was all a bunch of bullshit and wished the IA cock-suckers would try and work a real case once in a while.

His radio came to life again as more and more re-sources were dispatched to the search warrant scene at the far end of the county. The helicopter and a dozen more patrol cars were racing that way right now. Three detectives on a slow-speed surveillance didn't rate any resources. Mazzetti figured the media was on its way north as well. Why not? The SWAT team guys had cool uniforms and big guns and gave pretty good sound bites for the late news. He couldn't even say they were chasing a serial killer because they weren't. At least not yet. Byrd was only a person of interest.

It was after ten o'clock when he wondered how long it would be until they could safely corner this guy. It wasn't like the old days when no one cared how fast you chased someone or the reasons you were in the chase. It was all part of police work. But nowadays only certain cars could be in the chase and only with a sergeant on hand. And they had to be able to articulate the reasons they'd risk the public's safety. They had to be chasing a violent criminal who posed an immediate threat.

This might be a very long night.

* * *

About twenty minutes into the surveillance, John Stallings took the lead and let Patty back her Freestyle off the target vehicle. Just in case Daniel Byrd had been paying enough attention to recognize the same vehicle had been behind him for miles and miles of Jacksonville city streets. Mazzetti, in his more obvious police-car-looking Crown Vic, was the team's last choice to follow the crafty construction worker.

Byrd hadn't tried to get on the interstate, which made Stallings think his destination was relatively close by. As soon as Byrd stopped and got out of the truck, Stallings would make his move. At this point, Stallings didn't care what tactics he had to use. He had questions that needed answering. Right now Byrd was acting calm. He probably thought he'd lost them as soon as he left the construction site and was chuckling about how inept Jacksonville cops were.

Stallings saw their chance. The truck pulled into a surprisingly crowded McDonald's parking lot. He checked his watch, wondering where so many young people came from at eleven o'clock on a Wednesday night and why their parents would allow them out so late on a school night. He picked up the radio and said, "He's pulling into the McDonald's lot. I don't know that we can get him before he walks inside."

Mazzetti's voice crackled over the radio. "Let's trap him inside."

"There's lot of kids jammed inside."

"We'll be very low-key."

As Stallings drove into the lot he saw a JSO patrol vehicle with a young, burly officer talking sternly to three young men. He squeezed in right next the patrol car and badged the officer as he got out. The young cop immediately ignored the boys he was scolding and walked over to Stallings.

Stallings said, "Can you give us a hand real quick?"

"Absolutely. I'm working a contract here and they wouldn't let me leave to go to the scene of the shooting. I've been pissed off about it all night. What do you got?"

"Just a little jerk-off we need to question. He pulled up in the truck over there a minute ago and walked inside. I got two other detectives with me."

The burly patrolman scratched his short brown hair said, "I work here every Wednesday night because for some reason this place is a Wednesday-night gathering spot. There's only this door and the door on the opposite side and you can see both doors from both sides. I'd say we got this guy covered."

Stallings saw Patty and Mazzetti automatically walk to the opposite door. This time Mazzetti didn't draw his pistol. Daniel Byrd stood a couple of people back in the line to the counter. Stallings heard the patrolman muttering about missing out on the perimeter at the scene of the SWAT shootout. Thank God no JSO personnel had been hit. The jumbled reports coming in over the radio made it sound like there were two dead drug dealers and two that had run into the neighborhood.

As Stallings entered the door, the kids moved out of his way. He thought it was the big uniformed patrolman behind him who was making a path and he was glad he'd asked for the help. Then he realized his mistake.

Daniel Byrd looked over his shoulder and immediately noticed the patrolman. Like any good career criminal he picked up on Stallings and checked the rest of the room, making Mazzetti for another detective. Stallings prepared for a fight. But the wily parole violator was one step ahead of him.

Byrd shoved a young man standing next to him. Then he pushed another boy from behind. Within seconds a brawl had started at the counter and quickly spread through the McDonald's like a virus.

Stallings struggled to reach Byrd at the front of the counter and caught a glimpse of the smaller man as he leaped over the counter and bolted through the kitchen.

Stallings tried to get Mazzetti's attention, frantically pointing to the back of the restaurant. He turned around, worked his way to the door, and saw that he could cut off Byrd before he reached his truck. He could hear the patrolman inside shouting for everyone to calm down.

Byrd came from the corner of the building, saw Stallings, and instantly reversed direction. Stallings gave chase, and as he cleared the corner of the McDonald's he saw Byrd forcing a young man off a Honda motorcycle. The man had been in the drive-through lane. Before Stallings could reach him Byrd jumped on the bike again and screamed out of the lot.

All Stallings could do was get back to his car. Now it was a chase whether anyone had authorized it or not.

FORTY-ONE

Patty saw Stallings and Mazzetti jump in their cars and race north on the New Kings Road but she couldn't, in good conscience, leave a single patrolman to handle all the fights erupting inside the McDonald's. She drew her expandable baton from her pocket and popped it open, catching the attention of all kids closest to her. They took one look at the extended metal pipe and the woman wielding it and scattered.

The uniformed cop worked his way across the room to Patty and the kids slowly calmed down. The patrolman used a good, military voice to shout, "This restaurant is closed. Anyone I put my hands on after the count of thirty goes to jail."

Patty liked this guy and the way he got things done. The kids scurried like cockroaches when he shouted.

Patty chuckled with the patrolman, who had to listen to the McDonald's manager complain about losing all of his business for the night. The heavyset manager said, "I pay JSO to send an extra deputy here every Wednesday and Saturday night to keep things calm so I can make money, not to chase away all my customers."

The patrolman had taken it because this was a special situation. Most sheriff's offices offered a contract position whereby restaurants and other businesses could hire a deputy off-duty. It was more expensive than a regular rent-a-cop but much more effective because the deputy had a gun, was trained to use it, and could make arrests.

The uniformed patrolman looked at the manager and said, "Some of your customers are hanging around, getting tire irons and knives to make the fights more interesting. You want me to call them back in?"

The manager turned around and started shouting at the staff instead.

Patty hustled out to her Freestyle and headed north, picking up the radio. "Where are you guys?"

Stallings came on the radio and said, "The son of a bitch has led us all over Jacksonville and now we're coming south on U.S. one back by you. He's calmed way down and I don't think he realizes we're still after him. Tony stays one street east and I stay one street west, and somehow we've kept him roughly in sight."

Within five minutes Patty had pulled behind the motorcycle. Daniel Byrd had not seen any of their vehicles at the McDonald's and had no reason to think the mundane family SUV was a police vehicle. When he took a ramp onto I-95 southbound, Patty let Stallings take over and follow him onto the interstate. She hit the gas and raced along the surface streets to keep pace with the motorcycle. Most people on the streets had no concept of all the surveillances that went on with unmarked police cars. Patty's father always said he could pick out the unmarked police cars, but he meant the ones that looked like police cars. The Ford Crown Victorias or Dodge Chargers. He had no idea about all the other cars that were thrown into a modern police department's fleet, specifically for these types of operations. To the average person on the street she looked like a frantic housewife rushing home at 11:30 at night.

Stallings came on the radio and said, "He's getting off the interstate and we're close to his apartment. I bet that's where he's headed."

Patty had the address on an information sheet and knew the area well. Mazzetti came on the radio, "I'm on my way over there now."

By the time Patty pulled past the apartment building, Byrd was walking in the front door and the motorcycle was parked on the sidewalk a few feet away. Stallings had called it right.

You couldn't buy that kind of experience.

John Stallings didn't use the radio. Instead he pulled alongside Tony Mazzetti's Crown Vic a block away from the apartment building. They had things to discuss that didn't need to be put out over the radio no matter how rarely the frequency was monitored.

Stallings rolled down his window so they were almost face-to-face, saying, "You think we need help on this?"

Mazzetti shook his head. "Fuck no."

"Sounds like the SWAT thing is resolved and there'll be a lot of cops on the street."

"And what do we say? We really need to talk to this guy? Or maybe we have the SWAT team hit his apartment for stealing a motorcycle."

"Then the question is: do you want to wait or go in?"

Mazzetti said, "We gotta wait. He could barricade himself inside and then we would really need to call the SWAT team. If Patty stays where she is and we stay on this end we can cover that front door easy. That's the only way in or out of the building and the way he parked the bike means he's not staying too long."

Stallings nodded and pulled his car to the other side of the street. He settled in to watch the motorcycle. He glanced at his watch; nearly midnight and he was exhausted.

This could be the big break in the case. He couldn't think of another reason why this guy would run from them so hard. They had to get him in custody and interviewed as quickly as possible. There was no way Stallings was leaving this neighborhood without Daniel Byrd.

FORTY-TWO

John Stallings rubbed his eyes hard and shook his head, trying to wake himself up. It was after 2 A.M. and he was wondering when Daniel Byrd would be out of the apartment and back on the bike. Mazzetti had been stealthy and walked along the sidewalk to yank the spark plug wire loose on the Honda. It would only take Byrd a second to figure out what the problem was, but that would give them enough time to grab him.

Stallings had used all the veteran police tricks to stay awake over the years. He ate sunflower seeds one at a time, knowing that the activity of pulling them apart and eating them would occupy his mind enough to stay awake. He had gone the caffeine route, first with coffee then the various energy drinks, but he never cared for them much. He tried the old trick of drinking water constantly so he had to pee relentlessly and therefore couldn't doze off. The downside of that was he kept filling and emptying a Gatorade bottle he kept in the car. Tonight he was using an old standard. He would hold his breath for as long as he possibly could, sometimes as much as a minute and thirty seconds.

That kept him awake and supercharged his heart rate; it took ten minutes to recover completely before he'd do it again.

As he was about to measure another breath on his Timex Ironman watch, the radio crackled and he heard Patty Levine say, "Someone is at the front door."

A few seconds later Mazzetti said, "Gotta be him. As soon as he goes to the bike let's grab him."

Stallings was close to the bike. All he had to do was pop out of his car, and with a sprint, be on top of Byrd before the shithead ran. Stallings mumbled, "Is today the day that changes my life?"

Patty came on the radio again. "I don't think it's him. It looks like a female. She stepped outside for a moment and then stepped back into the lobby. It's a white female in a yellow dress with the flower pattern on it."

Stallings was one step ahead and slipped out of his car with the radio in his hand. He crept along the sidewalk, sticking close to the scraggly bushes and occasional garbage can. Then he heard Patty say the woman was out of the building. A moment later he saw the yellow dress and was surprised to see the woman walk directly to the motorcycle.

Stallings paused a few feet away looking through an untrimmed ficus hedge. After a moment he realized what was happening. Daniel Byrd had slipped on one of the dresses they'd seen in his closet. He had a small satchel slung over his shoulder and was wearing a baseball cap. From a distance he would look like a woman.

Patty realized it at the same time and said over the radio, "That's him, that's him. Byrd is wearing the yellow dress."

Stallings had the radio low and close to his ear so Byrd wouldn't hear. But he couldn't help but notice Mazzetti's car roar to life as he mashed the gas and raced down the street toward him.

Byrd's head snapped as he held on to the satchel tight and started to sprint like only lean ex-cons could sprint. He was like a rocket as he started down the sidewalk. He was smart enough to wear tennis shoes instead of high heels with the dress, which barely slowed him at all.

Luckily for Stallings all he had to do was step out from behind a hedge and swing his arm in a classic clothesline move. He caught the fleeing felon at the top of his chest and the momentum carried Stallings's arm into his chin, not only upending Byrd, but damn near knocking him unconscious as well.

Stallings looked down at the moaning man, and all he could say was, "Sweet."

FORTY-THREE

An hour after capturing Daniel Byrd, Stallings sat across from him in an interview room in the Land That Time Forgot. Stallings liked the way Mazzetti was playing this slow and cool. He had purposely left the room to allow Byrd to stew in his own paranoia. He was letting the wily suspect imagine the worst. Stallings knew to just sit there and look mean.

Mazzetti hated calling so late to advise Sergeant Zuni that they were interviewing someone. He told her not to rush down to the PMB and he'd let her know if something came of it.

For Byrd's part, once he was caught he'd offered no more resistance. He was still in the patterned yellow dress and had a red mark across his cheek where Stallings's arm had ridden up his chest during the clothesline. Byrd was putting on a cocky act, but Stallings knew jerks like this started to crumble as soon as they realized they were going back to jail. The key was finding what Byrd wanted. If they had a carrot, they didn't need to use the stick.

Mazzetti came back in, settled into the empty chair,

and stared hard at Daniel Byrd. Byrd leaned back in his chair, but there was only so much coolness you could have with your hands cuffed behind your back while you were wearing a dress.

Mazzetti said, "Anything you want to talk to us about, Daniel?"

"Not a thing."

Stallings could hear the North Florida twang in those few words. He had known several families named Byrd in the Jacksonville area. One of them over in Baker County. These Byrds had a similar accent but a different outlook on life. The Byrds he knew worked hard and valued education above anything else. It made him want to smack this Byrd right in the face.

Byrd said, "What charges are you holding me on?"

"You got to be kidding me."

"Do I look like I'm kidding?"

Stallings had to cut in at this point. "You're wearing a yellow dress. So I would have to say, yes, you do look like you're kidding a little bit."

Byrd tried to give him a hard look, but he was an amateur trying to fight in the heavyweight division.

Mazzetti said, "We got a lot of questions and in the long run it'd help you out to be our friend."

"You didn't tell me what the charges are?"

Mazzetti stood quickly, scooting the chair back with his legs. "First off, a violation of parole. There's the grand theft with the motorcycle. Assault on the motorcycle rider. Fleeing and eluding the police. And resisting arrest."

"How did I resist arrest?"

Stallings said, "Really? All those charges plus your past history and you're worried about a misdemeanor resisting arrest? Son, have you got some kind of learning disability we should know about?"

"The only thing I'm ashamed of is that I let an old geezer like you catch me."

Stallings gave a chuckle. "That'll go over big at Raiford."

The comment hit home and caused Byrd to lose some of his cockiness. His brown eyes darted around the room and he fidgeted in his seat. But he didn't ask for a lawyer and had told Stallings he was considering cooperating. He was in custody so they had already read him his Miranda rights. Stallings was a little surprised he hadn't asked for an attorney then, but as the questioning had continued he was shocked the man was willing to sit there. He really didn't want to go back to prison.

Finally Byrd said, "What kind of questions do you have?"

Stallings and Mazzetti had already worked out this little dance. Stallings would ask general questions about Leah Tischler; then Mazzetti would build up to the homicides.

Stallings said, "I'd like to ask you about this girl." He slid a photograph of Leah Tischler across the table, and Byrd seemed to take a good long look at it.

Byrd said, "I've never seen her before."

"You run into her within the last two weeks?"

Byrd shook his head. "No, no way. I've been working every shift I could the last month trying to get enough money together to pay off my traffic fines so I could get a job driving a cement truck."

Stallings studied the younger man's face carefully and looked over at Mazzetti, who made a few notes but was also trying to get a fix. Stallings said, "So you don't want to say anything about this girl?"

"That's not what I said. What I'm saying about her is that I never met her and have no information on her."

Now Mazzetti got involved and said, "What about Kathy Mizell over by the health education building? The girl at the bus stop."

Once again Byrd kept calm and looked Mazzetti directly in the eye. "I have no idea what you're talking about. Why am I here really? Why were you guys chasing me? I've done a lot of shit, but I don't know what you guys are asking about."

Mazzetti said, "Whose dresses were those in your apartment?"

Byrd looked down at his dress and then gave a flat stare back to Mazzetti. "Really, dude, you can't figure it out?"

Stallings admired the young man's attitude.

Byrd said, "Take a wild guess why I can't let the guys at work know I wear them. Construction workers aren't known for their tolerance. This is the first time a dress ever really helped me out, other than to make me feel special and better than I really am."

That caught Stallings by surprise, but he had to admit the man was very cool and calm if he had really killed anyone.

The door opened to the interview room and Patty Levine stepped in. This was a very unusual move among the detectives. Mazzetti and Stallings immediately knew something big had happened. Stallings looked at her, waiting to hear whatever vital news she had. The way Byrd looked at her, Stallings could tell he might've been a cross-dresser but he wasn't gay.

Patty said, "He's not our man."

At the same time Mazzetti and Stallings said, "Why?"

"Because they just found a body in the courtyard at Shands hospital. She'd been strangled with a ligature sometime between ten and midnight. We were on Byrd the whole time and he never came close to the hospital."

Stallings knew there was a lot of information to verify and forensics to ensure that this was a victim of the same killer, but somehow, in that moment and looking at the lack of response from Daniel Byrd, he knew there was still a serial killer loose on the streets of Jacksonville.

FORTY-FOUR

Buddy sat straight on a stool as he ate his chicken salad sandwich on whole wheat at the counter in his kitchen. The last jar needed for his work of art sat on the counter next to him. He stared at it with mixed emotions. It was the ending of so many things. He'd taken extra time to blow it just right and the glass glistened in the overhead light of his kitchen.

It was early for lunch, not even quite eleven o'clock, but most of the work he was doing today was in the shop and any time he felt hungry he could run upstairs and grab a quick bite. That's how *Men's Health* suggested men eat. Lots of small meals staggered throughout the day.

The TV was off and he didn't have a newspaper open in front of him. He was enjoying the satisfaction he felt from completing another section of his work of art. He had also learned not to jerk on the cord too hard or you could break the subject's neck. He had been lucky last night to be able to grab Katie's final breath, but it had been just that, luck.

He'd hardly slept after the ceremony to put Katie in

her rightful place. From the first moment he put his plan in action it had gone almost perfectly. He'd surprised her, calling pediatric endocrinology from the phone in the lobby. He'd been in the hospital enough to know they were cheap on security cameras and both cameras in the lobby pointed to the front. Easy enough to avoid. He'd worn an oversized Jacksonville Jaguars Windbreaker because it disguised him a little bit if someone had happened to see him and it had giant pockets where he had stored one of his homemade jars.

Buddy still had his pass from earlier in the day and had the sticker on the outside of his windbreaker so no one would ever doubt he had permission to be inside the hospital.

Katie had wanted to meet him in the coffee shop, but he met her at the elevator and led her out to the rear garden. It was a well-maintained courtyard designed to give patients a place to step outside into a world that wasn't windy and usually had shade from one side of the building or the other. Even if there had been cameras out there it was too dark in most places to pick up anything. No one was out enjoying the night. Not with the things you could see inside, like *American Idol* or *America's Next Top Model*. Sometimes Buddy wondered how culture could continue with crap like that on the airwaves, drawing so much attention. He wished people took more of an interest in serious art. If more people appreciated art, maybe he could've made a living at it instead of doing it as a sideline to his plateglass business. Sometimes he forgot how bitter he was about people's shallowness.

He was glad that for one evening people had been occupied and hadn't bothered to come out to see the natural beauty of the gardens or the moon or the brilliantly lit constellations. As they sat on a hard patio bench in the corner of the courtyard near a low, manicured hedge of decorative plants, Katie had appreciated the majesty of the heavens, staring with those beautiful eyes and a relaxed, pleasant expression. He had wasted no time pulling out the cord and slipping it around her neck so quickly she'd never even realized it was there. Then he pulled as hard as he could with both hands to give her that shock and awe he needed to start his own artistic process. But her graceful neck did not have the muscle girth to withstand the stress and he felt a sickening snap.

He'd moved quickly, not releasing the cord until he had the jar in place. It'd been awkward and he had felt a little panic as he rushed through his process, but as he released the cord he realized there was just the slightest exhalation on Katie's part. Not enough to fog the jar, but he could feel it gently on the fingers of his right hand as he held the jar to her lovely mouth.

He had not been able to sit and enjoy the process for fear of being discovered at any moment. He quickly dragged her limp body from the round patio table and laid her between two rows of decorative plants. She would be easy to find. He'd have enough time to slip out the south door, which had no camera and no security personnel. He took a moment to look down at Katie's pleasant face. She looked very peaceful. He wondered if it was because her death came so swiftly. There were some marks on her neck, but her beautiful face had not been distorted and his memory of her would stay just like that.

The experience had been so positive he'd found himself whistling the theme to *Hogan's Heroes* while working earlier in the morning. He couldn't remember the last time he had whistled. Sometimes whistling set off a coughing fit so he had all but abandoned his childhood habit of whistling to keep himself focused.

He finished his sandwich and was about to turn on the radio to see if there were any news reports about a body being found in one of the city's finest hospitals. As he stood from the stool he heard a familiar sound and froze in his place, wondering who it could be.

Someone was on the stairway to his apartment.

John Stallings lay on the double bed, in his drab bedroom, in his lonely house in Lakewood. He'd slept for a couple of hours, but now, midmorning, he was wide awake and staring at the ceiling. He knew that at forty he shouldn't be working thirty-six hours in a row. But sometimes that's what the job called for. He'd been fitfully asleep until his cell phone had rung a few minutes ago. It was an analyst with JSO who hadn't realized he'd worked all night long. She had a question about the body found in the gardens at Shands hospital. Stallings explained that aside from hearing about it early in the morning he had no details.

Sergeant Zuni had been in a tough position personnel wise and had sent another team to handle the scene at Shands. She had put Sparky Taylor in charge of the crime scene investigation and sent Tony Mazzetti home to grab a few hours' sleep.

Now Stallings realized he couldn't sleep wondering about the new victim. He got dressed, ate a bowl of cinnamon sugar oatmeal, and headed over to the hospital.

But he was still dog tired.

* * *

Detective Luis Martinez was relatively new to the crimes/persons squad. He'd been brought over from Auto Theft less than a year ago to work on the Bag Man case. While he missed his friends over in Auto Theft and even the guys from patrol, he liked being a detective. Now, because of a whole line of strangulations, he had finally been assigned his own homicide. He worked with a partner named Bill Talbot who was all but useless and constantly had an excuse not to go out on interviews or work at night. Luis couldn't very well rat him out to the sergeant; that was not the way things were done. But that didn't mean he had to stop moving at his own pace.

Since the discovery of a female body in a car parked at Jacksonville Landing last Saturday, he'd been in almost constant motion. He was so excited about being allowed to run his own investigation that he wasn't jealous about not being included in this new serial-killer case. He liked working with the people in crimes/persons and knew he could learn a lot from Tony Mazzetti. The guy was a legend in JSO for his clearance rate and work ethic.

John Stallings was another guy he could learn from. The guy had been through everything life could throw at him and still kept a positive attitude and knew how to look out for other people. He was a cop's cop.

Instead, Luis Martinez had been saddled with a detective who had retired three years ago but apparently had failed to tell anyone. John Talbot was a nice fella who loved his wife and kids. He also loved donuts, beer, ESPN *SportsCenter*, and, way down the list, police work.

Luis didn't allow that to slow him down. He'd always give Talbot the option of coming with him on interviews, but if the older detective was busy or had other plans, Luis just went on his way.

The victim in this case, Cheryl Kazen, had been found dead from multiple stab wounds in the backseat of her Chrysler 300. She'd been a very attractive woman, but the more he looked into her background, the more suspects he found. She had a string of former boyfriends who all had records, and all the ex-boyfriends he'd questioned hated her guts.

The only real forensic evidence gathered from the car was a second blood sample. The lab had developed a DNA sample for both blood types. One matched Cheryl and the other was not in any of their databases. Luis had taken several DNA test kits on interviews, but only found two of the former boyfriends worth asking for a swab.

Now he was down to the second line of interviews. People the victim knew and dealt with occasionally. He was hoping to pick up some speck of information that, when viewed with the whole case, might point Luis in the right direction.

He was at a building owned by the victim and her family and rented to some kind of glass company.

Luis Martinez was in a shirt and tie with his Glock .40 caliber on his hip and his JSO detective's shield next to it. There was no reason to hide who he was in a homicide investigation, and having the gun and badge in view tended to intimidate people. That made up for the fact that he was only five foot six. At least in his mind it compensated for his lack of height.

All the doors to the shop were open, but it looked empty. An air-conditioner unit that cooled the second floor was running, so Luis started up the wooden stair-case to the door at the top.

FORTY-FIVE

Tony Mazzetti shuddered at the amount of information he needed to get from hospital administrators. He'd already been appalled at the lax security measures around the hospital and learned only half of the very few security cameras even worked. There was also the issue of visitors coming and going. The names were listed on the computer alphabetically but not always with a date associated with the visit.

The initial impression he'd gotten of the victim, Katie Massa, was that she was an extremely well-liked and friendly young lady who had no obvious enemies around the hospital. Two detectives had already questioned her ex-husband, by phone because he was in Afghanistan with a private security firm.

In most cases where a woman was missing or killed, if the cops automatically arrested her husband they'd be right more than they were wrong. But Mazzetti knew this girl wasn't killed by any ex-husband, no matter where he was on the globe. Even without the equipment and the lab he saw the marks on her throat and recognized the intricate pattern of the cord that had been wrapped around it and used to snap her neck. He had to work on the assumption that the killer had intended to strangle her but used too much force at just the right angle.

There were two news trucks in front of the hospital. Normally Mazzetti would've been champing at the bit to talk to them, but today he was exhausted from his efforts to catch Daniel Byrd and he was disheartened that there was no way Byrd was the killer. Byrd had been booked on assault and grand theft charges, and the lieutenant was pushing the fact that his parole should be revoked immediately.

But the real problem was they had no more suspects and were not any closer to catching the killer or clearing homicides.

Buddy hesitated at the door after he heard the steady, authoritative rap. He took a quick look around, wiped the sweat from his palms on his shirt, and opened the door with as calm a demeanor as he could muster.

"Arnold Cather?" The short man asked as he held up a wallet with police ID.

Buddy nodded his head and said, "What can I do for you?"

"My name is detective Luis Martinez with the Jacksonville Sheriff's Office. I was wondering if you could answer a few questions for me."

Buddy was not used to hearing his full name, and the way the detective spoke sent a jolt of nervous energy down his spine. He looked past the detective quickly to see if he was alone. Finally Buddy said, "Sure, come on in." He allowed the detective to walk past and noticed how the sharp-eyed young man scanned the whole apartment very carefully, as he kept his hand hovering near the black pistol on his hip.

Buddy motioned toward the couch and said, "Grab a seat. I need to wash my hands real quick." Buddy used the excuse to run his hands in the cool water and then wipe the sweat from them. As he left the kitchen to join the detective on the couch he noticed a heavy butcher's knife sitting on the counter. Without thinking, he grabbed it and stuffed it into the small of his back so his shirt covered it completely. Buddy plopped down on the couch next to the detective.

The detective said, "I'm here about Cheryl Kazen."

"I heard what happened to her. It's terrible."

"How'd you hear about it?"

"I saw it on the news and her sister called me."

"When was the last time you saw her?"

Buddy tried hard to stay calm, but his face flushed and a trickle of sweat ran down the side of his face. His eyes roamed around the room and fell on the bullet hole in the wall of the kitchen. The hole put there by Cheryl before he plunged the knife into her chest. And while he was looking over the detective's head at the bullet hole, his eyes dropped and he noticed, for the first time, a thin splash of blood at the base of his breakfast bar. If he had noticed, how long would it take before the detective picked up on it?

Finally Buddy was able to say, "Cheryl came by with her sister Donna one evening last week. Like Wednesday or Thursday."

"Why'd they come by?"

"They're my landlords since their father died and wanted to look around to make sure the place was in good shape and asked me if I wanted out of my lease."

He knew Donna would've told the story and he wasn't about to give this guy any reason to hang around.

The detective made some notes and let his gaze drift around the apartment. Buddy could hardly keep his right hand from slipping behind his back, like it had a mind of its own. He found himself considering if the detective would have called in his location or if someone might be waiting for him outside. It didn't seem to matter to his hand.

All that mattered was the magnetic pull of the butcher's knife's handle.

Patty Levine snapped awake on her couch about lunchtime. She had managed to doze off without the aid of Ambien or any other narcotic after the long surveillance and interview of Daniel Byrd. This single night's simple victory lifted her spirits slightly until she remembered some of the things she had to be anxious about.

The image of the injured homeless man and his snotty attorney using words like "careless" and "negligent" in the IA office yesterday left Patty shaken. Her stomach growled and felt like someone was doing a ballet at the top of her intestines. She slowly stood, shaking off the stiffness of lying in an awkward position, and through force of habit padded back to the medicine cabinet in her bathroom. She looked through the rows of amber pill bottles, found the oldest vial of Xanax, and automatically took two just to get her day started.

Her back throbbed so she reached for an odd assortment of painkillers, poking through the variety of shapes and colors to find a Vicodin. Before she placed it in her mouth, she hesitated, then looked at her image in the mirror of the medicine cabinet. Was this really what she wanted to be doing with her life? Even though she had been out late working and not partying, she looked like hell and it was almost noon.

Patty tried to trace her exact anxiety and realized it wasn't really about being sued. From her first day in the academy she'd heard that any good cop doing her job couldn't avoid being sued at some point in her career. But this didn't have anything to do with enforcement, it was just an accident. And it was her fault. Even if the homeless man was exaggerating his minor injuries and the lawyer was trying to milk the system. The sheriff's office was constantly getting these kind of complaints because of the perception they had deep pockets. It was unusual, however, that Internal Affairs would get involved and allow a scumbag attorney to question a JSO officer directly. There was a lot more to this than Patty could decipher. She wondered if Ronald Bell was actually after something more serious than a minor car accident. He had insinuated that she had tried to cover up her activity, but there was still the rumor of the missing drugs. She wondered if she was a suspect in the drugs' disappearance. Why not? She was an addict. She had to be honest with herself and admit some of the things she'd done recently were as a result of her drug use. This was not the way she wanted to live her life.

Maybe it was time she told someone else about her problem.

Buddy had tried everything to get Detective Martinez out of his apartment. He'd answered the same questions over and over and now was concerned that the sharp little detective had his suspicions about Buddy's role in Cheryl's death.

Martinez said, "I have to ask this. Have you ever been in trouble with the police before?"

Buddy shook his head. "No, not even as a kid."

"Would you mind if I took a quick look around the apartment and your shop?" He made it sound so casual and easy that it would be hard for Buddy to say no without looking like he was hiding something.

Buddy hesitated. Finally he said, "I have no problem with it, as long as you don't make a mess."

The detective kept his dark eyes directly on Buddy as he shook his head and mumbled, "That's fine. I won't make a mess." He slowly stood from the couch, looking down the hallway toward the bedroom, then over Buddy's shoulder toward his work of art.

Buddy stepped back and reached behind him very slowly.

Detective Martinez turned and stepped toward the kitchen quickly. It took Buddy several steps to catch up to the energetic man. The detective was in the kitchen before him, but he could close the gap. Buddy felt he'd lost the initiative when the detective faced him in the small kitchen.

Buddy calmly picked up his newly blown glass jar and moved it from the counter to a shelf near the refrigerator. It was an instinct and it didn't capture the detective's attention.

Detective Martinez set down his notebook upside down on the counter so Buddy couldn't see what he had written. The detective actually opened one drawer and looked down at several carving knives and another butcher's knife. "The victim was stabbed a number of times. I'm learning a lot about knives as I work this case." The detective sounded casual.

Buddy relaxed slightly until he looked on the wall and realized the bullet hole was directly behind the detective. He couldn't keep his eyes from shifting down to the bloodstain he'd seen near the baseboard earlier. God, he hoped the detective didn't follow his gaze.

He had to either keep cool or take action. He couldn't risk being stopped when he was so close to completing his work of art.

FORTY-SIX

John Stallings knew the news media would be all over the story of a young nurse found dead at one of the area's major hospitals. But when he turned on the radio in his county-issued Impala the very first words he heard from a newscaster were "serial killer." The phrase made him flinch. Often news stations would use the term in the form of a question like, "Is Jacksonville stalked by a new serial killer?" In this case the answer to that question was, "Yes." And Stallings was pretty sure the command staff at the Jacksonville Sheriff's Office didn't want that term used loosely.

The phrase itself struck a primal chord with the public and often caused more problems than it solved. The weight of useless tips could crush a team of detectives doing their best to solve a serial crime. He listened to the radio as the announcer gave a few details about the investigation. The next story was about a Christian revival that had been going on at the municipal stadium on and off for two weeks. The controversy was that they had to dismantle the stage so the Jaguars could play one Sunday afternoon. The news coverage on the event had swelled the numbers of believers filing into the downtown arena.

All Stallings could think about now was what he could to do to stop the man who was strangling young women in Jacksonville.

Buddy focused on Detective Martinez's face, trying to catch any movement or expression that might give a hint to what the detective was thinking. He continued to ask Buddy simple, non-threatening questions. First about Cheryl and then about any friends or associates she'd had. He was particularly interested in boyfriends and asked Buddy if he'd ever been interested in her romantically.

Buddy let out a quick snort of laughter. "No, not at all." He didn't have to fake that answer or lie in any way.

The detective took that another way. He said, "Really? You sound pretty definite on that. Why? She was awfully cute."

Buddy saw the trap the detective had walked him into. If he said he didn't think she was attractive, the detective probably wouldn't believe him. Everyone thought she was a knockout. And if he said she was such a bitch he couldn't be around her, that would also make the detective more suspicious. He might even think that Buddy had a motive to kill her.

Buddy hesitated and the detective took a half step back. Buddy had his hand behind his back resting on the handle of the butcher knife. He was making the assessment of how he could dispose of a Jacksonville police detective and his car. He'd also have to answer a lot more questions because surely the detective had called in where he was going and who he was talking to. At that moment Buddy wasn't sure there was an alternative.

Then the answer to the question came to him. Buddy said, "I don't really like to talk about it."

"Talk about what?"

"Look around. I'm in my mid-thirties, I'm neat, I've never been married, and I talk to my mom every day." Only one of those things was a lie.

It didn't take long for the detective to catch on to what Buddy was trying to make him believe. The detective nodded and smiled, picking up his notebook and stepping around Buddy toward the front door.

Detective Martinez said, "If you think of anything please feel free to give me a call." He handed Buddy his business card, turned, and opened the door.

Buddy was in the clear again.

FORTY-SEVEN

John Stallings hated the way news channels would inflate stories and make them sound more lurid or interesting than they really were. But he also recognized, as a detective in the new millennium, there was a role reporters could play in major investigations. The story of the dead nurse found at Shands hospital had been tied to three other murders in the Jacksonville area. Sergeant Zuni, fast on her feet, used the media opportunity to show photos of the missing Leah Tischler. Less than two hours after the first broadcast, Stallings was on his way to talk to a witness.

He'd come across this witness in a less than official way. One of the downtown homeless people had gone to the only person she could trust: Liz Dubeck. Liz had called Stallings directly and told him she'd entertain the witness at her office until he came down and talked to her.

The call was what he needed to pull himself out of his funk. It was not only his father's descent into Alzheimer's but the erratic behavior of his wife, Maria. She was gone from the house so often that all he could figure was she had a boyfriend. He felt like his hopes of getting back together with her had completely fallen apart. Somehow, just going to visit with Liz Dubeck cheered him.

Walking along the sidewalk to the front door of the four-story hotel, Stallings immediately noticed work being done on the building. A tall, stooped man was measuring the floor for new carpet and another man was measuring the front bay window. Inside, Stallings could tell the walls had been recently painted.

Liz Dubeck greeted him with a bright smile that instantly lifted his spirits.

Stallings said, "What's going on here?"

"I got a federal grant to fix up the old place. I'm going to replace some of the carpet that was ruined by a leak, have the whole place painted, bring the wiring up to code, and even replace the cracked front window."

"That sounds great." He felt a little awkward since their last conversation and really didn't know what else to say. As usual, Liz was able to take up the slack.

Liz looked around the lobby to ensure that none of the workers could hear her as she motioned Stallings around the front counter and said, "This woman is really scared about talking to the police. I promised her that you and I were friends and you'd use the information without implicating her."

"No problem. What kind of information does she have?"

Liz led him back into her office. "You can ask her yourself."

Stallings looked at the fifty-year-old woman wearing a plain but clean dress and eating a Krispy Kreme doughnut. Her greasy, gray hair had been recently brushed and pulled back in a ponytail. She looked up with bloodshot eyes but didn't say anything.

Liz introduced Stallings to the woman, who didn't want to give her name. But her first question took Stallings by surprise.

"Are you any relation to James Stallings?"

"He's my father."

"If James Stallings is your father, you can't be too bad, even if you're a cop. Your pop has done more to help me and the other homeless people in town than just about anyone I know."

For possibly the first time in his life Stallings felt real pride about his father. He settled down into the chair next to the woman and asked why she wanted to talk to him.

"I seen the photo of the missing girl on TV at the community center. I seen the girl."

"Which girl are you talking about?"

"The missing one. Leah something."

Stallings felt his pulse increase as he reached in his notebook and pulled out the familiar picture of Leah Tischler and held it for the woman to look at.

"That's her. I seen her two Saturdays ago. I remember because it was before that revival started down at the stadium. She was wearing jeans and a man's plaid shirt. Like a lumberjack's shirt. Way too hot for this time of year."

Stallings made a couple of quick notes and wanted to confirm the timeline with her. "How can you be sure it was a Saturday morning?"

"Because some businesses were closed and they don't serve breakfast at the community center on Saturday. I had to walk to the Christian relief center on

Davis. When I was coming out I saw that girl at a bus stop. We talked for a minute. That's why I remember."

She spent a few more minutes giving Stallings enough details for him to believe that she had seen Leah Tischler at least one day after she had been here looking for a place to stay. That meant Leah was alive and not wearing the belt found wrapped around Kathy Mizell's throat.

The woman said, "Leah said she was going on a trip. She was tired of J-Ville."

"Where was she going?"

The woman shrugged. "She just said she was leaving."

As Stallings thought of a new set of questions, he looked out of the open window in the office at the white construction van with a magnetic sign that said CLASSIC GLASS CONCEPTS stuck on the side.

Buddy was relieved the sharp young detective left without asking any more questions. After the meeting he decided he needed to get away from the shop for a few hours. He had estimates to make and was still looking for the final piece of his work of art. He doubted he'd be bothered about Cheryl's death any more. In a way she had gotten the opposite of eternity. It seemed like her case would be unsolved and she'd be largely forgotten in a very short time.

His first estimate was at a crappy motel that catered to homeless people and probably got a ton of federal money to house them. It was a simple job. Replacing a cracked window. No etching or decoration. Pretty much just manual labor. He'd make his estimate high so that if the woman accepted it at least he'd have a few bucks in his pocket. There was no way he wanted to get stuck on a job like this unless it set him up for free time later. The only thing that mattered now was his work of art. He had to find the right subject to fill that last slot.

As he made a few notes and walked back to the open door of his van, a young woman dressed like she worked at a bank stopped him and said, "Your sign says Classic Glass Concepts—does that mean you do more than just replace windows?"

"What are you interested in?"

"We were looking for a glass sculpture for the entryway to our house. You do anything like that?"

He didn't want to giggle and babble about how fantastic it'd be to make something like that so he took a second to think about it and look cool. In that moment he recognized how stunning the woman's eyes were. She had wonderful full lips and a pretty smile too. Finally he said, "I have some photos I could show you of my work."

"When can I see them?"

All Buddy could think was, *Anytime you want and for all eternity.*

FORTY-EIGHT

Not long after meeting with Liz Dubeck and her witness, John Stallings found himself in a big conference room of the Land That Time Forgot. Yvonne the Terrible was holding court with Mazzetti, Patty, and Sparky throwing out all the information they had gathered on the homicides.

Sparky said, "The chemical found on the body in the playground and Lexie Hanover's apartment matched. The lab says it's an industrial cleaner with specks of potash and other burned byproducts. They're checking to see what some of the uses of this chemical combination would be in the real world."

Patty said, "We've sorted the two hundred twenty leads that have been called in since the press conference this morning. Most are things that we've already covered and a few are about specific suspects. Nothing earthshaking right now, but we'll keep working on them."

Sergeant Zuni turned her pretty face to Stallings, obviously saving Mazzetti, as the lead investigator, for last.

Stallings said, "I just talked to a witness who says she saw Leah Tischler, out of her school uniform, after she disappeared from home. That means she could have discarded the belt found around Kathy Mizell's throat." That caused a humming in the room as almost every detective had a question. Stallings held up his hand and said, "This may not be the most reliable witness in terms of time frame, but I believe she did see Leah and she was very specific about what she was wearing. Jeans and a man's plaid shirt. She said it looked like a lumberjack's shirt. Leah was at a bus stop and mentioned something about going on a trip."

Sparky went on about some technical issue and what policy demanded, but Stallings tuned him out as he stared at the photos of the dead girls and Leah Tischler laid out on the table. He'd done this a number of times, staring deeply into each girl's face, trying to see what the killer might have seen. Why had he chosen these specific girls? They ranged in age from seventeen to thirty-five. None of the hair colors or even facial features appeared similar to Stallings. Yet there was something about each of them that seemed noticeable. They were each pretty, but not flawless or gorgeous. In each photo the victim was smiling, and they all had appealing smiles and bright eyes. If Stallings were going to attribute any single feature, he would have to say they all had an innocent look. Maybe a pleasantly naïve look. Would that be enough to attract the notice of the killer?

Tony Mazzetti started to talk, then cleared his throat loudly until Stallings looked up from the photos. "From the position of the body and the fact that the killer is never seen on any of the surveillance cameras in the hospital, I believe the killer knew the layout of the hospital fairly well. That might mean he's an employee and we're checking on that thoroughly. He used a cord around her neck that left a small pattern. It appears to be very similar to the pattern left on Lexie Hanover's throat. There was no chemical residue found anywhere and really no other forensic evidence from the body so far."

"The thing I've been wondering is why has the body count jumped so quickly in such a short amount of time? I can't believe that this guy just decided to start killing and in a week had four identifiable victims."

Patty said, "Maybe he's very young and developed a taste for it."

Sparky said, "I'm checking prisoners released in the last month from any prison in the Southeast. It may be that he's trying to make up for lost time."

Mazzetti shook his head. "I don't know. I get the feeling that this creep has been at this a long time and recently picked up the pace. He's got some specific goal in mind. If we figure out that goal we might get ahead of him."

Sergeant Zuni said, "The news media is already building on the story. An Atlanta station is running the same story that was run here and will broadcast Leah Tischler's photo from Daytona to Tennessee. We're going to get awfully busy so I intend to call in more help."

As the sergeant opened the conference room door everyone froze. Standing there, in a beautiful Burberry suit, was Ronald Bell.

Stallings knew his day just gotten worse.

*   *   *

Buddy felt the excitement grow as he drove his van into an elegant subdivision near Hyde Park. He'd removed the magnetic sign from his plain white work van and pulled into the driveway of the beautiful two-story home with a giant oak tree out front.

The woman who had approached him while he worked at the hotel had asked him to show her some of his work and give an estimate for an actual sculpture he could blow from glass to go in this ostentatious but beautiful house.

Her name was Janet and she did have a lovely smile. He had no idea what she did for a living, but it looked like it was lucrative. He was torn about using her as a subject in his work of art when she was the first person to ever ask him to create a glass sculpture for money. He tried to figure out a way to do the work, get paid, and use her as a subject, but he didn't see any chance of doing that. Time was too short.

She met him at the front door and extended a delicate hand in greeting.

Buddy said, "What were you doing all the way downtown when you live out here in Hyde Park?"

"I was at the revival in the football stadium. I find Brother Ellis to be completely entertaining and absorbing. I'm going back for his last sermon tomorrow."

Buddy nodded. He liked the idea that this girl was religious. It meant she would be able to understand what he'd done for her by preserving her memory for eternity. He peeked over her shoulder into the long entryway that opened to a spectacular family room. She stepped aside and welcomed him into her home. Buddy tried to get a sense of who else was in the house. He had his final jar and special cord out in the van. A euphoric feeling swept over him as he realized this could be the final piece of the puzzle. Janet could be the linchpin for his work of art.

Janet said, "I have a warm feeling that I will love your glasswork."

"Somehow I know you will."

Patty Levine's stomach rumbled with anxiety. Ronald Bell stood talking to Sergeant Zuni and Patty outside the conference room. Patty couldn't believe what seeing him did to her nervous system. She could hardly stand up straight.

Bell said, "I'm sorry it has to be this way, but we have to go overt with our investigation and I'm going to interview several of the detectives." He focused his pale blue eyes on Patty without naming her specifically.

Sergeant Zuni said, "Ronald, I recognize you have a job to do, but this is not a good time. We're in the middle of a major homicide investigation."

"I understand and wish things could be different. I was hoping someone might confess and save us all a lot of heartache and trouble." Again he looked at Patty.

From farther back in the conference room Sparky Taylor cleared his throat, stepped forward, and said, "There may be an explanation for what happened to the missing pills."

Bell snapped, "When I want audiovisual advice or to hear policy recited, I'll give you a call, Detective Taylor."

Sergeant Zuni said, "We've got too much to do for this bullshit. You need to get out of our hair. And I mean right now."

Bell said, "There's nothing I'd like to do more. But

first I need to do an interview. Not an arrest. Just a simple interview now that this is an official inquiry." Once again his attention was completely focused on Patty Levine.

Now Patty understood why guys on the street would run from cops. She felt like sprinting out of the office and away from Ronald Bell right that second.

From behind her Sparky Taylor spoke in a clear voice, saying, "Policy demands that I be heard." It was the most forceful thing anyone had ever heard him say. And everyone turned to look directly at Sparky Taylor.

FORTY-NINE

Buddy made some calculations in his head. He'd been at the house almost ten minutes with his plain white van sitting in the driveway. How many neighbors would have noticed him in that time? Did it really matter anymore? He'd be done with his work of art very soon and that was all that was important. His monument to eternity, displaying the gifts God had given him.

His eyes followed Janet as she walked through the cavernous house as graceful as a dancer with a pleasant smile the whole time. She'd showed him two different sketches of etchings she liked on two large panes of glass that would set off the living room from the entryway. One etching was of a cross with Christ crucified on it and a faint shadow cast below him and the sun above his head. She had drawn it herself and it was moving in its own way. Certainly a unique and important skill that could be remembered forever.

Buddy brought in a leather work pouch that contained two measuring tapes, a carpenter's square, several pencils, and a grease pen. In addition, the special cord and the last jar were in the bag. He was ready. He had decided. He reached in and pulled out his jar.

Janet said, "What's that?"

He handed her the jar. "Something I made."

Janet held the dark green jar to the light, not bothering to conceal her admiration. "This is wonderful."

Buddy was ready to make his move.

John Stallings felt like he wanted to strike Ronald Bell in the head. The only question in his mind was if he should use his fists or elbow. But Yvonne Zuni seemed to be able to read his mind and gave him a serious "chill out" look. With a nod of her head she sent him back to his desk, worried about his partner. While he sat there thinking, he realized, maybe for the first time, that Patty had somehow filled a void in his life and he viewed her as a daughter. She was a partner he trusted, but he had very strong paternal feelings about her welfare. Even though there was only thirteen years' difference between them, he worried about her like she was one of his own.

He took a few minutes to breathe deeply and concentrate on calming down. There was a lot of work to do and no matter how much satisfaction he'd take in laying out the noxious IA investigator, in the long run it wouldn't help his chances of catching and stopping this killer who had claimed so many lives in such a short time.

He wondered what Sparky was saying behind the closed door of the sergeant's office. Patty had been pulled in along with the sergeant and Ronald Bell. After a few minutes Stallings regained his composure and started going over the tasks he needed to complete.

Luis Martinez, a relatively new detective in the crimes/persons unit, plopped down in the chair in front of Stallings.

Luis inclined his head toward the sergeant's office and said, "What's going on in there?"

Stallings mumbled, "Usual bullshit." He liked the tough, direct former Marine who had recently been assigned his first homicide. "How's your stabbing case going?"

Martinez shrugged. "No one really cares about the Kazem stabbing. All anyone is talking about is the serial strangler. I haven't gotten anywhere on the stabbing except to talk to a lot of ex-boyfriends and associates." He opened his notebook and stared out the first sheet of paper. "Shit." He ripped out a sheet of paper, crumpled it, and tossed it in the garbage can by Stallings's desk.

Stallings said, "What's wrong?"

"I got some kind of kind of chemical shit on the paper when I was over at the glass company talking to a guy who leases the building from the murder victim."

"Is the guy a suspect?"

"No, he's okay. He had no real motive and definitely wasn't interested in her romantically." Luis stood and said, "I gotta get back to work, Stall. It's a lonely case."

Stallings mumbled, "Let me know if I can help." Then he looked down at the damp sheet of paper Luis had tossed into his can. He wondered if it would hurt Ronald Bell if he picked up the garbage can and smacked him in the head with it.

Buddy was lost in the image of Janet holding his homemade jar to the sunlight streaming in from a tall window—her light brown hair like satin, her full red lips, and that beautiful graceful neck. It was her neck that had him mesmerized as he held the cord loosely in his right hand. It looked like he just had a length of rope. Nothing threatening or unusual. It could've been a standard for measuring glass. His only concern was that if he moved too quickly she might drop the jar.

She turned and faced him, handing back the heavy jar. Those wide eyes and that brilliant smile grabbed his attention now. She said, "It looks like the jar has a specific use."

"I've made eighteen of them to hold one of the most precious commodities on earth."

She placed a hand on his shoulder and leaned in close. "What would that commodity be?"

Buddy decided he'd tell her as he was collecting the commodity. He placed the jar gently on a coffee table, faced her, once again taking in her beautiful face. He worked the logistics out in his mind of how to loop the cord around her throat and apply even pressure so he didn't have the same problem he'd experienced with the nurse, Katie Massa.

As he started to shuffle to one side he heard the front door and a male voice call out, "Sweetheart, where are you?"

She turned and took a step away from Buddy, yelling, "I'm in the living room with a true artist."

She was so sweet it hurt Buddy's heart that he couldn't make her part of eternity right now. It seemed unfair to her.

He watched the tall, well-built young man embrace his wife, then offer his hand to Buddy.

Buddy shifted, saying, "Nice to meet you."

Buddy smiled and nodded as he took another look at

his perfect subject. He even wondered if it would be worth killing the husband with a knife or a blow to the head. He figured in his current condition he wouldn't have the strength to overcome such a fit young man. And that made him even sadder.

He'd have to keep his eyes open for another subject. Then he brightened as he thought about the manager of the hotel. He had to concentrate to think of her name: Liz Dubeck.

FIFTY

Patty was in the sergeant's cramped office with Sparky Taylor and a clearly agitated Ronald Bell facing the stern sergeant sitting on her throne behind her desk.

Bell looked at Sparky and said, "What fucking policy do you want to quote now? It's too bad you didn't read policy about staying fit or maybe your fat ass wouldn't have gotten stuck in a bathroom window and you could've stayed in the tech division, where at least people care about your fucking opinion. Jesus Christ, I am sick of tech agents."

Yvonne Zuni said in an icy voice, "That will be quite enough." And it worked because Ronald Bell shut up and sat down like his third-grade teacher had struck him with a ruler.

For his part, Sparky seemed completely unfazed by the outburst. He said, "The policy says that when there is a large seizure of contraband that must be tested in the lab, a representative sample can be stored in temporary evidence downstairs while the overall seizure is secured."

Bell said, "So what?"

"So Dwight and I live by the same code of policy. He would know the policy and follow it. Since he's been injured and unclear about what happened, I wonder if anyone checked temporary evidence." He turned to give Bell a subtle, superior glance.

Patty had to stifle a chuckle, he'd done it so perfectly. What Sparky had said sounded so simple that it couldn't be true, could it? She had only used temporary evidence once. It generally involved holding part of a seizure in a standard-size locker with two separate locks at the entrance to the evidence room. An evidence custodian keeps a key to one lock in the evidence room and the seizing officer keeps a key to the second lock. That way the seizing officer can come back and retrieve the sample to take it to the lab while maintaining a strict and clear chain of custody. Not all departments used it and usually it only applied to narcotics.

The sergeant stood behind her desk and said, "I have an easy solution to this debate. Let's all go down to evidence and check the lockers. It sounds like it's something IA should've done long before the investigation got this far. And it will definitely be something I address with the captain later on."

Patty liked the support she was getting from the people on her squad and it was starting to give her some confidence. She followed the little posse of Sparky Taylor, Yvonne Zuni, and Ronald Bell down the rear stairs and through the corridor to the evidence custodian.

As they were walking, Bell said, "We never found a key around the scene of the fight or in Dwight's clothes."

Sparky said, "I've thought about that and there are a

number of possibilities. The key would have been out and possibly on the desk. Your people could've simply overlooked it. It could've been kicked all the way across the room during the scuffle. It might have even ended up going to the hospital with Dwight and being left there."

Patty followed along, realizing she was a suspect in the eyes of the sheriff's office. Even if it was only the IA division. She had to come to grips with idea that someone thought she'd committed the crime. It gave her a lump in her throat and upset her stomach. It made her think about all the times she'd purposely tried to upset suspects in her own cases in an effort to get them to confess or cooperate. This incident was giving her an entirely new perspective on the trick. She would have to look at the way she conducted business differently from now on. This sucked. She'd gone beyond pharmaceutical help. Patty was so nervous now that no amount of Xanax would calm her down. The crazy thing was that she was terrified over an administrative issue. She hadn't been this scared when she was held captive by the fucking Bag Man. Her life had been on the line, but she'd known someone was trying to help her. It was an odd experience to have someone question her integrity.

Stallings had tried to follow Patty and the group as they left the office, but a sharp look from the sergeant had kept him in his seat. It gave him one more thing to worry about in addition to his wife, his father, Jeanie, his kids, and Leah Tischler. He felt like he needed to burst out and do something to take action against one of the problems in his life.

He looked around the nearly empty office and decided to act. Now.

Fifteen minutes later he pulled into the driveway of his former residence, pausing at the front door before knocking firmly but politely and waiting for someone to answer. It was Charlie's smiling face that cheered him up as soon as the door swung inward.

"Hey, pal, is your mom around?"

"She's upstairs. Do you have time to kick with me?"

"Let me talk to Mom for a little while first."

The boy darted upstairs like a guided missile; almost a full minute later Maria glided down the stairs like she was at an awards show and had admiring crowds watching her. In his own way Stallings was an admiring crowd.

She gave him a weak smile and walked past him into the family room to sit on the couch. He knew the unspoken command to follow her and sit next to her. And he obeyed.

Stallings started. "We need to talk."

"Yes, we do."

"I mean about us."

"I do too."

That surprised him because she generally avoided any conversation about the troubled relationship.

"I thought we had made a connection the other night. I mean I did spend the night here."

"You fell asleep here. There is a difference. And I'll admit I liked having someone to cuddle up to. But as soon as the call of duty hit you, the house was empty and silent again. I understand your need to help people and I commend it. But the kids and I are people too and we need more than just a few minutes of your time every day."

He had considered a lot of reasons why Maria was acting the way she was. He thought it might be some reaction to seeing him with Liz Dubeck. He'd even considered the idea that she was using again. But this was not only the most logical and obvious explanation, it was also the one that stung the worst.

Maria continued. "The last two weeks have been a revelation to me. I've gone down to the stadium and listened to Frank Ellis for hours each day. The man has some amazing insights and made me feel a real connection to Jesus."

Stallings leaned back and stared at his wife. "That's why you were downtown. You were going to see the Holy Roller."

"That's a condescending term. It was a legitimate religious service."

"I wasn't trying to be insulting. I thought it was a legitimate Baptist religious service. You've been a legitimate Catholic your whole life."

"I thought you would have learned by now that nothing lasts a lifetime."

That brought Stallings up short. He looked at his wife and remembered their early married life with Jeanie running around and Maria smiling from early in the morning till she laid that beautiful head down on the pillow. It would be easy for him to say that was all he wanted back, but it was so much. He realized now it was more than any man should hope for.

Maria caressed his cheek and then let her hand drop to his. "You should be happy that I've gone to the service. It's taught me a lot about myself and what to expect from others. You are such a good man, John. And I've had a new hope instilled in my heart. I really do believe you can change. I believe in redemption. But you're going to have to earn it. You'll have to show me that you care about the family and that you can express all of your feelings, both good and bad."

"And how do I do all that?"

"You have to figure it out for yourself. It may take a while. You may not be able to do it. And until you figure it out, I can't have you living in this house."

Stallings stared into those luminous dark eyes and thought his heart might break. He had no idea how to change.

At some point in the process Patty Levine had decided to toughen up and take this shit like a cop. She did everything else on the job like a man. It was to the point that most cops didn't even notice she was female. Almost. That was the way she liked JSO. Anymore the only reason female cops were treated differently was because of an ingrained view or, as some called it, an "instinct" for men to treat women differently. On the road she occasionally saw patrolman instinctively keep her out of harm's way. When the truth was she usually could fight better than any man on road patrol.

Now she stood in the corner of the room while Ronald Bell questioned an evidence custodian and Yvonne Zuni kept the proceedings from turning into a witch hunt.

Bell said, "So you don't have a record of the detective using a temporary evidence locker?"

The heavyset, middle-aged man acted like Bell was a fifth grader. "I said this before and now I will repeat myself for the fourth time. He was checking in something, I don't know what, and took a temporary evidence key. Whoever took in the package and gave him the key expected him to be back in the next few minutes and didn't log it for some reason. It was a mistake that I accept responsibility for. But it happened and I do not have time to explain it to you even once more. Is there anything that confuses you in that statement, Mr. IA?" He had spoken slowly and clearly.

Patty smiled at his condescending manner, chalking it up to some past run-in with the Internal Affairs division.

Bell said, "If we don't have the key to the second lock how do we get into the locker?"

The evidence custodian rubbed his bald head and said, "We do have an emergency master key. But we don't use it very often."

Bell said, "I think this qualifies as an emergency. You can use it on my authority."

The evidence custodian chuckled, reached low under his counter, and handed him a three-foot-long set of bolt cutters, saying, "Ooh, your authority. I can't wait to see if these things work. I've never been authorized to use them before." The evidence custodian didn't even wait to see Bell's reaction. He rolled his eyes and went back to his usual work.

Bell, Sparky, and Sergeant Zuni walked across the outer room to the wall of fifty lockers. They scanned the numbers along the top row to find the locker the narcotics detective had used. The evidence custodian had given Sergeant Zuni his key to the second lock. Once they found the locker the evidence lock was opened and off instantly. Then Bell used the big bolt cutters on the second heavy-duty lock. He struggled as he pulled the handles together and let the giant clippers snap through the shackle of the padlock.

He wasted no time opening the locker and even

from her position, Patty could see a gray bundle. She stepped behind the group as Bell pulled it out and saw the initials and date written by the injured narcotics detective.

Sparky looked at Ronald Bell and said in a very moderate and cool tone, "Perhaps you people in IA should read up on policy a little more. We could've avoided this entire ugly incident had you showed a bit more interest in doing your job well."

Patty smiled at the portly detective's comment.

Sergeant Zuni summed it up more succinctly. She looked at the IA investigator and said, "You're a douche bag."

Patty Levine laughed out loud for the first time in a week.

FIFTY-ONE

Tony Mazzetti felt the week start to catch up to him on Friday morning. He had set up an interview room in the administrative section of Shands hospital. The management and security at Shands could not have been more helpful and open to the investigation. Their help sped along a number of tasks he had to complete on the murder case. He also felt a lift in his spirits when he heard that the missing narcotics had been found and no one would get in trouble for it. He was starting to realize that Patty Levine had been a suspect and it bothered him. It bothered him because he didn't understand how a great cop like Patty could fall into the crosshairs of Internal Affairs and he didn't understand why Patty had not wanted to talk to him about it at all.

He'd spoken to her last night, hoping she might suggest he come over. Instead she was polite and cool. Just before he ended the phone call she said the words he had been dreading, "I think we need to talk sometime this weekend."

He felt the same way, but based on the way she'd been acting and the tone of her comment, he suspected they each had two entirely different things to say. In his mind he was already trying to figure out how to arrange his life without falling back into the lonely routine he had lived before he met Patty.

He sighed and looked down at a notepad, trying to build an interest in talking to one of the thirty hospital employees who thought they might get to help him in his investigation. There were two other rooms with detectives taking down information. Mazzetti realized he should be coordinating information and supervising the investigation, but he needed to settle down to a simple task for a little bit.

As Mazzetti was about to call down for his next witness, a tall, odd-looking young man of about thirty poked his head in the door, pushed his dark brown glasses up on his face, and said, "Are you one of the cops looking into the murder of Katie Massa?"

"I am." The young man gave off an odd vibe and Mazzetti let his hand drop to the side where his Glock sat on his hip.

"I think I need to talk to you"

"You have information?"

"Yes, I know who killed her."

Mazzetti sighed, set down his pen, and finally said, "Really? And who would that be?"

"Me."

Buddy had parked his van with the magnetic sign slapped on the side. He couldn't believe how long he had agonized over the logo for Classic Glass Concepts. He had given a sort of a regal sketch to the sign company, which had made him five signs he could slap on his van. He'd lost two, one had been defaced, and one had faded. The best part was that he got the signs for free when he fixed a broken window in the sign company showroom. He charged them for materials and made the labor seem harder than it really was so they didn't think they were being ripped off.

He'd taken this job at the hotel for two reasons. The woman hadn't offered him his full estimate, but it wasn't bad money and she was a very likely candidate for his work of art. From a strategic standpoint it didn't make sense to use a subject that he'd worked so closely with. But the time to worry about covering his tracks was past and Buddy had come to terms with it.

Had Detective Martinez talked to him about Cheryl a year or two ago, he might have learned something about police procedure he could've used. Instead he had the sense Detective Martinez had a lot to do and not very much help on his investigation. He wondered if all police investigations were like that and if his constant worry over the years about being discovered had been a waste of time.

As he lay down his tools and cut the caulk from around the outside of the wide bay window he looked up to see the lovely Liz coming out the front door of the ramshackle hotel. She turned toward him with a steaming cup of coffee and a wide, bright smile.

She said, "I thought a good cup of strong coffee might start you off on the right foot."

He accepted it with a gracious smile.

"How long do you think this'll take?"

"I should be out of your hair by lunchtime."

"I wasn't trying to rush you. I just wanted to know if you'd like me to make you lunch around noon?" She placed a delicate hand on his shoulder.

That was all he needed. It was like an electric shock.

The combination of her sweet smile, pretty face and kind manner was all he needed to know for sure that she was the final piece of his work of art.

John Stallings checked in at the office, hoping the media coverage had generated a decent new lead. He was ready to go out and get something done. In the darkest corners of his heart he recognized he wouldn't mind punching someone. Someone who deserved punching. Just the thought made him feel better. He didn't like that side of his nature, but as he got older he'd come to accept it. There were many cops who never came to terms with their natural instincts. Really smart guys who tried to act tough. Tough guys who wanted to show how organized they were. Police work took all kinds of cops to complete.

The squad bay was very quiet as Sergeant Yvonne Zuni came in the main door and paused at Stallings's desk. She said, "How are you today, Stall?"

"Good, how about you?"

She let out a long sigh and sat down in the seat next to him. "Now that the IA cloud has been lifted from the squad I feel like I can focus on the mountain of information we're getting in from the tip lines and lab."

"We gettin' anything good?"

She pulled a random report from her pile in her arms. "We finally have the lab report on the chemical found with two of the bodies. You know, the stuff Sparky found at Lexie Hanover's apartment."

"What was it?"

"It says here that it is consistent with the residue from a commercial glass cleaner with trace elements including potash. Some of the manufacturers form their own glass components, and potash and other accelerants would be used in natural, non-electric furnaces."

"What does that mean?"

Sergeant Zuni looked off in space for a minute, then said, "Maybe it would be a good idea to look into construction workers that deal with glass in windows."

Stallings nodded his head, knowing that it would be another big drain on man power when there were so many other leads coming in. He remembered speaking with someone recently about a glass company. But he just couldn't recall the details.

Stallings knew it would bother him all morning until he could remember.

FIFTY-TWO

Tony Mazzetti looked at the lanky orderly who now sat directly in front of him. There was no one else in the small room the administration had given him as an office while he looked into the murder of Katie Massa. Obviously this guy was some kind of nut. The question was if he was a nut who liked to confess to murders he didn't commit or a nut who went around strangling women.

Years before, when he was new to homicide, Tony Mazzetti had been taken in by a man who confessed to killing a teenager with a knife. He'd been so proud of himself after he found the man by canvassing the neighborhood where the homicide had occurred. But when he took the confessed killer back to the office he was met with a chorus of laughter. The suspect's name was Gerald Conway, better known to the homicide detectives as "Conway the Confessor." For some reason the man felt compelled to confess to every homicide that happened in the south end of the county. He'd been institutionalized twice and was on heavy doses of psychotropic drugs trying to bring him back to reality. It was a bitter lesson Mazzetti had taken to heart. Over the years he'd had several more instances where caution had proven his savior by not accepting confessions on their face.

Mazzetti took a moment to assess the young man who had thinning dark hair, a long, hawklike nose, and ears virtually perpendicular to his narrow head. Mazzetti said, "How'd you kill her?"

"I choked her."

He could've heard that on the radio. "Describe how you choked her."

The young man took a moment, looked around the room to ensure they were alone and said, "I wrapped my hands around her throat and squeezed until she went limp in my arms."

Okay, thought Mazzetti, *this is bullshit.* One of the few facts they knew for sure was that Katie Massa had been strangled with a rope or a cord of some kind. But he didn't want to dismiss this guy yet. Obviously he would have to talk to someone about one of the hospital employees wandering around telling cops that he killed someone.

Mazzetti said, "Why'd you strangle her?"

"Because she met someone else."

"Was she your girlfriend?"

"She was, but she may not have realized it."

Mazzetti had to stifle a laugh. "You know the guy she met?"

"I know he gave her crosswords to solve. She loved her crossword puzzles."

Mazzetti nodded and smiled, trying to think how quickly he could deal with this guy. He stood from behind his table and said, "Let's go talk to your supervisor about this. Where would I find him?"

"Up in endocrinology."

Patty Levine approached Sparky Taylor's desk by the most circuitous route possible. He was one of the few people who knew she had been a direct suspect in the theft of the drugs. He was no dummy and probably realized there was a rationale behind Ronald Bell's theory that Patty had stolen the drugs.

She eased to Sparky's desk and saw that he was trying to make connections between pages and pages of phone numbers and names relating to the homicide. The same kind of stuff she was good at too. She cleared her throat until he looked up with that wide face of his and casually pushed his glasses back onto his nose.

Patty started slowly. "Sparky, I wanted to thank you for figuring out what happened to the missing drugs."

"There's no need to thank me, I was just doing my job. It's too bad that Ronald Bell doesn't know policy well enough to resolve something as simple as that quickly."

Patty nodded and said, "Thanks all the same." She turned and slowly started to step away when Sparky said, "Wait a sec."

Sparky took off his glasses and rubbed his eyes, motioning Patty to the chair next to his desk in the far corner of the squad bay. He lowered his voice and said, "You guys think all I care about is tech equipment and policy. But I'm a cop first. I've been on road patrol, in fights, two shootings, and nearly a divorce. I see how hard you push yourself. I also see your ups and downs. It gets to all of us, girl. You're not alone."

Patty stared at Sparky like it was the first time she had ever seen him. He had worked with her the least amount of time of anyone on the squad and he had seen directly to her problems. It was like he had taken an X-ray of her emotions. She nodded her head and mumbled, "Thanks, Sparky." She stood and started to shuffle away from the desk.

Sparky said, "I'm always around if you need to talk to someone."

Suddenly Patty realized John Stallings wasn't the only super sharp cop on the squad.

Stallings went over some notes at his desk, thinking about all the information that had flooded into his brain over the past thirty-six hours. He knew they had to do something quick to avert another homicide and it crushed him that he had no viable plan. They were all working hard and doing their best, but it didn't seem like it was nearly enough.

An elderly black custodian ambled through the squad bay randomly wiping down cabinets and emptying garbage cans. When he reached Stallings's desk he paused and said, "You look tired, John."

"Been a long week, Ben. It doesn't look to get any easier in the coming weeks."

The older man chuckled. He had a deep, warm voice that had always been comforting to Stallings. The old custodian said, "I can remember when you started here. I don't think you looked much different than you do now except for the scar on the bridge of your nose and a few lines around your eyes."

"Somehow I doubt the interior held up as well as the exterior."

"God tests us each in our own way." As he was talking the older man reached down and picked up Stallings's garbage can. "They first called you Stall because your engine ran so fast they were afraid you'd stall out."

"You've got one hell of a memory, Ben. I wish my dad could remember things as well as you." Stallings's eyes shifted to the garbage can and he got an odd feeling. He couldn't put his finger on it at that moment.

Mazzetti realized he'd broken a number of rules by not handcuffing the tall, dorky orderly named Marvin. He knew the guy was off by a couple of degrees and he'd clearly had nothing to do with Katie Massa's homicide even though he insisted he had. Mainly Mazzetti wanted to make sure the hospital realized they employed a nut and he figured Marvin's supervisor was the best person to talk to.

The corridors were crowded midmorning on a Friday. People hustled back and forth, and Mazzetti noted that several other orderlies nodded their heads as they passed Marvin. But no one seemed too concerned that he was walking with a cop through the halls of the hospital. Mazzetti had his suit jacket off, and his gun and badge were clearly visible on his hip. In addition, he had a identification badge around his neck and everyone had been told the police would be hanging around the hospital conducting the investigation.

Pediatric endocrinology was one end of the floor that also housed pediatric oncology and a wing for kids with other ailments. A little girl whose head was as bald and shiny as any old man's scuttled by in a long nightgown and waved at the orderly, saying, "Hi, Marvin."

For his part, Marvin seemed quite unconcerned he'd just confessed to a homicide and smiled at the little girl as he said, "Hello, Emma. I'll come by and see you later."

The little girl giggled and scooted on her way.

Mazzetti allowed Marvin to lead him to the wide nurses' station and immediately identified a woman of about thirty-five who was clearly in charge of the massive and busy station. She was tall and athletic, with pretty brown hair tied in a ponytail. She also wore runner's shoes, which gave Mazzetti the impression this was not a manager who sat back and watched others work.

He stood there for a moment until she looked up. She came from behind a round desk at the center of the console out into the hallway and nodded to Marvin as she looked at Mazzetti. "Is there a problem, Officer?"

"Can we talk privately?"

The woman looked at the other seven nurses, who were busy making notes or answering the phone, and said, "Will this take long? Is Marvin in trouble?"

Mazzetti wasn't sure exactly how to answer because technically Marvin had made a false police report or obstructed justice or bothered a police officer so badly that he was lucky he hadn't gotten his ass kicked. Instead Mazzetti said, "Are you his supervisor?"

The nurse surprised him by starting to laugh. First as a giggle, then as a loud guffaw. It took her a few moments to compose herself. Finally she said, "Did he tell you he worked here as an orderly?"

"I don't think I'd be here talking to you if he hadn't."

"Marvin is not officially employed by the hospital."

"I don't follow. He's dressed like he works here and he told me he works here and you obviously know him."

The nurse adopted Mazzetti's slow condescending speech pattern to say, "He is a patient here. He's treated three days a week in the psychiatric services section. But he's harmless and good for the kids' morale so we allow him to come and visit."

"Why's he dressed like that?"

"I think you'd have to ask him about that."

Mazzetti glared at the taller man, who shrugged and said, "I like to dress in white scrubs." The nurse started to laugh again. *Fuck,* thought Mazzetti. He looked back at the nurse and said, "Did he know Katie Massa?"

That sobered the woman instantly. She nodded and couldn't find words to speak. Finally she said, "He had a little crush on her. Everyone did." Then Mazzetti's eye caught something on the console. He reached past the nurse and picked up the single sheet of paper with a crossword printed out on it. "Marvin mentioned something about crosswords."

The nurse said, "Katie did them all the time. She'd print out some for us to do too."

Mazzetti looked at Marvin. "How'd you know Katie got the crosswords from a guy?"

"She told me she did."

Now the nurse, sensing where Mazzetti was going with his questioning, said, "She told me she got it from a guy too. She met him at Starbucks around the corner."

"Did she say anything else about him?"

The nurse shook her head. "Not really. She had just met him and liked him. She didn't describe him or give any details." This was a sharp woman who recognized that any new man entering Katie's life would be a suspect in her death.

Something told Mazzetti this was a serious lead.

FIFTY-THREE

John Stallings couldn't take his eyes off the garbage can in the custodian's hands. Something in the back of his head was screaming at him, but he couldn't hear what the voice was saying.

The older custodian said, "You guys keep some long hours. At least you're not as bad as narcotics with paperwork crumpled up and thrown everywhere and day-old food sitting on every desk. It's like cleaning a frat house."

Stallings nodded absently, then suddenly recalled his conversation with Luis Martinez about interviewing a man at a glass company. At that moment he couldn't pinpoint the source of his anxiety. He said, "Hold on a minute, Ben." He stood and peered into the half-full garbage can and saw the sheet of paper Luis Martinez had tossed into it yesterday.

Stallings plucked out the paper, pulled it out at the corners to clearly see the ring with a hint of moisture still visible. He looked at the custodian and said, "Gotta go." And hit the door of the squad bay at a full sprint.

* * *

Buddy couldn't recall when his nickname had really caught on. It wasn't long after he moved out of his mother's house and started working the odd construction jobs. He always felt his real name, Arnold Cather, was formal and stiff sounding. His parents had never called him Arnie. Until the day his father died when Buddy was twelve he called his son Arnold. His mother had been no better. When she was happy with something he did she called him Arnold; when she was angry she called him Arnold. Now she didn't call him at all.

He liked the informality and anonymity of the name Buddy. He especially liked the way the woman who ran the hotel, Liz, said it with such a pleasant smile and upbeat tone.

He had decided she was the final link. The chance to finish his work of art so it could stand for all eternity. He had the jar out, sitting on the rear shelf of his van along with the cord he had used on his last several victims. Now he was waiting for the right circumstance. He was certain he could do it sometime later today but was prepared to come back if he had to.

As he replaced the bay window, for the second time in less than a week he found himself whistling.

Stallings didn't like to bully people, at least people who hadn't committed a crime. But as he backed the lab tech into the corner, he realized the man was nervous because he feared actual physical pain. Stallings would never consider touching another employee of the Jacksonville Sheriff's Office in any kind of aggressive way. But he didn't have to let this guy know that's how he felt.

The tall, thin young man had initially told Stallings he wouldn't be able to look at the paper with the odd chemical ring on it for several days and that Stallings should submit it through official channels.

Stallings said, "I don't think you understand. This is urgent and relates to the multiple homicide investigation we have going on."

The young man stammered, "I won't be able to tell you exactly what the chemical is without checking a number of variables. Could take hours or even days."

"All I need you to do is compare it to a previous sample we submitted from two other victims. You don't have to tell me what it is, only if it's the same chemical found at the other crime scenes." Stallings stepped away from the man to let him relax slightly. "And I'm going to stand in the room until you get it done."

The young man scurried to the other side of the lab and grabbed a folder of recent reports. He came back and took the paper Stallings had given him in an open plastic bag and examined the stain, first through a large microscope sitting at the end of the bench and then with a magnifying glass as he looked into the light. The young man went to a bench and pulled out a bottle with a small eyedropper and placed one drop of clear liquid on top of the paper. He then examined the paper again with the magnifying glass and touched the drop of liquid with a small piece of litmus paper.

Stallings fidgeted, trying to conceal his impatience. At least the young lab technician was doing his job and doing what Stallings had asked. He didn't feel right rushing him if he was working diligently.

After a few more minutes and two more tests, the young man looked at Stallings and said, "It's the same chemical exactly."

FIFTY-FOUR

John Stallings rushed through the corridors of the Police Memorial Building like a maniac, at one point knocking a dispatcher out of his way with barely an apology or glance behind him. He'd dialed Luis Martinez's cell phone three times only to reach his voice mail. The secretary in the Land That Time Forgot had seen him earlier and thought he was in the building somewhere.

As Stallings headed back to the crimes/persons squad bay, he decided, on a whim, to check Luis's former unit, Auto Theft. As soon as he banged through the door he saw Luis chatting and laughing with a detective in fatigues and a T-shirt that had the JSO emblem on the chest.

Luis looked up and smiled at Stallings and started to introduce him to the other detective when Stallings gripped him by the arm and said, "What was the name of the guy you were talking to when you got the stain in your notebook?"

"Huh?"

Stallings resisted the urge to shake him. "Yesterday you told me about talking to some guy at a glass company."

"Oh, that guy. He's nobody. He knew the victim on my homicide, but there's no way that little fruit ball did it."

"Luis, what was his motherfucking name?" The tone and language clearly caught Luis Martinez by surprise.

"Arnold Cather."

Stallings grabbed a pen off whatever desk they were standing next to and snatched a piece of paper. "Spell it." He wrote out the name. "What was the name of the company?"

"Classic Glass Concepts."

For some reason that name rang a bell with Stallings too. He wondered if his father's memory problem wasn't genetic.

Liz Dubeck was having one of those days where everything fell into place. Her three employees actually showed up, sober and helpful. She had taken an hour right at sunrise to run, climb the four flights of stairs ten times, and finish with four sets of push-ups. The guy from Classic Glass Concepts had come on time and, although he appeared to be very slow and methodical, was making progress. She had eaten nothing but fruit and avoided any coffee. Mornings like this were rare indeed.

She'd been in a good mood for several days since the money from the federal grant had been deposited into her business account. She had been planning on it for some time and had everything in place to start sprucing up the hotel immediately. The only thing she was taking her time with was bringing the wiring up to code. It was not a cosmetic, superficial job and was proving to be much more expensive than she'd anticipated. She had two estimates scheduled after lunch and hoped one contractor might see the other and get into some kind of bidding war. Devious was not part of her nature, but she could justify her actions if it meant helping even one more runaway in greater Jacksonville.

She knew a lot of this was to cover guilt she felt over Leah Tischler. No matter how many people told her it wasn't her fault, she couldn't help but worry about the missing teen.

She sucked down half a bottle of water as she surveyed the lobby and approved of the job the carpet guy had been doing in the sitting area across from her office. The new glass that was being fitted in the window was so clear it took a moment for her to realize it was already in place.

Could this day get any better?

Tony Mazzetti was reeling from the discovery of the link between Katie Massa and a man who gave her crossword puzzles. The fact that Marvin wasn't really an orderly but a psychiatric patient didn't affect the information. It meant that someone at the hospital had to have seen Katie with the man. He delivered Marvin back to the floor where he was being treated. He was a noncustodial, voluntary patient and posed no threat to the public. But he was still as crazy as a shithouse rat.

Mazzetti's phone was in his pocket, and he dug it out to see Stallings's name. He flipped open the phone, "What do you need, Stall?"

"I might have a suspect's name. Can you check it out at the hospital?"

"How'd you get the name?"

"Tony, it's a long story. But Martinez talked to him on a different homicide and ended up with the same chemical residue as the one from Lexie Hanover's apartment on a sheet of notebook paper."

Stallings's information made his crossword seem lame so he kept his mouth shut and copied down the name Arnold Cather.

"Sit tight, Stall. I'll check this guy out and get back to you."

John Stallings had never been good at waiting patiently for anything. Now he paced while Luis Martinez gathered all the information he had on Arnold Cather and while Tony Mazzetti checked the guy out at the hospital. He forced himself to sit at his desk and write down the facts he had learned on one sheet of paper so he could explain it coherently if someone asked why it was important.

Finally Luis Martinez came over to his desk with several reports. The smaller detective said, "I don't know if this guy could be your killer. I didn't get that kind of vibe at all." He dug through a stack of papers and pulled out a report from the driver's license bureau known as a D.A.V.I.D., which recorded the address, vital information, and a large color photo taken when a driver's license is issued in Florida.

Stallings looked at it for a moment and realized where he'd seen the name Classic Glass Concepts before. "That fucking guy was replacing the bay window over at a hotel where a missing girl had been seen."

The look on Martinez's face told Stallings he might be onto something.

It didn't take long for Tony Mazzetti to track down the name Arnold Cather. He was on the log entering the hospital and when Tony ran down to records they immediately referred him to a doctor in the oncology unit.

The doctor was on rounds when Mazzetti caught him as he was entering a room on the fifth floor. "Excuse me, Doc." Mazzetti held up his badge. "Can I talk to you for a sec?"

The young Indian doctor sighed and rolled his eyes. "I'm really quite busy right now. Can it wait?" The doctor assumed that would be enough to stop Mazzetti and turned his back on the detective as he started to enter the room.

Mazzetti reached out and grasped the man's pencil-thin arm, perhaps too aggressively, then decided to go with it and jerked him back out into the hallway. "No, it cannot wait." He led the doctor down the hallway to the first empty room he found and all but shoved him into it.

The young doctor said, "I don't think I like this sort of treatment. Perhaps I shall have to speak to your supervisor."

"You can speak to whoever the hell you want after you answer a couple questions. This involves the murder of a nurse right here at the hospital and is absolutely time sensitive." That seemed to catch the attention of the doctor, who remained silent, but now his eyes focused on Mazzetti. "Do you treat a patient named Arnold Cather?"

The doctor hesitated. "Look, Detective, I understand you have a job and this is a serious matter. But ethically I cannot talk about who I treat or don't treat without a subpoena. I have to worry about being sued every minute of every day."

Mazzetti swallowed hard, trying to think of a counterargument. Instead, he thought about the faces of the dead women he'd looked at over the past few weeks. "Doctor, I'm going to give you immunity to talk to me. I will get you a subpoena later if I have to. But it is vital that I find out about Arnold Cather."

"I told you I'm worried about the legal consequences."

"Perhaps you should worry about the physical consequences." Mazzetti bowed up and stepped closer to the smaller young man with dark glasses and trimmed black hair.

The doctor stammered for a minute. "You—you can't be serious."

"We have women who've been strangled. One right here at the hospital. We also have a link to a suspect named Arnold Cather and I've already been told by the hospital he's being treated by you. Now I need to know about him. Right now."

The young doctor swallowed and nodded his head. "Okay, but if I'm forced to later, I will say that you threatened me."

"I can give you a black eye to back up your assertion if you'd like."

"No thank you. I think I'll be able to convince people myself."

"Then tell me about Arnold Cather."

"I wouldn't think that he'd be capable of crimes like that. He is a little on the odd side but seems perfectly harmless. His hobbies are glassblowing and crosswords."

Mazzetti took in the information, digesting its significance. He kept cool and said, "What are you treating him for?"

The doctor hesitated, knowing that this was a sensitive subject. Finally he said, "Mr. Cather is in the advanced stages of lung cancer."

"Is it debilitating yet?"

"It's terminal."

Mazzetti froze for a moment, looked at the doctor, and said, "How long does he have?"

"I'm surprised he's still alive and functioning so well. A couple of months ago I told him he only had six weeks to live."

Mazzetti instantly realized this was their man and why the pace of the killings had picked up so drastically.

The killer was trying to beat his own deadline.

FIFTY-FIVE

John Stallings hustled down the stairs to the rear parking lot, frantically dialing and redialing Liz Dubeck's cell phone. He'd left one quick message for her to call back but desperately wanted to reach her and tell her to just walk away from the hotel if the glass guy was there.

He was about to call Patty and the dispatcher to get someone to head over there when Mazzetti's name appeared on his phone. Stallings immediately answered it, saying, "What do you got, Tony?"

Mazzetti all but shouted into the line, "This is our man. He's a terminal cancer patient. That's why he's killing so often."

Stallings bounded through the rear door and out into the parking lot with the phone glued to his ear.

Mazzetti said, "You know where this guy is?"

Stallings said, "I think he's over at an old hotel that caters to the homeless and runaways. His glass shop is not too far from the PMB."

"Don't do anything stupid. I'm on my way now."

Stallings wasn't about to wait and didn't intend to do anything stupid.

Buddy had the jar and cord in his left hand as he casually strolled through the lobby, nodding to a stoned dude laying carpet. He paused at the empty counter to capture the full excitement of what he was about to do. He also needed to catch his breath and clear his throat with one long, hard cough. He wondered, once the artwork was completed, if he would even bother going back to see Dr. Raja, who'd done all he could but hadn't really helped in any way. Buddy's passion for blowing glass had also been his doom. His desire to capture the final breaths of beautiful women probably had led directly to his own imminent death.

When he had savored the feeling, Buddy glanced over his shoulder to make sure the carpet guy wasn't paying any attention. He scooted behind the counter and into the office. It was empty. He thought it was weird that a hotel, even a shitty one like this, didn't have anyone at the desk.

Then he noticed the rear door that opened into the alley behind the hotel was ajar. She was outside, where there was no one around.

Perfect.

Patty Levine was on her way into the office at the Police Memorial Building when John Stallings called. She rarely heard any hints of panic in his voice, but she instantly picked up on the urgency of his call.

"Patty, go to the hotel Liz Dubeck runs. Stick close to her until I get there."

"What's the problem, John?"

"There may be a guy there fixing her front window. His company is Classic Glass Concepts. He's our killer."

Although Patty would've loved to hear the reasoning, she knew she'd find out later. Right now her only job was to race over to the hotel.

Stallings said, "I'm calling dispatch, too. Don't do anything crazy, just make sure Liz is safe. Patrol will be on its way soon."

Patty said, "I'll be there in less than ten minutes." She stepped on the gas of her Ford Freestyle and shot through a red light. The idea that she could be in a position to catch this asshole gave her hope of redemption.

Buddy stuck his head out of the open office door into the long, empty alleyway. There was a Toyota Camry parked right next to the door that he assumed was the manager's. Beyond the car, about forty feet from the door, he saw the pretty manager named Liz shaking out a throw rug. He watched her for a moment with fascination as she inspected rug after rug and either shook out the dirt or tossed it in the Dumpster.

He immediately saw a chance to buy a few hours by tossing her body into the Dumpster when he was done. Sometimes things just worked out. He felt like this was another sign he'd made a wise choice of subjects.

Buddy peered through the crack in the door and savored the feeling once again as he checked the rubber seal on his homemade glass jar, then pulled on the heavy cord.

This was going to be sweet.

Stallings roared out of the lot of the PMB, almost knocking the metal gate out of his way. It wasn't a long ride over to the hotel, but it felt like an eternity as the acid ate away at his stomach. His mind raced through a thousand possibilities of what could happen. Unlike Tony Mazzetti, Stallings rarely thought about ensuring he had enough evidence to make a case. All he really wanted was to stop the killer. Any way he could. At the moment his absolute first priority was making sure Liz Dubeck was safe. He hadn't realized how much she meant to him until that very moment.

He didn't care if he stopped Arnold Cather, or if Patty Levine or a patrolman did. He just wanted it over. He knew Mazzetti was racing from the hospital so he could be the one to make the arrest. Stallings was fine with allowing him to grab all the credit.

He cut across a side street, swerving at the last second to miss a motorcyclist, then a homeless woman pushing a shopping cart full of tin cans. He still had several blocks to cover before he'd be at the hotel.

FIFTY-SIX

Buddy eased out of the office into the alleyway. He liked the fact that the hotel manager had no idea he was approaching her from behind. Her dark hair swayed from side to side as she shook out another small rug. She had a much curvier body than most of his subjects and he appreciated the shape of her hips in her tight-fitting jeans.

He carefully took one small step after another so as not to alert her. As he crept closer he considered the logistics of using the cord and grabbing the small glass jar at the critical moment. This was such a spur-of-the-moment action he hated to spoil it by planning it out so carefully. He stuffed the jar into his belt line so he could reach it quickly as he closed the distance.

The thrill of completing his artwork almost made him dizzy as Buddy took the two ends of the cord in each hand.

As Patty Levine pulled directly in front of the hotel, she saw a patrolman rolling up from the opposite direction. They stopped their cars on each side of the empty street and she hurried across to meet him.

Climbing out of his cruiser, the muscular thirty-year-old cop said, "Hey, Patty, you know what this shit is about?"

"We're checking on the hotel manager here and detaining any male workers until Stallings and Mazzetti can come over. Should only be a few minutes."

The uniformed cop said, "This has to do with a homicide?"

Patty nodded. She looked past the cop and saw the white van. The patrolman followed her toward the front door. She looked through the front window and saw a worker kneeling in the lobby.

Patty said, "This might be the guy they want to detain. I don't know what he looks like. It all happened really fast."

Patty burst through the front door of the hotel with the uniformed cop right behind her.

Liz Dubeck was distracted by all the things she could do to the hotel with her generous federal grant. She knew she was focusing on minor issues like buying new throw rugs or medicine-cabinet mirrors, but there was so much to do it was a little overwhelming.

Right now she stood in the alley behind the hotel assessing about thirty throw rugs from the hotel's bathrooms. She didn't mind the physical activity under the bright, North Florida sun. It was a beautiful day. Even stuck between two crumbling buildings, she liked being outside.

Liz had to admit that fixing the hotel wasn't the only

thing on her mind. She wondered what John Stallings was doing. She worried about the handsome detective and knew he was having a hard time in his personal life. Liz didn't want to seem like a vulture, waiting to pick him off when his wife kicked him to the curb permanently, which is what Liz thought would happen. She didn't know why, it was just the feeling. He was such a good guy, and it really did seem like good guys got treated like dirt by women.

Liz realized she should be back inside at the counter, but things were slow right now and she had two employees running other errands. As she shook out a rug that was in pretty good shape, she thought she heard a sound behind her.

As Patty and the patrolman rushed into the lobby, the man looked over his shoulder, then sprang to his feet. Before Patty could say anything the man said, "What do you cops want?"

The patrolman, whom Patty had worked with and knew was a badass on the street, took a step toward the man as Patty said, "What's your name?"

Without the patrolman even touching him, the man started screaming, "Police brutality, police brutality!"

Patty looked at him and said, "What are you talking about, you moron?"

The man said, "I know how you cops work. I want witnesses before I get hurt."

"Is that your van out front?"

The man screamed again, "Help, police brutality!"

The patrolman hovered a few feet away and said to Patty without taking his eyes off the man, "What do you want me to do? Should I make this a self-fulfilling prophecy?"

Patty said, "Stay here with this idiot. I'll find the manager." Patty hustled across the lobby past the counter and into the office. It was empty.

She had a bad feeling.

FIFTY-SEVEN

Patty Levine drew her Glock .40 caliber and stepped through the door into the alley. The first thing she saw was Liz Dubeck walking toward her quickly.

Liz said, "Hello, Detective. I heard someone yelling in the lobby and I was coming to check it out." Then she saw the gun in Patty's hand and said, "Oh my God, what's wrong?"

Patty said, "Where's the glass guy?"

"You mean Buddy? He was out front changing out the window the last time I saw him."

Patty motioned for her to follow and stepped back into the office, where the uniformed cop now had the guy from the lobby, cuffed behind his back and standing in the corner.

Liz said, "What's going on? Is Junior under arrest?"

Patty said, "That's not Buddy, the guy from Classic Glass Concepts?"

"No, Buddy is a little older and shorter than Junior."

Patty exchanged looks with the patrolman, then

headed out to the lobby. As soon as she looked out the window she froze.

The white van was gone.

Buddy sometimes wondered if his work of art had made him paranoid. He had no idea why the cops were hassling the carpet guy at the hotel, but he thanked God he'd heard them. He hustled around the outside of the hotel and peeked in through the office window to see a young woman and a uniformed Jacksonville patrolman pull the carpet guy roughly by his arm. They all seemed focused on the rear door so Buddy just slipped away. It couldn't be a coincidence. He knew they were after him.

The realization that his luck had run out had caused him to drive back home and rush around his apartment, packing a few almost random items, as well as assess how he would move his work of art. In his bedroom, he opened a dresser drawer to grab a pair of underwear and froze. There, sitting right where he had left it, was Cheryl's pistol. He hesitated but overcame his hesitation, stuffing it into the front of his pants like he had seen on all of the police shows.

Buddy came out in the living room and stared at his glass wall. He knew the dimensions off the top of his head. Fifty inches wide by forty-two inches tall. When his work of art was set on its base it stood almost six feet tall. Although he had hoped to keep it in one place to be admired by everyone for years to come, he had been practical and made it so that the actual glass structure could be transported separately from the base. He judged the glass to be about one hundred pounds. It would be tough, but he could muscle it down to the van. He'd already removed the magnetic signs. He could leave town at a safe speed. No one would notice a plain white van.

He grabbed the duffel bag full of keepsakes from his bedroom as well as the heavy comforter he intended to use to safeguard his work of art. His eyes were instantly drawn to the bottom right corner, the single empty slot left in the handmade blown-glass wall. He wondered if he'd be able to swing back by the hotel and use Liz Dubeck as his final subject. If not, he may not live long enough to find someone else. The idea of leaving it unfinished was the only regret he had in his life at this moment.

Then he heard a noise and froze to listen intently. There was someone on his flight of stairs. He reached for the gun in his waistband and hoped he'd watched enough TV to know how to use it.

It had taken longer than John Stallings would've liked to organize a few cops to come over to the warehouse of Classic Glass Concepts. Stallings left one patrolman with Liz Dubeck, who still didn't know exactly what was going on. Now he, Patty Levine, and a burly patrolman who had worked with Patty on the road were carefully surveying the inside of the open shop used by Classic Glass Concepts and Arnold Cather. Another patrolman ran around the rear of the building and more patrolmen were on the way. Tony Mazzetti had asked Stallings not to do anything until he got there. Always looking for the credit of an arrest. Stallings would gladly give him credit for this arrest, but he wasn't about to give this asshole a chance to slip away. They needed to act now.

Inside the shop, Stallings placed a hand on the grille of the white van. Still warm. He stepped back in the shop, looked at the curtained windows upstairs, and motioned for Patty and the patrolman to meet him at the base of the stairs. He took a minute to consider waiting for Tony Mazzetti.

Patty said, "Do we wait or do we go in?"

Stallings shook his head. "I wouldn't mind waiting, but we don't know who he might have up there. Maybe even Leah Tischler." He noticed Patty wince slightly and recalled her own incarceration at the hands of another crazed killer.

Patty said, "Let's get going." She nudged him slightly until he took the first step, then started climbing as quickly and quietly as possible. The footfalls of three cops on the narrow stairs had to make a racket inside.

Stallings barely had time to mutter, "Is today the day that changes my life?"

He had a feeling it was.

FIFTY-EIGHT

Tony Mazzetti wasn't sure he'd ever gone this fast in his whole life. The big Ford Crown Victoria was great on straight patches of road, but this was Jacksonville with stoplights and tourists and one-way streets and, possibly worst of all, Canadian drivers. Although he wanted to concentrate on the road, all his mind could consider was what was happening at the suspect's house. Stallings had given him a quick rundown of the situation. It didn't sound like he was going to wait specifically for Mazzetti no matter how much the lead detective protested.

Mazzetti had called Sergeant Zuni and laid out what was happening, expecting her to call Stallings and tell him to wait. All she'd said was she'd meet him at the scene.

Was he the only one who realized the lead investigator needed to be present at the arrest? How would it look on TV if he had to give credit to someone else?

* * *

As Stallings, Patty, and the uniformed cop neared the closed door at the top of the stairs, Stallings recognized that the situation had taken on its own energy. The longer it went, the more the cops were convinced Arnold Cather was the killer. That's how it always happened. It was also how mistakes were made in major investigations.

There was no way he would take any chances. With all the help on the way, no matter what happened here, Cather wasn't getting away. Not today. Another problem Stallings considered was the sheer number of cops that would be flooding the scene. Everyone wanted to say they were in on a serial-killer arrest. And sometimes that was the problem. With so many cops, things could get confused or out of hand.

He looked behind him at Patty and the patrolman two steps down with their guns drawn and pointed at the window next to the door. "Knock and announce or kick in?"

Patty said, "Crazy cop's choice. I'd say he knows we're here already."

Stallings turned like he was going to kick the door, stopped, and tried the handle and found that it was unlocked. He wasted no time shoving the door open and diving inside with his gun up. Scooting across an open space he slid behind a counter in a tiny kitchen. He peeked around the side of a kitchen bar and saw Arnold Cather standing next to a glass structure of some kind.

Cather had a gun in his hand.

Buddy had not considered eternity for himself. At least not in the terms he had to now as he held a gun to

his own head. It was one thing to have Dr. Raja say he
was going to die. It was another to know he'd be dead
in the next few minutes. At least standing there with
the gun to his temple had frozen all the cops in place.

He looked over at his work of art and the final slot
empty on the bottom far side. He'd worked this out in
his mind when he seemed to have more nerve, but right
now he hesitated. He intended to breathe into the jar,
seal it, and place it in his work of art, then pull the trigger before he took another breath. The way he figured
it, he'd have a few seconds to revere his ultimate accomplishment. The more he considered being part of it
for all eternity the more the idea appealed to him.

Buddy looked at the cops. One was crouched by his
kitchen counter and two more stood at the door with
their pistols all pointed directly at him. He knew he
couldn't give them any reason whatsoever to fire.

This was his final chance to finish his work of art.

Stallings had forced himself to scan the room
around Arnold Cather before he focused all of his attention on the crazed glass worker. He knew that Patty
and the patrolman would be covering the suspect and
wanted to ensure there was no one behind him and
nothing else in the apartment that could be a threat.

Stallings called out to him in a clear voice, as calm
as he could make it, "Arnold, put the gun down."

Cather said, "You don't understand."

Stallings said, "Why don't you explain it to me?"
The longer he drew this out, the better the chance he
had to resolve it.

Cather said, "I just want to finish my work of art."
His eyes shifted over to the glass wall next to him. "I

swear to God if you let me finish it, I'll shoot myself and it will be all over. I won't have to go to court or waste your time. It's better for everyone this way."

Stallings said, "Why is it better, Arnold?"

"I treasure each of the girls whose essence is stored in this wall. This is designed to remember them. Each jar holds a little piece of an angel."

Stallings took a quick moment to count jars. There were seventeen in place and one in Cather's hand. He wondered if Leah Tischler or even Jeanie was somewhere in the obscene wall. Stallings felt the anger rising in him as his finger slowly tightened on the trigger of his Glock.

Cather said, "Please, please, give me a few seconds. That's all I ask. Is that so much? I'll finish this, then finish myself." There was a hitch in his voice.

Stallings saw how much the man worshiped the crazy hulk of glass and figured out what he planned to do. A fury started to boil in Stallings as he realized the man was breathing into the final jar. From somewhere deep inside him he heard a voice and he followed it.

With both hands firmly on the butt of his pistol, Stallings started to fire. Four quick rounds blasted inside the small apartment. He struggled to keep the pistol on target as each round caused the barrel to recoil straight up.

The sound of the shots, the smell of the gunpowder, the afterimage of the shots fired from the pistol froze the entire apartment in Stallings's mind.

FIFTY-NINE

Tony Mazzetti brought his car to a squealing halt in front of Arnold Cather's shop. He saw Stallings's car and a patrol car in front of the shop. Mazzetti bolted from his car and darted inside. It was empty.

He heard Stallings's voice. He turned toward the steps, but before he could reach them he heard gunshots from the room at the top of the stairs. It was clear as day. Four quick, individual shots.

A uniformed cop and Patty crouched at the top of the stairs with their guns pointing inside.

Mazzetti drew his gun and took the stairs two at a time.

Sergeant Yvonne Zuni turned down the street where Classic Glass Concepts was located. She felt confident having a veteran like Stallings on the scene but knew that things could get out of control quickly. Over the main radio frequency she heard the emergency alert tone, then the panicky voice of a young patrolman shouting into his radio, "Shots fired, shots fired! Warehouse on Davis."

Sergeant Zuni picked up the handheld radio from her passenger seat, waited for dispatch to acknowledge, identified herself clearly, and said, "Is anyone hurt? I'm coming down the street in an unmarked Ford Taurus. What is your current location?"

Her calm tone and commanding presence forced the young officer to think for a moment, take a breath, and say, "I'm covering the outside rear of the building. The shots came from inside. I'm headed around front now."

Sergeant Zuni was quick to come on the radio and say, "Hold your position. I'll be there in less than one minute." She couldn't resist the urge to press the gas a little harder. Experience had taught her to be steady and calm as soon as she arrived on the scene. It was her job to inspire confidence and dissipate panic. But she was only human and she allowed herself a few moments of anxiety as she wished she were there right now.

The gunshots reverberated in Stallings's ears. Patty and the patrolman seemed to have suffered less having the open shop behind them. Stallings was relieved no one else had fired out of reflex. Often, one cop shooting spurred others. It had been a fact since the Boston Massacre.

Stallings kept his pistol trained on Arnold Cather's head even after he'd dropped his gun to the ground. The glass structure Stallings had just shot four times was shattered into thousands of pieces. Only the bottom row of jars remained intact and even that had cracks and fissures still erupting.

Cather started to tremble, then weep, and stumbled back against the apartment's flimsy wall and slid to the ground like he had been shot through the chest. Stallings had figured out that no bullet fired into the man could have caused as much damage as the ones fired into his obsession.

Arnold Cather would never harm anyone again.

Arnold Cather, known to the entire world as Buddy, lost all control of his limbs as he watched his whole world crumble into a pile of useless fused silica. Instead of his life flashing before his eyes, memories of endless hours over the hot furnace, blowing different pieces of the structure and painstakingly making each jar to fit each slot so exactly, flooded into his head. Even the pleasure he had derived from identifying each subject so carefully, then capturing her breath so lovingly, seemed like a dream to him now.

How could that cop be so cruel? How did he know it would hurt him so much to destroy his work of art? He wanted to strike back, but his whole body was fighting just to keep his heart beating. He felt worse at this moment than he had the day he was told he would never recover from the tumors growing in his lungs.

As he bumped the wall, his legs gave out and he slid to the ground with a graceless plop.

Why couldn't the cop have shot him and saved him all this sorrow?

SIXTY

John Stallings felt like a caged animal as he watched Tony Mazzetti and Sparky Taylor interview Arnold Cather at the PMB. He sat in a viewing room next door to the interview room, watching the proceedings on a closed-circuit TV with Yvonne Zuni in one chair and Lieutenant Rita Hester in the other. He couldn't sit still, standing and pacing in the back of the room, giving handwritten notes to Patty in the hallway so she could text them to Mazzetti.

Stallings recognized that, as the lead detectives on the case, Mazzetti and Sparky should be the ones in the room staring down the suspect. Since Arnold Cather liked to go by the name "Buddy," Mazzetti immediately started calling him Arnold and Sparky called him Buddy. They set up a good dynamic for the classic "heavyset compassionate good cop and annoying bad cop."

After the fifth question Stallings sent in, Mazzetti turned directly to the camera and shut off his phone. Once again Stallings sprang up and faced the back of the small observation room. He had tipped his hand

and it took an old friend and former partner like Rita Hester to call him out on it.

She lifted her wide frame, nicely hidden behind a brown pantsuit, and motioned him out of the small room into the hallway. As soon as he was clear of the door she wrapped her strong hand around his elbow and tugged him into the empty conference room across the hall.

She leveled those clear, brown eyes at him and said, "You trust me, Stall?"

He nodded his head, noting that she had not removed her hand from his arm.

"Then let me monitor this interview and I'll act as your proxy. I'll make sure Mazzetti questions him on every aspect of his activities and ensure that he never met Jeanie."

Stallings appreciated how she danced around saying something like, "We'll make sure he didn't strangle your daughter." Stallings looked at Rita Hester's pretty face, feared by every criminal in Duvall County. As usual, she was right. Not just professionally, but personally as well.

Stallings felt the energy seep out of his body and knew he was spent. The killings were over. He'd accomplished his goal. Now he had to trust the cops he worked with to look out for his own interests. Mazzetti was an asshole, but he could handle this.

It was time for John Stallings to step back and recapture as much of his life as he could.

On his way home to his small house in Lakewood Stallings stopped at the hotel to check on Liz Dubeck. As soon as he walked through the front door of the empty lobby she rushed from behind the counter and threw her arms around him. At that moment he knew she had realized how close she'd come to being part of that monstrous glass structure.

Liz said, "I heard that you figured out Buddy was the killer and sent the others to protect me. You're like my guardian angel."

Stallings wasn't sure he knew what to say. "Just glad you're safe."

She stepped back, smiled, and said, "Am I safe as far as you're concerned? Have I dropped into female-friend mode?"

"I'm not sure we ever progressed past that stage. And there's nothing wrong with being friends, is there?"

She stepped forward, ran her fingers through his hair, and planted a kiss on his lips. Then she stepped away from him and said, "I'll always be here for you."

"You can't know how important that is to me."

Stallings felt a stab of sorrow as he trudged to his car. He sat in front of the hotel for a moment wondering if he had enough energy to make it to his house and collapse in his bed.

As it turned out, that was exactly how much energy he had left.

Patty Levine had given Tony Mazzetti a good night's rest to recover from the investigation. She knew there was so much more to do, but at least they were confident the killings had stopped. The strangler was behind bars. As far as Tony Mazzetti was concerned they had cleared a bunch of homicides.

She looked across the table in the Caribbean-themed restaurant out on Atlantic Beach and smiled at him. She felt the effort it took to smile. It wasn't the organic, warm smile she could've produced a month ago.

Mazzetti said, "This is the first chance we've had to chat in almost a week."

"Not so good for people in a relationship, huh?"

"Anyone would acknowledge that these were special circumstances. Now we can focus on us."

"But for how long? Our whole lives are special circumstances." She took a moment, then reached across and grasped his right hand in both of hers. "That's why I wanted to talk. I think I need to focus on me for a while."

"What's that mean?"

Patty knew he didn't understand exactly what she was talking about. She could never go into the details of her concern. She wouldn't intentionally put anyone in that position. The fact that Sparky Taylor had shown the insight to figure it out had shocked her. She didn't want to seem like a whiner or admit there were days she couldn't handle the job. Tony Mazzetti would land on his feet now that she had taken him out of his comfort zone of ignoring everyone and everything except his job.

When Patty cleaned up her act, she'd be interested in talking to him about a life together, special circumstances and all.

SIXTY-ONE

On Sunday morning about ten o'clock, John Stallings's phone rang and he was surprised to hear Lois
Tischler on the other end. She was crying and asked
him to come by the house. When he hesitated she threw
in a "please" and hung up. He wasn't scheduled to take
the kids and his father out to lunch until one o'clock so
he hopped in his Impala and drove out to the beach,
wondering if it was some kind of domestic Mrs. Tischler wanted to keep quiet. Often grieving parents
identified with a cop investigating a missing child and
called the cop for any number of reasons. He saw no
harm in easing this woman's sorrow.

He pulled in the winding driveway and was met at
the door by Mrs. Tischler in simple jeans and a top that
showed off her athletic body. She surprised him by
jumping up and hugging him and kissing him on
cheek. While he was entangled with Mrs. Tischler, he
looked over her shoulder, and standing in the ornate
entryway was a young lady. That was the phrase that
came to his mind since she looked every bit of a youthful, graceful, cultured lady.

Her hair was cut differently, but Stallings knew immediately who it was. A smile broke across his face as he said, "Leah?"

The girl nodded, then rushed forward and joined the hug. Stallings felt a tear pop out of his eye as he said, "How? What happened?" He noticed in the hallway Bob Tischler bawling like the rest of them.

Ten minutes later, after everyone had settled down and he sipped a remarkably strong cup of exotic coffee, Leah sat across from him on a leather couch. Her parents were on either side like they intended to prevent any planned escape.

Leah said, "I saw my photo on TV in Tennessee. I made me realize how much pain I caused and I had to come home to face the consequences."

Eventually Stallings was able to ask if she'd ever met Arnold Cather.

"He gave me a ride from near the hotel downtown. But while I was at his shop two women came in and started arguing with him over rent or the lease. I jus got up and walked away. The next day I took a bus as far as Atlanta and then caught a ride with a truck drive to my friend's house in Tennessee."

Stallings marveled at the young woman.

Leah continued, "The guy at the glass warehous gave me an old flannel shirt and I had a pair of jean and my backpack. I left my school uniform and th backpack at his shop."

It was amazing how many questions were being an swered by a girl who had never even known she ha been moments away from death.

Stallings felt something that hadn't surfaced in long time: hope.

SIXTY-TWO

Almost a month after the capture of Arnold Cather, few days after Halloween, Stallings sat next to his fa-ler in the living room of the rooming house where he ved. His memory had not improved and he had pro-ided no more details about his brief visit with his lissing granddaughter. His prognosis remained grim. tallings felt the pain of never connecting with his fa-ler until recently, and now the old man was likely to rget him altogether. But the goodwill he had built up ver the years had provided a solid core of volunteers help care for the ailing James Stallings. It was grati-ing on a number of levels.

The father and son watched an Orlando Magic game at led directly into the local news. The lead story ught Stallings's attention when the announcer said, Arnold Cather, being held for the murder of at least ur local young women, has died of lung cancer in the edical unit of the city hospital. He had been trans-rred there from the county jail two days ago and had mained under constant guard."

Stallings noted, as the story continued, that the JSO

captain made a point of mentioning that Cather had suffered and wasted away. His defense attorney had the balls to say, "He lost his valiant battle with cancer."

To Stallings the only hero in the story was Leah Tischler. She had done more for him than he ever thought possible. Her return had allowed him to move on from not only a missing persons case but the murder investigation. It had given him motivation to deal with Maria and the kids differently. He and Maria were talking much more frequently and the kids seemed happy.

But most of all Leah Tischler had given him hope.

If Leah could make it back to her family, so could Jeanie.